Conquest of the Danelaw

By

H A Culley

Book two of the Birth of England

Published by

oHp

Orchard House Publishing

First Kindle Edition 2021

Text copyright © 2021 H A Culley

Principle Characters

Abrecan – The son of Deorwine and Cuthfleda

Æbbe – Ywer's sister, Skarde's wife and mother of Brandt and Frida

Ælfflæd - King Eadweard's second wife

Ælfweard –Eadweard's elder son by Ælfflæd

Ælfwynn – Æthelflæd's daughter

Æscwin – Abbot of Cæstir; elder brother of Cuthfleda, Ywer, Kjestin and Æbbe

Æthelflæd – Lady of the Mercians

Æthelstan – Eadweard's eldest son by his first wife. Lord of Mamecestre

Agnar – Gyda's second cousin

Alexis – Greek infirmarian at Hagustaldesham Monastery

Åmunde – Danish jarl ruling part of southern Northumbria

Anarawd ap Rhodri – King of Gwynedd

Arne – A Norseman, captain of Æthelflæd's warband

Aart, Kenric and Penda – Three members of Irwyn's warband

Astrid – A Dane, married to Wynnstan and head of Cuthfleda's household

Banan – Æthelflæd's captain after Arne

Bawdewyn – Wynnstan's successor as Æthelstan's captain

Bēomēre – The son of a Mercian fisherman

Beornrīc – Ealdorman of Dornsæte and ally of Osfirth

Berðun – A Northumbrian Angle, Æthelstan's body servant

Brandt – Son of Æbbe and the late Jarl Erik Fairhair, Skarde's half-brother

Cadda - Ealdorman of Herefordscīr

Cedric – A ship's boy, later a warrior on a Mercian longship

Cena and Broga – Two of Æthelflæd's scouts

Chad – A friend of Wynnstan's, later the captain of his hearth warriors.

Constantin – King of Alba

Cuthfleda – Ywer's elder sister and Æthelflæd's closest adviser

Cynric – One of Æthelstan's gesith

Deorwine – Hereræswa of Mercia and Cuthfleda's husband

Dyfnwal – King of Strathclyde

Eadsige and Mēserīc – two of Irwyn's companions

Eadweard – King of Wessex

Edith – Æthelstan's half-sister, later married to King Sigtrygg of Northumbria

Edwin – Eadweard's younger son by his second wife, Ælfflæd

Ealdred of Bebbanburg – Earl of Bernicia

Eohric – Wynnstan's body servant after Hengist

Frida – Daughter of Æbbe and the late Jarl Erik Fairhair, Skarde's half-brother

Hákon and Ulf – Danish jarls who ruled half of the Danelaw

Hengist – A potboy rescued by Ywer, later his body servant

Heoruwulf – Captain of the Saint Oswald, a Mercian longship

Hrotheweard – Archbishop of Jorvik

Hwgan – King of Brycheniog

Hywel Dda – King of Brycheiniog

Galan – Captain of Eadweard's gesith

Godric – A Dane, captain of Ywer's warband

Gyda – Ywer's Norse wife

Irwyn – Ywer's son

Kjestin – Ywer's twin sister, married to Odda

Leofdæg – Captain of Cæstir's garrison

Mildritha – Wynnstan and Astrid's daughter

Odda – Ealdorman of Dyfneintscīr

Ögmundr – Norse jarl holding lands to the north of the River Mǣresēa

Osfirth – Ealdorman of Wiltunscīr and Hereræswa of Wessex

Plegmund – Archbishop of Cantwareburh
Ragnall – King of Mann, later King of Northumbria
Sawin, Wardric and Tidhelm – Three of Wynnstan's scouts
Sicga – Wynnstan and Astrid's son
Sigehelm – Former shire reeve of Cent
Skarde – Jarl of Wirhealum
Stepan – A young Mercian archer

Uhtric and Leofwine – Physicians serving Æthelflæd

Wælwulf – Odda's son and Irwyn's cousin

Wilfrid – Member of Ywer's warband

Wirfrith – Bishop of Wirecestre

Wynnstan – Captain of Æthelstan's gesith, later Thegn of Rumcofen

Ywer – Ealdorman of Cæstirscīr

Place Names

Afon	River Avon
Alba	Scotland
Alse	River Axe
Alseminstre	Axminster, Devon
Apletune	Appleton, Cheshire
Banesberic	Banbury, Oxfordshire
Bardenai	Bardney, Lincolnshire
Bebbanburg	Bamburgh, Northumberland
Bedeford	Bedford, Bedfordshire
Bernecestre	Bicester, Oxfordshire
Branchetreu	Braintree, Essex
Brigge	Bridgenorth, Shropshire
Britannia	The island of Britain (Latin name)
Brunanburh	Location debateable, probably Bromborough, Merseyside
Brycheiniog	Brecknockshire, South Wales
Cœr Luel	Carlisle, Cumbria
Cæstir	Chester, Cheshire
Cæstirscīr	Cheshire
Cantwareburh	Canterbury, Kent
Casingc Stræt	Watling Street (Roman road)
Cedde	Cheadle, Cheshire
Celelea	Chowley, Cheshire
Cent	Kent
Ceolmaersford	Chelmsford, Essex
Ciropesberic	Shrewsbury, Shropshire
Corebricg	Corbridge, Northumberland
Cornweal	Cornwall
Deoraby	Derby, Derbyshire
Denmark	Denmark
Dēvā	River Dee

Dofras	Dover, Kent
Dornsæte	Dorset
Dornwaracester	Dorchester, Dorset
Dùn Breatann	Dumbarton, Strathclyde, Scotland
Dyflin (Viking name)	Dublin, Ireland
Dyfneintscīr	Devon
Ēast Seaxna Rīce	Essex
Eforwic	York, North Yorkshire (Saxon name)
Englaland	England
Execestre	Exeter, Devon
Fearndune	Farndon, Cheshire
Frankia	A large part of France, Belgium and Germany
Frodesham	Frodsham, Cheshire
Gewaesc	The Wash
Glowecestre	Gloucester, Gloucestershire
Grantebrycgescīr	Cambridgeshire
Grárhöfn	Near Birkenhead, Cheshire Hagustaldesham Hexham, Northumberland
Hamtune	Northampton, Northamptonshire
Hamtunscīr	Hampshire
Herefordscīr	Herefordshire
Hertforde	Hertford, Hertfordshire
Hochenartone	Hook Norton, Oxfordshire
Huntedone	Huntingdon, Cambridgeshire
Hwicce	Part of Mercia, most of Gloucestershire and Worcestershire
Íralandes Sǽ	Irish Sea
Íralond	Ireland
Jorvik	York, North Yorkshire (Viking name)
Ledecestre	Leicester, Leicestershire
Licefelle	Litchfield, Staffordshire
Liedeberge	Ledbury, Hereforshire
Lintone	Luton, Bedfordshire
Lincolia	Lincoln, Lincolnshire

Lindsey	Part of modern day Lincolnshire
Loncastrescīr	Lancashire
Lundenburg	London
Lygan	River Lea
Llyn Syfaddon	Langorse Lake, Breconshire
Malberthorp	Mablethorpe, Lincolnshire
Malduna	Maldon, Essex
Mamecestre	Manchester, Greater Manchester
Mann	Isle of Man
Mǣresēa	River Mersey
Nestone	Neston, Cheshire
Nordfolc	Norfolk
Norþweg	Norway
Nortone	Chipping Norton, Oxfordshire
Orkneyjar	Orkney Islands
Oxenaforda	Oxford, Oxfordshire
Oxenafordascīr	Oxfordshire
Portweg	Portway
Rumcofen	Runcorn, Cheshire
Sæfern	River Severn
Scrobbesbyrigscīr	Shropshire
Silcestre	Silchester, Hampshire
Snotingeham	Nottingham, Nottinghamshire
Somersaete	Somerset
Steanford	Stamford, Lincolnshire
Stane Stræt	Stane Street (Roman Road)
Sūð-sǣ	English Channel
Sūþfolc	Suffolk
Sūþrīgescīr	Surrey
Suth-Seaxe	Sussex
Sweartwæter	River Blackwater
Tamuuordescīr	Staffordshire (then based around Tamworth)
Tatenhale	Tattenhall, Cheshire

Temes	River Thames
Tes	River Tees
Theocsbury	Tewksbury, Gloucestershire
Tiddingforde	No longer exists, near Leighton Buzzard in Bedfordshire
Tomtun	Tamworth, Staffordshire
Totenhale	Tettenhall, Wolverhampton
Touecestre	Towcester, Northamptonshire
Uisge	River Great Ouse
Walingtune	Warrington, Cheshire
Waruwic	Warwick, Warwickshire
Wealas	Wales
Wendel-sæ	Mediterranean Sea
Wiltunscīr	Wiltshire
Winburne	Wimborne Minster, Dorset
Wintanceaster	Winchester, Hampshire
Wirecestre	Worcester, Worcestershire
Wirhealum	Wirral Peninsula, Cheshire
Wōdnesfeld	Wednesfield, Wolverhampton
Wrekichester	Wroxeter, Shropshire
Ynys Môn	Isle of Anglesey, Wales

Glossary

ANGLO-SAXON

Ænglisc – Old English, the common language of Angles, Saxons and Jutes.

Ætheling – literally 'throne-worthy.' An Anglo-Saxon prince

Avantail - a curtain of chainmail attached to a helmet to cover the throat and neck

Birlinn – a wooden ship similar to the later Scottish galleys but smaller than a Viking longship. Usually with a single mast and square rigged sail, they could also be propelled by oars with one man to each oar

Bondsman – a slave who was treated as the property of his master

Braies – underwear similar to modern undershorts. Worn only by males

Bretwalda – overlord of some or all of the Anglo-Saxon kingdoms

Brythonic – Relating to the Bryttas, especially the language spoken by them

Bryttas – Britons, essentially the inhabitants of Cornwall (Kernow), Wales (Wealas), Cumbria and Strathclyde at this time.

Burh - fortified settlement

Byrnie - a tunic of chain mail, usually sleeveless or short sleeved

Ceorl – a freeman who worked the land or else provided a service or trade such as metal working, carpentry, weaving etc. They ranked between thegns and villeins and provided the fyrd in time of war

Cyning – Old English for king and the term by which they were normally addressed

Danegeld - a tax levied in Anglo-Saxon England to bribe Danish invaders to leave

Ealdorman – The senior noble of a shire. A royal appointment, ealdormen led the men of their shire in battle, presided over law courts and levied taxation on behalf of the king

Englaland – England (meaning *Land of the Angles*)

Fyrd - Anglo-Saxon army mobilised from freemen to defend their shire, or to join a campaign led by the king

Gesith – the companions of a king, prince or noble, usually acting as his bodyguard

Hacksilver - Fragments of silver that were used as currency

Hearth Warriors - alternative term for members of a Gesith

Hereræswa – military commander or general. The man who commanded the army of a nation under the king

Hersir – a landowner who could recruit enough other freemen to serve under him

Hide – a measure of the land sufficient to support the household of one ceorl

Hideage - a tax paid to the royal exchequer for every hide of land

Hundred – the unit for local government and taxation which equated to ten tithings

Kernow - Cornwall

Pallium - an ecclesiastical vestment bestowed by the Pope upon metropolitans and primates as a symbol of their authority

Reeve - a local official including the chief magistrate of a town or district, also the person manging a landowner's estate

Sæfyrd – Members of the fyrd (q.v.) who served at sea

Sæ Hereræswa – Commander of the King Ælfred's navy

Scop - A travelling poet who entertained by reciting heroic poetry

Seax – a bladed weapon somewhere in size between a dagger and a sword. Mainly used for close-quarter fighting where a sword would be too long and unwieldy

Settlement – any grouping of residential buildings, usually around the king's or lord's hall. In 8th century England the term town or village had not yet come into use

Shire – an administrative area into which an Anglo-Saxon kingdom was divided

Shire Reeve – later corrupted to sheriff. A royal official responsible for implementing the king's laws within his shire

Skypfyrd – fyrd raised to man ships of war to defend the coast

Tabula – a board game introduced by the Roman which is similar to Backgammon

Tæfl – a board game similar to chess which simulates a battle between two unequal forces.

Thegn – the lowest rank of noble. A man who held a certain amount of land direct from the king or from a senior nobleman, ranking between an ordinary freeman, or ceorl, and an ealdorman

Tithing - a group of ten ceorls who lived close together and were collectively responsible for each other's behaviour, also the land required to support them (i.e. ten hides)

Wergeld - the price set upon a person's life or injury and paid as compensation by the person responsible to the family of the dead or injured person. It freed the perpetrator of further punishment or obligation and prevented a blood feud

Witan – meeting or council

Witenaġemot – the council of an Anglo-Saxon kingdom. Its composition varied, depending on the matters to be debated. Usually it consisted of the ealdormen, the king's thegns, the bishops and the abbots

Villein - a peasant who ranked above a bondsman or slave but who was legally tied to his vill and who was obliged to give one or more day's service to his lord each week in payment for his land

Vill - a thegn's holding or similar area of land in Anglo-Saxon England which would later be called a parish or a manor

VIKING

Bóndi - farmers and craftsmen who were free men and enjoyed rights such as the ownership of weapons and membership of the Thing. They could be tenants or landowners. Plural bøndur

Byrnie - a tunic of chain mail, usually sleeveless or short sleeved

Hacksilver – (or Hacksilber) Fragments of silver that were used as currency

Helheim – the realm in the afterlife for those who don't die in battle

Hersir – a bóndi who was chosen to lead a band of warriors under a king or a jarl. Typically they were wealthy landowners who could recruit enough other bøndur to serve under their command

Hirdman – a member of a king's or a jarl's personal bodyguard, collectively known as the hird

Hold – Title given to a jarl with significant territorial possessions.

Jarl – a Norse or Danish chieftain; in Sweden they were regional governors appointed by the king.

Konungr - King

Lagmann – Literally lawspeaker. He presided over the thing, worked as a judge and formulated the laws that had been decided by the people. Laws were not written down but memorised by the lagmann.

Mjolnir – Thor's hammer, also the pendant worn around the neck by most pagan Vikings

Nailed God – pagan name for Christ, also called the White Christ

Swéoþeod – Swedes, literally Swedish people

Thing – the governing assembly made up of the free people of the community presided over by a lagman. The meeting-place of a thing was called a thingstead

Thrall – a slave. A man, woman or child in bondage to his or her owner. Thralls had no rights and could be beaten or killed with impunity

Valhalla – the hall of the slain. Where heroes who die in battle spend the afterlife feasting and fighting according to Norse mythology

LONGSHIPS

In order of size:
Knarr – also called karve or karvi. The smallest type of longship. It had 6 to 16 benches and, like their English equivalents, they were mainly used for fishing and trading, but they were occasionally commissioned for military use. They were broader in the beam and had a deeper draught than other longships.
Snekkja – (plural snekkjur) typically the smallest longship used in warfare and it was classified as a ship with at least 20 rowing benches. A typical snekkja might have a length of 17m, a width of 2.5m and a draught of only 0.5m. Norse snekkjas, designed for deep fjords and Atlantic weather, typically had more draught than the Danish type, which were intended for shallow water.
Drekar - (dragon ship) larger warships consisting of more than 30 rowing benches. Typically they could carry a crew of some 70–80 men and measured around 30m in length. These ships were more properly called skeids; the term drekar referred to the carvings of menacing beasts, such as dragons and snakes, mounted on the prow of the ship during a sea battle or when raiding. Strictly speaking drekar is the plural form, the singular being dreki or dreka, but these words don't appear to be accepted usage in English.

Introduction by the Author

Although this series of novels contains some of the characters introduced in the previous series - *The Saga of Wessex* - it is a separate series of novels. It concentrates on the momentous events that led to the unification of the four kingdoms – Wessex, East Anglia, Mercia and Northumbria – into one realm called at the time Englaland – the land of the Angles.

Having succeeded in their struggle for survival, Wessex and the half of Mercia not under Danish rule gradually expanded their control over the rest of England. Initially this was due to the efforts of King Ælfred's children, Eadweard of Wessex and Æthelflæd of Mercia.

What they started was then completed by Eadweard's son, Æthelstan.

After his death, the union fractured for a time but the foundations were there and setbacks to the unification of Anglo-Saxon England proved temporary.

The books in this series are works of fiction but I have tried to stick as closely as possible to the history as outlined in the sparse written records of the early tenth century. Inevitably, the various sources contradict one another, especially as regards dates, but I have tried to piece together a logical chronology before putting pen to paper – or more correctly finger to keyboard.

I am particularly indebted to the following sources:

Ælfred's Britain – War and Peace in the Viking Age by Max Adams

Alfred, Warrior King by John Peddie

Pauli's The Life and Works of King Alfred translated by B Thorpe

The Warrior Queen – The Life and Legend of Æthelflæd by Joanna Arman

Edward the Elder and the Making of England by Harriet Harvey Wood

Æthelstan by Sarah Foot

Anglo-Saxon England by Sir Frank Stenton

PROLOGUE

The rain pattered down on the roofs of the various halls, huts and hovels that had sprung up haphazardly between the more substantial ancient Roman buildings, some of which had been repaired in a makeshift manner and some had been left as ruins. All lay within the walls of the old city that was now called Lundenburg.

As the rain intensified, lightening lit up the night sky and thunder crashed overhead. Unsurprisingly, very few ventured abroad in such conditions but nevertheless the man in the Black Monk's habit under a jet black cloak darted from shadow to shadow like a wraith.

When he reached the tavern with the wooden carving of an angel hanging outside, he pulled aside the cowl which covered his head and peered behind him to make sure he wasn't being watched. He glanced up at the carving above his head and, worried that the rotten wooden effigy hanging from a rusty chain might fall and brain him at any moment, he darted inside.

The smell that greeted him was a mixture of damp wool, stale urine and dogs' faeces emanating from the earthen floor covered in straw that should have been changed weeks ago. A half-starved cur slunk towards him, its tail between its legs, hoping for a morsel of food from the stranger but all it got was a swift kick. It yelped and ran to hide in a corner where it waited for a more sympathetic patron to enter.

The stranger glanced around without lowering his cowl and, spotting a man wearing a blue tunic and buff coloured cloak, he made his way towards where he sat alone in a small alcove.

'You received my friend's message then?' the man in the blue tunic asked unnecessarily.

'Obviously,' the Black Monk replied curtly.

He was no more a monk than he was King of Wessex. It was merely a convenient disguise. He wasn't here to exchange small talk and he decided to cut to the chase before the fool opposite him could indulge in any more pleasantries.

'Who am I to kill and what's your master offering?'

The man in the expensive blue tunic recoiled. He wasn't used to dealing with assassins and this man looked as if he'd cut your throat without a moment's thought if you displeased him.

'Er, Lord Æthelstan,' his companion replied in a whisper so low that the other man could hardly hear him.

Now it was the assassin's turn to feel uncomfortable. It was one thing to kill one or other party engaged in a land dispute or to settle a blood feud but to murder the king's son, whether a bastard or not, was quite another.

'Well, will you do it?'

'What's your master offering?'

'Six hundred silver pennies.'

'That's not nearly enough for the risk I'd be taking. Besides, Æthelstan is always accompanied by his gesith; no, I need to hire other men so the price will have to be a thousand pennies.'

The other man struggled to hide his pleasure. His lord had given him twelve hundred pennies to pay the assassin. That left two hundred for him to pocket, more than he would normally be paid in two years as his master's senior reeve. However, the Black Monk was no fool. He saw the look of greed that passed over the other man's face and knew that he'd been cheated.

The reeve's glee changed to fear as he felt a dagger prick his inner thigh under the table.

'Let me have all that your master gave you or I'll geld you here and now.'

Reluctantly the reeve handed the other man a hefty purse. The assassin put it on the bench beside him out of sight of the others in the tavern and loosened the draw cord.

'There's only a few hundred pennies in there,' he exclaimed after a quick glance at the contents.

He pushed his dagger deeper into the reeve's thigh.

'Half now and half when the deed is done,' the frightened reeve squealed.

'Three quarters now,' the other countered.

'That's all I have. Meet me here in two months' time and I'll give you the rest; provided, of course, that Eadweard's bastard is dead.'

The Black Monk grunted. The official story was that Æthelstan, the king's eldest son, was born out of wedlock but rumours that he had married Æthelstan's mother in secret were gaining in credence. Not that he could have cared less who ruled Wessex. He wasn't even a Saxon.

His father had been a Viking raider and his mother an Irish thrall. She'd been sold to a Saxon ceorl soon after he'd been conceived and he'd been born into slavery. When he was twelve he'd killed his master after he'd been given one too many whippings and ran away, leaving his mother to face the consequences. Doubtless she would have been hanged but he consoled himself with the thought that there was nothing he could have done about it. He'd been killing ever since.

A slatternly girl who looked no more than thirteen came and offered him a goblet of ale but he waved her away. When she persisted, saying that he had to buy a drink or leave, he waved the dagger with its point dripping blood from the reeve's thigh in her face. He'd expected her to get the message and leave him alone but he'd miscalculated. She dropped the jug of ale and ran away screaming like a banshee.

Half the men in the tavern got to their feet to see what was amiss. Not wanting trouble, the Black Monk quickly left the tavern and vanished into the night. In his absence the reeve found himself surrounded by an angry mob but he pointed to his bloody leg and claimed that he'd been robbed. A few men went outside to chase after the supposed thief but the foul weather soon persuaded them to return to the warmth of the fetid tavern.

The reeve left, limping on his wounded leg, wondering whether it had been such a good idea to arrange to meet again in the Angel tavern in two months' time. Then he realised something. The assassin didn't know who he was, nor the identity of the noble who wanted Æthelstan dead. He didn't need to return to the place after the man dressed like a monk had kept his side of the deal and, best of all, he could keep the other half of the man's blood money. All he had to do was to kill the intermediary who had put him in touch with the assassin and the trail would run cold.

PART ONE

The Quiet before the Storm

The Danelaw roughly comprised these fifteen shires:

Leicestershire, Yorkshire, Nottinghamshire, Deorabyshire, Lincolnshire, Essex, Cambridgeshire, Suffolk, Norfolk, Northamptonshire, Huntingdon shire, Bedfordshire, Hertfordshire, Middlesex, and Buckinghamshire.

CHAPTER ONE

SUMMER 911

Cedric scanned the horizon but it remained empty. He glanced down at the deck nearly fifty feet below him. From up here the warriors who manned the longship looked like pieces on a tæfl board. The ship suddenly hit a larger wave than normal and the boy lurched around. He instinctively clutched at the small projection from the mast on which he sat but it wasn't necessary; he'd firmly secured himself to the topmost section with a length of stout rope.

At twelve he was the youngest of the ship's boys aboard the *Saint Oswald*. She was the largest type of longship; the sort the Vikings called a drekkar – a dragon ship. It had been captured from the Northumbrian Danes the previous year and the fierce serpent mounted on the bows had been removed and burnt. Now the figurehead was a depiction of the saint whose name had been given to the vessel – a king of Northumbria from centuries ago who had converted his kingdom to Christianity. The carved wooden figure was dressed for war but held a cross aloft instead of a sword.

Cedric had heard the scops tell of a warrior called Wynnstan who had led a daring raid into Lindsey, part of hostile Northumbria, to recover the saint's relics a few years ago. Now Oswald's bones resided in a jewelled casket in the church dedicated to his memory in Glowecestre, the most important settlement in Mercia and the home of Æthelflæd, the Lady of the Mercians.

The boy was startled out of his reverie by the sudden appearance of something on the horizon off to the west. At first he wasn't sure if it was an illusion but then a second shape appeared near it. He carefully undid the rope around his waist so that he could stand up on the tiny seat, holding onto the top section of the mast like a limpet.

Satisfied that he hadn't been mistaken, he re-attached the rope and breathed a sigh of relief, the danger of falling onto the deck far below – or even worse, into the sea – having receded. At least hitting the deck would bring a quick death; plunging into the cold sea would mean the prolonged agony of drowning. Although he could swim, unlike many of his fellows, there was no chance of the longship turning about and finding him and they were many miles from shore.

Now he could see the shapes more clearly. There were three of them and they slowly became dun coloured sails. They were too far away for him to see any device woven onto the sails but they were coming from the direction of Íralond and that meant that they were more than likely Norse longships. That didn't mean that they were necessarily Vikings intent on raiding. They could be Norse knarrs, or even longships, crewed by traders. However, merchantmen normally came from the south bringing cargoes from the Continent or even from the lands around the Wendel-sæ. Whoever they were, they needed to be investigated.

'Ho there, below, three sails off the larboard beam,' Cedric bawled down in his treble voice.

The captain, a Mercian named Heoruwulf, cupped his ear to indicate that he hadn't heard the boy clearly above the noise of the wind, the sea rushing past the hull and the creaking of the wood from which the ship was made.

Cedric cupped his hands together to form a funnel and shouted his message again as loudly as he could. Heoruwulf nodded and peered to the west but he could see nothing except the endless grey sea from deck level.

'Can you make out any details yet?' he called up.

The lookout gazed at the oncoming grey shapes. Now he could just make out the foaming white surf at the bows and he could see that the dun coloured sails had a black device on them but he couldn't see what it was.

'They are coming on under full sail but I can't make out their device yet. They can't have a lookout at the mast top - or perhaps they have seen us and they want to close with us,' he bellowed back.

He glanced to landward where the other three ships of their small fleet lay. The Saint Oswald was the nearest to the oncoming Norsemen and so, even if they'd seen her, they wouldn't be aware of the other ships.

All four were large longships of a type called skeids and carried crews of between sixty and eighty men. Their task was to patrol the entrance to the Sæfern. The estuary was bordered by the coast of Somersaete – part of Wessex – to the south east, the Welsh kingdoms of Glywysing and Gwent to the west and Mercia to the east.

However large the three strange ships were, they were unlikely to be a match for the Mercian ships, especially as the latter each carried around twenty archers. Their task was to kill the enemy steersmen, the captains and as many of the rowers as they could before the enemy could close with their ships.

'I can make out the device now. It looks like a raven with spread wings. The hulls appear to be lined with shields,' Cedric called.

'Vikings then,' Heoruwulf muttered to himself, then more loudly 'Archers, ship your oars and ready your bows,' as he began to prepare the ship for battle.

✝︎✝︎✝︎

King Eadweard sat brooding in his personal quarters in the palace at Wintanceaster. He'd expanded it over the decade since his father, Ælfred, had died, including replacing many of the timber buildings in stone. He now occupied several rooms behind the main hall which provided him with a bedchamber separate from that of his wife and children, an ante-chamber occupied by his personal servants and the pages on duty, and an office.

Whenever he could he liked to get away from his officials and the demands made on his time ruling Wessex; unfortunately, that wasn't very often. However, today was one of those times and he took advantage of it to think about his son Ælfweard.

At nine the boy should have been fostered out to one of Wessex's noble families by now but his wife, the Lady Ælfflæd, insisted on keeping the boy by her side. Even worse, he was becoming a spoiled and selfish little brat. Consequently Eadweard was becoming increasingly concerned about his fitness to succeed him in due course. He dreaded having to confront Ælfflæd but he would have to insist on sending Ælfweard away to start his preparation for manhood.

Ælfflæd and he had another son called Edwin but he was only two and barely able to talk as yet. Ælfflæd doted on him nearly as much as she did on Ælfweard. They also had several daughters but his wife showed little or no interest in them.

He refused to admit it to himself but he knew deep down that he had made a mistake in labelling his other son – his eldest - a bastard. He had married his first wife in a moment of passion when he was fifteen. Although she was the niece of an ealdorman her father was a thegn with no wealth or power to speak of and Eadweard's parents had forced him to repudiate her. She had given birth to a son ten months after they'd wed and had named him Æthelstan but he'd been dispatched to Eadweard's sister, Æthelflæd, in Mercia to get him out of the way.

He'd arranged for the boy to be sent to a monastery, intending him to become a monk, but Æthelflæd had thwarted him. Had the boy taken his vows he'd be ineligible to inherit; instead Æthelstan was now making a name for himself as a warrior on the northern border of Mercia.

He should be angry with both his sister and his son for having disobeyed him but he was secretly glad that they had. Far from being disqualified as a future king, he was showing every sign of becoming an excellent candidate. Eadweard had been impressed by the young man when he'd met him a few months ago – the first time he'd seen him since he was a babe in arms - and Æthelstan had played a vital part in defeating the Northumbrian army at Totenhale the previous year.

He had been enamoured of Ælfflæd when they had first married and for many years afterwards but gradually he'd realised that she was selfish and avaricious. She was also insanely jealous of Æthelstan. Undoubtedly she saw him as a rival for the throne in due course and Eadweard was fairly certain that she would stop at nothing to make sure that one of her sons succeeded him.

He would like to have rid himself of her but he couldn't afford to. That would alienate her brother, Ealdorman Osfirth of Wiltunscīr, who was also Hereræswa of Wessex. Osfirth was both wealthy and powerful and Eadweard depended on his support.

The more he thought about it the more the situation depressed him. Eadweard was far from a coward on the battlefield and he had a sharp mind when it came to politics. However, he lacked courage when it came to confrontations with his wife, so he tended to avoid her as much as possible. He was happiest when he found reasons to escape from Wintanceaster.

Consequently he threw himself into personally supervising the construction of the new burhs, both on the border of Danish held Ēast Seaxna Rīce and to defend his newly acquired lands to the north of the River Temes in Oxenafordascīr.

It was a strategy he'd devised with his sister. Not only would the new fortified settlements help to protect Wessex and Anglian Mercia, in due course they would provide a bridgehead for the re-conquest of the Danelaw, or so he hoped.

Æthelflæd was to play her part by building similar fortified settlements in strategic places. She started with one at Brigge on the River Sæfern. The Viking leader Hæsten had built a small fort on top of the cliffs on the west bank in the winter of 895/6 and had died there. Now Æthelflæd intended to improve the original fort and enclose the settlement below it with a palisade. It would prevent any Vikings from raiding upstream as well as defending the nearby border with Wealas.

'It's not enough,' she told her closest adviser and friend, Cuthfleda and the latter's husband, Deorwine, the Hereræswa of Mercia. 'Our ships patrol the river estuary but it's a large stretch of sea and some are bound to slip past; besides, we only have a few ships and they couldn't defeat a large fleet.'

'We could improve the defences of Glowecestre,' suggested Deorwine.

'But it's at the head of an inlet, not on the river itself,' Cuthfleda pointed out.

'And it's quite some distance from there to Brigge,' Æthelflæd said thoughtfully.

It seemed an intractable problem. Brigge would be relatively easy to make into a burh but her resources weren't limitless - far from it - and there were other priorities. She had agreed with her brother that she would build frontier defences near the border with the Danelaw, which ran for the most part along Casingc Stræt, the old Roman road from Dofras in Cent as far as the River Sæfern at Wrekichester, once an important Roman centre but now abandoned.

Four new burhs were planned along this border, one of which was at Tomtun, the capital of Mercia before it was partitioned. However, she couldn't concentrate on just the Danelaw. Mercia was also threatened by Northumbria. She would need to improve the defences in the north as well. It was going to take years and she prayed that she and Eadweard were allowed the time to complete their line of fortifications.

Cedric scrambled down the shrouds which supported the mast and jumped onto the deck just as his fellow ship's boys finished lowering the mainsail. He helped the other three furl the heavy oiled woollen sail around the yard from which it was suspended and then lift it into the cradle and secure it. By this time the first of the Viking ships was a mere three hundred yards away.

The rowers bent their backs to propel the Saint Oswald away from a head on collision and made for the leeward side of the enemy craft. With the wind behind their arrows the archers would have a little extra range. The steersman brought the ship skilfully head on to the waves to give the archers as stable a platform as possible and the rowers let their oars drag in the water so as to slow their ship.

The boy watched as the first arrows climbed into the sky, shot at high trajectory so that they came down from on high into the mass of men in the other longship. Many of the score of arrows struck the ship's timbers or shields held above the Vikings' heads but a few found exposed flesh.

Three of the best archers had waited until the enemy had lifted their shields, exposing the owners' bodies before loosing. One killed the steersman and another wounded the man standing beside him, presumably the captain. The steering oar swung wildly with no hand on it and the drekar came close to broaching as a large wave struck it broadside on.

The Vikings were thrown here and there and chaos reigned. The next volley took them unprepared and this time eight were killed or wounded. Seconds later a third volley struck down a dozen more. The archers had done their job and Heoruwulf gave the order for the rowers to get the Saint Oswald underway again. It took some time before she picked up speed and by that time a smaller Viking ship – a snekkja with fifteen oars a side – was closing in on the Mercian ship's larboard side.

The Saint Oswald had twenty four oars a side and normally the smaller longship would have been no match for her but Cedric saw the third Viking ship making for the port side. This was a drekar similar in size to the Saint Oswald. Even with the assistance of the archers it was extremely unlikely that they could weaken the two crews sufficiently to make a difference. It meant that they would be boarded by perhaps a hundred and twenty warriors, enraged at the fate of their sister ship.

However, Cedric had forgotten about the rest of their fleet. The other three Mercian longships were closing fast and someone on the Viking ships had the sense to realise that there wasn't enough time to board and take the Saint Oswald before they were boarded themselves, and by overwhelming numbers. The two enemy longships sheered away and began to head back whence they'd come.

Heoruwulf waved his thanks at his rescuers and gestured for them to pursue the two Vikings. The first drekar was trying to limp away but, with only half the oars manned and an inexperienced man on the steering oar, they were making slow progress. The ship's boys, assisted by one or two of the less seriously wounded, were hauling on a halyard and the yard with its wildly flapping sail rose slowly up the mast. It showed how much of a panic the enemy were in – or perhaps it was because they now had inexperienced men in charge. Normally the sail would be hoisted whilst it was still furled and then the boys would climb aloft and release the sail from its bindings.

It didn't take long before the Saint Oswald overhauled the drekar, which was still being rowed as the ship's boys struggled to sort out the sail.

'Raise larboard side oars,' Heoruwulf yelled and one set of rowers lifted their blades out of harm's way as the prow approached the stern of the Viking craft.

The enemy rowers were still pulling at their oars as the Saint Oswald scraped down the drekar's hull, snapping off the ends of the blades as it went. The inboard ends shot backwards as the oars shattered, caving in the rowers' ribs or breaking their arms. Two Mercian warriors threw grappling irons aboard the other ship and hauled the two hulls together.

By now the rowers had exchanged their oars for weapons and shields and leapt aboard the enemy. Cedric followed gripping his dagger tightly. If he could kill a Viking he could keep whatever the man owned. The plunder the raiders had captured would be shared out but a warrior's personal wealth and equipment belonged to his killer.

At first Cedric couldn't see anything except the backs of his own crew but then he spotted the man standing on the rear deck who had been wounded by an arrow. It had struck his right shoulder making that arm useless. However he held a sword in his left hand and he evidently wasn't inexperienced in using it that way. He'd just killed one of the younger warriors in Cedric's crew.

The wounded Viking cast around for his next assailant but he didn't look low enough. Cedric crouched as he approached the man, who he assumed from the ornate helmet on his head was the captain. At the last moment he stood up, taking the man by surprise. Cedric thrust his dagger into his left armpit before he could react. He expected the captain to drop his sword but he was made of sterner stuff. He clumsily swung the blade at Cedric's head and the boy only just managed to duck just in time. Unfortunately, in so doing he'd let go of the hilt of his dagger and he was now unarmed.

The wounds in his shoulder and his armpit were beginning to trouble the captain and the consequent blood loss was weakening him. He blinked to clear the sweat from his eyes and looked around for his assailant. It gave Cedric a moment's respite and he risked looking down for his dagger. He couldn't see it but he yelled in excitement when he saw a hand axe lying close by.

He rolled away to escape the captain's next clumsy thrust with his sword and managed to grasp the haft of the axe as he did. He rose to a kneeling position and, as the Viking took another cut at him, Cedric lifted the heavy axe and, nearly overbalancing, managed to strike the back of the man's right knee with such force that it numbed the boy's hand. Now hamstrung, the man's leg collapsed under him and, as he lay in the deck, Cedric brought the axe down again and again trying to sever the Viking's head from his body.

Someone hauled Cedric to his feet and took the axe from his hand. He looked around blinking away the tears. He didn't know why he was sobbing but the others knew. It was the inevitable reaction to surviving his first battle and killing his first man.

He looked around and it slowly dawned on him that the fight was over. The Vikings were either dead or prisoners and for the last few minutes the crew of the Saint Oswald had been watching and cheering the youngest member of their crew as he fought the enemy captain.

Quite apart from the kudos he gained with his crewmates, the captain had a heavy purse of silver tied to his belt. Furthermore, he wore several gold and silver arm rings and his helmet, byrnie and weapons would fetch a fair bit back in Glowecestre. It slowly dawned on the boy that he was rich.

He'd only been taken on as a ship's boy because his father had been a warrior before he'd been killed in battle. Although he was a ceorl – a free man – he'd left his family destitute. They had had to exchange their home for a tiny rat-infested hovel and his mother had to work all hours as a laundry maid in an attempt to clear his father's debts. The alternative would have been to sell herself and her children into slavery.

Now he could pay off the creditors and purchase a decent hut in which to live as well as looking after his mother and his three younger siblings. He was euphoric and that, combined with his youth, ensured that it took very little of the ale captured on the drekar before he got roaring drunk that night.

At first the prisoners wouldn't talk but, after Heoruwulf had thrown one of them overboard and left him to drown, they changed their minds. It wasn't so much that drowning was an unpleasant way to die; it condemned a Viking to spend the afterlife in Helheim, rather than Valhalla - or so the pagans believed.

Heoruwulf learnt that the leader of the Vikings and captain of the second drekar was a man named Ragnall who called himself the King of Mann, a sizable island in the Íralandes Sǣ off the Cumbrian coast. The Vikings had been raiding the south east coast of Íralond and had planned to sail up the Sæfern to pillage southern Wealas and Mercia before heading home.

Most Mercians had heard of Ragnall. He was said to be one of the grandsons of Ivar the Boneless. He had been of the brothers who had led the Great Heathen Army; the Danes who had nearly overrun Wessex half a century before. Although Wessex and Western Mercia had survived, the Danes had conquered East Anglia, Northumbria and the other half of Mercia.

Legend had it that Ivar had abducted the daughter of the King of Strathclyde and sired several children with her. He'd sailed to Íralond where he'd become King of Dyflin but he'd died in battle a year or so later.

The Mercian longships returned to Glowecestre well content with having seen off the raiders and having captured a valuable longship to add to their small navy. Heoruwulf believed that they had taught Ragnall a lesson that he wouldn't forget in a hurry. He boasted that the man was unlikely to ever trouble Mercia again. Unfortunately that would prove to be far from the case.

CHAPTER TWO

NOVEMBER 911

Ywer, Ealdorman of Cæstirscīr in northern Mercia, groaned as he got out of bed. He was only thirty seven but a lifetime of fighting and being badly wounded on several occasions had left him feeling a lot older. He glanced down with fondness at his Norse wife, Gyda, who was still sleeping peacefully and snoring quietly. He pulled on a linen tunic and a thick woollen cloak before going outside to empty his bladder.

It was cold, even for early November, and his gut told him that this was going to be another harsh winter. Still, the store huts were full of grain and other supplies which should be enough to see them through to the spring. Nevertheless, there was time for one last hunt to lay in more salted and smoked game before the winter snows arrived. Irwyn, his twelve year old son, would enjoy getting out of Cæstir for a while too.

Thoughts of his son brought a warm glow to his heart. The boy's grandfather, Jarl Harald, had been proud of his grandson. It was such a shame that the old man had died before seeing the boy became a man. He frowned. The sudden death of Harald hadn't just been a tragedy for the family. Gyda was the old jarl's only surviving child but, as a woman, she was ineligible to succeed him. Consequently the local thing – the Norse equivalent of a witan - had elected Ögmundr, a man with no connection to Ywer's family, as their new jarl.

They couldn't have made a worse choice. Ögmundr hated Mercians and had refused to meet Ywer. It didn't bode well for future relations with their neighbours to the north. Harald had been the most powerful and influential of all the jarls who held land across the River Mǣresēa from Cæstirscīr. Although Ögmundr didn't have his predecessor's status – indeed he was very much an unknown quantity as far as his fellow jarls were concerned – he did command a sizeable warband, even without the other Norsemen living close by.

With that in mind, Ywer decided that it would be wise to take several of his nobles and his gesith when he and Irwyn went hunting. Harald had prevented his young men from raiding Ywer's territory but he was certain that Ögmundr would place no such restriction on his warriors; he might even encourage it to test Ywer's mettle.

The air was cold and frost still coated the ground when the hunting party rode out of the walled settlement of Cæstir under a cloudless blue sky. Everyone rode with care. The shod hooves of their mounts could easily slip on the frozen earth and a moment's inattention could send horse and rider crashing to the ground, often severely injuring both.

It was better once they entered the trees where the earth – if not exactly soft – wasn't quite so hard. They were after boar and each man carried two of the special spears used for hunting them. They differed from the spears used for war. There was the sizeable crosspiece at the base of the metal blade to stop the maddened boar forcing its way down the spear, even when impaled, to gore the man wielding it.

The riders also carried swords whereas the dog handlers and trackers, who accompanied them on foot, were armed only with daggers. The final group were servants, also on foot, leading packhorses to carry home the day's kills.

Boar hunting was popular, not just because of the succulent meat it yielded but because the danger involved added spice to the sport. Boars were cunning and had been known to wait in dense cover to ambush the hunters. Hunting wasn't necessarily an entirely one sided business.

'Will I be allowed to make a kill today father?' an excited Irwyn asked as the trackers and the dog handlers cast about for the spore of a boar.

'No, this is a dangerous sport, Irwyn. You are here to experience a hunt and learn what happens. You will have to wait until you become a man and a warrior before you can think of making a kill yourself,' Ywer explained.

Irwyn's mood changed instantly from eager anticipation to frustration. Warrior training began when a boy reached fourteen and became an adult legally. It usually took two years to complete and therefore Irwyn gloomily reflected that it seemed to him like an eternity before he'd be able to engage in a hunt himself.

He wasn't allowed to carry a boar spear, or even a bow. The only weapons he had were his dagger and the seax which had been a present from his father on his twelfth birthday. It was all so unfair when he considered himself perfectly capable of slaying a stupid animal.

It wasn't long after they'd entered the trees that the dogs picked up a scent. The huntsmen had difficulty in restraining their dogs as they ran after them through the undergrowth. The trail was faint and narrow; brambles cut the men's bare legs and one tripped over a tree root causing him to let go of the hound's leash.

Ywer roundly cursed the unfortunate man. His dog would try and tackle the boar on its own and would easily be killed. It wasn't the hound's task to attack the quarry; they were there to follow its spoor.

Stupidly some of the younger riders were overcome with excitement and galloped after the hound. Ywer and the more experienced of the mounted hunters called them back but to no avail. To his concern, Ywer saw that one of those who had joined the mad rush after the loose dog was Irwyn.

✝︎✝︎✝︎

Ögmundr looked at the man two of his warriors had brought into his hall. He was dressed all in black wool; he'd exchanged his habit for black woollen trousers which were wider than the Anglo-

Saxons favoured and were similar in style to those worn by the Danes and the Norsemen. However, his tunic, although made from good quality material was unadorned, unlike those worn by wealthy Scandinavian men who liked to show off their wealth by embroidering the hem and sleeves with silver and gold thread. Furthermore he was clean shaven whereas Scandinavians took pride in their beards and grew one as soon as they were old enough. When he spoke, his Norse - although fluent - had a trace of an accent. The man was an enigma.

'I'm told that you wanted to make me an offer I can't refuse,' the jarl said without preamble.

'And I'm told that you have no love for your neighbours to the south,' the man replied, his face expressionless.

'They believe in the White Christ, even the Norsemen amongst them; they are mistaken. My mission is to bring them back to the true religion, the worship of Thor, Odin and the other true gods.'

'Be that as it may,' the stranger replied. 'I can help you by killing one of their their leaders.'

'Ywer?'

'Him too, but I was thinking more of King Eadweard's son, Æthelstan. He is your most important enemy.'

'He's merely an irritant. I could take Mamecestre any time I choose,' the young jarl boasted, 'but the Danes in Northumbria would expect me to give it back to them. Why should I do them any favours?'

'You're not thinking clearly. Æthelstan is dangerous and he's ambitious. I'm told that, when he succeeds his father, he intends to fulfil Ælfred's dream of uniting Wessex, Mercia, East Anglia and Northumbria into one mighty kingdom.'

The stranger had heard nothing of the sort; it was merely a ploy to get Ögmundr to play his part in the killing of Æthelstan. What he didn't realise was how prophetic his words would turn out to be.

'If that's what he thinks, the man is a fool!' the Norseman responded with a laugh. 'Northumbria, East Anglia and most of

Mercia is firmly in the hands of the Danes and what isn't controlled by them is ruled by us Norsemen.'

'Think for a moment. Northumbria's power was all but destroyed at the Battle of Tatenhale. It will take a decade or more for them to recover. The rest of the Danelaw has no cohesion. It is governed by a myriad of jarls constantly bickering and fighting over territory. The glory days of the Great Heathen Army are long gone.

Even as we speak Eadweard and Æthelflæd are building burhs, ostensibly to defend their lands but in reality as bridgeheads from which then can launch attacks into Eastern Mercia. Once that falls East Anglia will follow leaving Northumbria isolated.'

What the man had to say gave Ögmundr pause for thought but he wasn't a man who ever considered the wider picture. His main concern was to consolidate his power over the jarls who surrounded him. However, it would enhance his reputation if he could capture Mamecestre. If he had to hand it over to the Danes of Northumbria subsequently he could, he supposed, demand a price for doing so.

'Tell me what you have in mind,' he said eventually.

✝︎✝︎✝︎

When he saw his son disappearing with the rest of the young hotheads Ywer's immediate instinct was to charge after him. However, common sense prevailed and he ordered his captain, Godric, to take charge of the rest of the hunting party. He set off accompanied by Skarde, a Christian Norseman who was Jarl of Wirhealum, a sizeable peninsula within Cæstirscīr.

Skarde had no children of his own but he doted on his nephew, Brandt, the son of his late half-brother and Ywer's sister, Æbbe. He had brought the boy along for much the same reason as Ywer had brought Irwyn – to experience a hunt for himself.

Ywer had a feeling that Skarde and his sister were lovers but, if so, they were being discreet about their relationship. The Church frowned on marriages between brother and sister-in-law but Ywer couldn't see why. It would need a Papal dispensation for them to wed, if indeed they wished to do so; he made a mental note to speak to his brother, Æscwin, the Abbot of Cæstir, about the possibility of obtaining one.

Skarde told Brandt to stay with Godric before following Ywer. The two galloped along the clear trail left by the excited youths but the youngsters must have been some way ahead of them because, when they came to a large clearing, they were nowhere in sight. Ywer dug his heels into his horse's flanks, urging it to go faster and slowly he drew ahead of Skarde.

Unbeknownst to the two men, Brandt had been no more obedient than his cousin and had chased after his two uncles, ignoring Godric's yelling to stop. The captain cursed the boy to hell and back and sent two of his own men and a couple of Skarde's warriors after them. The hunt was developing into a dangerous farce. He had no doubt that Ywer would severely discipline the fools who'd broken away from the hunt but that didn't help the current situation.

Skarde and Ywer rode through a stream but lost the trail on the far side; the ground there was rocky and there was no sign of either hoof prints or boar tracks. Ywer was getting desperately worried when the two men heard the faint sound of excited shouting quickly followed by ones of alarm. They raced off in the direction of the noise fearing the worst.

Meanwhile Brandt had fallen behind his uncles on the pony he was riding. By the time he came to the stream the two men had disappeared. Unlike them the boy had remained calm and, rather than casting about for signs on the far bank whilst still mounted as they had done, he jumped down and painstakingly looked for any signs. It wasn't easy to spot but several horsemen were bound to leave traces of their passing on even the stoniest of ground. One rock had a recent chip in its side made by an iron shod hoof and several other stones had been displaced. He re-mounted and set off in the direction indicated by the marks.

When Ywer reached the site from where the noise had emanated his heart sank. The youths following the hound had been ambushed by a large sow protecting a couple of piglets. The dog which had caused the problem lay dead with its stomach ripped open, its warm guts steaming in the cold air. It wasn't the only animal killed by the boar; two horses had also been gored to death. One of the riders had evidently been thrown clear but the other wasn't so lucky. His leg had been trapped under his dying horse and the sow had torn out his entrails.

The three surviving youths had managed to spear the boar but none of the strikes had been fatal; that had only served to enrage the animal even more. However, by the time that Ywer and Skarde arrived on the scene the sow lay dead.

One of the young men explained what had happened. The sow had attacked Irwyn next but he had guided his horse out of the way at the last minute so that the wicked tusks only managed to score a deep cut along her side. The boy had lifted his leg out of harm's way, otherwise the tusk would have seriously injured him. As the boar charged past him Irwyn had lost control of his rearing mount and had fallen off. The sow had churned up the earth in its efforts to turn around and continue its attack.

Despite being badly winded, Irwyn rolled to one side to evade her but one of the boar's tusks snagged on his tunic, ripping it and lifting him clear of the ground for a moment. At some stage the boy's seax had fallen out of its scabbard and now lay a few feet away.

The other three had ridden in to thrust their second spears into the sow as it renewed it efforts to gore the vulnerable boy but none of their thrusts proved fatal. In time she would have died through loss of blood but not before Irwyn had been killed. He realised that his salvation lay in his own hands as the others milled about not knowing what to do after using their last spears.

Irwyn scrambled along the ground on all fours and rolled out of the way as the sow made another lumbering charge. In doing so he managed to grasp the hilt of his seax. When the animal made yet another attempt to sink her tusks into his body he jumped up, twisting out of the way as he did so, and landed with his legs astride the animal's broad back. He knew he only had a second or two before he would be thrown off but the boar was so surprised that for a moment she came to a halt and stood there quivering as she tried to work out two things: where her quarry had gone and what the unexpected weight on her back was.

Irwyn ignored the sow's powerful stench and seized his chance; grasping the hilt of the seax in both hands, he drove it down with as much force as he could muster into the animal's skull. At first he wasn't sure that his blade had penetrated the hard bone and reached the soft brain matter underneath but the sow slowly dropped to its knees and rolled over, trapping his leg under her dead body.

Whooping in triumph the others dismounted and dragged the boar off Irwyn. So far he'd suffered no more than a few scratches but the sharp bristles tore his trousers to shreds and his leg was badly grazed in the process. Irwyn felt the pain but was too euphoric over his kill to pay it any attention. It was at that moment that his father and uncle rode into the clearing.

Far from congratulating him his father berated him and his companions for their folly, pointing out that it had led to the death of one of their number. Everyone hung their heads in shame and jubilation changed to contrite misery in an instant. All eyes were on the irate ealdorman and they had forgotten about the piglets. They were around a year old and close to the age when they would normally have left the sow. Although their tusks were still growing they were old enough to be dangerous and, seeing their mother killed, they attacked the group of hunters.

Irwyn was standing, as was Skarde having dismounted to check that the sow was dead. Both were therefore in the most danger when the piglets attacked. The boy was the first to react, jumping to the side just as one of the animals reached him. Ywer jabbed down with his boar spear, driving the point into the young boar's body. It squealed in fury but a second thrust found its heart and it collapsed beside its mother.

Skarde wasn't so lucky. Brandt came on the scene just in time to see the piglet drive one of its short tusks into his uncle's right calf. His leg collapsed under him and a second thrust of the young boar's tusks penetrated his other calf, severing his anterior tibial artery. Bandt was frozen with shock but the warriors who had followed Ywer and Skarde arrived at this point and one of them quickly dispatched the second piglet. However, the damage had been done.

Ywer dismounted and ran over to Skarde as he lay on the ground, his leg pumping out his lifeblood at an alarming rate. He undid his belt and used it to apply a tourniquet. It reduced the loss of blood to a trickle but the ealdorman knew the situation was serious. Without treatment the tourniquet was only delaying the inevitable. At best Skarde would lose his lower leg and at worst he'd bleed to death.

It was at that moment that Leofdæg, the captain of Cæstir's garrison arrived.

'Get a fire going,' he barked. 'Quick as you can. The wound needs cauterising.'

Men ran to gather kindling and wood whilst one got out tinder and flint from his saddlebag. Leofdæg had been trained in the rudimentary skills of healer at one stage in his long life by two brothers who had served Ywer and his father before him as physicians – Uhtric and Leofwine. They were now part of Æthelflæd's household but Leofdæg knew what to do. He washed the wound and then got one of the men to expose the wound whilst he applied the heated end of his seax to the tear in the artery.

The smell of roasting human flesh was nauseating but it did the trick. Skarde lost consciousness due to the pain but when he eventually awoke the wound had been sewn together, dressed with a poultice and bound with cloth torn from a clean tunic. He would probably walk with a limp once he'd recovered but Leofdæg's swift action had saved his life.

†††

The day after the hunt Ywer was still contemplating what punishment his son and nephew should suffer for their disobedience when Æthelstan arrived with his gesith. In addition to being the Lord of Mamecestre, a fortress on the border between Mercia and Northumbria, Ywer had recently made him the thegn of six vills on the south bank of the River Mæresēa, across from the territory ruled by Ögmundr.

The vills had been held by Rinan until his death the previous autumn. He had been the captain of the gesith of Ywer's father – Jørren – but he had never married nor had any children. It seemed logical to make Æthelstan his successor. Now he was responsible for defending the frontier all the way from Apletune to Mamecestre.

'Have you had any trouble from Ögmundr?' Ywer asked him once they were settled in front of the central hearth in Ywer's hall.

Æthelstan nodded his head as he sipped the spiced mulled mead that a servant had brought him.

'By God's grace, that's very welcome. I'm frozen after that ride. At least it's not snowing,' he said with a wry smile.

'There have been a couple of raids recently but they were minor affairs. In both cases Wynnstan tracked the culprits and hanged those he caught as a warning to others. They were scarcely more than boys – newly trained warriors eager to prove themselves. However, Ögmundr is rumoured to be gathering his forces for something more major, perhaps an assault on Mamecestre itself, but more likely a raid on one of my vills.'

'Why do you think that?'

'One of those who Wynnstan hanged had taunted him, saying that the time was coming when he and I would be killed by Ögmundr, along with all our men.'

Wynnstan was the captain of Æthelstan's gesith. He had grown up living in the woods as a boy and was the best tracker in Cæstirscīr, possibly in the whole of Mercia.

'Is Astrid still refusing to join him?'

Æthelstan sighed. Astrid was Wynnstan's Danish wife who served Cuthfleda, Ywer's sister and close confidant of Æthelflæd, the Lady of the Mercians.

'I'm afraid so and it's making Wynnstan miserable, especially as his son remains with his mother in Glowecestre.'

Both Ywer and Æthelstan had been vastly relieved when the Witenaġemot of Mercia had gone against centuries of tradition and elected Æthelflæd to rule them after her husband, Lord Æðelred, had died earlier in the year. Glowecestre was de facto the capital of Mercia and it was where Æthelflæd normally based herself.

However, she wasn't there much of the time. Her current preoccupation was building several burhs – fortified and garrisoned settlements – to defend Mercia. Cuthfleda accompanied her as did the latter's husband, Deorwine, the Hereræswa of Mercia. That meant that Astrid went with Cuthfleda, leaving her three year old son, Sicga, behind in Glowecestre to be looked after by his nurse. That added insult to injury as far as Wynnstan was concerned. He couldn't see how his son was better off in the care of slaves instead of living with his father.

'What do you want me to do about it,' Ywer asked, returning to the matter in hand. 'These rumours about Ögmundr's intentions may be just that, rumours.'

'I was hoping that you could send me reinforcements; that would send a message to Ögmundr that he wouldn't just be attacking me but the whole of Cæstirscīr. Hopefully that would be enough to deter him.'

'I could but, with winter coming on, you might have extra mouths to feed for several months. Do you have enough supplies for that? Besides, is Ögmundr really going to start a war at this time of the year?'

'Perhaps you're right,' the other man said reluctantly. 'I wish that Wynnstan hadn't been so quick to hang the braggart. We may have got more information from him under torture.'

Ywer grimaced. He wasn't enthusiastic about tormenting an enemy to get the truth out of them but he acknowledged that sometimes it was necessary.

'There may be more raids before the weather closes in and it becomes impossible so you may get another opportunity,' he said with an optimism he didn't feel. 'If you get concrete evidence that Ögmundr is planning something significant come back to me but for now I suggest we just keep an eye on the situation.'

It wasn't the outcome that Æthelstan was hoping for but he had little alternative but to accept his ealdorman's decision. He went to leave but Ywer called him back.

'Before you go, there's a favour I would like to ask of you,' he began.

CHAPTER THREE

NOVEMBER 911

In consultation with Skarde, Ywer had decided on the appropriate course of action following Iwyn's and Brandt's foolhardiness. Neither Æbbe nor Gyda were happy about it but they had accepted it; after all what was proposed was common practice amongst the Anglo-Saxon nobility - and even amongst the Vikings. At Ywer's request, Æthelstan had agreed to foster the two boys and bring them up as warriors until they became men at the age of fourteen. For their part, the boys had mixed feelings about it.

Irwyn had expected to be fostered before this and Mamecestre wasn't that far away. Naturally he was unhappy at leaving his parents but he consoled himself with the thought that at least he would see them from time to time. Had he been sent to one of the other ealdormen in Mercia he wouldn't have been able to do so. If one part of him was sad at leaving his boyhood home, the other part was excited at the prospect of being trained to be a warrior, and by a man he admired almost as much as he did his father.

Brandt was two years younger and the pain at being parted from his own mother and the uncle he'd come to regard as his father was consequently more intense, especially as Skarde was still recovering from his injury. Furthermore, he'd spent much of his life living in a Norse settlement. Now he'd be surrounded by Anglo-Saxons, some of whom might well be antagonistic towards him because of his Viking blood, even if he was a Christian and had a Mercian mother.

He'd also miss his friends back in Grárhöfn. He had Irwyn as a companion, of course, but he didn't know his cousin that well. Like Irwyn, Brandt felt some excitement at embarking on a new adventure but, at ten, fourteen seemed an impossibly long way off. Consequently, he embarked on the journey feeling dejected and lonely.

Æthelstan had been reluctant to take on the fostering of his new charges. He hadn't done it before and he had no children of his own, nor was there any prospect of fatherhood in the near future. His own future was too uncertain to think about wedlock and starting a family. The lack of a wife to look after the two boys was a distinct problem. At their age they still needed the maternal nurture of a woman and he didn't even have a mistress.

He glanced at his captain and close friend, Wynnstan. He could have handed them over to him to bring up had his wife, Astrid, been living with him. He didn't really understand why she wasn't. If she were his wife Æthelstan would have insisted that she and the couple's son joined him. Instead she preferred to stay and serve Ywer's elder sister, Cuthfleda. He sighed and admitted to himself that he didn't really understand women.

The weak late autumnal sun had put in a brief appearance whilst he was at Cæstir but the blue sky had disappeared almost as soon as they'd left. Now the clouds overhead turned dark grey and a cold wind caused Æthelstan to pull his thick woollen cloak tighter around him. He was not a man to moan about discomfort but he did look at the wolf skin cloak that Brandt was wearing with some envy. Wealthy Danes and Norsemen took pride in wearing cloaks of wolf and bear skin but it wasn't the sort of garment that an Anglo-Saxon lord could ever wear without being the subject of ridicule.

As they headed north east towards the south bank of the great River Mæresēa light snow began to fall. It wasn't long before the flakes increased in size and intensity and he pulled his scouts back closer to the main body. They could see little in the developing blizzard and there was a danger of them losing touch with the rest if they ranged too far ahead.

The road they were following was little better than a track and, as the swirling snow covered the hard ground, it rapidly vanished. Only the trees and undergrowth on either side showed where it ran. When they emerged onto open moorland even those markers guiding them home disappeared. Thankfully four of his scouts -

Wilfrid, Sawin, Wardric and Tidhelm - were adept at following a trail in the most difficult of conditions. They took it in turns for one pair to walk ahead of the cavalcade and lead the way. It made progress slow and Æthelstan began to worry about the effect the cold was having on his men and the horses. He was even more concerned about the two boys.

'There's a disused group of huts that used to be inhabited by charcoal burners not far from here, lord,' Sawin told him.

The young scout shared his lord's unspoken concern and was especially anxious about the two boys who looked blue with cold - even Brandt, despite his wolf skin cloak. Furthermore, trudging through the snow, which was now more than fetlock deep, was exhausting their mounts.

Æthelstan nodded and Wynnstan gave the order to follow Sawin to shelter.

✝✝✝

The Black Monk had intended to ambush Æthelstan on his way to Cæstir. Initially everything went according to plan. Ögmundr had played his part in seeming to threaten to attack Æthelstan and, as expected, the latter had ridden to discuss the situation with Ywer. What the assassin hadn't anticipated was the size of the escort his quarry had taken with him. He had assumed that in friendly territory, Æthelstan would only feel it necessary to take a few warriors as escort, especially as he would presumably want to leave as many men as possible to guard his vills and the threatened fortress at Mamecestre. The assassin had miscalculated.

Normally his assumption would have been correct but, with the possibility of running into a raiding party of Norsemen, Æthelstan had decided to take his complete gesith of thirty mounted warriors. Any attempt on his life was made even more difficult as Wynnstan had sent scouts ahead of the main body to ensure that they weren't ambushed.

The Black Monk had recruited twenty men – outlaws and mercenaries in the main - with a sprinkling of inexperienced young Norse warriors. They weren't a match for Æthelstan's hardened fighters, especially as the brigands would be significantly outnumbered. He decided that he would have to try something different on Æthelstan's return.

His new plan was to send the few archers he had up trees either side of the road with orders to concentrate on killing Æthelstan. He assured them that the rest of his men would hold off the man's gesith long enough for them to climb down and escape after the deed was done. Of course, he had no intention of tackling thirty trained warriors with the scrapings from the gutter he'd recruited. As soon as his quarry was dead he and the others would vanish into the trees leaving the archers high and dry.

He'd sent men along the track to give warning of Æthelstan's approach. When the snow started his men started to bitch about the cold. Then the advance piquet returned claiming that there was no point in remaining at their post as they couldn't see further than a few yards along the track.

The Black Monk cursed them to Hell and back but he was forced to acknowledge that the snow had made his plan unworkable.

'There's an old charcoal burners' encampment that we sometimes use about two miles in that direction,' one of the outlaws told him, pointing to the south west. 'We could shelter there until this blizzard stops. It's only about five hundred yards south of the road.'

'Can you find it in this snow?' the Black Monk asked dubiously.

The man grinned, showing a mouthful of missing and blackened teeth.

'I know these woods like the back of my hand,' he assured him.

It wasn't until they got within eighty yards of the collection of huts and charcoal burning mounds that they realised that the small settlement was occupied. Horses were tethered in the lee of the ruined huts to shelter them from the worst of the weather but there was no sign of any men. Presumably they were all inside the huts.

Despite the fact that some of the turf roofs had caved in, the walls and what remained of the roofs would give them a fair degree of protection.

His ruffians were all for attacking Æthelstan and his men inside the huts but the Black Monk realised that would be folly. Although there was no sign of any sentries, he was certain that they were being watched. The man's gesith were too experienced to leave the place unguarded. Furthermore, there would be little room to wield swords, spears and axes inside the confined space of the huts and it would come down to dagger work. Unprepared or not, he knew which side he would put money on in that sort of fight.

No, the sensible thing to do was to wait until Æthelstan emerged and use his archers to kill him.

✝✝✝

'I need to go outside,' Irwyn told Æthelstan.

'To piss?'

The boy nodded, hanging his head as it was something to be ashamed of.

'I do too,' Brandt added.

For a moment Æthelstan thought of telling the boys to go in a corner of the hut where the roof had caved in like everyone else but he realised that they felt shy at doing so front of the men. In any case there was bound to be a few ribald comments if they were made to do so which would embarrass the two youngsters.

'Very well,' he said reluctantly, 'but don't go too far.'

The door had long since vanished and so the area near the open doorway was deserted. Snow blew in to settle on the beaten earth floor. Irwyn went outside and Brandt followed. Once in the open, the biting wind and the icy flakes which found their way down his back nearly caused him to change his mind but his need was desperate, so he pressed on.

Standing in the lee of a large oak tree a warrior named Chad huddled into his cloak as he kept watch on the approaches to the huts. Wynnstan had decided to change the sentries frequently because of the cold and Chad waited impatiently for his relief to appear. The dense curtain of white flakes blanketed sound and so he had to rely on sight. At first he thought that his eyes were playing tricks on him but there was no doubt about it; dark figures were moving stealthily towards the group of huts.

Chad tried to sound a warning by hooting like an owl, something rarely heard during daylight and so a favourite way of sounding the alarm without warning an enemy that they'd been spotted. However, it evidently didn't reach his companions as there was no movement from the huts. Then two figures emerged. He could only make them out indistinctly because of the falling snow so he didn't realise immediately that it was the two boys. However, their diminutive size meant that it had to be Irwyn and Brandt.

No one followed them out and, as they made their way to a nearby bush, he realised that they had come out to relieve themselves. He had to do something or the strangers would either kill or capture his ealdorman's son. It was far from ideal conditions in which to use a bow but it was the quickest way of halting the intruders. If they came under attack, they would turn their attention on him.

He hurriedly took the bowstring from its oiled leather bag and strung his bow. Selecting an arrow, he nocked it in place and chose the nearest man as his target. It was a difficult shot as the man's cloak would slow the arrow if he aimed at his body. The man wasn't wearing a helmet, just a woollen cap, so that was where he was most vulnerable. For a moment the target was obscured by the falling snow but then he reappeared and Chad released the arrow.

It flew straight and true, piercing one side of the man's neck and reappearing on the other. On the way it nicked both carotid arteries and the man collapsed gurgling as his life blood drained away, staining the nearby snow a dark red.

Unfortunately none of the other men had noticed the death of their comrade. Chad moved closer and picked a man close to several others as his next target. This time a gust of wind blew the arrow off course and it lodged in a tree just in front of his intended victim. It didn't matter as the attackers did what he wanted and turned in his direction. He sent one more arrow towards the enemy, hitting a man in his thigh, before vanishing into the falling snow.

The Black Monk cursed as most of his men went chasing after Chad. He looked around and saw that only three had remained with him. It was at that point that one of them pointed out the two boys by the bushes. They were in the act of tying up the waist cord of their trousers before hurrying back to the hut. Unfortunately they were totally unaware of the drama being played out and so didn't hurry, especially as it was slow and exhausting work plodding back through snow a foot deep in places.

The Black Monk's men were also hampered by the deep snow but they were taller and stronger than the boys and they managed to reach them before they found safety. Irwyn stopped in surprise when he eventually became aware of the four men struggling towards him but he managed to pull his seax out of its scabbard before they reached him. Brandt wasn't so quick to react and stood like a deer at bay, not knowing what to do.

Irwyn ducked under the clumsy cut at his head from the first of the ruffians to reach him. He thrust up from a crouching position and felt his blade sink into human flesh. It was more resistant than he'd expected and he had trouble dragging his seax clear. His adversary screamed; the boy had managed to strike up between his legs, gelding him as well as doing irreparable damage to his intestines.

It was the first time that he'd fought a man in earnest and he stood there shaking and staring down as the man writhed in agony. The boy was totally unaware that a second man had reached him and was about to cut him down with an axe when Brandt came out of his stupor. Dragging his dagger clear of its sheath, he leaped onto the man's back just as he was about to bring the axe down on Irwyn's head. The boy stabbed at the man's neck time and time again as he clung on until the dead man fell into the snow and Brandt was thrown clear.

The sound of fighting had inevitably been heard inside the huts and Æthelstan's gesith came rushing out to see what was happening. The Black Monk swore vociferously as he spotted his target but there was nothing he could do. It was time to leave. He'd stayed at the rear, leaving his three hirelings to deal with the boys, and therefore had a head start on the Mercians. The last of his three men wasn't so lucky and he was quickly caught.

Meanwhile Chad had led the rest of the Black Monk's men in a circle which ended back at the charcoal burners' huts. He emerged a few yards ahead of his nearest pursuers. He was tiring and, had the chase gone on for much longer, he would have been caught and killed. As it was, his pursuers took one look at the warriors milling around outside the huts and vanished back into the trees.

The man who'd been caught didn't need much persuading to talk. The promise of a quick death instead of a slow death hanging head down over a fire pit had been sufficient to get his tongue wagging. His name was Kåre, he was fifteen and he was one of Ögmundr's newly fledged warriors. All he knew about the man who led them was that he was called the Black Monk and he'd arrived to see his jarl unexpectedly. It was rumoured that an attack on Mamecestre was planned but the older and wiser warriors thought it was merely a feint.

The young warrior said that he was an orphan and pleaded with Æthelstan to be allowed to live. If he was spared he would swear an oath to serve him loyally, even if it meant becoming a thrall.

'He's scum, lord,' Wynnstan said in Ænglisc so the young Norseman wouldn't understand. 'He'll betray you the first chance he gets.'

'I realise that but he's evidence that Ögmundr is working against me, and thus is an enemy of Mercia. The man has to be dealt with before he gets up to serious mischief. I need to keep the boy alive for now so that he can tell Ywer what he told us.'

He went over to his new fosterlings, who sat against a tree with their arms around each other. He remembered what it was like to kill your first man in a fight and these two were very young to have to deal with the reaction that inevitably followed. He crouched down in front of them and told them how proud he was of them and how gratified their father and uncle would be with the way they'd conducted themselves. He saw the two stiffen their backs and puff out their chests in response to his praise. Patting them both on the shoulder he got up and told them to return to the shelter of the huts until the snowstorm was over.

An hour later the dark clouds vanished and the snow ceased falling. However, it was still bitterly cold when Æthelstan's column set off again. Instead of continuing towards his home he turned back to Cæstir to report what had happened. This time he deployed six scouts – two ahead and two on each flank just to make sure the Black Monk didn't try again.

As they rode Æthelstan thought about the attack. Although the Norse boy didn't know who the assassin's target was, it was pretty obvious he was the intended victim. It wasn't the first time. Mercenaries had tried to abduct him when he was nine. He had a shrewd idea who was behind the attack on both occasions. The one person who most wanted him out of the way was Ælfflæd. If he was dead there would be no obstacle to her son, Ælfweard, succeeding their father in due course. However, he didn't think that the king's wife would be so foolish as to get involved in hiring assassins. It was more likely that her brother, Osfirth, had made the actual arrangements. The question was what should – or could – he do about it?

Ywer was extremely perturbed when Æthelstan returned and told him what had happened. It didn't help that Gyda blamed him for putting their son in danger's way. He was proud of the way that his son had acquitted himself and the incident hadn't changed his mind about fostering the boy with Æthelstan. He only hoped that Skarde would feel the same about Brandt. Doubtless Æbbe would react similarly to his wife, especially as her son was quite a bit younger than Irwyn.

After Godric and Wynnstan, captains of their respective gesiths, had joined the two nobles in Ywer's office he outlined what he saw as the tasks that lay before them.

'We need to find this Black Monk and bring him to justice and we also need to deal with the threat posed by Ögmundr before he becomes a major problem.'

'This Black Monk must have a base somewhere,' Wynnstan pointed out.

'Perhaps he's staying in Ögmundr's hall?' Godric suggested.

'I think that's unlikely for two reasons,' Ywer disagreed. 'This Black Monk needs to operate this side of the River Mǣresēa and, secondly, Ögmundr won't want to be too closely associated with him. He can always deny any association with the attack on Lord Æthelstan by saying his warriors were young hotheads acting without his permission.'

'I suggest that I send out several small groups of scouts to check all possible places the brigands might be using as a base, including isolated farmsteads,' Wynnstan suggested. 'It seems to me that's the most likely type of place to hide. Once they've killed the inhabitants, no one would know that they were there.'

'Good,' Ywer said, nodding. 'Meanwhile I'll think about the best way to get rid of Ögmundr without launching a major campaign against the Norsemen north of the Mǣresēa.'

Gyda had a shock when she told Irwyn that she didn't want him to return with Æthelstan. The fight at the disused charcoal makers' huts had changed the boy. His father's pride in him had helped. He no longer regarded himself as a young boy but as a warrior. After all, he'd just killed his first man. He therefore told his mother that he had every intention of continuing with the proposed fostering.

She didn't take it well and blamed his father for, as she saw it, driving a wedge between her and their son. She was still mourning the death of her father, Jarl Harald, and had been feeling depressed for some time. This rift with Irwyn made it worse.

Brandt felt much the same way as his cousin. However, Æbbe wasn't as shocked as Gyda had been at the change in her son. She realised that he was no longer a child, despite his young age. Besides it was better that he had the companionship of his cousin than he was fostered with another noble where he wouldn't know anyone. There was something else that reconciled her to the loss of Brandt; unlike Gyda she would still have a child at home. Her daughter Frida was only eight and so it would be several years before she left her side to marry.

Æthelstan decided to stay at Cæstir whilst his and Ywer's scouts scoured the area between Cæstir and Mamecestre for the Black Monk's base. In the following days there was no more snow, however a bitingly cold wind blew the fallen snow into deep drifts. This made movement difficult and the scouts had to take care not to succumb to the cold. However, it also meant that the assassins they searched for were unlikely to stray far from whatever place of shelter they'd found.

Wynnstan led one of the groups and it was one of his scouts, Tidhelm, who found their base. As the former had suspected, the Black Monk's thugs had killed a Mercian ceorl and his family and taken over their farmstead. The bodies had been left outside and, although they had become covered during the snowstorm, animals had fed on the remains at night leaving the grisly remains on view.

As he watched, a boy emerged from one of the huts and made his way down to the nearby stream to fill two wooden buckets with water. He was bare-legged and wore a homespun tunic and a dirty sheepskin roughly cut to fit around his torso. It was held in place by a belt made of rope. Evidently the boy was a slave who'd been spared by the Black Monk when the rest were killed and who now served his band of thugs.

The boy struggled back up the slope watched by a man wearing a tattered brown cloak. The hilt of a dagger poked out from its folds. From the state of the cloak and the man's unkempt appearance Tidhelm assumed that he was an outlaw. Presumably he was watching the boy to make sure he didn't run away, although to do so dressed as he was and with bare legs was to invite frostbite and a slow death in the desolate snowfields. The boy carried the buckets into the hut and the man followed him, slamming the door.

Tidhelm slowly edged away from his vantage point, lying beside a bush on top of a low hillock, brushed the loose snow off his clothes and made his way back to where he'd tethered his horse. He led it back to where Wynnstan and the others waited.

'We've found them, captain,' he reported. 'They've killed the family who farmed the land but appear to have left the slaves alive to serve them.'

Normally Wynnstan would have left two scouts to keep a watch on the place but it was too cold to stay immobile in the open for very long, so he took everyone back with him to report to Æthelstan and Ywer.

That afternoon sixty men rode out of Cæstir led by Ywer and Æthelstan. Irwyn had pleaded to be allowed to go with his father but Ywer had been adamant. The boy was to stay with his mother. Gyda was delighted to have one last opportunity to spend time with her son but her happiness soon changed to annoyance. The boy did nothing but sulk and wouldn't engage in conversation with her, apart from the odd monosyllabic grunt.

Wynnstan and his four scouts ranged ahead of the main body, following their tracks back to the isolated farmstead. The cold wind had died down and the sky overhead had changed from a leaden grey to light blue. Few birds sat on the bare branches of the trees and those that did flew away squawking in alarm as the column of armed men rode below.

Once they reached the spot where Wynnstan waited the warriors split into two groups. Forty men led by Æthelstan circled the farmstead and set up a cordon whilst Ywer led the remaining twenty warriors towards the small hall and the other huts. Some would no doubt house grain and other produce stored to see the family through the winter, whilst others would provide shelter to the ceorl's livestock.

Whilst Æthelstan expected the Black Monk and most of the men he'd hired to live in the hall, it wasn't large enough for everyone. He couldn't be sure of the exact numbers they'd encountered at the charcoal burner's huts but he didn't think that there could have been more than a score. There were two huts in addition to the ceorl's hall and two barns.

Tidhelm pointed out the hut into which the boy carrying the buckets of water had gone. Ywer nodded and gestured for him to take three warriors with bows. Anyone who exited the door when the fighting started would be a target. Tidhelm warned his archers that there were slaves in the hut as well as the men they were after but he only did it to salve his conscience. He knew that realistically his men wouldn't have the luxury of checking who was who in the small space. They would be fighting for their lives and any hesitation could be fatal.

Four other warriors headed for the other hut whilst Ywer and Godric set off for the hall with the rest. Once he'd checked that everyone was in position Godric went up to the door and pushed it. However, it didn't budge. Either it was barred inside or there was a latch. He knelt down and peered through the gap between the edge of the door and the end of the wall. He breathed a sigh of relief; it looked like a simple latch.

He put his ear to the gap and listened. He could hear muted conversation and the occasional laugh. A voice yelled for more ale so it sounded as if the occupants were relaxed, talking, drinking and no doubt gambling to pass the time.

Godric put his eye to the crack but he couldn't see much. There was a fat warrior in a byrnie covered in patches of rust sitting with his back to the door. He had a knife in his hand with which he was cutting slices of ham from a large hock and then cramming them in his mouth but his sword scabbard was empty. Doubtless the Black Monk had ordered his men to leave their weapons by the door to prevent them killing one another when the inevitable drunken arguments broke out.

He slid his dagger into the crack and gently eased the latch up until he felt the door give slightly. He turned his head and nodded at Ywer. The two men put their shoulders to the door and it crashed open. Half-a-dozen men sat at the table just inside the door. They turned and gaped at the intruders before panic set in and they scrambled for their weapons. Ywer glimpsed another six or so sitting at a similar table on the far side of the central hearth before he was faced by his first opponent, knife in hand.

The brigand made an attempt to slash the ealdorman in the face but Ywer stepped back out of the way. In doing so he crashed into one of his men coming through the doorway behind him and his arm was knocked off target as he stabbed at his adversary's neck. He cursed and drew back his arm for another thrust. However, the man was too quick for him; he crouched down and sank the point of his eating knife into Ywer's thigh.

It wasn't a serious wound but it made him realise that perhaps this wasn't going to be as easy as he had thought. It was difficult to wield a sword properly inside such an enclosed space and a man with a knife or dagger had a distinct advantage. He'd been a fool; he should have realised that.

He turned his sword so that it was pointing upwards and brought the pommel down hard on the man's head. He was bareheaded and he collapsed unconscious. He moved further into the room to allow the warriors behind him to enter the hall. Godric had killed his initial opponent and was now fighting against two men, also armed only with knives. However, one of the brigands had got behind him and had picked up a two-handed axe from the pile of weapons by the door. It wasn't an ideal weapon as there was little room in which to swing it but the axeman managed to bring it down on Godric's forearm.

Unlike most warriors, whose arms were unprotected below the byrnie which finished above the elbow, Godric wore steel guards on his forearms. There was little power behind the axe blow and the metal guards saved Ywer's captain from serious injury but the blow was enough to make him drop his sword. Now he faced two knife-men as well as the one with the axe unarmed.

Ywer thrust the point of his sword into the side of one of the brigands holding a knife and then let go of it. He pulled both his seax and his dagger out of their sheaths as they were more suited to fighting in confined spaces. He stabbed the other knife-wielding brigand with his dagger and a second later he chopped his seax into the side of the one with the axe.

By this time the rest of his men had entered behind him and set to work killing the remaining enemy. Ywer took a deep breath to recover and then the pain of the wound in his thigh hit him in earnest. It might not have been serious but he was losing blood and it hurt like hell. He sat down on one of the benches and Godric went to the door yelling for Hengist.

Ywer's body servant came running carrying a satchel. He had been a potboy in a tavern owned by his cousin but the man treated him more like a slave than a relative. He made the boy sneak into rooms at night and steal from travellers staying at the tavern. However, when Hengist had tried to take the purse of a supposedly sleeping Ywer, he'd been caught. Ywer had taken pity on the half-starved boy and had taken him with him when he left. He'd been the ealdorman's body servant ever since.

He poured water on the wound after cutting away part of his lord's trousers to expose it. Next he used tweezers to pluck out small pieces of material that had been pushed into the flesh. After washing the wound again, this time with vinegar, he sewed the two sides of the cut together with catgut and, before bandaging it, he applied a honey poultice to assist the healing process.

'Try to walk on it as little as possible, lord, to stop it opening up again,' he said when he'd finished.

'I have been wounded before, boy,' Ywer snapped, more because of the pain than through annoyance at being admonished like a child.

'Yes, and you never listen to me so it always takes twice as long for you to heal as it should do,' Hengist replied with a grin.

Ywer cuffed the boy around the head for his insolence but the slap wasn't hard.

'I don't know why I put up with you,' Ywer said.

'Because you couldn't do without me,' the boy replied, ducking out of the way of a second slap.

Ywer got to his feet gingerly and, putting his hand on the boy's shoulder for support, he made his way outside.

'We killed them all, lord,' Godric told him, 'but there's no sign of the one they call the Black Monk.'

Ywer cursed; then, out of the corner of his eye he saw one of the servants looking at him as if he wanted to say something. Apart from the boy that Tidhelm had seen fetching water, there were three other slaves: a man and two girls. The latter were in a poor way having evidently been raped by the brigands many times over. It was the boy who had attracted Ywer's attention. He stepped forward when he saw Ywer looking at him but the older slave tried to pull him back.

'Let him speak,' he ordered brusquely and the man reluctantly let go of the boy. 'Well, what is it? Do you know where the Black Monk is?'

'Yes, lord,' the lad stuttered nervously. 'I saw him go into the woods to shit in private just before you arrived.'

'Where in the woods?'

The boy pointed towards the north.

'You stupid little brat,' the older slave scolded him. 'He'll come back and kill us all.'

Ywer didn't blame the man for being afraid. He'd seen his master and all his family killed in front of him and evidently the leader of the brigands still terrified him, even though all his men were dead. However, the way that the man looked at the boy made him realise that the lad would suffer a bad beating for his disobedience after he'd gone.

After telling the slave to shut his mouth he asked the boy his name.

'Oisin, lord,' the boy said hesitantly.

'You're Irish?'

'Yes, lord. I was looking after my father's sheep when some Vikings attacked our village. They captured me and slaughtered my flock for a feast to celebrate their magnificent victory over a few peasants,' the boy said bitterly. 'They took me across the sea with a load of other women and children and sold me in a slave market. From there I was taken with other slaves to be sold again, this time to the Mercian who farmed this land.'

It was a familiar tale.

'Did you look after your new master's sheep?'

'No, lord. He didn't keep any, just a few pigs and two cows. I was used for menial tasks but I also looked after the chickens.'

'I have sheep, a lot of them, and I'm always looking for those who know how to look after them properly. Can you birth lambs?'

'Yes, lord,' the boy said, brightening up.

'Good, you'll come with us. Hengist, Oisin will ride double with you.'

Hengist wrinkled his nose in disgust when he got close to the boy.

'I'll take him down to the stream and give him a good wash first,' he said.

'You forget what you smelt like when I first found you,' Ywer reminded him.

'Do you want me to hunt down this Black Monk,' Æthelstan asked later when Ywer told him what Oisin had said.

'Why don't you send Wynnstan? The devil must have already been in the woods when you put your cordon around the buildings so he's had a good head start. However, he's on foot and you have the best trackers.'

Æthelstan nodded and five minutes later Wynnstan, Tidhelm, Sawin and Wardric set off in pursuit of the would-be assassin.

☦☦☦

The Black Monk was squatting behind a tree when he heard the sound of men making their way towards him. He knew that it wouldn't be some of his ruffians; he'd made it clear enough that he valued privacy when he defecated, which was why he never visited the latrine pit used by others. He hastily pulled up his trousers and lowered his habit before moving further into the woods.

He watched as Æthelstan positioned his men to cut off any escape from the farmstead and thanked Thor that he'd managed to escape the trap. However, things did not look good. He couldn't have cared less about the fate of the brigands and outlaws he'd recruited but his horse, saddlebags and money were back at the farmstead. He had other money stashed elsewhere but the nearest was a hundred miles away. He took off his habit and hid it up a tree; now dressed in Danish trousers and a black tunic he looked less conspicuous. At least he had a score of silver pennies in his pouch and a dagger and a sword at his waist. He set off to find another farmstead where he could steal a horse.

Ten minutes after entering the extensive woods Sawin spotted the black habit hidden in the branches of an oak. Following the assassin's tracks wasn't difficult. Although it wasn't deep under the bare trees, the man's footprints stood out clearly in the snow. Evidently he'd realised this and he'd found the branch of an evergreen bush with which to sweep the imprints away as he walked.   It was a waste of time; the marks made by the improvised brush were as clear to his pursuers as his footprints had been.

They followed the obvious trail, mounted for the most part, and Wynnstan knew they must be closing the gap. The assassin probably had over half an hour's lead on them but, at this rate of progress they should overhaul him in a couple of hours. Then they arrived at a wide stream.

It was fast flowing and knee deep in the middle. The place where he'd entered the water stood out clearly but finding where he'd exited it wasn't as obvious. It was as if he'd vanished into thin air. They checked the far bank in pairs in both directions but there was no sign of his passing on the rocks which had been washed clear of snow by the flowing water, nor on in the snow which lay beyond the far bank.

'He's climbed up and made his way from tree to tree so as not to leave any trace,' Wardric suddenly exclaimed. 'Look there's a tree close to the edge whose branches hang down over the stream.'

It didn't take long after that before they picked up his trail again.

The Black Monk pressed on as fast as he could but the snow became deeper and his progress slowed until he estimated that he was barely covering one mile in an hour. However, the deeper snow slowed his pursuers as well. They were now walking and leading their horses and had ceased to gain on their quarry.

Eventually the Black Monk came across another isolated farmstead. However, this one seemed larger than the one he and his men had used as a base. As he watched from the edge of the trees he saw a girl emerge and make her way to the nearby stream. She was too far away for him to reach her before she made it back to the hall but she would probably need more water before too long. He made his way slowly to the far side of the stream opposite to where she had filled her buckets and sat down in the lee of a bush to wait.

The cold seeped into his bones but he ignored the discomfort. His one chance of escaping lay in stealing a horse. He cursed the reeve who'd sent him on this fool's errand. He didn't even have all the money he'd been paid up front and he'd had to pay each of his men a few silver pennies as a token of good faith. He'd promised to pay a lot more once Æthelstan was dead; a promise he had had no intention of honouring.

He'd brought some of his ill-gotten wealth with him in a saddlebag which was buried in the ceorl's bedchamber back at the first hall. It even included the majority of the money he'd been paid for this task. It would have been folly to keep it on his person; the brigands he'd hired could have killed him and made off with it. Now he regretted being so careful.

He counted out what he had on him, inadvertently dropping one of the pieces of hack silver because his fingers were so cold. He grunted in disappointment. It amounted to the equivalent of no more than fifty silver pennies. He decided that, once he had a horse, he'd have to double back to the hall. The Mercians would be long gone by then and he could recover his saddlebag.

Just when he was beginning to think he'd have to move or freeze to death the door of the hall opened again. This time a different girl emerged. She was much younger than the original one; perhaps ten or eleven? He waited until she'd filled the first bucket and then rose up from his hiding place.

Unfortunately for him his muscles had seized up with cold and his movements were clumsy. As he splashed through the stream the girl screamed and fled back up towards the hall. Both of them floundered in the snow but, now that he was moving, the assassin had thrown off the stiffness caused by his cold vigil and was rapidly overtaking the much smaller child. However, her screams had carried through the icy air and must have been heard by those inside the hall. The door opened and a large Dane emerged carrying a battleaxe. He was followed by two much younger men, presumably his sons, one wielding a spear and the other a sword.

The Black Monk stopped and, as the three lumbered towards him through the snow, he hurriedly retraced his steps towards the stream and the trees. However, luck wasn't with him. He was still fifty yards from the stream with the Danes the same distance behind him when he looked up to see Wynnstan and his three companions waiting for him.

CHAPTER FOUR

December 911 to March 912

'We need the other jarls to stay neutral,' Ywer said, opening the war council meeting in the main hall of his residence in Cæstir.

The original timber hall had been replaced by a new one in stone with two adjoining bed chambers, one for himself and his family and one for important guests. The original hall had been divided up with partitions to provide more guest chambers. It had been Gyda's idea to whitewash the stone walls to lighten the sombre red sandstone walls and it had worked - to an extent. Unfortunately the smoke from the central hearth quickly darkened the roof beams and the top sections of the walls and Ywer's insistence on hanging shields and banners to decorate them had further reduced the amount of light they reflected.

The stone was also much colder than the timber hall had been, even if the mortared joints kept out the wind which whistled through the small gaps between the planks of the old hall. The single fire pit in the centre meant that those sitting close to it were too hot and those closer to the walls received little benefit from the blazing logs. Consequently the more senior men close to the fire had stripped down to their linen under-tunics whilst those by the walls kept their cloaks closely wrapped around them.

'Why, lord? Surely we should launch a campaign in the spring to wipe out the viper's nest and drive the Norsemen from our shores?' one of the Mercian thegns suggested.

'Because that would be stupid,' Skarde retorted angrily. 'It would cost us men we can ill afford to lose and it would stir up a hornets' nest. Northumbria would retaliate and an indiscriminate attack on all Norse settlements across the Mǣresēa would alienate many of the Christian Norse who live peaceably in Cæstirscīr.' 'Like me,' he added after a pause.

Ywer sensed that tension was growing in the hall. Many of the original Mercian thegns resented the Norsemen who had settled in their land, especially on the peninsula called Wirhealum. They seemed to forget that before Ywer's father, Jørren, was appointed as the shire's ealdorman, much of Cæstirscīr had been a sparsely inhabited wasteland. Jørren, with the assistance of Lady Æthelflæd, had brought law and order to the land and encouraged Angles, Saxons and even Danes and Norsemen to settle there, making it the prosperous place it was today.

Men began talking all at once, the Mercians insulting the Norse and the Danes who responded in kind.

'This isn't helping anyone,' Ywer said forcefully after banging the hilt of his dagger on the table to restore order. 'We all depend on one another. If we start falling out amongst ourselves, who benefits? Our enemies would like nothing better than disunity. You seem to forget that we are the bulwark who stands against encroachment by the pagan Vikings in the north and the lawless Danes to the east.'

He looked around the room slowly, his eyes blazing with anger. At least his nobles had the grace to look embarrassed.

'Good; that's better. As I was saying, if we can convince the other jarls on our northern border to remain neutral, then we can concentrate on dealing with Ögmundr. Lady Gyda still has contacts amongst her people and she tells me that their new jarl is far from popular, especially amongst the older and wiser bøndur. They're afraid that he will lead them into a war resulting in defeat and ruin. Whilst the young men may be dissatisfied with their lives as farmers, artisans and merchants, their elders are more sensible. Their priority is to give their families security and lives free from hunger and privation.'

'That's all very well, lord, but how do we go about removing this bellicose jarl without starting a war?' the thegn who had advocated driving out the Norse asked.

'Over the winter I'll send emissaries to the other jarls to secure their non-involvement - by bribing them if necessary – and contact the most important of Ögmundr's hersirs and other influential bøndur. My hope is that they will call a meeting of the thing to elect a replacement jarl.'

'Why do you think that the outcome will be different this time, lord?' Skarde asked. 'After all, they chose him before and he's in a more powerful position now as the incumbent.'

'Because this time the opposition to his rule will be better organised and I intend to attend myself with Irwyn as he's Jarl Harald's grandson.'

'You'll be walking into a hornets' nest,' Skarde exclaimed, 'and if you take your gesith that'll be seen as provocation.'

'No, Irwyn and I will be going alone.'

✝✝✝

Naturally Gyda was totally opposed to the idea. She was convinced that she would lose her only child and be left a widow because of what she called Ywer's pig-headed stupidity.

'At least let me go with you,' she pleaded when it became obvious that pleas, threats and tears weren't about to make her husband change his mind.

Ywer was about to reject the idea out of hand but, much as he hated taking his wife into danger as well as their son, the idea did have merit. Gyda had been left various farms by her father. They were managed by a number of bóndi on her behalf but she was an important landowner in her own right. It was unusual for a woman to attend the thing but not unheard of, especially if they were landowners. They could speak but not vote.

On the other hand all adult freemen could attend and everyone's vote carried equal weight. Irwyn was also a beneficiary of Harald's will but, although classed as a bóndi, he was still a child and normally wouldn't be allowed to attend. However, the lagmann who presided over the meetings, could make an exception in special cases.

On the day in March prior to that on which the thing was to be held Ywer and Gyda rode to Apletune where they were reunited with Irwyn. Their son had grown over the winter and now looked more like a gangling youth than a child. He was already as tall as his mother and Ywer had no doubt that he would soon become taller than he was.

Æthelstan wanted to come with them but Ywer pointed out that, should anything happen to them, then he would have to take over as ealdorman until the Witenaġemot could appoint a permanent replacement. Skarde was the shire reeve and thus Ywer's deputy but he had no wish to become an ealdorman, nor would he be accepted by some of the Mercian thegns.

They crossed the river on one of the small birlinns that Æthelstan used for river patrols and were met on the far bank by a small group of Norsemen who had brought three spare horses. Their leader was a man called Agnar the Hold: hold being a term used for a man who owned a large area of land and who led a significant number of warriors. Agnar was the son of the late Jarl Harald's cousin and thus related, albeit distantly, to both Gyda and Irwyn. On Gyda's advice he was the man Ywer had chosen as a suitable replacement as jarl.

The morning of the thing dawned and Ywer went outside to relieve himself. A light rain was falling and the temperature was low enough to make him shiver, despite the warm cloak he wore over the under-tunic in which he slept. He looked up at the dark grey sky and hoped that the miserable weather wasn't an omen of what the day would bring. He brought the silver crucifix which he wore on a chain around his neck to his lips and kissed it for good luck and then tucked it away out of sight beneath his tunic. The Norse hereabouts were all heathens and there was no point in antagonising them needlessly.

Agnar led the way to the thingstead – an open area of ground near Ögmundr's hall in the settlement called Walingtune. He was accompanied by thirty of his tenants, mostly on foot and on the way he was joined by another three landowners classed as hersirs – a term used to describe bøndur who led a significant number of warriors. In all Ywer's family were surrounded by some one hundred Norsemen by the time they arrived at the thingstead.

Ögmundr was already there, standing on a rocky outcrop ten feet above the large grassy hollow where others were gathering. The lagmann stood beside him – an elderly man wearing a long brown robe rather than the tunics and cloaks worn by the rest. Twenty heavily armed warriors stood at the foot of the outcrop and another ten guarded the hillside behind the outcrop. All were armed with spears and shields and wore byrnies or leather armour and helmets. They made a stark contrast to the bøndur gathering in the hollow who wore no armour and who were armed only with daggers and swords.

Ywer did a swift count of the numbers as new arrivals dwindled to a handful and estimated that there must be the best part of four hundred men in the thingstead.

The lagmann opened the thing by praising Odin, Thor and Freya and calling on all the Norse pantheon to bless their deliberations and grant them the wisdom to reach the correct decisions. As soon as he'd finished Ögmundr stepped forward.

'I see three people who have no right to be here. They are our enemies and should die for their impertinence in attending a meeting of our thing.'

He pointed at Ywer and his family.

'Take them prisoner. Tonight whilst we feast we will take great pleasure in giving them a slow and painful death.'

Many of the young men cheered his words and six of the spearmen standing below the outcrop started to force their way through the crowd to arrest the trio.

'Wait!' Agnar shouted back. 'They are my relatives and they are here at my invitation. Gyda is my second cousin and the daughter of Jarl Harald and the boy is his grandson. They both own land in this jarldom and I claim that they have every right to attend.'

'I deny them that right. The woman is married to our enemy, Ywer the Mercian who stands by her side, and their son is a child. Neither has the right to attend our thing.'

'Surely that's for the lagmann to say,' Agnar retorted.

The latter looked uncomfortable. He was fully conscious that he was surrounded by the jarl's henchmen and he wasn't a brave man.

'Well, it is unusual for a woman and a boy who has not yet become an adult to attend but it may be permissible in certain circumstances,' he temporised.

Catching the thunderous look in Ögmundr's eyes he hurriedly added: 'of course, they're not permitted to vote.'

'I assume from that somewhat ambiguous pronouncement that they may stay,' Agmar declared.

A rumble of assent from the majority drowned out the protests of the younger warriors. The former had been dismayed at the suggestion that the relatives of a man whose memory they honoured should be tortured to death.

'Very well, but that bastard Ywer has no place here. He's responsible for killing several of our young warriors and must pay with his life.'

'I'm here as the husband and father of two of your landowners, jarl,' Ywer shouted above the clamour for his death. 'As to your charge that I killed a few of your warriors, you can hardly hold that against me when you disowned them and claimed that they had joined a band of brigands against your orders.'

He turned to those surrounding him.

'You can kill me, of course, but you might like to consider the implications of such an unwise action. You number what? Three hundred fighting men at most? Should I or any of my family be harmed in any way Lord Æthelstan and Jarl Skarde are standing by, ready to attack with twelve hundred men. They will kill you, bring fire and destruction to your homes and sell your women and children into slavery. Is that what you want? Consider for a moment what your stupid and belligerent jarl has led you to? Is he the best leader for you? No, I say he is the worst.'

The six spearmen were still trying to force their way through to where Ywer stood but, where before men had moved out of their way, now they stood fast and wouldn't let them through.

'Lord Ywer might not be one of us but he talks a lot of sense,' one of hersirs who had joined Agmar on route called out.

'I agree; Ögmundr is a fool who'll lead us to disaster,' another shouted above the growing hubbub in the hollow.

'It's you who are the fools, aye, and traitors too,' an incensed Ögmundr shouted. 'We aren't alone; the other jarls along the Mǣresēa will join us and then we'll be unstoppable. The rich lands of Cæstirscīr are ours for the taking once we've driven out the Mercians and the Christian Norsemen who support them.'

Ywer sensed the mood of the crowd changing. He'd anticipated this moment and a horn blew for quiet before another voice joined the debate.

'What makes you think that we would support you, Ögmundr,' a man standing at the rear asked. 'Have you asked us? No, and none of us would support you in a war against Mercia. Look what happened the last time we tried to capture Cæstir. Do you have such a short memory?'

The speaker was one of the other jarls in the region. He had stood unnoticed, his head covered by the cowl of his hood, at the edge of the hollow. He nodded to one of the men standing beside him who lifted a horn to his lips and blew three short blasts. After a moment or two several mounted men rode up to the lip of the thingstead.

'These are my fellow jarls; the ones you confidently claimed would support you. We have no more love for the Mercians than you do but we aren't idiots. We need to live in peace with them. More and more Norsemen are crossing the Íralandes Sǣ to settle to the north of here. We are more concerned about them and their desire for good land than we are about the Mercians, and so should

- 72 -

you be. You do whatever you want, Ögmundr, but you'll do it without us.'

A rider rode down to the speaker with two spare horses. The jarl and the man with the horn swung into the saddle and a minute later the last horsemen disappeared from sight leaving a stunned silence behind them.

'I say that you are a deluded idiot who isn't fit to be our jarl,' Agmar called out.

'In that case you know the law,' Ögmundr replied with a sneer. 'Tell him, lagmann.'

'You have challenged the authority of your jarl and you must now meet him in single combat,' the man said, much more confidently now that he was on safer ground. 'The fight is to the death or until one of you submits. The loser's fate then rests in the hands of the victor. Whoever wins will be jarl.'

Ywer's heart sank. Agmar was in his early forties whereas his opponent was half his age. If Agmar lost, not only would his hopes of getting rid of Ögmundr fail, but he knew that the jarl would carry out his threat of torturing him and his family to death.

✝✝✝

Æthelflæd sat at the bedside of Cuthfleda, her lifelong companion and adviser, in the nuns' infirmary in Wirecestre Monastery. Astrid, Cuthfelda's head of household, had gone to fetch Cuthfleda's husband, Deorwine, and prepare him for the news that his wife was dying. She had been with the couple ever since they had wed and, although neither of them had been in the first flush of youth, they had been very much in love with one another.

Cuthfleda thought that she was too old to have children but they had been blessed with a son who was now six and a half. It was very young to lose one's mother and she wondered what Deorwine would do with the boy. As he was the Hereræswa of Mercia he was seldom at any one place for long, especially now that he and

Æthelflæd were busy touring her realm to decide where to build new burhs for its defence and supervising their construction.

She found Deorwine playing with his son and with her own child, the three-year-old Sicga. Normally both boys would have been left behind with their nurses in Glowecestre whilst their mothers were away but this time Cuthfleda had insisted on bringing them with her. Perhaps she had a premonition that she was about to die?

At forty three she had lived longer than most women but she had appeared to be in excellent health until she had suddenly collapsed the previous evening. Uhtric, one of Æthelflæd's most experienced physicians, attributed it to a weak heart. He said that her pulse was faint and fluttering and, when asked if there was anything he could do to make her better, he shook his head. The brother, who was the infirmarian for both monks and nuns, looked at him reprovingly and reminded him of the power of prayer. Uhtric was a Christian but he was also a realist.

'By all means pray for Lady Cuthfleda but I advise you pray for her soul not for her recovery. In my view that would take a miracle.'

Whilst Ywer was anxiously waiting for the outcome of the fight between Ögmundr and Agnar, his eldest sister breathed her last.

Astrid had served Cuthfleda ever since Wynnstan had brought her to Glowecestre as a young Danish girl and she took her sudden death very badly. The funeral gave her some closure but it wasn't until Deorwine asked her what her plans were for the future that she gave it any thought. She had assumed that she would remain as head of his household and look after him and his young son but - as he pointed out to her - that would hardly be seemly.

He was a man twice her age and they could hardly be seen to be living under the same roof without creating a scandal. He would have to appoint a steward to the role as soon as possible.

Whilst she was still debating what to do the decision was taken out of her hands. Æthelflæd was satisfied that the construction of the new burh at Wirecestre was proceeding satisfactorily and, as her strategy was to secure her eastern border first, she announced her intention of moving on to the location for a brand new burh in a loop in the River Sæfern that would make an excellent defensive site against incursions from Wealas. After that, she needed to improve her defences in the north. Only then could she turn her attention to the border with the Danelaw in the east.

There was already a small settlement at the new location – a place called Ciropesberic. She had arranged to meet the Ealdorman of Scrobbesbyrigscīr there to discuss the new, and much larger, fortified settlement she wanted him to build there. What he didn't know was that she had also decided that he should move his hall there so that it could become the administrative centre of his shire.

'We won't remain at Ciropesberic any longer than necessary,' she told Astrid. 'From there I intend to go on to Cæstir and discuss the building of two new burhs with Lord Ywer. Of course, it will also give you the opportunity to be reunited with your husband.'

Astrid's reaction wasn't what she'd expected. Evidently she had assumed that, now Cuthfleda was dead, that Astrid would want to return to Wynnstan with their son and to live with him at Mamecestre. However, after years of living at court and putting her service to Cuthfleda before her duties as a wife, she wouldn't blame Wynnstan if he didn't want her back.

She supposed that she still loved her husband but, apart from brief visits, they had lived apart for so long she didn't know how he would react to her sudden return to his side. For all she knew, he could be living with a mistress. Whatever he felt about her, she knew that he would be overjoyed at seeing Sicga again and perhaps that would help. She sighed; she really didn't have any other alternative so she would just have to make the best of it.

✝✝✝

Ögmundr crouched, moving his weight from one leg to the other as he waited for the lagmann to start the fight. Agnar stood stretching and swinging his sword arm to and fro to ease his muscles. Both men stood at the edge of a circle some twenty yards across formed by those attending the thing. Agnar had dressed in his padded leather jerkin and donned his chainmail byrnie and helmet, all of which his opponent had already been wearing.

They had each been allowed a shield and a choice of axe or sword. Agnar had opted for a sword but Ögmundr had chosen a heavy long handled battleaxe with a curved blade at the end on one side and a wicked looking spike on the other. The axe was a dangerous weapon but it required the wielder to use both hands and so Ögmundr had slung his shield around so that it was hanging on his back. Both men also had a dagger.

'I thought that the thing elected the jarl,' Ywer whispered to his wife. 'I wasn't expecting this.'

'They do, but only after a challenge has been issued and accepted,' she replied quietly. 'The winner is usually elected.'

'Well, they would hardly choose the loser,' he muttered.

At that moment the lagmann raised his hand and then lowered it. Ögmundr sprinted towards Agnar, evidently eager to end the challenge to his rule as quickly as possible. Agnar didn't move until the last moment and then he stepped to one side as his adversary tore past him and ended up running into the crowd of onlookers. One man's cheek was torn open by the spike on the jarl's battleaxe and his companions angrily shoved Ögmundr back into the ring.

He whirled around, fully expecting Agnar to take advantage and attack him from behind. He swung his axe blindly expecting to catch Agnar unawares but he wasn't there. When the axe met no resistance Ögmundr nearly lost his footing and he struggled to retain his balance. It made him look foolish and he burned with anger at the laughter and insults that were directed at him.

Whilst the older man remained calm and composed, his adversary let his fury affect his judgement. Once again Ögmundr rushed at Agnar but this time he came to an abrupt halt just as the older man went to step aside. The jarl had anticipated the move and swung his axe at Agnar. The latter was caught by surprise but he managed to bring his shield up to take the blow.

Had Ögmundr been more in control, he should have been able to smash the spike through the other man's shield and into the arm that held it. However, in his rage the blow was mistimed and the curved blade hit the shield instead, glancing off it. It jarred Agnar's left arm and cut a chunk out of the leather which covered the lime-wood shield but it did no real damage.

Agnar now seized his moment and stabbed down at the other man's legs, driving the point into his right thigh. Instead of slowing him down, the wound just infuriated Ögmundr even more and he raised his axe over his head, intending to bring it crashing down on Agnar's head. Had the blow landed it would have smashed through the heavy steel helmet and split his skull in two.

Instead, Agnar ducked out of the way. The blade still struck the back of his byrnie but it was a glancing blow. It chopped through several metal links and badly bruised an area near Agnar's spine but it didn't put him out of the fight. Ignoring the pain, he deliberately dropped his sword so that he could pull his dagger out of its sheath.

Whilst his opponent was trying to recover the heavy axe ready for another blow he moved in close and stabbed the shorter blade up into Ögmundr's right armpit, severing the tendons between the scapula and the humerus. The jarl staggered back, no longer able to use his axe; it was far too heavy to use one handed. He dropped it and clumsily unsheathed his own dagger with his left hand before going on the attack once more, limping because of the injury to his thigh.

Agnar waited for his opponent to launch his next attack but, when he did, he leapt forward to meet him instead of sidestepping. He thrust the point of his dagger into the jarl's chest. He didn't expect the blade to penetrate the chain mail very far but he was hoping that the blow might cut through some of the links and strike his ribs, thus winding him.

However, this time it was Agnar who was taken by surprise. Ögmundr turned his back on him at the last moment so that the blade struck the shield hanging on his back. Caught by surprise, Agnar wasn't quick enough and the jarl's dagger slashed across the exposed biceps of his right arm, forcing him to drop his dagger.

Ögmundr should have had Agnar at his mercy but the jarl's manoeuvre had put weight on his injured leg and it gave way under him. He fell to the ground, yelling in both pain and frustration. He landed on his side but managed to roll out of the way as Agnar brought the copper-bound edge of his shield down where the jarl's throat had been a split second before.

His right arm was useless so Agnar threw away his shield so that he could retrieve his dagger with his left hand. As Ögmundr tried to get to his feet Agnar moved behind him and drew his blade across the jarl's throat, severing one of the carotid arteries.

Ögmundr knew that his lifeblood was pumping out of him and he only had moments more to live. He had let go of his dagger and now his hand groped for it. Agnar knew what he wanted but instead of giving him the dagger to hold, he handed him the axe. It would serve as well and there was no danger that the dying man could use it for a last attempt on Agnar's life. The jarl gave a grunt of thanks and died with a weapon in his hand; convinced in his own mind that he would be taken by the Valkyries to reside with Odin in Valhalla.

CHAPTER FIVE

Summer 912

Wynnstan waited for the arrival of Æthelflæd, Lady of the Mercians, with some trepidation; not because her visit was anything to worry about – quite the contrary – but she was accompanied by his wife, Astrid, and his young son, Sicga. It had been two years since he'd last seen her and the boy. His son would be nearly four now and he regretted not being there when he'd learnt to talk. He wouldn't be a toddler anymore; he'd be a young boy. He would be devastated if his son didn't remember him.

He'd taken all of Æthelstan's gesith to escort his lord to Cæstir. They no longer had to worry so much about the Norse across the River Mǣresēa. Ever since Agnar had become a jarl the raids into Mercia had dwindled to almost nothing. If Agnar and his fellow jarls weren't exactly allies, they had at least remained neutral. In any case, they had other things to worry about. Norsemen from Íralond continued to flood into Northumbria and, although most headed into the hinterland, the numbers that had settled along the north-west coast continued to grow.

They had even invaded Cumbria, which was part of the Brythonic Kingdom of Strathclyde but had been given a bloody nose by the Bryttas. These were the original inhabitants of Britannia at the time the Romans invaded and were the same ethnic stock as those who lived in Wealas and Kernow. It was rumoured that one of the leaders of the Irish Norse was Ragnall ua Ímair, King of Mann, whose fleet had been defeated by Heoruwulf's ships the previous year.

Wynnstan was startled out of his reverie by a cry from a sentry alerting everyone to the approach of a large number of riders. He shaded his eyes against the bright sun and peered down the road which led to the bridge over the River Dēvā to the south. The sentry had good eyesight; all he could see was a cloud of dust. Gradually the cavalcade got closer and he could make out the riders ahead of the dust thrown up by hundreds of hooves. One of them carried the Wyvern banner of Mercia but the lead riders appeared to be scouts. Evidently Æthelflæd wasn't taking any risks, even this close to the walls of Cæstir.

He hurried down the steps and across to the stables where Hengist was already waiting with his horse. Seconds later he was joined by Ywer, his captain, Godric, and Æthelstan. The four rode out of the gates and headed for the near end of the bridge. When the approaching screen of scouts reached the far bank they dismounted and allowed their horses to drink. Two minutes later the Lady of the Mercians trotted over the bridge followed by her own captain, Arne, who bristled when he saw Wynnstan. The two did not get on.

'Greetings Lord Ywer, nephew, I trust I find you both well?' Æthelflæd asked with a smile.

Wynnstan's attention was diverted from the formalities as soon as he saw the carriage near the bridge. He had no doubt that it contained Astrid and his son as well as Æthelflæd's personal maids. Had he not been so preoccupied he might have seen movement in the bushes that lined the far bank.

Suddenly a figure rose from his hiding place and pulled back his bowstring. The arrow struck Æthelstan in the chest but he managed to keep his seat in the saddle. The assassin nocked another arrow to his bowstring but he never had a chance to fire it. Chad, one of the scouts further along the bank, had spotted him as soon as he rose from cover. Reacting without conscious thought he pulled back his arm and threw his spear at the assassin. For most men the distance would have been too great but Chad practised throwing his spear most days and had built up the muscles of his right arm and shoulder.

The spear point dropped towards the ground as the man pulled back his bow and Chad thought that it wasn't going to reach him but then it struck into his thigh just above the knee. The arrow spun away harmlessly and the man dropped his bow before limping away towards the edge of the forest.

Chad hauled himself into the saddle to give pursuit but one of the other scouts had already grabbed his bow and was stringing it by the time that Chad was ready to give chase. He hadn't gone more than a few yards when the other scout's arrow took the limping assassin in the back and he collapsed. When Chad reached him he dismounted, drew his dagger and turned the assassin over. He didn't have to check for a pulse to know that the man was dead.

Meanwhile Wynnstan had jumped out of the saddle and helped Æthelstan to dismount. He laid him carefully on the ground and yelled for someone to fetch a physician. A few minutes later both Uhtric and Leofwine appeared and cut away Æthelstan's expensive embroidered woollen tunic and linen under-tunic so that they could examine the wound.

'Thankfully, the arrow head struck a rib and was deflected. Otherwise it might have reached his heart or one of the blood vessels around it,' Uhtric told Æthelflæd as his brother carefully pulled the arrow out.

As soon as he did, blood started to pour out of the wound and Leofwine pressed a clean linen cloth on it to staunch it. Uhtric searched in his bag and produced a poultice which placed over the wound as soon as Leofwine had washed it clean with wine vinegar and checked that there were no pieces of cloth in it.

'We'll need to sew it up later but we must get him to the monastery infirmary first,' Uhtric told Æthelflæd.

'Will he be alright?' she asked.

'He should be, lady, the wound isn't too deep. The major danger is infection.'

Wynnstan looked up as Chad brought the body of the assassin over the bridge draped across his horse. He recognised it at once.

'The Black Monk!' he exclaimed in surprise.

†††

When he had last seen the man he was running away from the Danes who were chasing him towards the stream. Wynnstan and his companions had tried to head him off but the bushes growing along their side of the stream were almost impenetrable and they had to head further into the wood to get around them. By the time they'd been able to join the stream again they found that they were close to a cliff edge.

The stream fell fifty feet into a pool at that point but it wasn't an unbroken sheet of water. Rocks protruded on the way down, forcing the waterfall this way and that. As they watched, the water swept the black monk past them and flung his body against one rock and then another before it plunged into the pool at the bottom. They watched for some time but he didn't resurface. Satisfied that he was dead, they retraced their way back to join Æthelstan at Mamecestre.

Somehow he had survived both drowning and the bitter cold, although how he'd done so with the injuries he must have sustained was a mystery; one that was never likely to be solved now that he was dead.

Fortunately, Æthelstan had recovered quickly from his injury, although it would take a month or more before the catgut stiches could be removed. Thanks to the precautions that Uhtric and Leofwine had taken there was no sign of any infection and, after a few days' rest, he was well enough to attend Æthelflæd's war council. In addition to Ywer and the two captains – Wynnstan and Arne – the Hereræswa of Mercia, Deorwine, was present.

'I congratulate Lord Ywer on removing the immediate threat to us from across the Mæresēa but, as I'm sure you're all aware,

Northumbria continues to pose a danger,' Æthelflæd began. 'I need to secure Mercia's other borders before my brother and I can turn our attention to reclaiming that part of Mercia which is called the Danelaw. King Eadweard is also determined to bring East Anglia under his rule.'

There was a stir of interest in the room at this. The southern part of the present Danish Kingdom of East Anglia - Ēast Seaxna Rīce - had originally been an independent Saxon kingdom before being incorporated into Mercia two and a half centuries ago. Later it had been ceded to Wessex before being lost to the Danes.

However, the rest of East Anglia between Ēast Seaxna Rīce and the Gewaesc, the rectangular bay on the north-west corner of East Anglia, had always been an independent Anglian kingdom. If Eadweard intended to incorporate this into his kingdom it meant that his ambitions went beyond regaining lost territory; his aim appeared to be the creation of an Anglo-Saxon kingdom encompassing all of Englaland south of Northumbria.

'I have already begun building burhs along the River Sæfern to defend us against the various kingdoms of Wealas, now I need to reinforce our defences against Northumbria.'

'We have fortresses here, at Frodesham and at Mamecestre, lady,' Ywer pointed out. 'Where would you site new burhs and how would we populate them?'

'Frodesham is a small fortress, not a burh, and although Mamecestre is ideally situated to protect the north-east of Cæstirscīr, it can't control the entrance to the Mǣresēa from the Íralandes Sǣ. Cæstir is too far inland to protect the Wirhealum peninsula,' she pointed out. 'Deorwine, please continue.'

The hererǣswa cleared his throat and outlined the plans for the two new burhs, one at Rumcofan where the estuary of the Mǣresēa narrowed to become a river and one at Brunanburh, on the other side of the estuary, half way down the east coast of Wirhealum.

Both burhs would include a small harbour in which they planned to base longships to patrol the estuary and the sea approaches.

'Brunanburh is on Jarl Skarde's land,' Ywer objected.

'Which is why we intend to make him the Earl of Brunanburh,' Æthelflæd said with a smile. 'He will be responsible for building it and manning it.'

Earl was a title that Ywer had vaguely heard of before. He had heard that Eadwulf, the ruler of the independent Anglian enclave between Viking Northumbria and the Kingdom of Alba in the north, called himself Earl of Bebbanburg. It appeared to be a corruption of the ancient Anglo-Saxon title eorl, meaning a man of noble birth, and the Scandinavian word jarl, meaning anything from prince to chieftain.

'Does that mean Skarde becomes independent of me as ealdorman of the shire?' Ywer wanted to know.

'You need to understand, Lord Ywer, Lady Æthelflæd needs to offer something to Skarde in return for his new responsibilities. It also means that you will need to find a new shire reeve, I'm afraid,' Deorwine told him. 'However, even if you've lost the tax income from Wirhealum, your new burh at Rumcofan will attract more settlers to it and the surrounding land.'

Ywer glowered at him but he held his tongue. There was nothing he could do or say if the lady had made up her mind.

'At the moment Rumcofan is one of my vills. Am I to give it up too?' Æthelstan asked a trifle belligerently. 'And who is to be its lord?'

She frowned, upset at his attitude. 'You're a man now, nephew. I want you by my side,' she snapped, then continued in a more conciliatory tone. 'You will retain your deeds to Rumcofan and your other vills but you'll need to appoint another to be responsible for the new burh and a reeve to look after your lands. Ywer, you will also need to find someone else to take charge at Mamecestre.'

'And me, lady? Am I to remain as captain of Lord Æthelstan's gesith?' Wynnstan asked, looking pointedly at Arne.

The two detested each other and, if they were to serve together now that she had effectively appointed Æthelstan as her senior counsellor to replace Cuthfleda, that would only sow disharmony amongst the ranks of the two gesiths.

'It's a matter for my nephew, of course, but perhaps it would be better if you remained in Cæstirscīr, especially now that you have been reunited with your family,' Æthelflæd replied with a glance at Æthelstan. 'Perhaps Lord Ywer can find you a suitable appointment?'

Wynnstan's reunion with Astrid had gone better that he had hoped. The two had been hesitant when they'd met but little Sicga had rushed into his father's arms and he had whirled him around, evoking squeals of delight. That broke the ice and Astrid smiled at their son's evident joy. Wynnstan had put the boy down and taken her by the shoulders before kissing her tentatively on the lips. She'd responded by hugging him and pushing her tongue between his lips to tangle with his own. After that, it was as if they'd never been apart.

'Perhaps Wynnstan would like to take over the responsibility for building and commanding the new burh at Rumcofan,' he suggested.

'Nothing would please me more, lord.'

He would miss Æthelstan, of course. They'd been close friends ever since they were boys but Æthelstan was an ætheling and was obviously being groomed by his aunt for kingship, of Mercia if not for Wessex as well. He would need other, more wealthy and powerful, friends by his side if he was to succeed.

✝✝✝

Æthelstan did more than support Wynnstan's appointment to command the new burh; he made him a gift of the deeds so that his former captain now ranked as a thegn, and a fairly wealthy one at that. Along with the settlement of Rumcofan itself, which represented twenty hides of land, there were six tenanted farmsteads with a total of ten more hides. Each hide represented a land-holding that was sufficient to support a ceorl and his family. There were bondsmen and their families and slaves as well who worked the land but they were forbidden to bear arms. The family of each ceorl or freeman could provide between two and three warriors on average and so the Rumcofan fyrd would number close to fifty men.

It wasn't anywhere near enough to defend the new burh and, even if Wynnstan could afford to keep a few hearth warriors as well, they wouldn't be sufficient to make a difference. He would have to depend on new settlers but they wouldn't come straight away. Eventually the burh would include other ceorls such as artisans, merchants, shopkeepers, tavern keepers and the like. Moreover there was plenty of uncultivated land to lease to new tenant farmers but it would all take time.

He was also tasked to build a harbour. This wouldn't be just a base for the three longships that Æthelflæd would send him to patrol the estuary and the approaches but in time it could become a trading port to rival Cæstir itself if he could persuade the Norse merchant shipping to use it.

However, that was all a fantasy at the moment. To start with he would need to build a suitable hall for himself, his family, servants and a few hearth warriors. It was his priority; after that the construction of the perimeter palisade with towers and at least two gateways – one to link up with the road and one to give access to the harbour. He had some money but not anywhere near enough for that type of undertaking. He began to suspect that Æthelstan's gift of the vill was likely to prove something of a poisoned chalice.

He approached Chad, Sawin, Wardric and Tidhelm and asked them if they would be prepared to serve as his hearth warriors. Chad and he had been friends for some time and the others, although young, had been with him when he'd recovered the sacred remains of Saint Oswald. He would trust all four with his life. They instantly agreed so he went and asked Æthelstan to release them from their oaths to him. He was reluctant as they were amongst the best of his scouts but, now that he was to serve in his aunt's household, perhaps his need for them wouldn't be so great.

'How are you going to fund the building of your new burh?' Æthelstan asked as Wynnstan turned to leave.

'I've no idea; it's something that's been troubling me. Perhaps I'll have to approach Lord Ywer for a loan?'

'Obviously Lady Æthelflæd has forgotten to tell you,' he said with a grin. 'She'll send carpenters and labourers to you just as soon as they've finished work on the burh at Ciropesberic. They are being employed at her expense, although you'll have to provide the lumber free of charge.'

'That's not a problem, lord,' Wynnstan said, smiling with relief. 'I need to clear some of the woods to provide more farming land in any case.'

✝✝✝

The Lady Ælfflæd was far from happy. She scowled as she re-read the letter for the third time before throwing it into the brazier which heated her chamber. She felt like screaming in frustration; instead she cuffed her maid around the head to relieve some of her anger and told her to get out. The frightened girl stopped putting away the clothing that her mistress had tried on and then rejected that morning and, leaving it strewn all over the bed, she hastily scuttled out of the room.

The letter had been from Ælfflæd's brother, Osfirth, Ealdorman of Wiltunscīr and Hereræswa of Wessex. In essence he had told his sister that his reeve had heard nothing from the Black Monk and he had to assume that his assassin had failed to kill Æthelstan. In confirmation of this, he had heard a rumour that Eadweard's bastard had returned to Glowecestre with his aunt. If that was the case, he would be much more difficult to kill than when he lived in the borderlands.

She decided to tackle the matter head-on and the next time that the king came to her bed – which wasn't nearly as often as she would have liked these days – she broached the matter as soon as he'd rolled off her, having sated his lust.

'Cyning, you promised me some time ago that you would formally declare our son Ælfweard to be your heir and ask the Witenaġemot to recognise him as such.'

'Did I? I think that's extremely unlikely. By tradition the Witenaġemot waits until the old king is dead and buried before deciding which of the æthelings should succeed,' he replied, giving her a sour look.

Trust the woman to spoil the moment by trying to wheedle something out of him, he thought bitterly. Normally he would have stayed in her bed for a while until he'd fully recovered from his exertions but, to her alarm, he got up and pulled on a robe.

'I find your constant harping on what happens after my death to be both indelicate and a trifle depressing. If you raise the matter again I will avoid your company completely, do you understand?'

'You can't afford to alienate me, Eadweard,' she said complacently. 'You depend on my brother's support to keep the ealdormen of the western shires in line, not to mention the debt you owed him for the money he's lent you over the years.'

'That may well have been true when I was younger but I assure you, woman, that all of Wessex is firmly under my control now. As to the loans, perhaps the easiest way of freeing myself of that particular burden is to replace Osfirth as ealdorman and as my hereræswa as well. I'm sure that whoever I select as his replacement will be only too happy to pay off my debts in return for the governorship of such a prosperous shire.'

The last thing that Eadweard wanted at this juncture was disharmony amongst his nobles. If he was to incorporate East Anglia into his kingdom and help Mercia recover the Danelaw he needed everyone's wholehearted support. Nevertheless, his wife had overplayed her hand and he knew that the time was coming when he would have to get rid of her.

When Æthelflæd had told him that she intended to groom his firstborn as a potential heir Eadweard had reiterated his claim that he was a bastard. However, the more the king got to know Æthelstan the more impressed he was with him. In his heart he knew that he would make a much better king than the self-centred Ælfweard. However, to recognise his eldest son as legitimate after all the years he'd maintained that he was a bastard would make him look both dishonest and a fool.

'Sister, you know that Æthelstan was born out of wedlock...' he'd started to say but his sister interrupted him.

'You know that's not true and I can prove it. I've seen a copy of the marriage certificate.'

'You can't have! It was destroyed.'

'Two were produced and one was given to Jørren, your wife's uncle.'

'Do you know where it is now?'

'Yes, but I'm not going to tell you. It will be kept safely hidden away until either you change your mind and acknowledge Æthelstan as your eldest legitimate son or you die. Then he can produce it and claim his inheritance.'

For a moment she thought that her brother was going to strike her, such was his anger at being defied. However, Eadweard needed his sister's help in wresting back control of the Danelaw and he managed to restrain himself.

When he had time to think things over he decided on a compromise. He couldn't undo what he'd said in the past but perhaps he had something to offer which would appease his sister.

'I will recognise him as an ætheling, but in Mercia, not Wessex. After all, he's been brought up there and he is your nephew.'

Æthelflæd thought about it. It was probably the best offer that she could wring out of Eadweard and it gave Æthelstan the status of royalty that he currently lacked. Eventually she nodded and Eadweard smiled in relief. He would have preferred not to have made his son an ætheling of Mercia but he would make sure that it didn't compromise his long term plans.

Æthelflæd was nearly five years older than he was and he fully expected to outlive her. If so, he had no intention of letting his eldest son succeed her as Lord of Mercia. It would be incorporated into Wessex as a step on the road to uniting the Anglo-Saxon people and create one kingdom called Englaland. That had been Ælfred's dream and Eadweard's greatest wish was to triumph where his father had failed.

✝✝✝

Cedric looked about him with interest from his vantage point at the masthead. Once again it was his turn to be the lookout as the Saint Oswald led the three longships around the north-eastern point of Wirhealum and headed into the Mæresēa estuary. The palisade around the new burh of Brunanburh was taking shape, as were the two new longships being constructed by its Norse inhabitants.

However, the Saint Oswald and her consorts were headed for Rumcofen at the far end of the estuary. There were a number of fishing boats ahead, some casting their nets in the river but most heading out to try their luck in the open sea. The only other craft in sight was a knarr which was also heading out to sea, probably a Norse merchantman trading between the Norse settlements along the north bank of the river and either Mann or Dyflin.

In 902, the Irish kings of Leinster and Brega launched a two-pronged attack on Dyflin and drove the Vikings out. However,

Viking colonies continued to exist along the south-eastern coast of Íralond and their trading ships were still welcomed in Dyflin itself. Apart from the usual trade goods, the Vikings supplied the largest slave market in Western Europe with a constant supply of captives for sale.

Cedric looked across into the knarr as it sailed past and looked at the score or more men, women and children who huddled miserably in the centre of the deck. Almost all of them had red hair, ranging from almost blond to bronze, and he guessed that they were Picts from Alba. He shuddered and hope that he never suffered the same fate. Death would be preferable to becoming a Viking's thrall.

As Rumcofen drew closer he was surprised to see that the defences were far in advance of those at Brunanburh. The palisade was complete and work on the towers at each corner and either side of a gate facing west were well advanced. At first he couldn't see the harbour and he was so distracted looking for it that he nearly forgot the reason that Heoruwulf had kept him up the mast in the first place. Normally the lookout would have been called down as soon as they entered a river.

He looked down into the clear water and was startled to see a sandbank close to the larboard side of the ship.

'Ware shallow ground off the larboard beam,' he yelled down. 'Another one dead ahead, steer to port.'

'Were you asleep, you dozy bastard?' the captain yelled up as soon as they had passed the danger. 'Run onto one of those and we'd be dismasted, never mind being stuck there until the tide turns again.'

'Another one dead ahead,' Cedric called, ignoring the captain's anger for now, although he knew that he'd be called to account for his indolence later.

'Come down, Cedric, we're getting the mast down.'

Obediently the boy clambered back to the deck where Heoruwulf handed him a length of rope with a metal weight attached to it. The rope was knotted every foot.

'Into the bows with you and call out the depth.'

As he ran forwards the other ship's boys secured the sail before releasing the rigging and lowering the mast into its cradle on the deck. As they were doing so the rowers slid their oars through the holes in the ship's side and started to slowly propel the longship through the water.

Cedric threw the weighted end of the rope forward and, as the ship's prow came level with the vertical rope he noted the colour of the ribbon tied to the knot just clear of the water.

'Six feet,' he called, embarrassed by his voice which was on the point of breaking and fluctuated between its accustomed treble and a deeper tone.

He threw the line again and this time it recorded a depth of nine feet. The boy glanced ahead and saw that they were drawing close to the point where the river narrowed. Now he could see the harbour. He cast the line once more before he dare look again. This time he could see a jetty which jutted out into the water.

The next time he cast the line it ran out before it touched bottom. That meant that there was at least twelve feet under the keel.

'No depth,' he called and was told to stop casting.

The channel would be free of sandbanks from thereon in.

The harbour itself was little more than a couple of jetties at each end and a wooden platform sitting on piles sunk into the muddy sand between them. A few sheds and larger warehouses were in the process of construction behind the harbour and he could see a palisade with another gate beyond that.

A rotund little man was gesturing the attract Heoruwulf's attention but the captain didn't seem to have noticed him.

'The port reeve is signalling to us, captain,' Cedric pointed out helpfully.

Instead of thanking him for his alertness, the captain clouted him hard about the head so that the boy staggered and had trouble in keeping to his feet.

'Do you think I'm blind, boy? He'll want us to moor in the worst berths so he can keep the best for merchantmen who'll bribe him.'

Ignoring Cedric reproachful look as his rubbed his head, he turned to the steersman.

'Head for the wharf near to what looks like a hall. I'll wager that's our accommodation.'

It made sense for the longships to be close to where the crews would be living. It made guarding them easier too as they could fence off that section of the wharf.

As soon as they'd tied up the port reeve came bustling up with two armed men who looked to be at least fifty.

'You can't moor there,' he shouted.

'Why not. Isn't this our hall?'

'Well, yes but you're to tie your ships up back there.'

Heoruwulf peered in the direction indicated.

'You mean near the outflow from the latrines,' he said with a grin. 'No. We're fine here and if you don't like it we'll go and see Lord Wynnstan. Perhaps you'd like to explain your reasoning behind giving us the worst berths. I'm sure he'll agree that it's not the sort of treatment that those who've come to protect you deserve.'

The port reeve's face paled and one of his elderly guards couldn't hide his amusement. The reeve gave him an angry look and stomped off.

'I think we'll need to leave a small guard behind to keep our berths whilst we're out on patrol, captain,' the steersman suggested.

'No, I can't afford the men. If he's put other ships here when we get back we'll cut the mooring ropes and let them drift away. Word will soon get around and it won't happen again.'

Astrid couldn't remember when she'd last been so happy. Her reunion with her husband had gone more smoothly than she'd dared to hope and he'd put her in charge of building their new hall.

She was used to running a grand household but she'd never been allowed to plan the layout and oversee the construction before.

Naturally, it was less grand than Cuthfleda's and Deorwine's quarters in Glowecestre and it would be built of timber rather than stone but she had got Wynnstan to make some concessions. The foundations under the timber walls would be made of stone, thus reducing the creeping damp that affected purely wooden halls and there would be a suspended floor of wooden planks instead of beaten earth.

Unusually, she had designed an L shaped hall: one wing would be the main hall for meetings, eating and drinking and where the servants and Wynnstan's few hearth warriors would sleep. The other wing would house private chambers for the family and two more for guests. She planned a colonnade using timber posts with a roof to provide a sheltered link between the hall and the bed chambers. Wynnstan thought it was far too fancy for a humble thegn but she'd insisted.

Wynnstan prayed to God every day at mass in the small timber church, thanking him for his good fortune. He realised that he would need to replace it with a larger building now that the population of the new burh was growing but it would have to wait until the towers were complete. Unfortunately, there wasn't time to do that before it seemed that the defences might be put to the test.

The first he knew of the trouble that was brewing to the east was when a few refugees from the Æthelstan's five vills along the south bank of the Mǣresēa arrived at his gates. The trickle quickly became a flood. The Northumbrian Danes were besieging Mamecestre and the nearby inhabitants had fled before their foraging parties could pillage their settlements and farmsteads.

Wynnstan immediately dispatched a messenger to Ywer and to the reeve in charge at Frodesham. He debated what else he could do. Even if he included every ceorl over the age of fourteen in his vill, those who had fled from the other vills and the crews of the three longships, the most he could raise was around four hundred, allowing for a small garrison to defend Rumcofen. Reports from those who'd fled from the Danes were wildly at variance with each other and possibly grossly exaggerated but, even so, it seemed likely that Mamecestre was being besieged by at least a thousand Vikings.

'We can't take on a thousand Danes,' Chad said, shaken at the thought of doing so.

Wynnstan had recently appointed him as his captain of his warband, not that four warriors could really be counted as such but the appointment also covered leadership of the fyrd, especially its training. He was the elder by several years and the obvious choice.

'I'm not suggesting that we do. Four hundred couldn't hope to overcome a thousand or more Danes, especially as half of them scarcely know one end of a spear from the other. Even if the garrison of Mamecestre sally forth to attack the enemy we would still be outnumbered. No, we harass their forage parties to lower their morale and deprive them of food.'

'I see,' Chad said thoughtfully, 'but they could still bring in supplies from Northumbria by river.'

'Which is where the Saint Oswald and the other longships come in. Their task will be to escort a couple of knarrs up river and sink them beyond the besiegers' encampment. The Danes will be forced to unload their cargoes some distance from Mamecestre and take it the rest of the way overland. Then we attack their resupply columns.'

'That way we not only deprive the enemy of their supplies but we can bring it down river and store it in our own storehouses in case we are besieged here,' Chad said with a grin.

'Precisely.'

PART TWO

Enter the Dragon

(Author's Note: The wyvern – the mythical beast that was the symbol of both Wessex and Mercia – was a two legged dragon)

CHAPTER SIX

Early Autumn 912

Chad, Sawin and four members of the Rumcofen fyrd watched as a dozen Danes emerged from the wood and made their way cautiously into the open meadow. They had deployed two of their number as scouts but they didn't spot the six men hiding in the trees at the edge of the next stretch of woodland.

One of the fyrd was Oisin, the former Irish slave boy released by Æthelstan. Wynnstan had leased him a remote farm which was only suitable for grazing sheep. The Irish lad was now fifteen and his skill as a tracker had brought him to Chad's attention. At his request Wynnstan had sent a bondsman called Belden and his family to help look after Oisin's sheep, thus freeing the boy to serve in one of the groups whose job it was to ambush Danish foraging parties. They had brought one of Belden's sons along with them to help with chores and to look after the horses.

Chad's small group were outnumbered two to one but they had surprise on their side. All were also adept at using a bow. After leaving their horses with Belden's eleven year old son deep in the wood, Chad sent three of his men to find vantage points up trees which gave them a good view of the track in both directions. The rest waited behind bushes close to the track.

The two scouts came into view first but Chad let them pass through the chosen killing ground. The pair of Danes either weren't very good at their job or they were complacent, being a mere three miles from their encampment outside Mamecestre.

A minute or two later four more Danes rode into view closely followed by two carts being driven by two more. The last four men brought up the rear on foot. The three archers in the trees sprung the ambush. Two brought down the scouts, hitting them in the back just as they were about to round a bend and disappear from sight.

The other bowman sent an arrow the other way into the chest of the leading Dane.

A split second later Chad and the other two emerged and stabbed the remaining three horses in the chest or cut their throats. One fell and trapped its rider beneath it as it thrashed about in its dying throes; another reared up, throwing its rider before collapsing and the third sunk to its knees. The Dane riding it leaped clear but ran straight into the spear being wielded by Oisin. The other two cut the throats of the other two riders before all three attacked the two on the carts as they jumped down.

The four in the rear of the carts stood transfixed for a second, wondering what exactly was happening. Then one of the archers in the trees sent an arrow into the shoulder of one of them and the other three turned and ran. However, they hadn't reached the edge of the wood before more arrows brought them down.

The two driving the carts put up a good fight and succeeded in wounding Oisin before they too were dispatched. Chad sent a couple of men to kill the wounded and loot their corpses whilst he had a look at Oisin's wound. He'd sustained a long but shallow cut to his upper right arm.

'You're lucky, boy,' Chad told him. 'It'll need cleaning but I don't think it even needs stitching, just bandaging for a week or two whilst it heals.'

When they got back to where Belden's son waited with their horses Chad went and fetched the leather bag in which he kept his rudimentary medical kit. He washed the shallow cut with vinegar and used a pair of silver tweezers to pull out as much of the fabric from the sleeve of Oisin's tunic as he could see, then applied a honey and herb poultice before bandaging it up with a strip of clean linen.

The carts contained what the Danes had managed to pillage from several deserted farmsteads and a settlement, not that it was of much value. The supplies were of much more interest. There were four deer carcases, a dead pig and five live sheep in addition to a quantity of root vegetables and a dozen bags of wheat ready for milling.

Pleased with the success of their ambush. Chad sent Sawin ahead as a scout and the small cavalcade headed south-west to give the besiegers' camp around Mamecestre a wide berth.

☩☩☩

It had taken Ywer over a month to muster a large enough army to tackle the Danish horde at Mamecestre. It was harvest time and the majority of the ceorls in the fyrd were farmers. They had been extremely reluctant to leave until all their crops were safely in. The weather hadn't helped. It had rained for much of July and August and a lot of time had consequently been lost. Wet grain would have just rotted in the barns.

They hadn't been on the road westwards for a day before a messenger reached Wynnstan to say that the stronghold had fallen.

'What happened?'

'They starved us out. We ended up eating the rats once the livestock and the horses had gone. The grain and the vegetables ran out a month ago,' the messenger replied. 'I only managed to get away by climbing over the palisade in the middle of the night before the surrender and stealing one of the Dane's horses.'

Wynnstan continued to question the man but he hadn't anything useful to add. At first he thought the Danes might be heading to Rumcofen but they might equally aim for Frodesham first. It lay some three miles to the south and, if it fell, it would cut Rumcofen off from Cæstir.

The settlement at Frodesham had no defences and would fall easily enough but the fortress up on the ridge would be much more difficult to take. He remembered capturing it from the Danes when he was a boy. They would have lost a lot of men assaulting it but they had managed to seize the open gates before the alarm could be raised. It was the time when he'd first met Astrid. She was a Danish servant who'd been foraging for mushrooms in the woods. Wynnstan had prevented any harm befalling her and, in return, she'd distracted the sentries, giving the attackers time to reach the gates before they could be closed.

Speculation as to the Danes intentions after capturing Mamecestre was fruitless. Wynnstan's first priority was to inform Ywer. For a moment he was tempted to go himself. He had a lot to be thankful for: life as a thegn and commander of an important burh was more than he could have ever aspired to, having grown up as a feral child in the woods. Furthermore, his reconciliation with Astrid and reunion with his son had made him extremely happy. That said, he missed the excitement and danger of his previous life. He sighed with frustration.

He realised that, if he rode out to inform Ywer himself, Astrid wouldn't understand and it could jeopardise their new found rapport. In any case, he told himself, his priority had to be the defence of Rumcofen just in case the Danes ignored Frodesham and lay siege to his burh next. So he sent Tidhelm and Wardric.

✝✝✝

Ywer was exasperated by the slow pace of progress. An army had to move at the speed of the slowest of its constituent members, in this case the supply carts pulled by oxen. He was tempted to leave the baggage train behind but it contained all the paraphernalia required to set up camp each night. Even if he did press on without the wagons, the vast majority of the fyrd were on foot and they couldn't march much faster than the oxen.

The heavy rain didn't help. The track was already muddy and the passage of so many feet, coupled with the water cascading down from the skies, was turning it into a quagmire. Men slipped and slid, cursing when they lost a shoe in the mire and the carts ground to a halt when confronted by the shallowest of slopes. Men got covered in muck as they pushed and heaved the heavy wagons up the slope and the oxen bellowed in protest as their drivers whipped them into making a greater effort.

'We'll be lucky to make it to Frodesham before nightfall,' Godric complained as he sat on his horse beside Ywer. Both men had pulled their hoods up and held their oiled woollen cloaks tightly around them in a vain effort to keep dry. The two men had halted just over the top of a rise to allow the fyrd to catch them up. Ywer had deployed most of his horsemen forward and to the flanks to act as a screen in case they ran into a Danish patrol, although he thought it unlikely this far from Mamecestre.

On the first night they had made it as far as the small settlement of Eltone, six miles from Cæstir. Ywer had hoped to reach Frodesham before dark, a distance for the day of no more than five miles, but so far they had travelled less than three and it was already past midday.

'It's another thirty miles from there to Mamecestre,' Godric muttered gloomily. 'It'll take the best part of a week at this rate.'

'There's nothing we can do about it,' Ywer retorted sharply, 'so we'll just have to bloody well get on with it.'

Like Godric, he was worried at the delay in setting off to relieve Mamecestre but voicing the frustration he felt at this further delay didn't help.

The heavy rain made it difficult for Tidhelm and Wardric to see very far so it was only by luck that they saw the Danes before they ran into them. They had just reached the edge of a wood and were about to cross the meadow down to the stream that lay at the bottom of a shallow valley when a large group of horsemen emerged from some scrubland on the other side of the valley.

They hastily backed their horses into the wood and dismounted, tying their reins to a tree. Tidhelm remained on the ground whilst his companion climbed a tall oak tree. He peered across the valley but the rain had intensified and he couldn't make anything out. After a few minutes it slackened off and then faded away to drizzle.

At first Wardric was puzzled by what he saw. The Danes appeared to have given Frodesham a wide berth and they were heading in the wrong direction to attack Rumcofen. He wondered if they were making for Cæstir but that seemed unlikely after the last attempt by Vikings to take it had ended in disaster. According to the reports he'd heard, the Danes had fewer men this time. Of course, the Vikings who had laid seize to it on the last occasion were Norsemen in the main but, even so, there had been some Northumbrian Danes present and word of what had happened would have spread.

He tried to picture in his mind what lay ahead along the Danes' line of march. He thought that they should meet the road from Cæstir to Frodesham a mile before the latter place. Then it came to him. The Danes weren't going to lay seize to Cæstir. They were going to ambush Ywer whilst his army was strung out along the road.

He clambered down the tree and had a brief discussion with Tidhelm before the two of them set off in an attempt to reach Ywer and warn him before his army walked into a trap. Thankfully, the Danes weren't moving much faster that the Mercian army. Although many more of them were mounted, their pace was still dictated by those on foot and by their baggage train.

Keeping to the trees and to dead ground out of sight of the Danes, the two scouts cantered ahead of the enemy column and half an hour later they encountered Ywer's screen of scouts. At first the latter thought that they were Danes but thankfully Ywer's men were led by Wilfrid who yelled for his men to put up their weapons.

'Any fool can see that they're not dressed like Danes,' he said scornfully. 'What are you two doing here? Is Wynnstan bringing a contingent to join us?'

'No, we need to speak to Lord Ywer urgently. Mamecestre has fallen and the Danes aren't far behind us. You're walking into an ambush.'

Wilfrid immediately sent a group of his horsemen to locate the Danes and took the two messengers to see Ywer. It didn't take the ealdorman long to formulate a plan. The one advantage he had over the Danes was his archers. However, a wet bowstring lacked the power to propel an arrow at the same speed and over the same distance as a dry one. He looked up at the sky. Drizzle was still falling but there was the odd patch of blue sky heading their way. Satisfied that it would soon be drying up, he told Godric his plan.

☩☩☩

Irwyn swelled with pride as he rode beside his foster father. Æthelstan didn't treat his charges like children. As far as he was concerned they were warriors who needed to grow a bit taller and stronger. He made no allowances for Irwyn's and Brandt's youth and expected them do everything his warriors did. The boys didn't complain, unlike some of the scions of the nobility who had recently joined his gesith. They seemed to think that their breeding should exempt them from standing their turn as sentries or looking after the horses.

They also made the mistake of looking down on the experienced hearth warriors that Æthelstan had brought with him from Cæstirscīr. However, they soon discovered that their lord didn't respect breeding; he was only interested in the qualities his men possessed. This didn't make him popular with some of the young nobles but those who were prepared to get their hands dirty soon came to respect him, even if he was said to be a bastard.

Irwyn had been selected to carry Æthelstan's standard that day. He found that it grew heavy after a while and the wind made the heavy material flap as if it was struggling to escape. That afternoon Æthelstan was due to meet his father and Irwyn was determined to display his lord's banner properly as they approached the king's camp.

Earlier in the year Eadweard had advanced north from Lundenburg along the River Lygan, which formed the border between Ēast Seaxna Rīce and the former Mercian shire of Middel Seaxna Rīce, until he'd reached Hertforda. He'd driven out the Danish jarl and was in the process of constructing a large new burh. It was divided into two parts with a fortress either side of the ford over the Lygan.

He intended to consolidate his hold on Ēast Seaxna Rīce and had asked his sister to send a contingent of Mercians to help him.

Æthelflæd had decided to send Æthelstan in the hope that would bring the two men closer together. Although, as Osfirth would be there in his capacity as Hereræswa of Wessex, he couldn't see that his presence would achieve anything except to bring disharmony to the king's war council.

Far from sweeping into the encampment and riding up to the king's tent, as he'd expected, Æthelstan was stopped at the perimeter by a group of sentries who either didn't recognise the banner displaying a white wyvern on a green background - the symbol of Mercia – or else they'd decided to have a little fun at the expense of the new arrivals.

'What's your business here?' the leader of the sentries asked aggressively, adding 'lord' after a pause that was long enough to be insulting.

Cynric, the second son of the Ealdorman of Herefordscīr and one of those who considered himself superior to those of lesser birth, dug his spurs into his horse and rode up to the belligerent sentry, only pulling back hard on the reins to bring his mount to a halt inches from the Saxon. The man stepped back a pace or two as the horse snorted in his face.

'This is Lord Æthelstan, the king's eldest son,' he hissed at the startled sentry. 'Now get out of our way!'

The sentries hurriedly stepped aside and Æthelstan rode past trying to hide the smirk on his face. Cynric might be a stuck-up prig but he had his uses.

Tent didn't adequately describe Eadweard's accommodation when on campaign. Whereas Æthelstan's was just large enough to accommodate a small bed, a table and chair and a place for his body servant to lay his head, the king's tent was enormous and was divided into three sections. He was shown into the main area where his father sat at a large desk. Not for Eadweard the muddy earth that others had to suffer, here it was covered by wooden boards. It was large enough for a dozen men to gather for briefing but there was only the one chair. Two chambers led off the main area; presumably the king's bedchamber and another for his servants.

The king didn't get up and embrace his son or give him any other outward sign of affection. However, he did seemed pleased that Æthelflæd had chosen him to lead the contingent of Mercians.

'I'm going to continue northwards when I leave here,' Eadweard told him. 'I want you to head east and establish a new burh at Malduna. It lies at the head of the Sweartwæter estuary and from there my ships can patrol the coast north of the Temes.'

Æthelstan had no idea where Malduna might lie, except that it must be to the east if it was near the coast. What was certain was that to get there he would have to travel for several days through territory controlled by the Danes. In essence his father had given him the task of subduing the rest of Ēast Seaxna Rīce whilst he moved into East Anglia.

He wondered what to do about his two foster sons. He'd brought Irwyn and Brandt with him because he didn't know what to do with them. He'd imagined that his contingent of Mercians would join the main army and that they would be safe with the baggage train. However, now he was being sent into hostile territory with just a few hundred men they would be in a great deal more danger; he wished now that he'd left them behind.

He found out that Malduna was forty miles away and a major settlement called Ceolmærsford lay on his route. As it was a former

Roman city and the base of the jarl who ruled this part of Ēast Seaxna Rīce, he would have to capture it before attacking Malduna. To leave an enemy stronghold in his rear was asking for trouble.

'How many men has the king given us for this task?' Cynric asked when Æthelstan briefed his gesith and the captains of the Mercian fyrd.

Æthelstan regarded the question as impudent. He now wished that he'd appointed a new captain when Wynnstan left his service. At the time he didn't bother as he considered that he was quite capable of leading his hearth warriors himself but he now realised that having an intermediary between him and his men had its advantages. The bond between him and his sworn warriors needed to be as strong as possible and having to discipline them for every small error or incident of ill-discipline didn't help. He needed someone to stand between him and his men. They could resent, or even hate, their captain but it wouldn't affect his own relationship with them.

However, the choice of captain wasn't a simple matter. There were a couple of strong candidates from amongst those who had been in his original warband. None of them were high-born and, although skilled fighters, and in some cases excellent scouts and trackers, the score or so nobles who had been appointed by his aunt looked down on them. Conversely his hardened warriors had little respect for the newcomers.

Then he thought of Bawdewyn. He'd been one of those chosen by Æthelflæd but he was the son of a wealthy thegn but an illegitimate one. As such he needed to make his own way in the world. He had fought at the Battle of Totenhale when the armies of Wessex and Mercia had inflicted a crushing defeat on the Northumbrian invaders and so he was well-regarded by the original members of the gesith. There was only one question: would he accept the responsibility? Bawdewyn was popular but whoever was captain couldn't afford to have any close friends if he was to do his job properly.

After the meeting Æthelstan asked Bawdewyn to stay behind.

'What do you make of Cynric?' he asked.

Bawdewyn seemed a little stunned by the question and hesitated before answering.

'Well, he has a high opinion of himself and a loud mouth but under that somewhat arrogant exterior I suspect he lacks confidence in himself.'

Æthelstan was impressed. The man had summed up Cynric's character concisely and, he suspected, accurately. It hadn't occurred to him that the young noble's egotism was a front.

'I need someone I can trust implicitly to take Wynnstan's place as my captain. Who do you think capable of doing that?'

'Why are you asking me, lord? I've only been in your service for a few months; surely there are others who know you and the members of your gesith better who could advise you?'

'Yes, but they are either of low birth and, although completely loyal and excellent fighters, they would never be accepted by the young nobles. Conversely, they hold few of the latter in high regard as warriors. Nearly all have yet to prove themselves in battle.'

'I understand your dilemma as to who to appoint but not why you would want to discuss the matter...'

Bawdewyn's voice trailed off as the reason dawned on him.

'Surely you're not asking me to become your captain, lord? Or have I jumped to the wrong conclusion? If so excuse my presumption.'

'No, you are quite correct. I can't think of a better man to help me lead, not only my gesith, but also the fyrd who are here to support us.'

'Can I have a moment to consider it, lord? I'm most appreciative of the honour you do me but to be promoted from one of fifty hearth warriors to be both their captain and also lead the four hundred ceorls in the fyrd is a big step.'

'Of course. We leave for Ceolmaersford at dawn tomorrow. Let me have your decision tonight.'

The rain might have ceased but water continued to drip down from the leaves. It was still a month or so before the trees began to shed their summer splendour and the Danes huddled under their cloaks as the column wound its way through the wood in search of a good ambush site.

Six Danes had been sent ahead to locate the advancing Mercian army. Their orders were to return to give the Danish leader, a jarl called Åmunde, at least half an hour's warning of Ywer's approach. That would give him enough time to deploy his men.

Wilfrid watched as the six horsemen rode their horses slowly through the wood. They were alert and evidently watching for signs of Mercian scouts. However, they didn't bother to look up and so didn't see Wilfrid sitting on a branch above the road.

As soon as the scouts had passed him he gave three hoots like an owl and, after an answering hoot, he climbed down and went into the wood to retrieve his horse. He eased his sword in its sheepskin lined wooden scabbard to ensure it would slide free when needed and then, grasping his spear in his right hand and his shield with his left, he set off after the enemy scouting party. His job now was to stop any of them escaping to warn the main body of Danes.

There was a clearing a few hundred yards further on and the Danes fanned out into a V formation to cross it. That was a mistake because it gave the five archers waiting in the shrubbery on the far side of the clearing a clear shot at each man. The first that the enemy scouts knew of the danger they were riding into was the whisper of the air rushing past the feathers at the end of the arrows.

Only two of the Danes wore a chainmail byrnie. Three had on a leather jerkin and the sixth, the youngest of the group, wore no more than a woollen tunic. Two of the arrows struck one of the men wearing chainmail, one glancing off and the other pinning his right leg to his horse. It reared in response to the sudden pain and the rider was thrown clear. In doing so the arrow came out of the horse, which bolted, and the man lay on the ground, blood pumping out of his femoral artery. Satisfied that he wouldn't be going anywhere in a hurry, the two archers turned their attention to the rest of the scouts.

The other three archers had succeeded in killing the youth in the tunic and two of the horses with their first volley. One man was trapped under his dead horse but the other had been thrown clear. He scrambled to his feet and headed back the way he'd come. He didn't get far before one of the bowmen brought him down with an arrow in his back.

The remaining two scouts turned their horses and dug their heels in. Three arrows followed them as they galloped out of the clearing. Two struck the rearmost horse in the buttocks, causing it to rear up and deposit its rider on the ground, where he lay winded. However, the last man - the second one wearing a byrnie - got clear.

The archers ran into the clearing. There was nothing they could do about the man who'd escaped but they quickly killed the winded Dane and the one trapped under his horse by cutting their throats. When one of them went to do the same to the one with an arrow in his leg he found that he'd already bled out. The Mercians then searched the bodies for anything of value, stripped the body of its byrnie and collected the helmets, weapons and shields.

'They should fetch a reasonable sum back in Cæstir,' one of them commented in satisfaction.

Wilfrid rode into the clearing at that point leading a second horse with a body draped over it.

'Did he put up much of a fight?' one of the archers asked, noting the gore covering Wilfrid's body.

'No, it's his blood, not mine. Silly bugger was looking over his shoulder as he rode out of the clearing. By the time he looked where he was going my sword was already on its way to cleave into his neck. I nearly took his head clean off his body; nearly dislocating my shoulder in doing so,' he said ruefully. 'Strip him of anything valuable and tie it to this horse. Then kill the injured horses and drag all the bodies into the undergrowth. We don't want the bloodstains on the ground giving a warning to the Danes so use your swords to dig up some earth from under the trees and cover them as best you can. I must go and warn Lord Ywer that the Danes are coming.'

He went to ride away but paused.

'Make sure you're clear of here before the enemy get here, whether you've finished or not. Avery, you go up the trail to the edge of wood and keep watch. Come back and tell the others as soon as you see their vanguard appear.'

Avery who, at thirteen, was the youngest of the Mercian scouts, nodded and went to fetch his horse from deeper in the woods.

'How long do you think before they get here?' Ywer asked Wilfrid.

'No more than half-an-hour, perhaps less.'

The ealdorman nodded and turned to the men gathered around him. They included Earl Skarde and his captain, Godric, as well as the leading thegns of Cæstirscīr. The only one missing was Wynnstan but he was still at Rumcofen expecting an attack by the Danes. Ywer wished he was with him. Few had more experience of fighting the Vikings.

'Very well, you all know what to do. Remember to watch my banner bearer for my signal.'

The Danes spilled into the open ground in front of a long rise up to the top of a small hill. The meadow was enclosed on three sides by woods. Ywer stood in the middle of the front rank of his shieldwall. Seven hundred of his men stood with him in four ranks. Only the front rank was made up of his thegns, jarls and hearth warriors. The other three ranks were provided by the fyrd. It wasn't much with which to face the army of Viking warriors which formed up at the base of the slope.

For a time the Danes did little but bang their shields and shout insults at the Mercians. That gave Ywer plenty of time to estimate their numbers. There were more than a thousand of the heathen devils, more like eleven or twelve hundred. He took a firmer grip on his sword.

Priests and monks moved along the ranks of men on top of the rise as they waited. They said mass and dispensed communion bread as they went and were followed by boys with water skins. Fear always made men thirsty and anyone on the hill that day who said that he wasn't afraid was a liar.

Whoever commanded the Danes was no fool. Ywer watched as two sizeable groups of the enemy moved into the woods on each side to check that they weren't full of Mercians waiting to attack their flanks as they advanced. He cursed. He had stationed a hundred archers guarded by fifty spearmen in each wood. They would be no match for the Danes in the trees where the archers couldn't use their bows properly. He prayed that Wilfrid and Godric, who commanded the two contingents, realised what was happening and retreated before the enemy. He'd rather lose the element of surprise and have them with him on the hill top than see them slaughtered in the woods.

His servant, Hengist, climbed an oak tree to get a better view of the impending battle. He should have stayed with the baggage train on the reverse slope of the hill but he was desperate to watch. His greatest desire was that one day Ywer would let him train as a warrior but, at twenty two, he was beginning to lose hope of that.

From his perch near the top of a tall oak he could see the woods stretching away on either side of the open meadow and beyond. The woods weren't that large. Behind them there was more open pasture on which sheep peacefully grazed. As he watched, Wilfrid's men emerged from the right-hand wood and ran across the open area, scattering the sheep. A hundred and fifty yards behind them Danes emerged in pursuit. Wilfrid waited until most of the Danes were in open ground and they yelled for his men to halt.

The archers stuck a few arrows in the ground in front of them and drew back their bowstrings. A second later the air filled with a cloud of arrows. Some of the Danes were quick enough to raise their shields to protect them but many were too slow. Over a score of the enemy fell to that first volley.

Before the first arrows had arrived the archers sent another volley and then another. Although most of the Danes had sheltered behind their shields by the time they landed, several arrows found chinks between helmet and shield rim or pierced the Danes' exposed legs. Another dozen or so fell.

Having lost a third of his men, the Danish commander gave the order to retreat, happy in the knowledge that at least he'd prevented the Mercians from attacking the main body in the flank. As the Danes fled back towards the trees another volley struck them in the rear. Less than half the original number of Danes reached the wood.

Wilfrid's men cheered and a few started to slit the throats of the wounded and others started to loot the bodies.

'It's not over you fools,' he yelled. 'Lord Ywer needs us to attack the rest of the pagan scum. You can come back here later.'

Sheepishly his men stopped what they were doing and raced back into the woods.

Hengist lost sight of them at that point and his gaze swung around to the other wood. However, none of Godric's bowmen or spearmen had appeared in the pasture beyond the left-hand wood and he was left wondering what had happened there.

The thousand Danes at the base of the hill remained where they were, presumably waiting until the woods had been cleared of Mercians. Hengist had no idea what had transpired between Wilfrid's men and the Danes in the other wood but less than a dozen of the latter eventually emerged and ran back to report to their commander. Still nobody had emerged from the other wood.

It was then that Hengist saw a large body of men approaching from the north. His heart sank. The Mercians faced enough of the Northumbrian Danes as it was without reinforcement. He had to let

Lord Ywer know at once. He climbed down the tree as fast as he could, ignoring the grazes and minor cuts he suffered in his haste.

CHAPTER SEVEN

Autumn 912

Ceolmaersford proved to be a sprawling settlement on the north bank of the River Can. Æthelstan had been told that the Romans had built a fort there but, if so, it had disappeared long since. Just to the east of the settlement another river joined the Can from the north and then flowed east into the Sweartwæter estuary at Malduna.

The land all around was flat with strip fields interspersed with small areas of pasture. Apart from huts and storage sheds there was a hall surrounded by a palisade some ten feet high. Other farmsteads were dotted around but none were more than a couple of miles from the settlement. The rest of the surrounding land was heavily wooded.

He'd been expecting a more prosperous place. There didn't even seem to be many other buildings one would normally expect in a place of this size such as taverns, workshops and the like. There was smoke coming from one hut and he suspected that might be a blacksmith's forge but that was it. If there had been a church at one time, there was no sign of it now.

The gates that led into the palisade were open with two idle sentries sitting on stools. There didn't seem to be a watchtower nor was there any form of defence for the settlement itself, not even a thorn hedge.

He came to the conclusion that this part of Ēast Seaxna Rīce was a peaceful place which hadn't seen warfare for decades. Well, he thought grimly, that was about to change.

Eadweard had given his son a hundred men from Wessex to bolster the four hundred Mercians but Æthelstan didn't think that they would be of much help; on the contrary they might even be a liability. They looked down on the Angles, who made up most of the Mercian fyrd, as inferior to Saxons and there had already been a couple of fights between the two groups.

Their leader was a thegn called Hedwig who came from Sūþrīgescīr, as did most of the Wessex contingent. However, there were also a dozen from Wiltunscīr chosen by Lord Osfirth. Æthelstan didn't trust them, nor did he believe Osfirth's assurance that they were amongst his best men. True, they were all proper warriors, not members of the fyrd, but their leader, Ravinger, was struck him as rather smarmy. He was all charm and smiles on the surface, almost obsequious, but the ætheling had the feeling that he was sneering at him behind his back.

He spent what was left of the day studying the settlement with Bawdewyn and three of his scouts. As far as they could tell there were no more than twenty armed men in the hall compound and the Danes in the settlement were in the minority. However, the men were obviously all bøndur - the Viking equivalent of ceorls – whereas the Saxon inhabitants all seemed to be thralls. His best estimate was that there were no more than a hundred Danes of fighting age.

Æthelstan's men set up camp for the night two miles away in a large clearing beside the River Can. By the time their lord arrived his body servant, a boy of fourteen named Berðun, had set up his tent and covered the ground inside it with freshly cut reeds. When they arrived for the war council the boy served the captains, including the Saxon Hedwig, mead, ale, cheese and freshly baked bread and then made himself scarce. As he slept on the floor of the tent he had nowhere to go until the meeting finished and so he thought he would try his hand at fishing whilst he waited.

Although he was a slave, his master treated him well and Berðun didn't hold a grudge against Æthelstan. The person he hated was his father, a poor ceorl who was a tenant farmer. The man drank and gambled away what little money the family earned from the sale of spare produce from the few acres they farmed.

One evening he lost so heavily playing tabula that he could only pay off his debts by selling one of his children into slavery. Berðun was eleven at the time and the youngest and so he found himself auctioned off in the slave market in Lundenberg. He'd been purchased, along with several other slaves, by a merchant and he'd been forced to walk with an iron collar around his neck, connected by a chain to the other slaves, all the way to Glowecestre. Once there, the merchant had sold him at a significant profit to the chamberlain who served the Lady of Mercia.

His feet were bloody and so tender after walking all that way barefoot that he was allowed to recover before being put to work in the main hall as a spit boy. The heat from the fire over which the meat was cooked whilst being continually turned was intense but, unlike in some halls, the boys worked as a team so that they were given a respite to cool down and drink water before their skin turned red and blistered.

He suffered this miserable existence for over two years before he was replaced by a younger boy. He was thirteen – nearly at an age when he would have started training with the fyrd had he remained free - when he was sent to work in the stables. He hadn't been there for more than a month when Lord Æthelstan arrived. He had rushed to take his horse, not knowing who the man was, and took it away to rub it down, water it and give it a nosebag of oats.

It was a magnificent animal and he stayed to brush its coat until it shone like a copper mirror. He should really have been helping the others to muck out but he was fascinated by the tall stallion. It must have been at least eighteen hands, much taller than any other horse he'd looked after.

He was so engrossed in his task that the voice from behind him made him jump.

'His name is Thunor and he's not normally so placid when a stranger comes near him. He must like you.'

Berðun was so startled that he dropped the brush. He turned around to see that the man who'd spoken was the man who'd being riding Thunor, only now he was dressed in an expensively embroidered red tunic made of the finest wool and blue trousers with yellow garters tied around them up to just below his knees. The way that they were tied indicated that he was a noble. A gold chain hung around his neck. The emblem suspended from it was that of a wyvern – the two legged dragon that was the symbol of both Wessex and Mercia – inlaid with rubies for its eyes. He thought that the stranger might even be Lord Æthelstan, nephew of Lady Æthelflæd and, so some said, first-born son of King Eadweard.

He went down on one knee and bowed his head.

'I'm sorry, lord, if I did wrong. I should be helping the others clear out the other stables,' he gabbled in his fright at being confronted by such an important man.

'Get up and let me look at you.'

Berðun obediently stood but still looked at the ground a foot in front of his bare feet. Æthelstan put his hand under the boy's chin and lifted it up so he could look at his face. It was streaked with dirt, as were his legs and the filthy homespun tunic he wore. His fair hair was matted and contained wisps of straw and bits of mud – or something worse – and no doubt it was crawling with lice. Nevertheless he could see that the lad was good looking under the dirt and his eyes were bright with intelligence. He came to the conclusion that this was no ordinary slave boy.

'Come with me,' he said abruptly, forgetting that his reason to visit the stables was to check on Thunor and give him an apple.

Half an hour later Berðun emerged from the indignity of being bathed and scrubbed by two giggling servant girls and angrily grabbed the cloth from them before they could dry him as well. He was ashamed that the experience had excited him sexually, which was only too obvious in his naked state. He covered his groin with one hand as he dried himself with the other, which merely caused the girls to giggle even more.

'Get out,' an angry voice said and the girls fled as a man he hadn't seen before came into the room carrying some clean clothes. 'Silly little fools; you'd think they hadn't seen a naked male body before, although perhaps not one as young as you. One of them has even has a baby.'

It didn't seem likely to Berðun. Neither of them could be much older than he was. However, he didn't voice his doubts.

'Get dressed and come outside when you're ready; and be quick about it. It doesn't pay to keep Lady Æthelflæd waiting.'

That puzzled the boy. He thought that it was her nephew who had ordered him bathed. The clothes were plain but well made. In addition to a linen under-tunic and a plain brown tunic made of much softer wool than any he'd felt before there were trousers made of the same wool but dyed cream and a pair of soft leather shoes.

When he walked into the corridor the servant pushed him back into the room none too gently.

'Look at your hair! Don't you know how to comb it?'

Berðun didn't think he could remember ever combing it, although his mother had brushed it now and again before giving up, complaining she could do nothing with such a mop of thick hair.

The servant tried to drag a comb through it but quickly gave up.

'Sit down,' he ordered, indicating a three legged stool.

He used a sharp knife to try and bring some shape to the boy's thatch and in the end resorted to cutting most of it away so that he ended up with hair three inches long all over. This proved more amenable to brush and comb and when he showed Berðun the result in a polished silver mirror the boy didn't recognise himself; not that he had ever seen his reflection before - except in water which distorted the image.

He wasn't vain by any means but the boy who stared back at him looked like a stranger. His now tidy hair framed a face that was both handsome and intelligent. His eyes were a startling shade of ice blue and his skin was blemish free. He smiled and for the first time he noticed how white and even his teeth were. They were unusual in a world where even boys had lost a tooth or two, either extracted because they had rotted and caused pain or had been knocked out in a fight.

'Stop gawping and follow me,' the man barked at him.

They walked along the corridor past two more doors and then emerged into a colonnade around all four sides of a small garden. He was led to a double door guarded by two unsmiling sentries carrying spears and with swords at their waists. One knocked on the right hand door and opened it a fraction.

'The boy's here, lord.'

He opened the door more fully and the servant pushed him in the back none too gently so that he stumbled rather than walked inside.

'Well, well,' a female voice said. 'There's a sight that will get every female in the palace excited.'

He looked up to see who had spoken. At first he thought it was the Lady Æthelflæd but she was said to be in her late thirties; this was a young woman in her early twenties. He bowed to her and then looked about him. There were two other people in the room. One was the man from the stables and the other had to be Æthelflæd. He bowed to both.

The older woman was glaring at the younger one but she didn't say anything.

'Aunt, this is the stable boy I was speaking about,' the man said. 'I need a body servant and I thought that this boy might be suitable; however, he's your slave and so the decision must be yours.'

'I don't know how you've managed up until now,' Æthelflæd said with a disapproving sniff.

He shrugged. 'I've made do with whichever servants were available, usually those who've also looked after my men.'

'And now you want to steal one of mine; one who has cost me money I might add,'

'You want me to buy him from you?' he asked incredulously.

'No, of course not,' she retorted. 'I'm just making the point that you should have found one yourself long since. You're too close to your men and you shouldn't be sharing with them.'

'That's why they follow me, because I'm one of them, not some stuck-up noble like some of those who you've foisted in me as hearth warriors.'

'Get used to them,' she snapped angrily. 'You need their support if ever you're to become king.'

Berðun was stunned by the conversation. He had a feeling that he shouldn't be hearing this but then servants were part of the furniture and they'd probably forgotten he was in the room.

'You're right, of course,' Æthelstan said insincerely. 'I'll have to get used to sycophants and two-faced nobles who pretend to be my friends whilst working behind my back for my downfall.'

'Yes, you will. It's how you'll keep your throne if you're fortunate enough to sit on it.'

'The boy's still here you know,' Æthelflæd's daughter said sweetly.

The other two glared at her before Æthelflæd told her nephew that she'd make a gift of Berðun to him. The boy should have felt annoyed at being treated like an inanimate possession but instead he felt unaccountably happy at becoming Æthelstan's servant.

He was busy thinking how he became a body servant when the makeshift fishing line jerked and a minute later he landed a nice fat trout. He went back to the camp thinking how pleased his lord would be at having fresh fish instead of the pottage he normally ate when on campaign.

As he passed through the part of the camp inhabited by the men from Wessex he caught a snatch of conversation coming from inside a tent before someone told the speaker to be quiet. Nothing more was said, or not that he heard anyway. However, the fragment he heard worried him. The speaker had said 'we should go for the bastard tonight, the sooner we get it over with, the sooner we get paid by Osfirth...'

Some men might have dismissed the snatch of conversation overheard by Berðun as tittle tattle or even mischief making, but not Æthelstan. He hadn't known his body servant for more than a few weeks but what he knew he liked and instinctively he trusted the boy.

That night ten men led by Ravinger crept towards Æthelstan's tent. He was surprised that there were no sentries stationed outside the entrance but that just made their task easier. Motioning for eight of his men to set up a cordon in case anyone came along, he cautiously pushed aside the woollen cloth that covered the entrance. There was a solitary candle burning in a sconce on the table. It was marked with horizontal lines, each one an exact distance apart to show when an hour had passed during the night. It had been one of King Ælfred's inventions.

By its flickering light he could see the ætheling's body wrapped in furs laying on the small bed by the far wall of the tent. A second body, that of his servant, lay curled up under a couple of blankets at the foot of the bed. He and another Saxon slowly made their way towards the two sleeping men with daggers clutched in their right hands.

Whilst his companion dealt with his body servant, Ravinger stabbed the body in the bed repeatedly but he was surprised at the lack of resistance. He threw back the furs to reveal an under tunic and trousers stuffed with straw. It was the same with the other body. Realising that they'd been tricked, Ravinger ran towards the entrance just as the sound of fighting erupted outside.

The woollen curtain was thrust aside before he could reach it as Æthelstan and two of his warriors burst into the tent. Both were armed with seaxes whereas Ravinger and his companion only had daggers. The two Saxons stood side by side in the small space daring the three men standing a few feet away to make a move.

They were so intent on watching the three Mercians that they either didn't hear the sound of a sword cutting through the wall of the tent behind them or they ignored it. Suddenly the man standing beside Ravinger arched his back and screamed as a spear sliced through his flesh. A second later he fell forwards and lay still, the spear jutting from his back, as Bawdewyn stepped into rear of the tent and pricked Ravinger's neck from behind. For a second the Saxon thought of resisting but, when Bawdewyn pushed the tip of his dagger into his neck so that it drew blood, he threw down his own weapon.

✝✝✝

Hengist had trouble forcing his way through the ranks of the fyrd and when he did he emerged in front of the shieldwall to find himself looking at the advancing Danish army no more than three hundred yards away. He gawped at them for a moment and then a volley of arrows from the woods on the right tore into the Danes left flank – the one unprotected by their shields. Around two score were killed or wounded but, before they had a chance to react, another volley struck home.

The Danes advance faltered until the blast from a horn called for quiet and Jarl Åmunde ordered his men on the right flank to clear the woods. Hengist watched for a moment as more than two hundred of the enemy ran towards where the archers stood. Another three volleys of arrows fell on them but this time the Danes had their shields raised to protect them and only a few were hit. The archers melted back into the trees pursued by the angry Danes.

Hengist looked left and right along the line looking for Ywer. At first he couldn't see him but then he thought of looking for his banner. There were several of them being held in the second rank but only one was blood red with a rearing white horse. He ran towards it past angry men who shouted for him to get out of the way as they concentrated on the men surging up the slope towards them.

'Lord, more Danes are coming,' Hengist panted when he finally found Ywer.

'More Danes? Are you certain?'

'There are hundreds, lord. Who else could they be?'

'I only hope that you're wrong. Now get to the rear before you're cut in two by a Danish axe.'

Hengist did as his master had bid him, forcing his way through lines of men standing shoulder to shoulder ready for the enemy attack. A few minutes later the two shieldwalls collided. Thankfully the long run up the slope had robbed the Danes of most of their momentum and they arrived out of breath and drained of energy. Their leader, Åmunde, would have done better to have made his men walk most of the way before launching their assault but the Danes' blood was up and all they wanted to do was to kill Mercians.

As they pressed home their attack, several arrows struck down a few men in their rear rank. Then the archers began their attack in earnest and many more arrows killed and maimed a significant number of the rear rank. They and the rank ahead of them were forced to turn and defend themselves with their shields. Consequently, the front two ranks, no longer held in place by their weight, were forced back several paces. That gave the Mercian shieldwall a distinct advantage and they pushed the enemy line further back down the hill.

Hengist had run back to his oak tree and clambered up again. Evidently Godric's men had fought a long and bloody hand-to-hand battle with the Danes sent into the right-hand wood and had eventually emerged victorious. As he watched some fifty Danes emerged from the lower part of the wood, many of them wounded but still able to walk with the assistance of their companions. He didn't know how many men Godric had lost but, to judge by the volleys of arrows peppering the rear of the Danish main body, half of his archers were out of action.

The approaching Danish reinforcements were now no more than half a mile away but, hidden as most were by trees and shrubbery as they made their way to the front edge of the wood, Hengist still couldn't make out any details.

When the leading horsemen appeared on the open ground at the bottom of the slope Hengist was elated. It wasn't more of the heathen devils, it could only be Wynnstan. He could clearly see the wyvern banner of Mercia being held aloft by one of the riders at the front of the column. As if in confirmation, the horsemen charged into the Danes fleeing from Godric and slaughtered them.

Three blasts on a horn by one of Wynnstan's hearth warriors drew Ywer's attention to their arrival on the field of battle. The Danes glanced behind them to see what the horn meant and, seeing the Mercian reinforcements, they panicked. They were already being assaulted on three sides and now their escape route had been closed off.

Several turned to flee before Wynnstan's fyrd could form up and advance up the hill; that started the rout. Soon all but a handful of Danes were trying to escape. Only Åmunde and the warriors of his hird remained. He had failed the man who'd tasked him with the capture of Cæstirscīr and he would rather die in battle and enter Valhalla than be put to death painfully for his failure. It wasn't so much being tortured that bothered him; if that was the way he died he would be condemned to spend the afterlife in Helheim.

His hirdmen had sworn an oath to protect him and, if he died they would die with him. Ywer had no stomach for such slaughter now that the battle was won. Besides, he wanted to question their leader and find out why he'd embarked on the invasion of his shire. He ordered his men to fall back and, after his gesith had forced the more hot-headed of the Mercians to obey, they formed a circle around the remaining eighteen Vikings.

'Surrender and I'll send you to Glowecestre for trial by the Lady of the Mercians. Your men may depart unharmed once they've given me their oath never to invade my lands again,' he said in

Danish. 'Resist further and you'll be used as target practice by my archers. I've no intention of losing any more of my men than I already have.'

Åmunde spat in Ywer's direction and his men growled their approval of his defiance.

'Ragnall will kill me anyway for my failure. I've rather die here than face his contempt.'

Ywer was taken by surprise. He had no idea that the Norse King of Man was behind the Danes' attack.

'What's Ragnall got to do with it? From what I hear he doesn't venture off his island unless it's to raid Wealas or Cumbria.'

'Then you heard wrong, Saxon scum. He's busy extending his realm into western Northumbria.'

Ywer didn't feel like pointing out that he was a Jute, not a Saxon, and the Mercians he led were, in the main, Angles who detested the Saxons. If Ragnall was trying to bring the Norse who inhabited the coastal strip between the Mǣresēa and Cumbria, part of the Brythonic Kingdom of Strathclyde, under his rule that didn't bode well for Mercia. Northumbria had ceased to be a significant threat after the last joint kings of Jorvik had been killed at Tatenhale two and a half years ago.

Earl Eadwulf of Bebbanburg, an Angle who ruled the northern half of Northumbria, had claimed the vacant throne but most of the Danish jarls opposed him and, as he was said to be ailing, they were left to rule their own petty fiefdoms without interference from a central authority.

It was a situation which suited both Eadweard and Æthelflæd admirably. It meant that the Northumbrians would be unable to come to the aid of their fellow Danes in East Anglia and Eastern Mercia. However, if Ragnall had designs on Jorvik and Northumbria south of the River Tes, that could scupper their plans; especially if Eadwulf was too ill to pose a threat to Ragnall from the North.

However, that was a matter that needn't concern him at the moment. He needed to decide what to do about Åmunde and the Danes who'd been routed.

'Shall we kill them, lord?' Skarde asked. The newly created Earl of Wirhealum had fought by his side and he and his Norsemen were plainly itching to resolve the matter so that they could chase the fleeing Danes and, no doubt, loot the bodies.

Ywer glanced down the slope and saw that Wynnstan had deployed his fyrd to cut off as many of the Danes as possible. Inevitably many hundreds would escape but they were destroyed as a fighting force and he knew that Wynnstan would collect the loot so that it could be divided properly with Ywer getting his share. That was important because he never had enough money to do everything that needed doing. He liked Skarde and his brother-in-law had proved a loyal friend but he didn't trust him not to keep whatever plunder he found.

'I give them to you, Skarde. You can do what you will with them. Sell them as thralls if you can disarm them; just make sure they are in no position to invade my shire ever again.'

†††

Eadweard read the letter from his son with dismay. Ravinger had bought his life with a confession, although his men – those who had survived the fight outside the tent that is – had all been hanged. Æthelstan had sent Ravinger back under escort with the letter. What happened to the man afterwards was in the king's hands. Eadweard read it a second time to make sure he hadn't mistaken what it said.

Cyning,

I send you greetings along with this miserable wretch who, with ten others, tried to assassinate me in the middle of the night. The attempt failed and I executed the rest of those who survived, only sparing this man so that he could confirm the veracity of what I have to report.

It was unnecessary to torture the leader of the assassins, Ravinger, to get him to betray the name of the person who sent him and the others to kill me. The promise that I would spare him and deliver him to you for trial was sufficient to get him to confess and to name the man who was responsible.

I regret the need to accuse your brother-in-law of ordering my death but he is the man Ravinger named and, as you doubtless know, the man is one of Ealdorman Osfirth's gesith. I leave Lord Osfirth's fate in your hands but this isn't the first time that an attempt has been made to kill me and hope that whatever steps you can take will ensure that there won't be another.

I am your loving son and servant,
Æthelstan,
Ætheling of Mercia.

Eadweard was shocked that Osfirth had tried to procure Æthelstan's death but he was annoyed by the tone of his son's letter. It was almost as if he was trying to force his king to put his hereræswa on trial. It would have served Æthelstan better if he had stated the facts and not tried to pressure the king into taking action. Osfirth was the most influential of the ealdormen in western Wessex and Ælfflæd would never forgive him if he put her brother on trial. Furthermore, Osfirth was his son Ælfweard's idol. If he acted as Æthelstan wished it would turn Ælfweard against him. He might only be ten but in a few years' time he would become a man, legally at any rate.

Eadweard felt aggrieved at being put in a difficult position. Whatever he did he would alienate one of his sons. The more he thought about it the more he cursed Æthelstan for the dilemma he faced. It didn't seem to occur to him that Osfirth was the only one who deserved any blame. In the end he decided on a compromise and wrote back to Æthelstan.

To Lord Æthelstan,
Ætheling of Mercia,

I am relieved that the attempt on your life failed. You will no doubt be pleased to hear that I have hanged Ravinger for his treachery.

Of course, I only have the assassin's word that he was carrying out Lord Osfirth's bidding. It isn't enough for me to formally accuse him of being behind it but he knows of the allegation and I have made it clear that there must be no further moves against you or he will incur my utmost displeasure.

Please let me know when you have secured Malduna,

Eadweard,
King of the Anglo Saxons

'Utmost displeasure? What does that mean, a slap around the face and a fine if he tries to kill you again?' Bawdewyn asked scornfully when Æthelstan showed him the letter.

'All it means is that Osfirth needs to be more careful the next time. I don't like to speak ill of my father but, between the two of us, I think he's been weak and pathetic. If he cared for me at all he'd have done more, a lot more. I fear that he thinks more of my half-brother Ælfweard than he does of me. His letter contains no indication that he feels any affection or real concern for me, nor does he address me as his son. He even signs it formally, not as my father.'

Æthelstan was fuming. He would calm down but his father's reply had also sapped his self-confidence. He'd always been confused about where he stood. His aunt told him that his mother had been wed to his father and therefore he was no bastard, as many claimed. He had asked for proof but all Æthelflæd would say is that she would show it to him when the time was right. On the other hand, Eadweard maintained that he had never married his mother. He realised that he did so in order to appease the Lady Ælfflæd and her family but what did that say about his father?

In the time it had taken to write to the king and receive his reply he'd taken Ceolmaersford without much of a fight. The Danes were heavily outnumbered and he'd only lost two killed and half a dozen wounded against twenty five dead Danes and a hundred captured, including women and children, who would be sold off as slaves. The Saxons who had worked for them now found themselves granted their former status as ceorls or bondsmen and reclaimed the land they'd previously owned or tenanted.

Of course, there were disputes which Æthelstan had to resolve and which he found all rather tedious. However, unless he left a stable situation when he moved on, his work would have been wasted. As it was he heard rumours that the Danes who lived in other vills in the district were banding together to attack him. Until he defeated them and re-imposed Saxon rule over the whole area he couldn't move on towards Malduna.

He knew this and Bawdewyn knew it but Eadweard's letter had induced an apathy in his son which he found difficult to overcome. Whilst he sat on his arse in Ceolmaersford his enemies were getting stronger. Bawdewyn and the thegns accompanying Æthelstan were getting increasingly concerned and not a little impatient. In the end Bawdewyn took matters into his own hands and sent out scouts to determine the enemy's location and strength. They came back to say that six or seven hundred Danes had gathered eleven miles away at Branchetreu.

The threat they posed was just what was needed for Æthelstan to throw off his lethargy and call a war council.

'The muster point for the Danes is at Branchetreu,' he began. 'It isn't a defensive position but it does lie at the junction of two old Roman roads: one leading directly from here and another called Stane Stræt. As such, it is an easy place for them to reach. Our scouts have confirmed that the number of warriors is around seven hundred, rather more than we have. There are also a number of women and children, mainly boys; evidently camp followers brought along to look after the warriors and their horses. All told they number about twelve hundred.'

He paused to allow the hubbub that followed his remarks to die down.

'They are only a day's march away and so we need to act quickly before they move south to attack us. The Roman road to Branchetreu is easy to follow, even where the paving is damaged or has completely disappeared. We shoukd therefore be able to move into position tonight and attack at dawn.'

This caused even more of a furore but this time he banged on the table with the pommel of his sword to restore quiet.

'If anyone has a better plan, then I want to hear it.'

No one said anything at first, then Cynric spoke out.

'Lord, I'm not saying that attacking the enemy at dawn isn't a good idea but they will still outnumber us and their warriors are better fighters than the fyrd; and there is always the risk that men will get lost at night, even following a Roman road.'

'You make a couple of good points. Each man is to paint a white patch on their shields. Worn on their backs on the march everyone will be able to follow the man in front, even if there is no moonlight. As to the attack, I have a plan to even the odds – and I have greater faith in the fighting ability of our fyrd than you seem to have, Cynric.'

✝✝✝

It was a close run thing. Æthelstan had underestimated the time it would take to cover the distance to the outskirts of the enemy encampment in darkness. Even with white patches on their shields some were so slow in the darkness that they lost sight of the man in front of them in the pitch black until the moon made a brief appearance and they caught sight of them again. More than once the column had to stop to allow stragglers to catch up.

Bawdewyn had arrived with a score of experienced warriors an hour ahead of the rest. A number of Danes patrolled the makeshift paddock full of livestock and the horse lines. It was enclosed by cut branches, thorn bushes and the odd stretch of post and rail fence and the Danes seemed content to walk along it. As far as he could see, there were no sentries hidden in the trees.

He and his men silently slit the sentries' throats. Bawdewyn found the task distasteful as nearly all were boys aged between twelve and fourteen but it was necessary. That left four Danes who sat around a fire drinking and gambling. They were silhouetted against the flames and he left their deaths to those of his warriors with bows.

To make sure all were killed at the same time, three bowmen were assigned to each man. When Bawdewyn gave a call like a screech owl the dozen archers released their bowstrings simultaneously and the Danes slumped forward. One fell with his face in the fire and the smell of roasting flesh carried towards the Mercians on the breeze, causing the youngest archer to go behind a bush and puke his guts up.

'For Christ's sake do it quietly,' one of the others hissed at him.

By now it was almost sunrise and Bawdewyn urged his men to hurry and remove the section of the fence nearest to the enemy camp. At the same time other warriors ran to cut the leather leading reins attaching the horses to long lengths of rope to keep them from straying into section where the sheep and cattle were grazing.

'Are you ready?'

Bawdewyn was surprised to see that the person asking the question was Irwyn. Not only did he think that he'd been left behind at Ceolmaersford with the wagons, the servants and the wounded but the boy had crept up on him without being heard.

'Did Lord Æthelstan send you,' he asked suspiciously.

'Not exactly,' Irwyn whispered. 'I borrowed a shield with a white splodge on it and snuck into the column in the dark. When my foster father asked for someone to go and find out if you were all set, I volunteered. I don't think he knew it was me or he wouldn't have allowed me to go.'

'He'd have done more than that. I wouldn't want to be in your shoes when he finds out. Yes. We're all set.'

'Then stampede the animals as soon as you can. The sun is already above the trees.'

With that, the boy disappeared as silently as he'd come.

Using the Danes' fire to ignite their torches, Bawdewyn's men formed a line behind the livestock and the released horses and started to advance, waving their torches and yelling. It didn't take long for the panicked animals to head for the gap in the barrier around the paddock and by the time they'd reached the first row of enemy tents they were running as fast as their legs could take them.

The galloping horses quickly took the lead and, although they knocked a few men down and a few died under their hooves, they avoided most of the tents and the terrified Danes as they scrambled to get out of the way. The cattle weren't as agile. They flattened the tents and crushed anyone still inside. Many of the men who had emerged were either impaled on their horns or were trampled to death.

The piteously bleating sheep in the rear did comparatively little damage but they prevented the Danes from forming a shieldwall before Æthelstan's warriors attacked them. They never stood a chance. Few had managed to grab a weapon or their shields in the chaos and the Mercians and Saxons tore into them stabbing and slashing until their arms felt as if they were dropping off and they could kill no more.

Æthelstan stuck his sword in the ground and leaned heavily on it, gasping for breath. Like most of his men, he was covered from head to toe in gore; thankfully none of it was his. He looked around; bodies lay everywhere. Most were of Danish men but the stampede had been indiscriminate and the mangled bodies of at least a hundred women and boys lay scattered amongst the men.

Once the count had been done Æthelstan was relieved to find that he'd lost no more than a score who'd been killed and a similar number were too badly injured to ever fight again, even if they recovered. When they'd finished counting, the Danish corpses numbered nearly four hundred. Another two hundred had been captured and Bawdewyn estimated that around five hundred had escaped. However, they were mostly women and children.

When his captain told him that it was Irwyn who had taken his message to him Æthelstan was furious at first. He sent for his ward, intending to punish him severely but, when he saw him covered in as much blood as he was himself, he relented. His men told him that Ywer's son had slain three Danes himself and therefore now counted himself a warrior.

'Very well, Irwyn. You've proved yourself today and I'll forgive you; but any repetition of this type of disobedience will see you sent back to your father in disgrace. Do you understand?'

'Yes, lord. Thank you.'

'Oh, by the way, where's Brandt? Did he come with you on this hare-brained adventure?'

'No, lord. He didn't know I was going. He was sleeping when I left.'

Æthelstan had a feeling that Brandt would be upset that Irwyn had crept away without telling him. He only hoped it didn't blight the friendship between the two boys.

The rout at Branchetreu had broken the back of Danish resistance in Ēast Seaxna Rīce and he spent the rest of the autumn re-establishing Saxon control over each of the vills. There were isolated pockets of resistance but they were quickly dealt with and, by the time he reached Malduna, he was welcomed like a hero. The

Danish residents had sailed away with their families several days before his arrival.

He returned to Ceolmaersford to overwinter with his men well pleased with what he'd achieved. He only hoped that his father would now realise what an asset he had in his eldest son.

CHAPTER EIGHT

913 - 914

Æthelstan had been right. Brandt had been furious with Irwyn for not taking him with him. He was also envious of the way the members of the gesith now treated his friend. Just because he had killed a few Danes they seemed to think that Irwyn was a warrior now, whereas Brandt was still treated like a boy. He resented it and, although he tried to hide it, their relationship was never quite the same again.

A year later Irwyn reached the age of fourteen and became a man. After he'd left to return home Brandt realised how much he missed him. Despite that, his resentment at being left behind grew. He was eleven when Irwyn left and it would be three more years before he too could return to his family as a warrior. In the meantime he carried on with his training and acted as a page for Lord Æthelstan with as good a grace as he could muster.

He got to know Berðun quite well in this new role and, although he initially looked down on the other boy because he was a slave, he gradually got to know the personality underneath and liked what he saw.

Once Ēast Seaxna Rīce was firmly under his son's control, Eadweard thanked Æthelstan for his service and presented him with a sword made in a country called Hispania. It was a ceremonial weapon, not one meant for fighting with, but Æthelstan had never seen such a fine blade, nor such a sharp one. The pommel was a large ruby held in place by gold wire and the hilt was covered in red leather, also bound with gold wire. It came with a scabbard lined in finest sheepskin and covered in red leather and embedded with gold studs.

It was a fine gift and one which must have cost Eadweard a small fortune. However, that was all the reward Æthelstan got for conquering the shire for his father. He received no glowing words of praise from him nor, as he'd half-expected, was he made its ruler. In the past the king's eldest son was created King of Cent; he didn't expect that but he did think he might be appointed as Ealdorman of Ēast Seaxna Rīce. However, that honour went to Hedwig, the thegn who'd commanded his contingent of Saxons.

If Æthelflæd had expected the former Mercian shire to be returned to her she too was doomed to disappointment. By appointing Hedwig Eadweard had clearly signalled that it was part of Wessex. Similarly his conquest of East Anglia had resulted in the appointment of West Saxons as ealdormen of the newly created shires of Nordfolc, Sūþfolc and Grantebrycgescīr.

In the summer of 913 Æthelstan returned to his aunt's side. At the time she was at Tomtun, at one time the capital of the Kingdom of Mercia. It lay on the River Tom just to the north of Casingc Stræt, the accepted demarcation line between Anglian Mercia and the Danelaw. It therefore lay in Danish territory but she had driven out the local jarl and was busy making it into a burh.

The Danes might have united to oppose this transgression but they were more concerned with King Eadweard's advance towards the Five Boroughs. These were the independent jarldoms centered around Ledecestre, Snotingeham, Deoraby, Steanford and Lincolia. He had already captured several of the main Danish settlements between Wessex and the Five Boroughs including Bedeford and Hamtune.

Eadweard had halted his conquest after capturing the latter two settlements in order to consolidate his gains. He was now busy building burhs in order to defend what he'd gained before winter set in.

When he arrived at Tomtun Æthelstan found his aunt fuming at the king.

'He takes land which belonged to Mercia before the Danes seized it and now he declares that it is to remain part of his domain,' she protested as soon as she'd greeted him.

'Ēast Seaxna Rīce should be ours as well but instead of giving it to me, the man who restored it to our control, he appoints a Saxon as Ealdorman with scarcely a word of gratitude to me.'

Evidently the matter still rankled but Æthelflæd wasn't overly concerned about a shire inhabited largely by Saxons far away to the east. Her focus was on those still under Danish rule whose people were Mercians.

'We need to move more quickly than we have done to recover what's left of Eastern Mercia,' she declared.

However, it seemed that her brother might have over-extended himself.

✝✝✝

Ulf waited impatiently in his hall at Ledecestre for the arrival of his cousin, Hákon. He couldn't understand why the man had taken so long to answer his request for an urgent meeting; after all Hákon's base, Snotingeham, was less than thirty miles to the north of Ledecestre. Between them they ruled almost half of the Danelaw and they could muster close on three thousand spears.

He had also invited the jarls of the three other boroughs - Deoraby, Steanford and Lincolia – to the meeting but the former was busy improving his defences in case of an attack by Mercia and the other two were worried about an incursion from the newly conquered East Anglia.

When Hákon eventually arrived he blamed his cousin for taking him away from hunting a pack of wolves that had been raiding his tenants' farms. It took the wind out of Ulf's sails just as he was about to berate his cousin for his tardiness.

The two men couldn't have looked more dissimilar. Whereas Ulf was small and fine-boned, Hákon was a hulking brute who stood six inches taller than any of his men and whose arms were as thick as most men's thighs. Ulf took pride in his appearance, bathing regularly and combing his beard daily. His tunic and baggy trousers were always freshly laundered and his leather shoes waxed.

Hákon looked as if he'd slept in his filthy clothes for a month, which he probably had. A puckered scar ran from just above his right ear and across his cheek to his crooked nose. He tied the finger bones of his dead enemies into his greying, unkempt beard and shaved his head. Ulf could have sworn that he saw lice moving in the hairy mass that hid his mouth and chin. He shuddered and hoped that they didn't decide to leap across into his own hair.

'The other jarls are chicken-livered cowards,' Hákon exclaimed when his cousin told him that they were on their own.

'They serve their purpose,' Ulf said, trying to calm the volatile Hákon.

'How?'

'Whilst the bastard Saxons face strong Danish forces on the borders of Grantebrycgescīr and Nordfolc, Eadweard will be forced to leave enough of his warriors there to defend them. That means less are available to defend Wessex itself.'

'You plan to strike at the heart of his kingdom?'

'Yes, I propose a two-pronged advance, one through the former jarldom of Bedeford towards Lundenburg and one into Oxenafordascīr and across the River Temes into the heart of Wessex.'

'What about all the burhs he's built along the Temes and in Oxenafordascīr to the north, not to mention the difficulty in taking Lundenburg itself. It's far too well defended and we have no siege engines.'

'I'm not so daft as to suggest we besiege his strongholds; my intention is to burn his settlements to the ground, lay waste the countryside, kill as many of the Saxon scum as we can and pillage Wessex's wealth. With the gold and silver we seize we can attract more Vikings from Denmark and Norþweg to join us.'

'It sounds plausible,' Hákon said doubtfully.

'What other choice do we have?' Ulf asked impatiently. 'Wait here until either the Mercians or the Saxons – or possibly both - invade our jarldoms?'

'Very well, I agree. When do you propose to launch this raid?'

'In early autumn when the crops are in. We can burn their stored crops and kill their livestock, leaving those we don't kill to starve to death over the winter.'

Hákon grinned and raised his drinking horn to toast the success of his cousin's plan.

The plans of the two jarls were disrupted by the weather. In the middle of September 913 their army had mustered at Ledecestre when the heavens opened. Rain continued to fall off and on for the next month and the despondent Danes dispersed to their homes until the spring of the following year.

Nevertheless, the abortive gathering of so many warriors hadn't gone unnoticed by Eadweard's agents and it gave him all winter to prepare for the coming onslaught. All that he lacked was information about where the Danes would strike.

'I need someone to infiltrate the enemy camp when they re-muster and find out what their target is.'

He was sitting at the head of a long table in his hall in Lundenburg. After his masons had repaired the ancient Roman walls he had commissioned a stone-built church in the eastern sector and, at the same time, work began to repair the basilica on the northern edge of the old forum. Once it was completed, Eadweard used this as his palace in the east. Wintanceaster remained as his capital officially and that was where his treasury was kept. The court moved around the kingdom with the king but increasingly he overwintered in Lundenburg instead of Wintanceaster. The rest of the year he was on campaign or touring his conquests and supervising the construction of new burhs.

His wife and her children remained at Wintanceaster, which was another advantage of basing himself at Lundenburg. The more he saw of Ælfflæd the more he detested her. He regarded her now as little more than a brood mare. She had given him eight children in the fourteen years they had been married but the last five had all been girls and he worried about the succession. It was plain that she was unlikely to bear any more boys; she had conceived readily enough during the first eleven years they were married but she hadn't been able to conceive since the birth of their daughter Æthelhild.

The fact that he hadn't slept with Ælfflæd often enough recently to make another pregnancy likely hadn't occurred to him. Now one of his wife's ladies had caught his eye. Her name was Edagifu, daughter of Ealdorman Sigehelm of Kent who had died at the Battle of the Holme a dozen years before. She was just fourteen and, as Sighelm's only child, she had inherited his lands in Kent. Officially she was the king's ward until such time as she married.

Eadweard wasn't anxious about the betrothal of Edagifu to another before he was ready to marry her. Although her mother had procured a place with the court in Wintanceaster to find her daughter a husband, as her guardian he had the final say in whom she could wed. His problem was how to dispose of Ælfflæd without creating a scandal. However, that would have to wait until he'd dealt with the threat posed by Hákon and Ulf.

'It will have to be someone who can pass as a Dane,' Odda, Ealdorman of Dyfneintscīr, said thoughtfully.

Eadweard nearly retorted that he was stating the obvious but he held his tongue. The king was cultivating Odda as a staunch ally to counter the influence of Osfirth of Wiltunscīr in the western shires.

'My nephew, Irwyn, is half Norse and speaks Danish fluently,' Odda continued.

The king had forgotten that Odda's wife, Kjestin, was Ywer's twin sister. He had given Ywer's fifteen year old son a place in his gesith at the request of Æthelflæd. It had cost him nothing to grant his sister's wish and, for her part, she had repaid Ywer's loyalty, at least in part, by securing the post for his son; serving in the King of Wessex's gesith was a great honour and Ywer had been suitably gratified, even if his wife was unhappy at losing her son again so soon after he'd returned to Cæstir.

'You understand what you have to do?' Eadweard asked the lanky boy after Odda had briefed his nephew about the mission.

'Yes, cyning. Once I've discovered the strength and intentions of the Danes I'm to make my way to Lundenburg where you'll be with the army of Wessex.'

Eadweard was doubtful about entrusting such an important mission to an untried boy about whom he knew little but he'd accepted Odda's proposal rather than upset him by rejecting his nomination. At the same time he'd asked Osfirth, who was still his hereræswa, to find him a reliable man and gave him the same task. He deliberately hadn't mentioned this to either Odda or Irwyn.

†††

Wynnstan was bored. After the life of a warrior and scout for the past twenty four years he found the humdrum existence of a landowner and settler of minor disputes tedious. Naturally he enjoyed living with Astrid and his son again and her evident pleasure at their lovemaking, the frequency of which had abated little since their reunion, was undiminished; so much so that she was pregnant once more.

Nevertheless, even the expectation of becoming a father again hadn't quelled the restlessness he felt. He told himself that, at thirty seven, it was time he hung up his sword and enjoyed however many years the Lord God saw fit to grant him.

Apart from bedding his wife and playing with his son, the other pleasure he looked forward to was hunting. Boar seemed to be increasingly rare along the southern bank of the Mǣresēa and the immediate hinterland but there were plenty of deer.

Hunting them wasn't the only pastime he now indulged in. Astrid had brought an activity which was unfamiliar to Wynnstan north with her. For some time nobles on the Continent had hunted using hawks and this had recently crossed the sea to Wessex. Eadweard had made a present of a pair of breeding merlins to Æthelflæd and she, in turn, had encouraged the ladies of her court to take up the sport.

Hawks and falcons were subsequently imported from Frankia and Cuthfleda had often accompanied Æthelflæd before she'd died. Astrid was dubious about following suit, mainly because training a hawk, in her case a young goshawk, required a great deal of patience on her part, even though the bulk of the teaching was done by the falconers. Patience wasn't something that Astrid possessed a great deal of but she loved the feeling of achievement when she sent her hawk hunting and it returned with some small mammal or a bird taken on the wing.

She had taken it badly when Wynnstan forbade her from hawking, or even riding, when the baby began to show but she knew he was being sensible, however much it went against the grain to obey him.

Even when he was called away she'd resisted the temptation to go hawking again. She was in her thirties and few women gave birth successfully that late in life; indeed many had died before they reached her age – usually in childbirth or due to complications in pregnancy. So she steeled herself to taking life more quietly for the next few months - but it wasn't easy.

Wynnstan had read the letter from Ywer with mixed feelings. He'd been informed by Odda that his son was to undertake a perilous mission as a matter of courtesy and, resisting the temptation to rush south, had decided that Wynnstan was the obvious person to look after Irwyn. Not only was he fluent in both Norse and Danish, but he was the best scout Ywer could think of and he had undertaken secret mission in Danish territory before – notably the recovery of Saint Oswald's relics.

Ywer didn't want it known that his son had a protector and guide. The mission was his son's and he didn't want him to think that he didn't trust him to carry it out. However, he didn't see the harm in asking Wynnstan to join him on the road north through hostile territory. That way he could ensure that the boy reached the Danes' camp safely and afterwards Wynnstan would leave him once they were safely back in Eadweard's domain. The place chosen for the meeting was Bernecestre in the north of Oxenafordascīr, the shire ceded to Wessex by Mercia as part of the price for Eadweard's support for his sister's enthronement as Lady of the Mercians.

As agreed, Wynnstan arrived first and took a room in the only half-decent tavern in the settlement. It wasn't a burh, as such, but it was surrounded by a palisade for defence, given its proximity to the Danelaw. Irwyn, dressed a Saxon, would make his way there camping in woods and avoiding habitation as much as possible. Although armed as a warrior, he could easily fall prey to men attracted by the purse at his waist.

Just as Wynnstan was getting concerned, Irwyn arrived. He handed his horse over to a stable boy with instructions as to its care and then made his way into the taproom carrying his blanket roll and saddlebags. He dumped them on a bench at a spare table and sat down.

As a slovenly girl came to see what he wanted to drink, Irwyn let his eyes wander around the room. If he spotted Wynnstan sitting on his own in a corner near the stairs leading up to the sleeping chambers above, it didn't show on his face.

Having ordered a flagon of mead and a bowl of pottage – all that the hostelry had to offer in the way of nourishment – Irwyn let his eyes wander around the room again. Half a dozen artisans sat at one table complaining loudly about the taxes they had to pay these days to support the king's establishment of burhs across the land. A group of apprentices sat at another boasting about how many girls they had bedded and another traveller sat on his own near the fire eating his pottage.

Irwyn relaxed; none of the usual labourers and petty criminals seemed to favour the place as a watering hole which, given the price he'd had to pay for inferior mead and no doubt watery pottage, was hardly surprising.

He had just started to eat the pottage, which was as thin as he'd feared, when the door banged open and three men entered. They were obviously warriors but poor ones. Not one of them possessed a byrnie and the helmets they wore were of poor quality and had several dents which hadn't been repaired. The sword hilts were of plain wood screwed through the metal tang of the blade and the scabbards were cheaply made. One had a seax which looked to be of much better quality – probably taken from a dead man – and all three also wore a dagger. Irwyn's first thought was that these were warriors who'd fallen on hard times.

The three newcomers scanned the room until their eyes found Irwyn.

'Looks like we've found our quarry,' the one who was presumably the leader said in satisfaction.

'Come with us, boy. There's someone who wants a word with you.'

The boy got to his feet and, leaving his sword alone, drew his seax and dagger. He knew that a sword nearly three foot long would be more of a hindrance than a help in such a confined space.

'Whoever wants to speak to me can do so in here,' he replied, crouching and watching his opponents to see which of them would be brave enough to make the first move.

He risked a quick glance at Wynnstan but he continued to sit and quietly sip his ale. The other occupants of the small taproom had backed up against one of the walls in an effort to stay well out of the way of the impending fight.

'No need to be like that, lad,' the leader of the trio said, trying to sound conciliatory. 'We mean you no harm.'

'I'm not in the habit of repeating myself so I'll only say this once more. If whoever this mysterious person is wants a word with me, then bring him here and I'll listen to whatever he has to say.'

'You're coming with us, like it or not,' the man snapped. 'Now, you can come willingly and unharmed or we can cut little bits off you until you are unable to stop us dragging you out of here by your ankles.'

'What makes you think that you three miserable bastards aren't the ones leaving here feet first?'

As the last words left his mouth Irwyn made his move. He darted towards the far wall and then spun on his right foot as one of the mercenaries made a feeble attempt to stab him. The seax flashed once in the firelight and the man dropped his sword, his right biceps cut through to the bone.

Before the other two could react, Irwyn kicked a nearby bench towards their leader. The end crashed into his knee evoking a howl of pain just as Irwyn stepped close to him and thrust his dagger up into the join between chin and neck. The seven inch long blade pierced his mouth and continued upwards until the point embedded itself in the base of his brain. Unable to control his heart or his breathing, the man died before he hit the floor.

Irwyn fully expected the third man to make a run for it but he was brave to the point of folly. The boy let go of his dagger and leapt away, narrowly avoiding a cut from the man's sword. In doing so he stumbled and lost his balance. With a cry of triumph the third mercenary chopped down towards the boy's right shoulder.

It would have been easier for him to have chopped at the exposed back of the neck but that would have killed the lad. The man was all too aware that the man who sent him and his companions wanted the boy alive and, if he killed him, his own death was assured.

However, the blow never landed. As he lifted his sword Wynnstan threw a knife which impaled itself in the man's right shoulder. The sword dropped from his hand and Irwyn straightened up, bringing the pommel of his seax into contact with the point of the mercenary's jaw. He dropped like a stone.

'You took your time coming to my aid,' Irwyn complained.

'You seemed to be doing well enough on your own until you tripped over your own feet,' Wynnstan replied with a grin. 'That's the trouble with being your age; your brain hasn't yet learned how to control your growing body.'

'We need to question that one to see who's paying them and what they wanted from me,' Irwyn said, pointing to the man sitting against the wall and clutching his injured arm.

'Yes, but not here and now. I don't suppose for one moment that these three came alone.'

So saying he strode to the door and lifted the locking bar into place.

'Is there another exit?' he asked the terrified tavern keeper.

'Yes, through here, the man stuttered. 'There are steps in the back room that lead down into the cellar. There's a hatch that we use for deliveries. Stand on a barrel and you can climb up into the street at the back of the tavern.'

On hearing this, the other men in the taproom made a rush for the door but Wynnstan barred their way, waving his sword at them in warning.

'We'll go first and check that the way is clear.'

Grabbing the boy's blanket and saddlebags, Wynnstan led the way into the cellar. He heaved the boy through the trapdoor so that Irwyn could scramble up into the street, which proved to be little more than an alley just wide enough for a small wagon.

'Go and check both ends,' he whispered and the boy scampered off, returning a minute later to say that there were half a dozen more ruffians at each end of the alley.

Wynnstan climbed out before turning to help the others. Two minutes later everyone was standing in the alley.

'That way is clear,' Wynnstan told them, indicating the way that led to the back of the tavern.

'But...' Irwyn started to say before his companion kicked him hard on the shin.

As soon as the men rushed off Wynnstan grabbed Irwyn.

'Quick, back into the cellar.'

They dragged the trapdoor shut just as the sound of a commotion reached them. Evidently the drinkers had run into the mercenaries at the back of the tavern and a scuffle had started whilst they searched through them for the boy they were after.

Hearing the disturbance, the other mercenaries pounded down the alley and disappeared around the corner. As soon as they'd gone, they emerged from the cellar once more and ran around to the front of the tavern. The stables lay opposite and, whilst Irwyn helped the stable boy to saddle their two horses, Wynnstan went into the tavern and grabbed the wounded mercenary. Ignoring his shouts of protest he kicked him across the street into the stables before knocking him out.

He threw him across the front of his horse and the pair rode out of the stables just as the mercenaries re-appeared. They chased them for a little way but no one on foot was going to catch a cantering horse.

'Get a move on! It's almost sunset,' Wynnstan called.

The gates would be shut for the night at any moment and so they increased their pace to a gallop. Horses were restricted to walking pace within the settlement and so this immediately attracted attention but no one was brave enough to try and stop them. The sentries who were in the act of closing the gates stopped what they were doing and grabbed their spears but they were too late. They rode through the partially open gates, knocking the two sentries aside as they went.

✝✝✝

'Who else knew about your assignment, apart from Odda, your father and the king?' Wynnstan asked Irwyn once they were well clear of Bernecestre.

'No, one. Oh! Except for his hereræswa, of course.'

'Osfirth knew about you coming north to spy on the Danes?' Wynnstan exclaimed. 'Naturally he would; I should have thought of that.'

'You think he was the one who hired those brigands back at the tavern?'

'Him or someone working for him.'

'But why? What's he got against me?'

'Perhaps we'll find out when we interrogate our friend here,' he said, indicating the unconscious figure in front of him.

Irwyn followed Wynnstan along a track which led from the road across a meadow and into a wood. Five minutes after entering the wood they entered a clearing where four men were waiting. The boy recognised them immediately. Sawin, Wardric and Tidhelm came forward and greeted him before lifting the still unconscious mercenary down from Wynnstan's horse. A fourth warrior stood guard at the edge of the clearing and, to his surprise, Irwyn saw that it was Hengist.

'Are you a warrior now, Hengist?' he said, approaching the former body servant.

The young man grinned.

'Yes, at last. It wasn't for the lack of asking but eventually Wynnstan gave way. This is my first mission,' he said proudly.

'And your last if you don't keep watch properly,' Wynnstan barked at him.

A small boy who Irwyn hadn't seen before appeared out of nowhere and took charge of the two horses, unsaddling them and leading them away to where the others were tethered.

'Who's the urchin?' he asked Wynnstan.

'Eohric, he's my new body servant. His father was one of my tenants but both he and his mother died last winter. His elder brother stood to inherit the land but couldn't pay me the tax due so he decided to sell Eohric as a slave. I couldn't allow that to happen so I took the boy as payment but not as a slave. He's only ten but he's strong for his age and he's a quick learner.'

Privately Irwyn thought that Wynnstan had been too soft-hearted. Selling a member of a poor ceorl's family into slavery to pay a debt happened all too often. He could understand Wynnstan taking him on as his body servant but a slave didn't need paying, a servant who was free did.

Just as they sat down to eat a brace of brown hares that Wardric had brought down with his bow, the mercenary groaned and looked about him, straining against the rope which bound him to a tree.

Initially the captive refused to talk but, as soon as Wynnstan ordered his men to erect a tripod over the fire so that he could hang the mercenary upside down over it and boil his brains, the mere threat made the man eager to talk.

He didn't know much. He was an outlaw who had been hired, along with a few others and master-less warriors seeking employment, to find and kill Irwyn. He didn't know why or the name of the person who wanted him dead but he thought that it had something to do with the Danes who were said to be mustering an army twenty miles or so to the north.

Once he was satisfied that the man knew no more than that, Wynnstan ordered him to be hanged and the men settled down for the night. Irwyn couldn't get to sleep. He kept pondering over who would want to capture him and why. Evidently whoever it was didn't want him killed, perhaps because that would lead to awkward questions and, if the person responsible was identified a blood feud would result. Not only would that involve his father and his family but also Lord Odda, who was his uncle by marriage.

He'd been proposed for this task by Odda, of course, and he knew from gossip at Eadweard's court that Osfirth was jealous of Odda's rise in the king's favour but what would Osfirth gain by his failure to report back on the Danes' strength?

He was about to drop off to sleep at long last when suddenly it came to him. If Osfirth had sent his own man to spy on the Danes' camp and discover their intentions, his success would make Odda look a failure and Osfirth would gain Eadweard's gratitude. He only wanted Irwyn delayed until it was too late. That had to be it. He was tempted to wake Wynnstan and tell him but the thegn was fast asleep, to judge by his soft snores, and so he decided to wait until the morning. Five minutes later he was fast asleep himself, only to be woken an hour later when the heavens opened. No one was going to sleep through the deluge and so he went and told Wynnstan about his suspicions.

CHAPTER NINE

April 914

Irwyn realised that riding into the Danish camp alone in broad daylight was likely to arouse suspicion and so he waited at the edge of a wood until just after nightfall and then walked into the camp leaving his horse with Hengist, who had accompanied him in the last part of his journey. Wynnstan and the others were still somewhere to the south following the trail of the mercenaries who'd tried to kill Irwyn in Bernecestre.

For his part Wynnstan hoped that the man who'd been sent on the same mission as Irwyn was likely to remain with the mercenaries and follow Wynnstan's trail in the hope of killing the boy before he reached the Danes' encampment.

The boy and he had parted company at a stream. When Wynnstan and his party had climbed up the far bank they had left signs that even a blind man could follow. Irwyn and Hengist had continued upstream for half a mile before exiting. Even if their enemies checked as far as their exit point, they had chosen a place where the stream ran over rocks so only the most expert of trackers could have found it.

Nobody seemed interested in him as he meandered his way between the rows of Danish tents. He noticed other men going to and from the woods around the campsite; some went to find wood for the cooking fires, several others came back with small game they'd trapped or killed with an arrow and a few had been to relieve themselves rather than use the stinking communal pits.

The latter were filled in and new ones dug every few days but all they consisted of were planks placed over the pit for people to squat on with a gap between them. Inevitably the planks got splashed and filthy. It was no wonder they stank. Irwyn drew unfavourable comparisons between them and the communal latrines used by his people. They consisted of a long box with holes to sit on, which meant all the crap ended up in the pit. Furthermore, there was usually sawdust to throw down when you'd finished. This helped the faeces decompose and kept the smell down.

Despite the stench, Irwyn headed for the communal latrine. Men tended to gossip whilst using it and he thought that he might hear something interesting there rather than try and eavesdrop on conversations around the campfires. All the men around the latter knew each other but obviously that wasn't the case in the latrines.

He squatted until he thought his thigh muscles were going to seize up but he didn't hear anything of any value. He was just about to give up and go for a wander around the camp instead when two men came in who looked wealthier than most of the others.

'By Thor's hammer, it stinks worse here every day. It's time it was moved again,' the taller of the two complained, wrinkling his nose.

'Hardly worth it,' his companion grunted as he lowered his trousers and hitched the hem of his expensive tunic out of the way. 'We'll be leaving in three days.'

'Do you think Hákon and Ulf are wise to split their forces?'

The other Dane shrugged.

'Well, it'll force the Saxon bastards to split theirs as well,' he replied.

'No, it won't,' the other man retorted. 'The whole idea is that we march into the heartland of Wessex and destroy as much as we can before they realise that we're there.'

One of the men glanced across to where Irwyn was squatting and lowered his voice. The boy had to strain to hear them after that but he was blessed with unusually acute hearing.

'Then what's the point of trying to reach Lundenburg and Oxenaforda?' he whispered. 'We don't have the means to capture them quickly and we'll have the bloody Saxons and Mercians on our backs if we try and besiege them for any length of time.'

'Yes, of course,' the other man said impatiently. 'The idea is to lay waste the countryside en route and destroy the harvest to halt that bastard Eadweard's campaign to take our lands. When the bloody Saxons are starving next winter he'll have something else to worry about rather than attacking us.'

Irwyn smiled to himself. His knowledge of Danish swear words wasn't extensive but he knew what kusse meant. Both men had stopped talking and were giving him curious looks. They had finished their business and were tying their trousers back up whilst he was still squatting and had been for a long time. He hurriedly pulled his own trousers up and made a quick exit before anyone could question him. One of the Danes went to follow him but just as that moment a group of five men walked past Irwyn and entered the latrine enclosure. By the time that the man whose suspicions he'd aroused had pushed his way past them the boy had disappeared amongst the tents.

His heart was in his mouth. At any moment he expected to be challenged but he reached the outer fringes of the encampment before anyone questioned him.

'What do you think you're doing, boy,' one of the men sitting around a fire called out.

For a moment Irwyn was tongue tied; all he could do was stare at the man who'd spoken. His brain seemed frozen and he was unable to offer one of the many explanations he had prepared for such a moment.

'Alright, uncle. I'll go and clean your armour now,' a boy replied, sounding fed up.

Irwyn hadn't seen him at first. He peered into the darkness and saw a boy of about eleven get up from where he'd been sitting and chatting to other boys before going into a nearby tent.

Breathing a sigh of relief Irwyn walked unhurriedly towards the wood. He found it a great strain when all he wanted to do was run and it seemed like an age before he reached the treeline. Once there he set out to find where he'd left his horse with Hengist but he got disorientated despite the soft light given off by the new moon and he realised that he must have followed the wrong path into the wood.

'Where are you off to in such a hurry, boy?' a voice suddenly said out of the darkness.

He whirled around and saw a man standing not ten feet away and staring at him, sword in hand. Instead of panicking, Irwyn calmed his breathing and tried to think what was odd about the way that the man had spoken. Then he realised. The man had used the Norse word strákur for boy and not the Danish dreng. His accent wasn't quite right either.

'Well, well,' the man said in Ænglisc, raising the point of his sword. 'What a stroke of luck. My guess is that you're Æthelstan's little bumboy, Irwyn.'

Irwyn saw red, not so much at the implication that he was a catamite, but because of the insult to his former foster father who he greatly admired. Without thinking the boy dragged his knife from its sheath and launched himself at the man. Osfirth's agent was totally unprepared for the boy's sudden attack. He had expected him to be frightened and to cower away. Instead he barely had time to raise his sword before the boy cannoned into him.

Irwyn batted the sword away with his left arm, scarcely noticing the cut to his forearm as he did so, and thrust his knife into the soft underneath of the man's chin.

The knife was three inches long, not enough for the point to penetrate the man's brain and it got stuck in the roof of his mouth. The wound was painful but far from fatal. The man bucked furiously in an effort to throw the boy off him as he lay on the ground with Irwyn on top of him. He almost succeeded but Irwyn threw his legs astride his opponent's body and clung on whilst sawing his blade to and fro desperately seeking to sever one of the man's two carotid arteries.

Having failed to unseat his assailant, the man grabbed the boy's wrist with one hand and tried to push the thumb of his other hand into one of Irwyn's eye sockets. The wound he'd suffered might not be fatal but he was losing a lot of blood and that made him weak. He made one last desperate effort and at last he managed to heave the boy off. However, Irwyn clung onto the hilt of his dagger and, in flinging him clear, the man caused the blade to slice horizontally across his throat, thus cutting across the artery.

It didn't take him long to bleed out and Irwyn got shakily to his feet, drenched in blood, and shaking uncontrollably. It wasn't so much the fact that he just killed a man, after all it wasn't the first time, but it was the reaction to the adrenalin rush that had enabled him to overcome a man twice his weight, not that he knew what had given him that extra burst of energy and strength.

He bent double and was violently sick before sitting down with his back to a tree. He'd nearly recovered when two more men discovered the body and turned on Irwyn.

'What happened here, boy? Who's this man you've killed?'

'We'd better take him to explain himself to Jarl Ulf,' the second man said firmly. 'Come on lad, on your feet.'

Irwyn couldn't believe it. Just when he'd discovered the Dane's intentions and killed Osfirth's agent, he was about to be taken to one of the Danes' leaders. His chances of coming up with a credible story were zero. He couldn't take on these two men, even if he hadn't left his dagger sticking out of the agent's throat. His sword was still in its scabbard whereas both of these men had drawn theirs. He'd be lucky if they just hanged him; it was more likely that he'd be given a slow and extremely painful death.

✝✝✝

'The situation across the Mǣresēa is getting worse,' Godric remarked as he stretched his chilled feet out towards the fire.

He was sitting with Ywer and Skarde in the former's hall in Cæstir. Whilst the men sat on stools around the central hearth, Gyda, Æbbe and Astrid sat in a corner embroidering a blanket for the latter's baby, which was expected in the next couple of months. She had come to stay with Gyda until after the birth and Ywer's sister, Æbbe, had come on a visit with her husband and her daughter, Frida.

The girl was playing with six year-old Sicga at the moment but her childhood was slipping away. She'd soon be twelve and her mother and stepfather had already been discussing possible matches for her. With Brandt still with Æthelstan, Æbbe would miss Frida enormously when she left. However, she consoled herself, with any luck that wouldn't be for a year or two yet.

Her attention strayed and she put down her needle for a moment to glance over to where the three men were deep in earnest conversation.

'What are you thinking about?' Gyda asked softly.

She was well aware that Æbbe envied Astrid. She hadn't been able to conceive a child with Skarde, however much they tried for one. However, her sister-in-law's reply surprised her.

'I'm worried about King Ragnall of Mann and whether he'll bring war to destroy our peaceful existence. We've seen so much of it in the past and I was hoping we'd seen the last of it.'

All three women were well aware that Ragnall was consolidating his hold over western Northumbria before, so it was said, making a bid for the vacant throne of Jorvik. They had even heard rumours that he was planning to oust the Earl of Bebbanburg from his stronghold and take over the area between the River Tes and the Firth of Forth called Bernicia.

The previous earl, Eadwulf, had died last year and had been succeeded by his son Ealdred, who was just fifteen and was said to be something of a weak character. If Ragnall ever became King of all Northumbria and succeeded in taking over Bernicia as well, he would rule a territory that stretched from the Rivers Mǣresēa and Hymbre in the south all the way to the Firth of Forth and the border with Alba in the north, a vast area greater in size than Mercia was before the Danes conquered half of it.

Gyda looked sympathetically at Astrid whose face had paled. With Wynnstan away God knows where, she had to be feeling vulnerable; after all their home would be a key stronghold that Ragnall would need to take if he decided to strike south into Mercia.

'Surely your cousin, Jarl Agnar, would resist Ragnall if he decided to seize the land north of the Mǣresēa?' Astrid asked her, as if in answer to Gyda's unspoken thought.

'He has a treaty with Ywer but I doubt that he and his fellow jarls are strong enough if Ragnall demands their loyalty,' she replied quietly.

'Anyway, we're safe here,' Æbbe said brightly. 'The pagan Norse failed to take Cæstir the last time they tried.'

She steered the conversation away to Astrid's forthcoming baby.

Later that day, when Gyda was away talking to the reeve, Astrid told Æbbe something which had been preying on her mind.

'I hate it when Wynnstan is away but I have a good reason to be grateful that I'm here and not in Rumcofen, quite apart from the threat of an attack by Ragnall,' she began.

She paused, unsure whether or not to confide in Æbbe but the other woman urged to carry on. She took a deep breath and continued.

'It's Chad,' she said at last.

'The captain of Wynnstan's hearth warriors?'

Astrid nodded, looking down at the ground.

'He's been most solicitous for my welfare since my husband left.'

'Surely, that's a good thing?'

'Too solicitous if you know what I mean. He makes me feel uncomfortable whenever he's near me. I think he lusts after me.'

'What, even in your present state?'

'The fact that I'm heavily pregnant just seems to excite his interest even more.'

'Has he tried to force himself on you or given you any evidence of a desire to seduce you?'

No, it's just my intuition but I know I'm not wrong.'

She looked at the disbelieving look on the other woman's face and knew that she'd made a mistake in telling Æbbe.

'Never mind; forget I said anything. No doubt I'm being foolish,' she snapped.

She got up from the chair she'd been sitting on and rushed out of the hall and into her guest chamber where she lay down on the bed and curled up, crying her eyes out. She knew she was right about Chad. Her only hope was that she didn't have to return to Rumcofen before Wynnstan came back to her side. She daren't think what might happen if he didn't return.

†††

Wynnstan crept closer to the top of the escarpment and edged into the underside of a gorse bush before peering over the rim. The group of mercenaries they'd been following had camped below and were busy cooking a meal before night fell. There was one obvious sentry along the narrow track leading to their campsite but he couldn't see any others. The horses were tethered to posts sunk into the ground in a grassy corner of the clearing well away from where the men were. He was surprised that there didn't appear to be anyone guarding them.

He carefully examined the men again. Most were dressed as Angles or Saxons but two were either Danes or Norsemen to judge by their baggier trousers and the different type of ribbon around their lower legs. They were all poorly dressed and none had the appearance of being warriors serving a noble. He concluded that Osfirth's agent had already left them to infiltrate the Danes' encampment.

He edged away from the top of escarpment unsure what to do. He only had three men with him, not counting Eohric – insufficient to attack the mercenaries without risking their lives even when they were asleep.

In any case what would that achieve? It was Osfirth's man they were after and he might have even reached the Danish camp by now. He decided that the time had come to forget about the mercenaries and head for the rendezvous with Irwyn.

✝✝✝

Irwyn obeyed the Dane and got groggily to his feet. He swayed for a moment, appearing to be dazed, if not wounded, but it was all an act. As soon as one of the Danes lowered his sword and stepped forward to grab his arm Irwyn kicked him as hard as he could just below his kneecap. The man yelped in pain as his leg gave way and he toppled forward. The other Dane tried to plunge his sword into the boy but he was hampered by his colleague who was between him and Irwyn.

The boy twisted away from the blade and hared off into the trees, not noticing the thorns and small branches that got in his way, tearing at his sleeves and trousers and slicing into the flesh of his face. The two Danes ran after him, one outstripping the other who hobbled as fast as he could on his injured knee.

When he calculated that the second man had dropped back far enough for him to tackle the first man on his own he hid behind a tree with his sword drawn and waited for his pursuer to run past. When he did, he thrust his sword out just above the ground so that it tripped the man up. He fell heavily on his front and, before he could roll over, Irwyn stabbed his sword down with two hands at the base of the man's neck. The blade severed his spinal cord and sliced into his jugular vein.

The Dane was paralysed and at the rate he was bleeding he would soon be dead. Irwyn grabbed the man's dagger to replace the knife he'd lost and sliced through the leather thongs that attached the man's purse to his belt. Tucking the purse into his tunic, he sheathed the dagger and waited for the other Dane to reach him.

He'd found killing the second man easier than the first but he was tempted to flee from another fight. However, he didn't want the survivor going back to the camp and raising the alarm. If he could kill him as well that should give him several hours of a head start on any search for him. Perhaps the Danes might even think the two missing warriors were deserters and not even bother to search the woods for them. He squared his shoulders; first he had to kill the man limping towards him.

The Dane had sheathed his sword and now had hold of a two-handed battleaxe that had been hanging down his back by a strap. It was a weapon against which Irwyn had no experience and the thought that he'd be better off running crossed his mind, even if the man would soon have groups of mounted Danish warriors searching for him.

He pushed the thought to the back of his mind and picked up the other Dane's sword in his left hand. The Dane advanced at a slow hobble whirling his axe in front of him.

'I'm going to cut you into little pieces, boy. Aren't you terrified?' he asked with an evil grin on his face.

'Why should I be? I've killed two men like you already tonight and I prefer to do things in threes.'

The Dane rushed at him with a roar of rage and too late Irwyn realised that, however hard he might have kicked his knee, the man had recovered sufficiently to overcome any lingering pain. Irwyn did the only thing he could think of and darted behind the tree. His opponent appeared a foot or so to the side of the tree and swung his axe at Irwyn. If he'd stayed where he was the blow would have decapitated him but he ducked just in time.

The heavy axe head hit the tree and embedded itself in the trunk. The Dane pulled it this way and that to free it but, by the time he'd done so, Irwyn had stabbed one of his swords into the man's thigh just above the injured kneecap and the other into his armpit.

The Dane stepped back. He was bleeding heavily and he couldn't use his left arm. He dropped the axe and drew his sword just as Irwyn lunged at him again. Unfortunately the boy couldn't put enough power behind it and it did no more than break a couple of links in the man's chainmail.

However, the blow did make his adversary take a step back and his leg gave way under him. Before he could recover, Irwyn stabbed him again, this time in his throat. The edge of the blade sliced through one of his carotid arteries and the Dane fell to the ground, gurgling incoherently as his life blood pumped out of him.

Irwyn slumped down and leaned his back against a tree. He felt drained mentally and physically exhausted. Some time passed before he recovered sufficiently to get to his feet and take the purses and silver arm rings off the two dead Danes. One was obviously a wealthy hersir or even a jarl as he wore five arm rings on one arm and three on the other; his purse was full of hacksilver and a few coins, including a rare gold mancus. The other man's purse contained far fewer pieces of hacksilver and no coins but all told the boy was now wealthy enough to buy a good horse as well as a new byrnie made to fit him and a decent helmet.

He thought of taking the byrnies, helmets and weapons of the dead men but that would only encumber him. He did, however, hang the heavy battle axe on his back before trying to retrace his steps back to the body of Osfirth's agent. It wasn't long before he realised that he was lost and he sat down once more, this time it was to try and work out what to do.

Whilst he sat there lassitude overcame him and he drifted off to sleep.

Half a mile away Hengist was getting increasingly worried. He'd left the horses tied to a tree and crept forward to the edge of the treeline to keep watch for Irwyn. Several Danes had made their way to and from the wood, presumably to defecate, but all of them were too big to be the boy. Some time ago he thought he saw him come out of the camp and head for the wood but he entered it three hundred yards to the west of Hengist's position.

He wasn't sure whether to abandon his vigil and go and see if it was Irwyn but then a man followed the boy into the wood and he assumed that they were from the camp and treading a well-worn path to relieve themselves.

He estimated that it was now the early hours of the morning and Irwyn had said that he wanted to be well away from Ledecestre before dawn. What made it worse was there was nothing he could do. Despite his concern he found his eyelids closing and he was about to drift off to sleep when he heard the call of a pigeon coming from nearby. As they were not nocturnal he became alert immediately, then relaxed. It was one of the calls used by Wynnstan and his men to give warning or attract attention.

He put his hands together over his mouth and repeated the call several times. Five minutes later he jumped when Wardric tapped him on the shoulder.

'Where's Irwyn?' he asked in a whisper.

'I've no idea,' Hengist replied, putting his mouth to the other man's ear. 'He went into the camp several hours ago.'

Wardric gave two more calls and a few minutes later they were joined by Wynnstan and the others.

'Right,' Wynnstan said decisively after he'd been briefed, 'if Irwyn has been captured there's nothing we can do but it's possible that he was the boy Hengist saw and he's just got disorientated in the darkness.'

'What about the man who followed him?' Tidhelm asked.

'There's no point in speculating. We need to find where they entered the wood and then see if we can follow their trail.'

Hengist led the way to where he thought that the two must have entered the wood and a few minutes later Sawin found an animal track leading into the trees. It didn't take them long after that to find the body of the first man that Irwyn had killed.

'Looks promising,' Wynnstan remarked. 'I think we've found Osfirth's agent.'

'There's a clear trail leading away from here into the heart of the wood,' Tidhelm pointed out. 'There's two sets of men's footprints as well as a smaller set,' he added.

Ten minutes later they found the bodies of the two dead Danes.'

'It seems that Irwyn has done the impossible and killed all three adversaries,' Sawin said in disbelief.

'So it would appear,' Wynnstan said nodding, 'but where is he?'

'There's a branch snapped off here and a set of smallish prints heading further into the wood,' Tidhelm called.

'Shhh,' Wynnstan whispered, gesturing for everyone to be quiet.

They froze where they stood and listened intently. After a moment or two they could hear a number of Danish voices coming closer. It sounded as if they were teasing one another good naturedly and chatting so it was unlikely that they were searching for Irwyn. However, it sounded as if there were quite a few of them and if they came across the boy he wouldn't stand a chance.

'We're going to have to kill them just to make sure they don't find Irwyn inadvertently or encounter us when we're unprepared,' he whispered.

'We don't know how many of them there are,' Hengist pointed out.

'No, but if we ambush them we'll have the advantage of surprise.'

He led his warriors towards the sound and came out on a track leading through the wood. The voices were quite close now so Wynnstan and Hengist hid in the bushes on one side whilst the others faded into the trees on the other.

They didn't have long to wait. A few minutes later the Danes appeared illuminated by the weak moonlight that filtered down through the tree canopy. Two were mounted and one had a dead deer slung across the front of his horse. Eight more followed on foot carrying a few small animals they'd caught in snares. None wore armour or helmets and they had evidently been hunting.

As they drew level with the ambushers the first rays of the coming sunrise appeared, illuminating dappled patches of the track. Wynnstan and his men all carried bows and, at that range, they could hardly miss. In a split second the carefree group of returning hunters were thrown into chaos. Wynnstan and Hengist brought down the two horses whilst the others killed three of the men on foot. Whilst the rest stood there in shock a second volley of arrows tore into them. One of the riders had jumped clear whilst his companion was trapped under his dead horse. The former was hit as were two more of the Danes on foot.

That left three and the trapped rider. All three were swiftly disposed of and all the bodies were dragged into the undergrowth. Most warriors carried their wealth on them as leaving their silver and other valuables in their tent would have been foolish. It didn't take long for the Mercians to deprive the bodies of everything of value.

'Now all we have to do is to find Irwyn before the camp begins to stir,' Sawin said sardonically.

The sun was now well above the horizon, which would aid their search but it wouldn't be long before more Danes entered the wood to empty their bowels rather than use the stinking latrines.

They retraced their steps to where they'd last found Irwyn's footprints and followed his trail. Less than a quarter of an hour later they found him fast asleep and covered in blood. Amazingly, apart from a flesh wound to his arm, none of it was his.

CHAPTER TEN

May/June 914

If Irwyn expected to be thanked by Eadweard he was doomed to disappointment. He had even seemed to doubt that the boy was telling the truth. However, Odda had convinced him that it would be foolish not to prepare for such an invasion.

Whereas Eadweard was sceptical about the boy's report, Osfirth was positively seething with rage because the Mercian boy had evidently outwitted his own man. As time passed he became baffled that the latter hadn't returned to his side. Naturally Irwyn wasn't about to tell him that his wait was in vain. Irwyn only hoped that Osfirth would conclude that the Danes had discovered his agent and killed him.

Irwyn left to march north with the rest of Eadweard's gesith and Wynnstan bade him farewell, intending to head home with his small group of warriors. However, before he could do so a messenger found him. Whilst Eadweard moved to confront one of the Danish armies Æthelflæd and Æthelstan led a mixed Saxon and Mercian force into northern Wessex to confront the army of Danes heading for Oxenaforda. Æthelstan invited him to join him and his aunt at Oxenaforda in order to take command of the army's scouts. Wynnstan sighed. He could hardly say no; it might be phrased as a polite request but it was tantamount to a royal command.

He would normally have been all too happy to join them but he was worried about Astrid this close to the birth. He was therefore reluctant to comply. It wasn't the only reason: he'd have to come into contact with Arne, the captain of Æthelflæd's warband, again. The man loathed him and the sentiment was reciprocated. Inevitably Arne would try to make trouble for him. However, it couldn't be helped and he'd have to put up with it.

Æthelstan gave his old friend an enthusiastic welcome, gripping him by both shoulders and smiling broadly. Æthelflæd also greeted him warmly, if not quite so effusively as her nephew. His arrival was only slightly marred by the scowling face of Arne and his cronies in the background.

'We believe that Ulf is the jarl leading the raid into Oxenafordascīr,' Æthelstan told him once the war council had gathered. 'At the moment our scouts have found elements of what appears to be their vanguard south of Casingc Stræt near Touecestre. However, a few groups have also been spotted on our side of Casingc Stræt several miles from Touecestre so it's difficult to be certain about their exact line of march. That's where you come in. I want you to deploy our scouts on a broad front and establish where the lead elements of the main invasion force are heading. Make sure that they aren't just groups of Danes who are raiding and foraging.'

In addition to the four scouts who'd accompany him, Wynnstan was given command of another twenty who varied in age, quality and experience. He chose the most experienced of them to lead one of the scouting parties alongside Sawin, Wardrıc and Tidhelm. He allocated four men to each of them and retained Hengist and two of the other scouts, called Cena and Broga, to make up his own group. He debated whether to leave Eohric at the main camp but in the end he decided to take him along.

Whilst he made his way cautiously towards Touecestre the other groups - spaced at intervals of three miles - advanced on a line running roughly north-west to south-east; in other words parallel to Casingc Stræt, the de facto border between the Danelaw on the one hand and Wessex and Anglian Mercia on the other.

Wynnstan hadn't encountered any Danes before nightfall and so he and his men spent the night in a thegn's hall some twenty miles south-west of Touecestre. During the night messengers arrived from the other groups to report that so far they'd seen no sign of the Danes either.

Overnight the weather broke and Wynnstan went out to relieve himself in driving rain. Not only would this make travelling conditions miserable but it would restrict visibility, making it harder to spot the Danes at any distance. Just after midday they'd reached Banesberic. Wynnstan had expected to have encountered the Danes by now if they'd been at Touecestre a few days previously. He decided to stay there for the rest of the day and sent out his scouts to call in the other groups. All arrived before dark and the news they brought was not good.

Tidhelm's group had heard a large cavalcade of horsemen approaching through the driving rain and had managed to hide in the undergrowth before they came in sight. Had they not been making so much noise, laughing and joking amongst themselves, they could have ridden straight into them.

'I estimate that there were at least three hundred warriors,' he told Wynnstan.

'How long ago was this?'

'At least three hours, although it's difficult to tell in this damn weather.'

Wynnstan drew a rough map in the dirt floor of the hall where they'd taken refuge from the rain.

'Can you say whereabouts this was?'

Tidhelm scratched his head for a moment and then pointed to a spot to the north-west of where they were.'

'About five miles away?'

Tidhelm nodded. 'That's about right, given the time it took to ride here once they'd passed us.'

'It has to have been the vanguard of the main Danish army but where are they headed for? They're well to the west of the main route between Snotingeham and Oxenaforda.'

'Perhaps they intend to cross the River Temes to the west of Oxenforda and then advance along the south bank?' Cena suggested.

'Yes, thank you Cena. That must be it. We must warn the Lady Æthelflæd.'

Oxenforda lay twenty five miles due south of Banesberic and, although the Danes didn't appear to be moving very fast – probably because they needed to forage and live off the land – there was little time to ride to Oxenforda and then reconnoitre the Danes' line of march before locating a suitable site at which to engage them. Broga, who came from the area, suggested the ridge above Hochenartone. Wynnstan didn't know the man sufficiently well to trust his judgement but, from the man's description, it sounded a possible location.

He sent Tidhelm and his men back to Oxenforda whilst he rode to Hochenartone.

'Tell the Lady Æthelflæd that I'll meet her at Nortone in two days' time.'

He realised that the army was going to have to cover twice the distance the Danes did to reach the proposed battlefield in time if Hochenartone was as promising a place to defeat the Danes as Broga said it was. Nortone lay eleven miles from Oxenforda and Hochenartone was four miles further on. It was going to be a close run thing. The Mercians had one advantage; they didn't need to spend time foraging as they had brought a supply train with them.

✝✝✝

Irwyn had volunteered to join King Eadweard's scouts as he was a good tracker and, as he'd proved, capable of moving undetected through the countryside. However, the king took the view that it was beneath the dignity of nobles, and especially his gesith, to act as scouts. The fact that he'd sent Irwyn to spy on the enemy seemed to have been conveniently forgotten.

Some of his fellow hearth warriors – mainly the younger ones – regarded him as something of a hero following his solo mission whilst others derided him for it. Evidently they shared their royal master's views on the appropriate behaviour of nobles. Irwyn therefore tended to shun the company of his elders and cultivated a clique amongst the younger warriors.

This disturbed Galan, the captain of the king's hearth warriors. There was already enough division within the army caused by the rivalry between Osfirth and Odda for Eadweard's favour. The fact that Irwyn was Odda's nephew through marriage increased the polarisation into two camps. As Osfirth was the hereræswa and Galan came from Wiltunscīr, he tended to side with Osfirth. He also identified naturally with the older warriors and this predisposed him to regard Irwyn as a trouble maker.

Consequently, Irwyn tended to get the worst tasks, including sentry duty in the early hours of the morning. He wouldn't have been human if he didn't come to resent his treatment at Galan's hands and he determined to get even. One morning, when he was saddling his horse alongside that of Galan he pushed a cutting from a thorn bush under the captain's saddle.

His somewhat childish act of revenge was intended to make Galan look an incompetent horseman when he mounted the animal and the thorns dug into its flesh. However, the thorns were unusually long and he lost complete control of it. It bucked against the pain and eventually rolled over in an attempt to get rid of the rider whose weight was causing it so much distress. In doing so it broke Galan's right femur and several of his ribs as well as fracturing his forearm.

It wasn't the outcome that Irwyn had intended and he felt awful about it. He and several others grabbed the horse and pulled it off the unfortunate captain and, whilst doing so, he surreptitiously removed the length of briar. He deeply regretted the prank that had gone wrong but remorse didn't stop him thinking clearly. Had he thrown the length of thorn bush away it would have doubtless been found and awkward questions might have followed. Instead, he tucked it inside the sleeve of his tunic to be disposed of later.

Doubtless Galan would recover in due course but Eadweard was furious at the loss of his captain for the foreseeable future. Luckily for Irwyn the man hadn't been a good rider; Galan regarded a horse as purely a means of getting from one place to another more quickly than on foot and looked like a sack of potatoes when doing so. Therefore nobody thought it that strange that he had lost control of his mount.

The king ordered the horse killed and, if anyone noticed the bloody spots when it was unsaddled, they didn't say anything. That was the end of the matter but it prayed on Irwyn's conscience and he determined to ask Eadweard's permission to return to Cæstir . Obviously he couldn't do anything until the campaign was over; to ask for permission to leave now would look like the act of a coward.

It was with a heavy heart that he rode northwards towards the advancing Danes. It didn't help that the new captain was one of the older warriors who disliked him intensely. However, the man's petty vindictive attitude towards Irwyn did go some way to lifting his feeling of guilt. He even welcomed the unwarranted punishments that came his way, regarding them as just retribution for his stupid act.

'They say that the Danes have halted at Lintone,' one of his friends said as a group of them sat around a fire cooking pottage in a small cauldron.

They had crossed from the area north of Lundenburg which Eadweard had established control over during the past two years and were now in the Jarldom of Bedeford, an independent realm outside the Five Boroughs – the region that used to form the eastern part of the old Kingdom of Mercia. Lintone was a large settlement with a population of several hundred. Many were Angles who'd been enslaved by the Vikings when they conquered the area half a century before but a substantial minority would be Danish bøndur. If they and the Danes living in the rest of the jarldom had joined their compatriots from the Danelaw, the army of

Wessex could be facing an enemy force of anything up to two thousand strong.

Eadweard had only bothered to muster the fyrds of Sūþrīgescīr, Cent, Lundenburg and Ēast Seaxna Rīce to deal with what he perceived as a minor raid. They provided fifteen hundred men but some of those were newly baptised Danes from Ēast Seaxna Rīce whose loyalty he wasn't entirely confident about. Furthermore, the fyrd weren't as experienced in warfare as most of the Danes they'd be facing. However, in addition to his own gesith he also had the warbands of those ealdormen who formed part of his court – Osfirth, Odda and Hilderinc of Hamtunscīr and they were all well trained and well equipped warriors. In total his army numbered some eighteen hundred. He was therefore likely to be outnumbered.

He was well aware of the dissention between Osfirth and Odda. Thankfully the other four ealdormen hadn't taken sides in their quarrel, nor had thegn who led the contingent from Lundenburg. They were all loyal to him. Whatever strategy he came up with for the coming battle, those two would have to be kept apart. Their men were just as likely to attack each other as they were to fight the enemy.

Mist covered the ground on the morning of the engagement. As the sun slowly burned it off Eadweard moved his men into position along the west bank of the river that ran close to the settlement. The Danes had occupied the hills to the east. His best chance of victory was for the enemy to charge downhill and attack him across the river. However, as the day wore on the Danes showed no inclination to move from their hilltop position.

The king was getting impatient and Osfirth took advantage of this to urge him to advance to meet the Danes but Odda and the other nobles dissuaded him. Eadweard was no fool, however frustrated he might be, and he knew that attacking uphill against an enemy superior in both numbers and experience would be suicidal. The mere fact that Osfirth had urged him to do just that convinced the king that he wasn't fit to be his hereræswa. Nevertheless, to remove him from his post just before a battle wasn't possible, especially given the divisions within his army. This only added to Eadweard's frustration.

Irwyn sat on his horse behind the king surrounded by the younger members of the gesith. The more senior warriors positioned themselves closer to Eadweard. Ywer's son was equally exasperated by the stalemate but he finally decided to do something about it.

'I say we charge the Danes and throw our spears into their midst,' he whispered to those closest to him.

'What good will that do?' one of his companions asked, looking puzzled.

'With any luck they'll chase us back down the hill.'

'It's worth a try,' another youth said.

'Anything's better than sitting here getting a sore arse,' a third agreed.

They spread the word to the others who'd been out of earshot during the muted conversation and five minutes later they peeled away and cantered around the left flank of the fyrd before splashing across the shallow river. They found the far bank was boggy and they had to dismount to lead their horses through the morass.

Once on firmer ground, and now covered in slime from the waist down, they re-mounted and walked their horses up the slope towards the Danes' shieldwall. The enemy hunkered down behind their shields waiting for the horsemen to charge them. Had they done so the spears that protruded from behind their shields would have killed the horses and the Danes would have made short work of the handful of dismounted warriors.

However, that did not happen. Irwyn and his companions walked their horses until they were nearly within arrow range and proceeded to hurl insults at the Danes. The enemy wouldn't have understood those who were shouting in Ænglisc but Irwyn and a few others spoke Danish. The enemy understood only too well their accusations of cowardice and the ribald allegations about the unfaithfulness of their mothers.

The roar of outrage from the enemy shieldwall grew and they shouted similar abuse back. Quite a few had lowered their shields to be heard better and,when Irwyn yelled 'now', his companions dug in their heels and the horses leapt forward. As soon as they were about twenty yards from the Danish line, they drew back their right arms and hurled their spears at the enemy.

A few of those in the front rank of the enemy shieldwall managed to raise their shields in time but ten of them were killed. The Danes had some archers but they'd been positioned in the rear and they couldn't see their targets. A scattering of arrows shot skywards but they landed without hitting any of the Saxon horsemen.

Immediately after throwing their spears, Irwyn and his companions wheeled their mounts about and trotted slowly away downhill. Irwyn had decided against cantering or galloping for two reasons: there was always the risk of taking a tumble on the steep slope and, more importantly, he wanted the Danes to think that they had a chance of catching them.

Despite the command from Hákon to hold their position, nearly half of the Danish army streamed away from the summit in pursuit of the Saxon horsemen. When they saw them dismount and flounder in the marshy ground at the base of the hill, they were spurred on to greater efforts to catch and kill them.

All twenty of Irwyn's companions made it safely to the far bank to the cheers of their fellow Saxons. Few realised that the leader of the daring sortie wasn't a Saxon like themselves, or even an Anglian, but one who was born of a Jutish father and Norse mother. The fyrd parted to allow them to pass through and they re-joined the rest of the gesith around the king.

Eadweard was about to vent his wrath at them for deserting their post but then he saw half the Danish army was struggling through the marshy ground a hundred yards in front of him. The rest of the Danes had followed the others' example and were now streaming down the hill.

'Archers,' Odda bellowed, seeing Osfirth staring open mouthed at the oncoming horde. 'Kill as many as you can before they cross the river.'

Osfirth had placed two hundred archers at the rear of the Wessex shieldwall and fifty on each flank. Although Eadweard was in overall command, he had taken the advice of his hereræswa as to deployment. Osfirth might have many faults but he was a dependable, if rather conventional, tactician.

The Danes struggled to hold their shields in front of them whilst wading through the boggy ground and several score fell to the first volley. More and more fell to subsequent volleys until the more fainthearted of the enemy tried to retreat back to firm ground. However, they were in the minority and the casualties being inflicted on them only served to inflame the rest.

When the first Danes reached the bank where the Saxons were drawn up they tried to carve their way through the shieldwall but they were at a distinct disadvantage as they struggled to climb up the far bank whilst defending themselves from the axes and spears of the Saxons.

It wasn't long before the water turned red with the blood of the dead and wounded. However, more and more Danes had now reached the far side of the river and in places the ferocity of their attack forced the Saxons back. More and more gaps appeared in Eadweard's front rank and, whereas it had initially been composed of well-armed and trained warriors from the nobles' warbands, their replacements from the second – or even third –ranks were members of the fyrd.

'Your action in drawing the enemy to us was commendable,' Eadweard said begrudgingly to Irwyn and his companions, 'but you disobeyed orders and deserve punishment. You are to dismount and take the places of those warriors in the front rank who've been killed.'

The order was both unfair and inappropriate as the gesith's task was to protect the life of the king. Normally they would only fight if he himself was in danger. Admittedly, his mounted attack on the Danish ranks was also wrong but Irwyn felt that it was justified in the circumstances. That didn't apply to the king's order. Nevertheless, Irwyn didn't hesitate but dismounted and gave the reins to a servant. His friends did likewise and they pushed their way forward through the rear ranks.

Irwyn found himself behind a boy no older than he was. He stood in the second rank clutching his spear in sweaty hands as he nervously waited for the man in front of him to fall. Irwyn pulled him to one side and told him to stand behind him. With a grateful nod the boy did as he was bid. A couple of seconds later the man in front of him was cut down by a Danish axeman. The boy's wail told Irwyn that he was a relative – an uncle perhaps or even the lad's father. There was no time to comfort him and he stepped over the man's corpse, bringing his shield around to cover his torso and jabbing the point of his sword into the axeman's left armpit as he did so.

The Dane had lifted the two-handed axe on high to bring it down on Irwyn's head but he lost control of his weapon when he tried to wield it one-handed. The axe blade glanced harmlessly off Irwyn's shield just as the boy thrust the point at his opponent again. This time he aimed for his throat and he felt the resistance as it penetrated the man's mouth before driving home into the base of his brain. The man dropped like a stone but unfortunately, in doing so, he wrenched his sword out of Irwyn's hand.

Another Dane stepped forward into the gap but this one wasn't an experienced warrior; he looked to be even younger than Irwyn and his tentative thrust at the older boy with his spear confirmed his suspicion that he was a novice who had yet to make his first kill. Irwyn had no trouble in knocking the spear point away with his shield whilst he pulled his seax out of its scabbard. The young Dane looked at him open mouthed, seemingly bemused by the fact that his spear hadn't had the result he'd expected. Irwyn couldn't bring himself to kill the boy and that was nearly his undoing.

Normally a warrior standing in a shieldwall would attack the enemy standing in front of the man to his immediate left because his right side wasn't covered by his shield. Irwyn had forgotten this basic principle and the Dane to the left of his young opponent used his momentary hesitation to thrust his sword into Irwyn's right side. It was a quick opportunistic thrust and lacked the power to penetrate his byrnie but the boy felt a sudden pain and he realised that one or more of his ribs had been fractured or broken. If the latter, there was a real danger that the sharp end of a broken bone could penetrate his lung.

He was furious with himself for being so stupid. The sensible thing to do would be to go to the rear and get his chest tightly strapped up but Irwyn gritted his teeth and ignored the pain. The man who had struck him was already dead and a second later so was the Danish lad he had hesitated to kill, chopped down by the Saxon warrior standing to Irwyn's left.

His next assailant was a somewhat rotund Dane who stood at least six inches taller than Irwyn. He had no shield but wielded a sword in one hand and a small axe in the other. The pain in Irwyn's side was now intense and he had difficulty in standing, let alone fighting. Luckily the Dane lost his footing as he reached the top of the bank and slid part of the way back down to the river's edge. Irwyn managed to thrust the point of his sword into the joint between the man's neck and shoulder before something hit his helmet and he passed out.

When he woke up it was all over. A monk had just finished strapping his chest up and one of his companions was trying to force a drink between his lips. The pain was intense, especially in his head, but he gritted his teeth. He was damned if he was going to let anyone call him a weakling.

'The monk says you've broken three ribs,' his companion told him. 'Luckily there is no pink froth and so it looks as if you haven't punctured a lung but you have to keep still until the bones mend. That's not what made you pass out though.'

The warrior held up Irwyn's helmet so that he could see it. It was badly dented on one side.

'Luckily it was the flat of the axe head which hit you. Had it been the blade....'

He shrugged, feeling it unnecessary to state the obvious.

'You've a nasty bruise on your scalp but your skull is still intact,' he continued cheerfully. 'You must be as thick-headed as people say,' he added with a grin.

The monk gently lifted the boy's head.

'Here, drink this. It contains herbs to dull the pain and make you sleep.'

Irwyn sipped the concoction and grimaced at the unpleasant taste; nevertheless, he drank it all. Satisfied, the monk left to deal with his next patient.

'What happened? Did we win?' Irwyn asked, wincing at the effort involved in talking.

'Not only were we victorious but we killed over five hundred Danes including their leader, Jarl Hákon. Our horsemen are still chasing their routed army. I doubt that the Danes of Snotingeham will trouble us again.'

'How many did we lose?'

'Less than a hundred and about the same number wounded. One of the ealdormen was killed though.'

'Which one?' Irwyn asked a little drowsily as the medicine took effect.

'Lord Odda.'

✝✝✝

Æthelflæd and Æthelstan rode forward with Wynnstan to inspect the terrain he'd selected to halt the Danish advance. The captain of her gesith, Arne, and her hearth warriors accompanied her. Whilst Wynnstan was explaining his logic for choosing the site, Arne kept making snide comments to his cronies until Bawdewyn, Æthelstan's captain, quietly threatened to beat him to a pulp if he didn't shut up. As Bawdewyn was several inches taller and much heavier and more muscular than Arne, the threat wasn't an idle one and Æthelflæd's captain kept his thoughts about the chosen battlefield to himself after that.

The settlement of Hochenartone lay to the north of a wide stream. It wasn't much of an obstacle but it might tire attackers eager to wade through it at speed to come to grips with their enemy. A few hundred yards to the south of the first stream there was a second one. There were also several small ponds and areas of marshy ground.

A hill to the west of the settlement lay between the two streams and on the other side of a shallow col to the west of the hill there was a ridge at roughly the same elevation which ran in an arc from the south-west to the north-west of Hochenartone. This ridge was where the source of the two streams lay and the whole area below the ridge was boggy.

Both Æthelflæd and her nephew saw the possibilities of such a site and, having discussed the deployment of their army, they withdrew to spend the night at Nortone. Wynnstan and his scouts didn't have the luxury of a good night's sleep. He led them forward widely spaced as a screen to locate the enemy. He saw their campfires some six miles north of Hochenartone astride the road that led through Hochenartone and Nortone before turning south-east towards Oxenaforda. Obviously, they were using the road - which was little more than a track - as the axis of their advance.

Satisfied that it would take them the best part of the morning to reach the site chosen for the battle, he led his men back to Hochenartone to get what sleep they could before dawn.

In the hours before the Danes' expected arrival the Mercians marched the five miles to their positions. However, those who were mounted were sent ahead of those on foot and, under Wynnstan's direction, they cut timber to use as sharpened stakes and tied them around the middle in bunches of three to form obstacles along the far bank of the southern stream. This was where the archers and spearmen stationed on top of the hill would retreat when driven from the high ground.

Æthelstan had drawn up the battle plan, assisted by Wynnstan. He didn't want to just defeat the Danes of the Ledecestre Jarldom, he wanted to destroy them. That meant trapping them in an area from which they couldn't escape.

The Danish scouts appeared first and, after taking one look at the five hundred men holding the hill to the south of the settlement, they raced off to give the good news to Jarl Ulf. Next to appear were the vanguard of several hundred Danes. They were eager to attack the Mercians on the hill but their leaders restrained with difficulty. Had they charged up the hill on their own they would have suffered severe losses, outnumbered as they were by over two to one. It was a pity as such an easy victory would have stiffened the resolve of the more faint-hearted of the fyrd.

More and more Danes appeared from the north until Wynnstan reckoned there might be as many as fifteen hundred, perhaps more. It was a greater number than the Mercians were expecting and he began to worry about the likely success of Æthelstan's plan.

Such worries didn't bother either Æthelstan or his aunt. He was confident of victory and she believed that the more Danes they could kill here the fewer she would face when she marched into the Danelaw to recover Eastern Mercia.

Stepan was the youngest of the archers who waited on top of the hill for the Danes to attack. He had just celebrated his fifteenth birthday and, whilst most boys who had recently reached an age to serve as warriors were placed in the rear rank of the shieldwall, Stepan had the broad shoulders, strong back and muscular arms required to use a war bow.

His father was a fletcher by trade who also made bows and his two sons had been brought up to use a bow since they were young.

He was therefore picked to join the other bowmen. His father stood on one side of him and his elder brother, Hyrpa, on the other.

Stepan watched fascinated as the Danes chanted and beat their spears, axes and swords against the lime wood shields they all carried on their left arm. He was overawed by the mass of the enemy gathered between the settlement and the stream below him. However, at this distance they looked incredibly tiny and for a moment he forgot his fear of what was to come.

The first wave of Danes waded knee deep through the stream. When they reached the far bank they found it difficult to climb. The Mercians had spent some time that morning wetting the precipitous slope between the water and the top of the bank to make it as slippery as possible. It didn't delay their foes for long but it required considerable effort and then they were faced by the marshy ground between the stream and the firmer ground at the base of the hill. Therefore they were already tired before they began the climb up towards the Mercians on the summit.

Stepan strung his first arrow and was eager to rain death down at the advancing heathens but his father hissed at him to wait for the order. A good bowman could perhaps kill or wound someone onc hundred and fifty paces away, especially if they were below them, but not all the archers were that adept with the bow and many arrows would be wasted.

Besides, as his father explained, at the moment the oncoming warriors were concentrating on climbing up the slope as fast as possible and most had their shields by their sides. Once the first volley or two of arrows hit them, they would slow down and bring their shields across to protect their torsos. They should therefore wait until they could inflict the maximum number of casualties. Stepan could see the sense in that but his impatience grew nonetheless.

Wynnstan had been given command of the hilltop and he waited until the leading Danes were eighty paces away before he gave the archers the order to fire. A hundred and twenty arrows flew at low trajectory into the front rank of the Danes and over fifty of them fell, killed or too badly wounded to pose a threat anymore.

Some of the rest managed to raise their shields before the next volley struck home but most were too slow. Over forty more fell to the Mercians' arrows. The third volley was less successful, despite the shortening range, and it caused less than a score more casualties.

'One more volley at high trajectory and then retreat,' Wynnstan called.

Stepan raised his bow and sent his arrow skywards. Without waiting to see where it fell, he followed his father, Hyrpa and the rest of the archers over the brow of the hill and down the far slope. He splashed across the stream at the bottom, holding his bow high so that the bowstring didn't get wet, and squeezed his way between the obstacles on the far bank before entering the boggy area on the far side. He struggled through the mire and arrived panting on the firmer ground fifty yards further on. This was where they reformed and waited. This time Stepan was in no hurry to use his bow. He needed to get his breathing back under control first.

Meanwhile the Danes were struggling to break through the Mercian shieldwall on top of the hill. One end of the line was protected by a rocky crag but the other end ended in a gentle slope down to the saddle. Naturally the Danes thought they could outflank the Mercians but, as they made their way around the end of the shieldwall fifty more Mercian archers appeared on top of the ridge to their left. After two volleys across the saddle the Danes decided not to risk losing more men to the archers on their flank. They therefore did the sensible thing and drew back.

Having lost nearly a third of his men, firstly to the archers and then when attacking the shieldwall, the Danish leader of the first wave withdrew back down the hill. Ulf was furious with him for failing to take the hill and led the rest of his army forward.

Stepan was naturally unaware of what was going on over the hill in front of him. He took his father's advice and sat down after unstringing his bow. He took a long swig from his leather water bottle and chewed on a lump of hard cheese. He didn't feel much like eating but, as Hyrpa said, 'you never knew when you'll get another opportunity.'

The clash of steel against steel and the screams of wounded men reached them but the boy felt strangely detached from what was happening out of sight a few hundred yards away. He felt drowsy in the warm midday sun and had almost dozed off when suddenly he was jolted back to wakefulness. Wynnstan and the rest of those who had been left to hold the hill were streaming down the rear slope and heading towards them. Not far behind them came a horde of Danes.

He jumped to his feet and re-strung his bow. After sticking five arrows in the ground in front of him, he waited. He no longer felt fear, just an impatience to send arrow after arrow into their foes.

This time the archers didn't wait for an order. They could see that the leading Danes were about to catch the laggards amongst the fyrd as they fled towards the stream. One by one they let fly at the Danes more in an attempt to slow them down rather than inflict serious casualties. To avoid hitting their own men they had to shoot at high trajectory and so their arrows fell amongst the mass of the pursuers rather than striking down the leading Danes.

Half a dozen of the slowest Mercians were caught and killed before the rest reached the stream. It slowed them down but the Danes were also hindered by the three foot deep water. Most made it safely through the line of three pointed obstacles before the Danes reached them but they still obscured the line of fire of the archers.

Wynnstan reached the archers and paused to regain his breath before yelling at the fyrd to lie down. It was something they had practiced and all except a few panic-stricken men dropped and lay prone on the ground. Now the archers had a clear view of the oncoming Danes. They couldn't squeeze through the line of obstacles whilst holding their shield in front of their bodies and as soon as they turned them sideways on they were exposed. Arrow after arrow tore into them and dead bodies now filled many of the spaces between the sharpened stakes.

The Danes tried to pull the dead and the obstacles out of the way but more and more of them fell to the bowmen's arrows. Some managed to get through the defences but they were in small groups which the spearmen and swordsmen of the fyrd quickly dealt with.

After what seemed to Stepan like an hour but was in reality no more than ten or fifteen minutes the Danes retreated to the far bank of the stream and formed a shieldwall to protect themselves from the archers. Had they but known it, the Mercians were down to their last few arrows.

The Danes this side of the stream now numbered less than four hundred. Initially, Ulf had held the rest back on the summit of the hill. Ignoring the situation at the bottom of the hill, he ordered his men to descend into the saddle to attack up the far side to drive the archers who stood on the ridge off it. Once he'd disposed of them, his plan was to traverse the line of the ridge well above the marshy source of the second stream and attack the Mercians holding the south bank on their left flank.

The archers on top of the ridge took one look at the hundreds of Danes heading their way and fled. With a cry of triumph Ulf led his men up towards the top of the ridge. However, just before they reached it Æthelstan and seven hundred Mercians appeared on the skyline and the archers returned to send volley after volley down at the now hesitant enemy.

As soon as Ulf realised it was a trap, he ordered his men to retreat. It was now the turn of the Mercians to chase the Danes down the hill but, instead of allowing them to retreat towards Hochenartone, they herded them back towards the hill they'd just descended. They tried to reform to defend the hilltop but they didn't have time to get their defence organised before the Mercians were upon them and they were forced down the hill towards where the rest of their army stood.

Ulf realised the battle was lost and he led his men along the firmer ground between the two streams in a bid to escape to the east. What he didn't know – and the Mercians did – was that the two streams converged a mile further on and formed a small lake.

When they saw the lake in front of them the Danes tried to ford the two streams that fed it but it took time to cross and the Danes crowded into the ever-decreasing triangle of land waiting for their comrades to get out of the way. Desperate to escape, Danes started to fight each other to get to the front of the queue.

The Mercians hacked down those at the rear of the routed enemy, making the rest even more desperate to get away. Some tried to surrender but it did them no good. The Mercians' blood was up and all they wanted to do was to kill the Danes whose ancestors had stolen their land.

Wynnstan had led his men further along the bank so that they could cut off those Danes trying to cross the southern stream and escape that way. Apart from his bow, Stepan was only armed with a dagger. However, there were a lot of weapons lying on the ground where their owners had either died or had discarded them during their flight. He scooped up a sword and a spear and followed his father and brother along the bank.

Stepan saw a Dane scrambling up the bank and, screaming insults at him, he waded through the boggy ground and thrust his spear through the man's chest. He fell back into the stream but in doing so, he tore the spear out of the boy's hands. Exultant at killing his first man face to face, he ploughed on through the soggy ground looking for his next victim.

He saw his father and brother standing a few yards away trying to stop three Danes from climbing out of the stream. He rushed to help them, the wet ground sucking at his feet. He scarcely noticed when he lost a shoe in the mire but a second later he saw a Dane climb the bank behind his father. He shouted a warning but to his horror he saw the Dane grab his father from behind and saw a dagger across his throat. He fell into the stream which carried his body away.

Stepan stood there rooted to the spot by the horror of what he'd just witnessed. In a way it seemed unreal; his father just couldn't be dead. Hyrpa was equally stunned but, when the big Dane turned to attack him, his brother reacted quickly, using his own dagger to block the Dane's thrust at his chest. Stepan ran forward to help his brother but he was too slow. The Dane punched Hyrpa on the nose, breaking it and temporarily blinding him. A split second later he thrust his blade into Hyrpa's chest.

As he fell, the Dane turned to make good his escape but, with a yell of fury, Stepan leaped onto the big man's back and stabbed at his neck again and again until he crashed to the ground. Stepan rolled clear and ran to Hyrpa and, pulling his dead brother's head into his lap, he sat there as tears rolled down his cheeks.

Arne reached the spot a minute or so later. He yanked the boy to his feet and slapped him in the face.

'There'll be time to grieve later, boy,' he yelled, his face inches away from Stepan's. 'There's more Danes to kill, now get on with it and stop crying like a baby.'

Arne stomped away followed by his cronies who sneered and made crude remarks as they passed the mortified boy. He wiped the spittle from Arne's mouth from his face and stood there bemused for a moment before returning to embracing his dead brother once more.

Wynnstan had been a few yards away and had seen what had happened. He was furious at Arne's insensitive attitude. After all, the battle was won and whether or not the boy joined in killing the last of those trapped mattered not one jot. He went and knelt by Stepan and gently prised the boy's arms away before lifting Hyrpa's body in his arms.

'Come with me, lad; we'll go and find a priest to bury him,'

He didn't know the boy from any of the other youngsters who had fought and died that day but something drew him to the disconsolate young archer, quite apart from Arne's heartless treatment of him. The boy seemed in a daze and, after they had found a priest and handed his brother's body to him for burying with the rest, he told Eohric to take care of Stepan and make sure he had something to eat.

Gradually the boy came out of his trancelike state and the realisation struck him that he was now the only male left in his family. That meant that he was now responsible for his mother and three younger sisters. He had no idea how he might support them as he'd only just started his apprenticeship as a fletcher and no one was likely to employ him. Even if they did, apprentices only received free lodging, food and training in return for their work. That wouldn't help his family. Despair washed over him until Eohric said something that gave him a glimmer of hope.

'Lord Wynnstan seems to have taken you under his wing. I don't know what your situation is but rest assured he'll take care of you from now on; that is, if you want him to.'

CHAPTER ELEVEN

Autumn 914

The more Irwyn delved into the death of Ealdorman Odda the more convinced he became that there was something suspicious about it. His uncle was no coward and yet he'd been killed by the thrust of a sword into his back. He couldn't find anyone who'd seen his death and that in itself was strange. Somehow he'd become separated from his hearth warriors during the fierce fighting and, although one or two said that the men around him at the time of his death weren't known to any of his gesith, one man thought that he'd seen one of them later in the camp. He was with others from Wiltunscīr – Osfirth's shire – but he couldn't be absolutely certain it was the same man.

It didn't stop him from feeling concerned when he heard rumours that Osfirth had importuned the king on behalf of a wealthy thegn who wanted to become the next Ealdorman of Dyfneintscīr.

However, Odda had a son. He had married Ywer's twin sister, Kjestin and they had three children – two girls and a boy. The daughters were now married and had consequently left home. The son - Wælwulf - was seventeen and therefore old enough to succeed his father.

Eadweard wasn't about to appoint someone to such an important shire who was an ally of Osfirth's and he hastened to recommend Wælwulf to a hurriedly convened Witenaġemot consisting of the ealdormen, senior thegns and churchmen who were with the army. Only three, including Osfirth and his protégé, spoke against the appointment of Odda's son, claiming he was too young and inexperienced, but the rest supported the king.

Needless to say, Osfirth was furious and Irwyn wondered whether he might arrange for Wælwulf's assassination. He wouldn't put it past him, given the attempts that had been made on Æthelstan's life. From what he'd been told Osfirth was almost certainly behind them. Irwyn had never met his cousin as he hadn't accompanied his father on campaign. However, he decided that he should write to him and warn him.

Wælwulf sat in what was now his hall, although he could scarcely believe that his father was dead and that he was now the ealdorman. When his mother announced her intention of retiring to a monastery he suddenly felt very alone.

'Why, mother? I need you here,' he said, trying not to sound plaintive.

'You're betrothed to Cwenhild and she'll want to be mistress of her own hall. My presence, watching her every move with a disapproving eye, will only lead to conflict and disharmony.'

Wælwulf knew that she was right. Their wedding was planned for two months' time and Cwenhild was a strong minded girl, despite being only fourteen. Kjestin was an equally strong character and they would clash from the first moment his new bride moved in.

'Where will you go?'

'It's years since I have seen my two brothers. I'll go to Cæstir and ask Æscwin for permission to enter his monastery. It'll enable me to spend what's left of my life close to my twin, Ywer, as well.'

Mention of Ywer reminded Wælwulf about the letter he'd received from Ywer's son. He'd never met his cousin but he had no reason to doubt what Irwyn had told him. He'd never liked Osfirth, nor had his father, but he was wary of starting a blood feud based on Irwyn's suspicions. If he was correct, that was a different matter. Honour demanded that he take the life of Osfirth, or one of his family, in retribution.

He decided to talk to those of his father's gesith who'd survived the Battle of Lintone individually and see if they knew anything which would confirm his cousin's suspicions.

†‡†

'I'll train you as a fletcher,' Wynnstan told Stepan, 'but everyone in my small warband has to offer more than one skill. Perhaps you'll make a warrior in due course but first I want to see if you've got the makings of a scout.'

'You're more than kind, lord,' the boy replied, pausing before daring to continue, 'but I have a family to support: my mother and three younger sisters.'

'How do you propose to do that?'

'I've no idea, lord, but I can't abandon them.'

Wynnstan smiled. He admired the boy's devotion to his family and his courage in standing up for himself. Many would have accepted his largesse and conveniently forgotten about their obligations.

'There is a limit to my generosity, boy. Does your mother have any special skills?'

'She's a miller's daughter and was brought up to help her father in the mill before she married my father.'

There was already a mill at Rumcofen but the miller was old and had no sons to succeed him. The mill seemed less and less able to cope with the demands of the local farmers and some had started to take their wheat and barley to the mill at Frodesham. As Wynnstan took a cut of the mill's profits, this irked him and his ceorls disliked having to pay the extra cost of transportation.

'Where does your family live?'

'In a small settlement in Scrobbesbyrigscīr, lord; you won't have heard of it but it's on our way north.'

'Very well. Does your family own a cart?'

'Yes, lord. And an ox to draw it.'

Wynnstan groaned. Ox carts were notoriously slow and he was anxious to return to Astrid as quickly as possible. Many poor ceorls only owned oxen because they could be used for ploughing as well as pulling a cart to market. They were cheaper to buy than a horse as well.

'You can sell the ox and I'll loan you the money to buy a horse to pull your cart.'

He paused and looked speculatively at the boy. Instinctively he trusted him but he didn't know him at all.

'If you are lying to me or exaggerating your mother's ability as a miller, I'll have the hide off your back and leave you and your family to fend for yourselves. Do you understand?'

'Yes, lord,' Stepan said, grinning with pleasure. 'You won't regret it, I promise.'

The boy had never ridden a horse before and found being perched on the gentle mare he was given a daunting experience. He doubted that he'd ever be able to ride a horse like the stallions his companions rode; even the gelding that Eohric was mounted on seemed huge compared to the small mare. At first he jogged along uncomfortably until Eohric took pity on him and showed him how to grip with his knees and match his motion to that of the horse. It was more comfortable but that night the insides of his thighs were badly chafed and his bum felt as if it had been beaten with a heavy stick.

As he hobbled around collecting firewood Sawin took him to one side and pressed a small pottery flask into his hand.

'Go and find somewhere private and smear this on your sore thighs,' he advised. 'You will get used to it. As for your arse, rise and fall more gently when you're trotting using your leg muscles. They'll ache for a while but they'll get stronger with exercise.'

Stepan thanked him and reflected how different Wynnstan's warriors were to the people in his settlement; they'd have laughed themselves silly to see him gingerly walking bow legged to keep his thighs apart, especially his friends.

By the time they reached his home and collected his mother and sisters he was more used to riding and felt superior to his friends, mounted on a horse in the company of a notable thegn and his hearth warriors. If he expected them to be impressed he was disappointed; they were jealous of his good fortune in escaping the drudgery of life trying to eek a living out of the poor soil and shunned him in consequence. Even his closest friends scowled at him. He was glad when the cart was loaded and he could leave.

He drove the cart sitting beside his mother with his sisters perched on top of their paltry possessions in the back. It made a nice change from riding but his mother had little to say to him and he got the impression that she was sorry that he was the one who had survived instead of his father or brother.

When he told her he'd secured a position for her assisting the miller at Rumcofen he'd expected her to be pleased. Instead she told him that she'd had enough of breathing in flour dust and heaving heavy bags around when she'd been forced to help her father.

'Well, you'll have to make the best of it,' he snapped, fed up with her attitude. 'It's that or starve.'

'You're the man of the family now,' she told him. 'It's up to you to provide for us.'

'No, although Lord Wynnstan will pay me, I'll need the money to buy a byrnie, a decent helmet and weapons, not to mention paying off the loan for my mare' he retorted. 'Besides, the only reason he's offering you a home is as the miller's assistant. He's an old man with no family so you will be able to take over the mill in due course.'

She sniffed and said nothing to him for the rest of the day. The next day he decided that he'd had enough of the morose atmosphere and he mounted his horse, leaving his mother to drive the cart.

Wynnstan was well aware of her ingratitude towards her son for securing a position which would enable her to look after her daughters as well as herself and decided to intervene.

'Mistress, I gather that you are unhappy at the thought of helping to run my mill. If so, you are welcome to turn around and head back whence you came. I will, of course, expect you to pay me for the horse I bought you before you leave.'

A look of panic replaced the sullen expression on the woman's face. Contrary to what he thought, she didn't blame Stepan for surviving the battle where her husband and eldest son had perished; she did curse the misfortune which had had deprived her of her comfortable life as the wife of a fletcher. Now that she was presented with a stark choice of returning to a life of poverty, made worse by the inevitable ridicule of the others in her settlement, or a chance to earn a decent living, even if it did mean hard and unpleasant work. There was really no doubt over which she would choose.

'Lord, I am most sensible for the kind offer you have made me,' she said smiling sweetly. 'I don't know why you think me ungrateful. I am delighted at the prospect of working at the mill.'

Her simpering insincerity didn't fool him for a minute and he felt sorry for Stepan. She obviously didn't love her son and he doubted if she had ever loved anyone. She struck him as selfish and only interested in her own comfort and well-being. However, he did need someone to work at the mill so he would put his misgivings about the woman aside for now. If she failed to live up to his expectations, however, he'd dismiss her without a moment's hesitation.

They eventually arrived at Cæstir where he found, to his relief, that Astrid hadn't yet given birth.

'The good wife says that it's overdue,' Astrid told him tearfully as soon as they were alone.

'Does she know by how much?'

'No but she says that the baby is big and she worries that it will be a difficult birth if it's delayed any longer.'

'Can't she give you something to bring on labour?'

'Yes, but I wanted you to be here.'

'Well, I'm here now so I think we'd better get this baby born,' he said, giving her an affectionate kiss on the cheek.

It was a difficult birth which lasted over twelve hours. By the end of that time Astrid was exhausted and because she had lost a lot of blood, and was still bleeding, she was very weak. The baby was another boy who cried lustily from the moment of his appearance. It was small recompense as far as Wynnstan was concerned for his wife's suffering.

'Is she likely to die?' he asked the good wife bluntly.

'She might if the bleeding doesn't stop soon.'

'Why is she still losing blood?'

'She's torn inside, lord,' she said nervously, wringing her hands in agitation. 'There's nothing I can do to stop it.'

'Show me,' he ordered.

The woman looked aghast.

'That's women's business, lord. Men cannot see their wives in that state. It's too intimate.'

'Don't you think we've been intimate in every possible way? I know full well what women have between their legs. Now get out of my way.'

Astrid lay on the bed, the white linen cloth under her stained a bright scarlet. She was pale to the point of translucence and could only manage a wan smile when she saw her husband. He examined her and immediately saw where she was torn. He wished that either Uhtric or Leofwine were here but they were far away in Glowecestre. Without a physician the best he could do was to summon the infirmarian from the monastery.

He fretted, alternately pacing up and down and sitting on the blood-stained bed to hold Astrid's hand. Finally the monk appeared and listened to what Wynnstan wanted him to do. He looked doubtful and it was outside his experience and hesitated until Wynnstan spoke again.

'It's a wound, brother, just like any other, only not where you're used to. It needs sewing up before my wife loses what blood there is left in her body,' he said, trying to keep his exasperation in check.

The infirmarian nodded and set to work. Ten minutes later he straightened up and washed his bloody hands in a bowl.

'That's the best I can do. The bleeding appears to have stopped but how it will heal I don't know. Get the good wife to wash the blood away and feed her some broth.'

'Thank you, brother. I'm most grateful.'

All he could do now was wait and pray.

✝✝✝

Cedric arrived at Rumcofen exhausted and bleeding from several flesh wounds. Those who'd known him as a ship's boy would scarcely have recognised him. Now a few months short of his sixteenth birthday he'd filled out and sported a beard that was the envy of other seamen his age who served on the *Saint Oswald*. He felt grief wash over him; they were no more, nor was the ship itself. It had been sunk by Norse longships whilst patrolling the River Mæresēa beyond Mamecestre.

He was immediately taken to Chad, Wynnstan's captain who was responsible for the defence of the burh. The reeve, a man called Beorht, was in charge of the burh's administration and Chad sent for him so that they could listen to Cedric's tale together.

'We were on a routine patrol along the river when we saw several longships coming towards us in line.' Cedric began. 'The ship's boy on lookout at the masthead counted six but there could have been more around the bend. He said that the lead ship was a drekar with a snake's head mounted on the prow.'

Chad and Beorht looked at each other in concern. Like Cedric, they knew that the pagans only mounted that type of figurehead when they were at war or on a raid.

'We couldn't engage so many longships so Heoruwulf ordered us to turn around and warn the garrison at Mamecestre. Unfortunately, it took us too long to turn and the leading drekar caught up with us. We gave a good account of ourselves until a second drekar pulled alongside and its crew boarded us. I saw Heoruwulf cut down and our crew tried to surrender. It made no difference and the heathens kept on slaughtering us.

'I was lucky to escape. Many of my fellow crew who had leaped overboard drowned. Those like me who could swim were hunted down by the Norsemen on land. As far as I know, Mamecestre is still in Mercian hands but it may well be under siege.'

Chad thanked him and sent him to get his wounds attended to and to get some rest.

'What will you do?' Beorht asked worriedly.

'Send messengers to warn Frodesham and ask Ywer for help, I suppose,' Chad replied morosely.

He wished Wynnstan was there to take charge. However, he was still at Cæstir.

With her husband constantly at her bedside, Astrid was slowly recovering. Wynnstan was shattered, not having slept for some time, but when he was sure that she was out of danger he went to get some much needed sleep. However, he'd only managed three hours of slumber before Ywer woke him to tell him about the Norse fleet.

'I must get back to Rumcofen,' his said, slurring his speech in his exhaustion.

'You need more rest first. Set out tomorrow. I'll send a messenger to let Chad know. I'm sure he's perfectly capable of calling in those who live in the surrounding vills and preparing the burh's defences. Meanwhile, I'll call out the shire's fyrd but it will probably be a week before everyone has assembled.'

Wynnstan nodded and went back to bed. At first he couldn't sleep; his mind was full of what needed to be done, not to mention his concern at leaving Astrid and the baby. However, he eventually drifted off and didn't wake until dawn the next day. Now feeling thoroughly refreshed, he dunked his head in a horse trough before going to join his men.

Stepan rode out of Cæstir beside Eohric at the rear of the small column. He was glad to leave his mother behind; the cart would have slowed them down and besides the mill stood on its own beside a stream and might well be destroyed if the Vikings besieged Rumcofen. The boy felt a heady mixture of excitement and trepidation. He'd fought Danes before, of course, but the Norse Vikings had a fearsome reputation.

A few hours later they rode in through the gates of Rumcofen. Wynnstan was relieved that they hadn't encountered any Vikings en route nor was there any sign of their longships on the river. However, when he heard the reason he became very concerned.

A messenger from Jarl Agnar, who led the independent Norse jarldoms to the north of the Mǣresēa, was waiting for him. Ragnall had already consolidated his hold on the Norse holdings in north-western Northumbria; now it seemed that co-ordinated attacks had been launched by sea, along the river and by land to bring the southern half of western Northumbria under his rule.

†††

Wynnstan ran to the ramparts with Chad close behind him when the sentry in the watchtower rang the bell to alert the garrison. His few hearth warriors were supplemented by two hundred of the ceorls who inhabited the burh and a further hundred of the fyrd who had arrived from the surrounding vills.

He breathed a sigh of relief when he saw Ywer's banner. The ealdorman had brought fifteen hundred men with him despite knowing before he set out that the threat was to the lands north of the Mǣresēa, not to his shire. He had a treaty with Åmunde and his neighbouring jarls and, although that didn't oblige him to come to their aid, it was in Mercia's interest to keep their northern border in friendly hands.

'What do we know of the current situation?' Ywer asked as soon as Wynnstan and he were alone in his private chamber.

'I've sent the only survivor from the *Saint Oswald* up river to find out where the longships landed and in what strength. Wardric and Sawin have gone across the Mǣresēa to make contact with Jarl Agnar to find out what's happening in his territory. We'll know more when they return.'

Cedric sailed the fishing boat up river with his two companions. One was HēahswīÞ, the boat's owner, and the other his twelve year old son. Their task was to find out where the Viking longships encountered by the *Saint Oswald* had landed. Fishing boats normally sought their prey in the estuary or close offshore but a few ventured further upstream so the sight of such a boat shouldn't arouse suspicion, or so Cedric hoped.

HēahswīÞ was nervous and wouldn't have contemplated hiring out his boat if Lord Ywer hadn't offered him ten silver pennies. It was more than he could earn from his fishing for several months and so, against his better judgement, he'd agreed.

Fishermen didn't venture out at night and so the reconnaissance had to take place in broad daylight. It was easier to carry the task out when visibility was good but it added to the danger.

As they passed the last of several small settlements and neared Mamecestre, HēahswīÞ grew increasingly nervous, much to the disgust of his son. The boy had respected his father hitherto. HēahswīÞ's byname was Lucky because he found shoals of herring and brought in significant catches when others came back with little to show for their efforts. However, his timidity on that day had undermined his son's unquestioning belief in him as a man. On the other hand the boy, whose name was Bēomēre, found himself suffering from a bad case of hero worship when it came to Cedric.

The latter was only three years older than Bēomēre but he was both an accomplished sailor and a warrior. Moreover he didn't stink of fish. It didn't take the boy long to decide that he wanted to exchange a life of poverty as a fisherman for that of a sea warrior.

His father was a ceorl, albeit an impoverished one, and so he could theoretically apply to become a ship's boy on a longship or a birlinn but he would need a sponsor. As the gentle breeze blew the small boat eastwards he allowed himself to imagine that Cedric might recommend him. After all, if their mission was successful, Lord Ywer would be pleased with Cedric and well might reward him. He knew his father would oppose him leaving so he would have to find an opportunity to speak to Cedric in private. That wouldn't be easy.

Hēahswīþ had two sons and four daughters. Bēomēre was the eldest and his father needed his help on the boat. His brother was only four and so it would be a few years yet before he was old enough to fill Bēomēre's shoes. In the meantime his father would have to hire someone. As he didn't pay his son, it would eat into his meagre profits. The boy shrugged. He had his own future to consider and the fact that his father beat him when he was drunk didn't encourage him to stay.

They'd set out just after dawn but Mamecestre was over thirty miles from Rumcofen. Cedric estimated that they weren't making more than four knots through the water. They'd had the incoming tide to help them initially but it was now on the turn. By this time they'd reached Walintune. Originally an Anglian settlement on the north bank where a Roman bridge crossed the river, it was now owned by one of the Norse jarls loyal to Agnar. This was the limit of the tidal reach of the Mǣresēa.

It was a cloudy day and so he couldn't use the sun to estimate the time but, with the help of the tide, they'd probably covered a third of the journey. That meant it was now between eight and nine o'clock in the morning.

Cedric studied the settlement as they went past it. It seemed deserted. No doubt the men had all gone to the muster called by Agnar to help defend their lands from Ragnall's horde. It would

leave their women and children defenceless and doubtless they had
fled into the hinterland pro tem. It would also explain why there
was nothing living to be seen; even the livestock and the chickens
had gone. It left the place with a somewhat eerie feel and Cedric
was glad when the wind carried them around the next bend and out
of sight.

Another hour passed before they came across the Viking fleet.
There were a dozen ships – five drekar and seven snekkjur –
moored along the north bank. As soon as the fishing boat came
around the bend those left to guard the ships came to the edge of
the river to watch it. Cedric realised that they were too far
upstream to be fishing and the enemy were right to be suspicious.

He had the information he came for. The longships had
probably brought a total of between five and six hundred warriors.
Those left to guard the fleet would be the ships boys and a few
elderly warriors. Nevertheless, there were more than enough of
them to crew one of the snekkjur. As thirty of them rushed to man
the smallest longship, Cedric yelled at his companions to go about.

Now the bitterly cold wind was against them and they would
have to tack downriver under sail or row. The snekkja had cast off
by the time that the fishing boat had turned around and started on
its first tack across the river. The snekkja was four hundred yards
behind them but it was being rowed and, even crewed by boys and
old men, they were gaining on the boat. Cedric realised that they
would be caught in less than a quarter of an hour.

†††

'I fear it's bad news, lord.'

Wardric and Sawin stood around the central hearth in
Wynstann's hall trying to get warmth back into their bodies.
Although it was still October a cold wind had swept down from the
north bringing with it icy rain and an occasional hailstorm. The two
scouts had been caught out in one of the latter. They thanked the

Lord God that they had been wearing byrnies and helmets when lumps of ice the size of silver pennies pelted down on them.

Their horses hadn't been protected and had consequently suffered bruising and injury. The animals had panicked and the two riders had quickly dismounted before the horses bolted in an effort to get away from the torment. The two men had been forced to walk the rest of the way to their rendezvous with the knarr that had been hired to ferry them back across the estuary to Rumcofen.

'Agnar and his fellow jarls engaged Ragnall in battle four days ago but they were betrayed. Many of their younger warriors deserted to Ragnall's banner and most of the jarls and the other leading Norsemen allied to us were killed.'

Both Ywer and Wynnstan felt has though they'd been dealt a hammer blow. With no allies left north of the Mǣresēa, northern Mercia faced a possible invasion from Northumbria just at a time when the rest of Mercia was fully engaged with the Danes to the east. Furthermore, there were growing rumours of trouble brewing in Wealas to the west.

'Lord, we need to determine what Ragnall's next move will be,' Godric suggested.

'Yes, you're right; and I need to let Lady Æthelflœd know of this development.'

✝✝✝

Cedric peered through the reeds at the side of the river. He could see the mast of the Norse snekkja several hundred yards away but there was no sign of the ship's crew.

It had been a close run thing. HēahswīÞ had refused to head for the bank and abandon his little boat as that was his only means of livelihood. He was too pig-headed to see that by staying on the river he was condemning all three of them to death. Thankfully Bēomēre had more sense and supported Cedric's plan to try and escape inland. As the land on the south bank was part of Mercia he hoped that the enemy wouldn't follow them too far before abandoning the chase.

Whilst the other two rowed in an effort to stay ahead of the longship, Cedric ordered Bēomēre, who was at the tiller, to head into the reed beds until they found the bank. The boy had done so but his father had cried out in protest and let go of his oar in an effort to grab the tiller. Bēomēre tried to resist him but the man was too strong and, pushing his son out of the way, he turned the bows towards the centre of the river once more.

By this time the Norse ship was less than a hundred yards away. Cedric had to act quickly. He swung his oar, catching the fisherman a hefty blow to his shoulder. Hēahswīþ staggered and tried to retain his footing. He failed and a moment later his lower leg hit the gunwale and he toppled over the side into the water.

His son gave a despairing cry and knelt down in an attempt to grab his father as he came to the surface, spluttering and cursing. However, Hēahswīþ was swept out of reach by the current. He began to swim back to the fishing boat but suddenly became aware of the approaching longship and turned towards the reed beds instead. Hēahswīþ reached them just before the snekkja could catch him. It continued into the rushes in search of him, which gave Cedric time to sail the boat into the bank a hundred yards further along.

Bēomēre was distraught and insisted on going in search of his father until Cedric managed to convince him that to do so was to risk capture by the pagan Norse. The boy had heard too many tales about what Vikings did to their Christian prisoners - usually inaccurate but he wasn't to know that - and reluctantly followed Cedric away from the abandoned fishing boat.

A few hundred yards further on the reed bed only grew close to the bank; that was where Cedric halted to check on the pursuit. At first he heard no one moving through the reeds but then he saw the tops waving. Only a few at a time were being disturbed and so it was likely to a be a single person, or at the most two. Cedric waited, confident that he could kill one or two ship's boys or old men, especially as surprise was on his side. He readied his seax as the waving reed heads indicated that someone was very close and was about to stab his foe when he realised it was HēahswīÞ.

'You cost me my boat,' he accused Cedric, looking furious.

'There's no time for this,' he replied tersely. 'We need to get out of here before they find us.'

'I hope they chase you and catch you. That'll give me a chance to retrieve my boat,' HēahswīÞ said viciously. 'Come on son; we'll double back.'

'No, father. It's too risky.'

'You'll do as you're told,' he shouted.

'Shut up you fool and listen,' Cedric snapped.

The man glared at the young sailor but then he too heard the sound of rustling reeds. They could see the tops moving which indicated a large group of people were no more than a hundred yards away.

'Come on,' the young Mercian sailor whispered and started moving away from the river towards the bushes which grew at the edge of the reed bed.

When he got there he crouched down and looked behind him. Bēomēre was behind him but there was no sign of the boy's father. Obviously he'd gone back to try and retrieve his fishing boat. That gave Cedric an idea.

Half an hour later Bēomēre and he emerged from the bushes and studied the reed bed between them and the snekkja. There was no sign of movement in the reeds but they could hear faint voices coming from the longship. They crawled through the reeds until they were within a few yards of the ship. By this time they were soaking wet and shivering with cold. Two boys no older than eleven or twelve were leaning on the gunwale and peering downriver. The sound of voices came from the deck out of sight from where Cedric and Bēomēre crouched.

After listening for a while Cedric came to the conclusion that there were only two speaking and both sounded quite young. Evidently the Vikings had left the four youngest ship's boys to guard the snekkja whilst the rest went ashore.

The longship was moored bows on to the soft mud of the bank. Followed by Bēomēre, he waded through the ice cold water along the hull until he reached the steering oar towards the stern. It was slippery but he managed to work his way along it until he could look along the deck. As he'd thought, two more boys, slightly older than the other two, were sitting chatting and playing a game of some sort whilst their juniors kept watch. Then he heard the soft sound of someone snoring. He looked down and immediately below him an elderly man – presumably the steersman - was fast asleep.

Cedric didn't hesitate; their lives depended on killing or subduing the watch so that they could escape on the snekkja. He leant over the gunwale and thrust his seax into the old man's throat. He died with a soft gurgle as the Mercian anxiously checked that none of the ship's boys had heard anything. They hadn't and he sighed with relief.

Two minutes later Bēomēre joined him on deck and they crept towards the two boys sitting by the mast. Suddenly one of them looked up and gave a startled cry. Cedric rushed at him as he was getting to his feet, pulling a dagger from its sheath. He never got the chance to use it. Cedric slashed his blade across the Norse boy's throat and blood gushed out as he toppled sideways.

The other boy was slower to react and Bēomēre jumped on top of him pointing his knife at the boy's throat but he hesitated. He'd never killed anyone before and he found he was reluctant to do so.

'Keep him alive,' Cedric hissed at him. 'We'll need help to sail the ship.'

The two boys standing by the side of the ship had turned and had drawn their daggers by this stage. Cedric advanced towards them, menacing them with his seax. He was three years older, bigger and was covered in blood. Thankfully the boys dithered instead of attacking him.

'Throw down your daggers and I'll let you live. You've three seconds to decide,' he told them.

He'd had spoken in Ænglisc and cursed himself for a fool. He spoke some Norse because they sometimes sold their catch to the Norsemen who lived across the other side of the river. His mistake had given two opponents time to recover from their surprise and they now advanced towards him. He was several years older, more experienced and had killed several times before. That gave him an advantage but one might dart in and wound him whilst he was engaged with the other. He had to act quickly.

He moved to his left and the boy on that side went to counter him but, before he'd realised he'd been duped, Cedric changed direction and chopped his seax down on the other lad's right forearm. He dropped his dagger with a howl of pain and a second later the other boy dropped his own weapon when Cedric pushed the point of his seax into his neck.

Cedric scooped up the daggers and threw them over the side.

'Bind up his arm – it's only a flesh wound,' he snapped at the second boy, this time remembering to speak in Norse.

Once that was done, he threatened the three boys with his seax and forced them over the side, jumping down beside them to ensure that they didn't run off.

'Now push her off the bank,' he ordered, cutting the mooring line with his seax.

As soon as it floated clear he gestured at the boys with his seax and they clambered back aboard. The rearmost one tried to kick Cedric back into the water after he'd sheathed his seax in order to climb up but Bēomēre, who'd stayed on board, hit him hard and he fell to the deck. As they drifted away from the bank Cedric ordered the boys to hoist the sail and sheet it home whilst Bēomēre grabbed the steering oar. Once underway, Cedric got the ship's boys to throw the two dead bodies over the side.

He searched the chests along the deck which were used by the rowers for their personal possessions and on which they sat to row. Having found two bloodstained wolfskin cloaks, he pulled one around his chilled body and passed the other to Bēomēre.

Two minutes later they passed the rest of the Norse crew on the south bank. Cedric counted seven men and a score of boys. They vented their fury, promising dire retribution, so Cedric went to the side and exposed his bare arse, knowing that would infuriate them even more.

A minute later his good mood vanished. A body floated face down in the water and, once the ship's boys had hauled it aboard, he saw that it was that of Hēahswīþ.

'I'm so sorry,' he told Bēomēre but there was no time to say more before they had to tack.

They worked their way upstream for the rest of the day. Cedric promised to release the Norse boys on the north bank once they reached Rumcofen and they gave him no further trouble. As the burh hove into view the eldest of the ship's boys approached Cedric and he put his hand on the hilt of his seax, expecting trouble.

'We don't want to go back and join King Ragnall,' he said. 'He's an unforgiving man and he will blame us for the loss of this ship. A quick death is the best we could hope for. It's more likely he will torture us first as a lesson to others.'

'You want to stay and join a Mercian ship?'

'Yes. We'll even swear to worship the Nailed God if we have to.'

'I can't promise anything but I'll talk to Lord Wynnstan on your behalf.'

After Cedric had given his report he was thanked but the defeat of Agnar meant that the information about the enemy fleet was worthless now. However, one of the Norse boys had told him about a rumour in the Norse camp that Ragnall wasn't interested in attacking Cæstirscīr. Once he'd established control over western Northumbria his next target was Bernicia – the area of ancient

Northumbria between the River Tes and the Firth of Forth ruled over by the Anglian Earl Ealdred. Once he'd secured Bernicia he would move on the Danish Kingdom of Jorvik and declare himself King of all Northumbria.

Ywer and Wynnstan questioned the three Norse boys at length before they were satisfied that they weren't trying to mislead them. It was something of a relief to know that they didn't face an immediate invasion by Ragnall but a strong and united Northumbria to the north of Mercia would be a serious threat in the future.

'Lord Ywer has agreed to take on the three Norse lads,' Cedric told Bēomēre sometime later. 'He'll replace the Saint Oswald with the snekkja we captured but he has something else in mind for me.'

He looked at the boy speculatively. He'd been impressed with how the boy had handled himself during the capture of the snekkja.

'What will you do now?' he asked casually. 'Return to your family?'

Bēomēre shook his head.

'My mother will blame me for my father's death and the loss of our boat. My uncle – my father's brother – always liked my mother and he'll look after her and my family but he is bound to blame me for his brother's death. He might even kill me in revenge.'

The boy looked downcast but then looked at Cedric hopefully.

'Do you think that I might be able to become a ship's boy here?'

'I'm not sure what Lord Ywer has in mind for me but I'll take you with me if at all possible.' Cedric replied.

CHAPTER TWELVE

November/December 914

Irwyn hadn't got very far with the investigation into his uncle's death. As winter approached, the armies of Wessex and Mercia returned home. All he'd managed to achieve was the possible identification of one of Osfirth's hearth warriors as a man who'd been seen close to Ealdorman Odda when he'd been killed.

When he asked Odda's own gesith how they'd become separated from their lord they looked shamefaced and all they'd say was that somehow other Saxons had moved forward into the first row of the shieldwall to take the places of the fallen and had come between Odda and his men, apparently both those to his left and to his right. After that it appeared that a man in the second rank had thrust a blade into the ealdorman's back, piercing the chainmail of his byrnie and driving on into his heart.

The young warrior realised that he had no evidence to present to the king and he very nearly gave up hope of finding the killer. One evening he returned to his tent to find a scrawled message telling him to stop his enquiries into his uncle's death or he would be joining him in Hell.

He returned to Lundenburg, where King Eadweard was spending the winter with his household warriors and his administrators. It made sense; it was a secure base for the winter months whilst being close to East Anglia and the newly recaptured south-eastern part of Mercia. Irwyn suspected that it might also be because it enabled the king to avoid being confined with his wife in Wintanceaster during the long dark, cold days ahead.

Spending the winter idling, gambling and drinking in Lundenburg wasn't something he looked forward to himself, especially when he believed that his cousin's life might be in danger. He therefore approached the king to ask permission to go to Execestre in Dyfneintscīr to spend Christmas with Wælwulf.

Much to his surprise, permission to go was readily given and he made preparations for the journey.

It would have been foolhardy to travel alone. Wessex was far from lawless but robbers and dispossessed outlaws lurked in some of the sparsely populated areas. He was also aware that a lone traveller could fall prey to thieves in some of the taverns he'd be staying in along the way. He therefore went to see Galan, the captain of Eadweard's gesith, to ask for his advice.

'There are a good few warriors looking for employment in Lundenburg,' he said. 'For many of them there is a good reason they don't have a lord and I wouldn't recommend that you put your trust in any of them. If I were you I'd go and see Eohfrið.'

'The old warrior who trains new recruits for the Lundenburg fyrd? Why would he want to come with me? He has a family here and I doubt that he'd want to stray far from his hearth once the snow arrives.'

'You misunderstand me,' Galan said with a chuckle. 'Of course, he won't want to go with you but he can probably recommend a few of the boys who are nearing the end of their training who might like a bit of an adventure. He trains the better ones for the garrison as well as teaching the fyrd how to fight; it's the former you need.'

The next day he met half a dozen fifteen-year-old boys and chose four to accompany him. One of them, Eadsige, asked if they could take his twelve-year-old brother, Mēreīc, along as a page to look after them. Irwyn was dubious as he thought that the younger boy might be more of a liability than an asset but, as Eadsige was unwilling to go without him, he eventually agreed.

The bitterly cold weather of late October had given way to a mild spell at the start of November. The roads were muddy but not unduly so. Nevertheless, Irwyn and his new companions were glad to reach the paved Roman road called Portweg that led from Lundenburg all the way to Dornwaracester. Once there it was only sixty miles along the coastal road to Execestre, Ealdorman Wælwulf's home. The whole journey was around two hundred miles and, thanks to the firm going on cobbled paving for much of the way, he hoped to reach Execestre in less than a week.

He planned to reach the old walled settlement of Silcestre by the end of the first day. Even if it hadn't been a convenient oplace to spend the night, Irwyn had always wanted to visit it. It was the first vill that his grandfather, Jørren, had been granted by the then King of Wessex, Æthelred – Ælfred's elder brother.

He reflected with some pride on his grandfather's achievements. By the age of sixteen Jørren had accumulated enough wealth to pay the purchase price by looting the Danes he'd killed whilst rescuing his brother who'd been captured by them in battle. During his quest he'd been joined by Leofflæd, who he'd later married. She had been Irwyn's grandmother. In due course Ælfred had banished Jørren from Wessex and he'd travelled to Mercia. There Lord Æðelred promised to make him the Ealdorman of Cæstirscīr, then a lawless land, provided he subdued it and brough it back under Mercian rule.

Silcestre wasn't how Irwyn had imagined it. The current thegn had allowed the walls to fall into disrepair and the fields surrounding it were full of weeds. Even the hovels and huts inside the walls appeared uncared for. The people looked at the ground when his small group passed them and gave the appearance of being downtrodden and demoralised.

The single sentry on the gate gave them a cursory glance as they rode in and spat in the dust as he continued to lean on his spear. His helmet was rusty and the leather of the jerkin he wore was cracked. Evidently it hadn't been waxed for a long time to keep it supple.

Like the other buildings in the settlement, the hall looked to be in a poor state of repair. He waited for a moment but no one appeared to see who the visitors might be, nor did any ostlers or stable boys come to take care of their horses.

Irwyn dismounted and, followed by his warriors, he stalked up the few steps to the door. Mērerīc was left holding the horses and after waiting in vain for someone to take them, he went in search of a water trough and the stables. The latter was empty apart from a sorry looking nag that appeared as uncared for as everything else in the rest of the vill. He unsaddled their horses and used his currycomb to groom them, getting as much mud out of their coats as possible, before filling two mangers with hay. As the nag looked half-starved, he filled a trough for it as well.

Meanwhile Irwyn had entered the hall and stood for a moment to let his eyes adjust to the gloom. Four windows let in some light but they were small and when the shutters were closed in inclement weather the place would have been as dark as the grave. The floor of beaten earth was devoid of the normal rushes and it consequently stank of urine and dog faeces – at least he hoped it was dog and not human.

Two elderly men sitting at the hall's only table lay slumped across it, presumably drunk. A slatternly looking girl appeared from behind a curtained alcove at the end of the hall. She had evidently dressed in a hurry because she had omitted to put on a dress over her soiled linen shift, nor was she wearing shoes or a belt. Irwyn assumed that the curtain screened off the area of the hall where the thegn slept. He strode towards it and pulled back the curtain.

A man sprawled naked on a bed of furs. The latter looked moth-eaten and were heavily stained. His skin was pasty white and his distended belly betrayed the fact that he drank and ate to excess. Irwyn doubted that he could run more than a few yards before collapsing. He couldn't imagine him taking his place in the shieldwall; a requirement of every noble in the kingdom unless they were disabled or too elderly.

The man stared blearily at Irwyn before raising himself onto one elbow with some difficulty.

'Who the devil are you and what do you mean by invading my private chamber?' he demanded, his voice slurred to the point of near incomprehensibility.

'My name is Irwyn, son of Ealdorman Ywer and grandson of Ealdorman Jørren. I'm a member of the king's gesith come to seek a night's shelter, as is my right.'

'Irwyn? Jørren? He's not the thegn here anymore; hasn't been for decades. I was a boy when he left,' the man said sounding confused.

'Yes, I'm well aware of that,' Irwyn said patiently. 'My grandfather is dead in any case. If you remember him from when you were a boy here then I take it that you're the reeve, not the thegn.'

'Er, yes, lord,' the man said uncertainly.

He realised that he was in the presence of an ealdorman's son and, even if Irwyn wasn't actually entitled to be addressed as 'lord', the reeve was his social inferior by some margin. He hastened to pull on a tunic, stand up and incline his head as a gesture of respect.

'Who's the thegn now?' Irwyn asked. 'I take it he doesn't visit often, judging by the state of the place.'

'Er, it belongs to King Eadweard,' the reeve replied, swallowing nervously.

'Does it indeed. Well, be assured that I will inform him of its dilapidated state when I next see him.'

Irwyn spent the night in the stables with his warriors in preference to the flea and rat infested hall. The next day the fine weather had given way to dark clouds which threatened rain before they'd gone too far. In the event they were lucky and it was early in the afternoon before the heavens opened and they got soaked. By that stage they'd made good progress, having covered another twenty five miles. They came across a small monastery and decided to stay there for the night, rather than press on in such miserable conditions.

He was surprised that the community consisted of a mere six monks and a few lay brothers until the prior explained that they were a daughter house of the monastery at Wintanceaster. He was chary of offering them hospitality at first, concerned about the paucity of provisions in store so close to the start of winter. However, when Irwyn and Eadsige offered to go hunting, despite the wet conditions, he brightened up.

It was the first chance that he'd had to talk to Eadsige on his own since they'd set out.

'You accent doesn't sound as if you were born in Lundenburg,' he observed.

'No, Mērerīc and I come from Cent. We were the second and third sons of a minor thegn.'

'Why did you leave? Did your father throw you out?'

'No, he died a few months ago. Our mother was his second wife but we have an elder brother, Betlic, born to his first wife, Ælfwen. He never got on with our mother and resented the fact that she'd taken Ælfwen's place in the marital bed a mere seven months after her death.'

'What happened when your father died? Surely he made some provision for you and Mērerīc in his will?'

'If so, we weren't aware of it and Betlic never showed it to us. He loathed us as much as he did our mother. Once father's funeral was over, he'd expelled the three of us from our hall. Mother was sent to a monastery and at least Betlic had the decency to pay the abbess enough for her to accept the recently bereaved widow as a resident without the necessity of becoming a nun.

'We arrived in Lundenburg with nothing except our clothing, our daggers and our horses, which had been a present from father. We'd only been there a week or so when I was accepted for training as a warrior by Eohfrið. The rest you know.'

It wasn't a particularly remarkable story and the fact that Eohfrið had chosen to train him meant that the two brothers had fallen on their feet. However, the failure of Betlic to make any payment to them out of his inheritance was unusual. He was sure that their father would have made some provision for them; no doubt Betlic had cheated them out of it and intended to leave them desititute as an act of petty vengeance. However, that wasn't his problem.

Irwyn had never given much thought to his own situation. As the eldest son of an ealdorman he had wanted for nothing as a child. His foster father was the most powerful man in Mercia and he'd been made one of the king's companions because of his birth, not on merit. Despite their rather different situations, he felt an affinity with Eadsige and his brother; an affinity which would grow with time.

They returned to the monastery with a large doe that Eadsige had brought down. The prior's attitude towards his guests changed immediately. Once hung and then smoked, the venison would supplement their normal diet of cereal crops, carp from the monastery's pond and root vegetables, for some time to come.

The rain had ceased by dawn and, as they'd managed to dry out their clothes overnight, they set off again in high spirits. Three days later they reached the end of the Roman road at Dornwaracester. From there on they would be travelling on a muddy track along the coast. It would be much harder going for the horses and Irwyn decided to stay for two nights to allow them to rest. Furthermore, it would do no harm to allow his companions a chance to recover from spending so long in the saddle.

What he'd forgotten was that Dornwaracester was the home of Ealdorman Beornrīc of Dornsæte, a close friend of Lord Osfirth. Trouble erupted on the first night. The best two taverns were expensive and Irwyn had opted to rent two rooms in one which was respectable but which wouldn't deplete his purse too much. Unfortunately, it was also the one favoured by Beornrīc's gesith.

Four men, who were obviously warriors were seated at a table near the central hearth when Irwyn and his five companions came down from their rooms. They shared two rooms with just the one large bed in each but at least it was better than camping in the open.

They'd hoped to have had a bath after nearly a week on the road but the tavern didn't boast such luxuries. Instead, they'd had to pay for cold water to be carried up to fill a large basin in each room. They'd washed as best they could and donned clean clothes before going down to the taproom to eat.

They'd left their byrnies and helmets in their rooms for Mēreric to clean the following day together with their swords but they wore both seaxes and daggers on their belts. One never knew how safe one would be in a strange place.

They took a table on the other side of the hearth from the four warriors and waited to be served. When the only girl serving appeared to ignore them, Eadsige sent his brother to order ale and something to eat from the man standing behind the trestle table at the far end of the taproom.

As the boy was returning with six leather tankards on a tray, one of the four warriors got up and approached him. He smirked at Irwyn and took one of the tankards off the tray before taking a swig out of it and wiping his sleeve across his mouth with a grunt of satisfaction.

His companions laughed and Mēreric saw red. Without thinking, brought his knee up to connect with the man's groin. With a howl of pain, the man dropped the tankard and doubled over. Mēreric continued on his way and put the tray down on their table.

'Looks like I'll have to go thirsty,' he said grumpily.

'On the contrary, it looks as if we aren't going to have time to enjoy our ale,' Irwyn commented dryly.

The man's friends were coming around the central hearth with their daggers drawn.

'Your friend got what he deserved for stealing another man's ale. Now put your daggers away before anyone gets hurt,' Irwyn said, getting up and putting his hand on the hilt of his seax.

'You don't know who you're talking to, boy. Your little guttersnipe just attacked one of Lord Beornric's gesith.'

'It would appear you don't know who you're dealing with either,' Eadsige retorted hotly. 'This man is the son of an ealdorman and a member of the king's gesith.'

Irwyn groaned inwardly. He'd wanted to keep his visit to his cousin a secret. Now Osfirth was bound to hear he was in the vicinity and there was no way back without going through either his shire or Beornrīc's unless he went by sea, which could be hazardous in winter. However, that problem would have to wait; first they had to extricate themselves from their present predicament.

Eadsige's statement had caused the four men to hesitate but that didn't last long.

'I think you had better come and explain what you're doing here to our captain.'

'I don't answer to him, only to the king,' Irwyn replied as authoritatively as he could.

'Nevertheless you are in Lord Beornrīc's jurisdiction now and he'll want to know what you're doing here.'

'We aren't guilty of any crime and you have no justification for detaining us.'

'On the contrary,' the leader of the Beornrīc's warriors countered. 'This boy assaulted one of our companions. That's a crime.'

'So is theft. If you pursue this, I'll enter a counter claim against your friend and a defence that my page was only acting in retaliation against a thief. I suggest you let the matter drop before you get into more serious trouble by interfering with someone on the king's business.'

It was a lie, of course, but Beornrīc's men weren't to know that.

'Very well. If your page apologises, then we'll let the matter drop,' the man agreed with reluctance.

'That's fair, if your man asks for forgiveness for stealing my ale.'

Both mumbled some sort of apology and everyone returned to their tables to continue drinking. The serving girl hastily brought a fresh tankard to Irwyn's table to replace the spilt one. No doubt the tavern keeper was grateful that a fight hadn't broken out and thought that a free pint was a price worth paying.

'We'll need to keep a watch tonight.' Irwyn told Eadsige later. 'The man that Mērerīc assaulted may have apologised but the look he gave your brother tells me that the matter is far from over as far as he's concerned.'

'I presume that you have given up the idea of resting here for a couple of days?'

'Yes, that would be stupid. We may have talked our way out of trouble last night but Osfirth dislikes me intensely. I'm not sure what he'd do if he got his hands on me but I'm not staying around to find out. The sooner we reach Dyfneintscīr the better.'

✝✝✝

It was the middle of the night before Eadsige, who was on watch, woke Irwyn.

'Someone is trying to lift the latch on our door,' he whispered.

He'd already roused his brother who was standing looking nervously towards the door with his dagger drawn.

'Stay here and protect your brother,' Irwyn said quietly before climbing out of the window armed with just his seax.

He edged along the lean-to roof below the window until he could knock on the shutters of the room occupied by the other three members of his entourage. Once one of them opened the shutters he put his finger to his lips and climbed into the room. Moving to the door, he slowly opened it a crack until he could see into the corridor. It was only illuminated by a single torch at the top of the stairs but he could see the backs of three men crouching by the door to his room whilst one of them used his dagger to try and lift the latch.

'Grab your kit and climb out onto the roof of the lean-to,' he told them before returning to the window of his own room. He told the other two to do the same and five minutes later the six of them dropped down to the ground and ran silently over to the stables. It took another five minutes to dress and saddle their horses before riding out of the tavern's courtyard.

'We've got a problem,' Irwyn told them when they halted several streets away. 'The gates won't open before dawn and by that time the watch will be looking for us as well as our friends back there.'

'Why would the watch be looking for us?' one of his companions asked.

'Because we left the tavern without paying for our rooms or stabling for the horses.'

'What do we do?' Eadsige asked.

'I doubt if there are more than a few men guarding the gates at night. We're going to have to force them to open the gates for us.'

As it happened those guarding the gate were fast asleep, not something that would ever happen at Cæstir, Irwyn thought wryly. Whilst the others watched them, having deprived them their weapons whilst they slept, Irwyn and Eadsige opened the gates. A few minutes later they cantered out of Dornwaracester and took the coast road westwards.

It was twenty seven miles to the crossing over the River Alse which marked the border between Dornsæte and Dyfneintscīr. Once there they'd be safe but their horses hadn't fully recovered and their trail would be easy to follow. Irwyn doubted that a hue and cry would normally be launched for a traveller who didn't pay what he owed a tavern keeper but he was willing to bet that Beornrīc's gesith would seize on it as an excuse to hunt them down. He had no doubt that Osfirth wanted his death if it could be accomplished without attaching any blame to himself and Beornrīc would be well aware of this.

Irwyn therefore decided to leave the coastal road as soon as possible and head north-west to the settlement of Alseminstre, which was just across the shire boundary. Once there, they could rest for a couple of days before riding the final twenty five miles to Execestre.

The night was cold but the blanket of cloud meant that the temperature hadn't fallen below freezing. However, it also hid what light the moon gave off. Of necessity, they only made slow progress in the near darkness and by the end of the first hour Irwyn reckoned that they had covered no more than five miles. They still had another dozen miles to go before they could turn off the coastal road and head inland to Alseminstre.

He thought about his four companions. Apart from young They were amongst the best young warriors that Eohfrið had taught but they were yet to be tested in battle. He felt that he could trust Eadsige to give a good account of himself but he wondered about the other three – Aart and Kenric and Penda. They were inexperienced and had shown signs of nervousness when the confrontation in the tavern looked as if it could turn nasty.

As they plodded on, the sky overhead got darker and the first snowflake struck Irwyn on the cheek. It was the first of many. Ten minutes later the snowflakes had stopped melting as they struck the damp earth and began to settle. Snow would make their journey more difficult but it would also cover their tracks.

Irwyn sent Eadsige back to watch their back trail. He had no intention of being caught unawares by any pursuers. By the time that they reached the point where the track leading to Alseminstre left the coastal road the sun had risen, not that it could be seen through the clouds overhead. The snow was falling quite hard now and it was over an inch deep even under the tree canopy. When they came out of the wood onto open moorland it was over two inches deep and beginning to form drifts.

The track was only just discernible as it snaked away an inch or two below the tops of the heather and grass that peeked through the layer of white. In places where the track was exposed to the strong westerly breeze it had disappeared completely under drifts a foot deep in places. The icy wind had begun to chill them and their horses and Irwyn knew that the time had come to seek shelter when Eadsige appeared behind them, galloping as fast as he dared to catch them up.

'There's a dozen armed men less than a mile behind us,' he panted.

✝✝✝

Ywer decided that there should be one last hunt to provide meat for his larder before winter set in. He invited Earl Skarde and Wynnstan to join him and the former brought along his son Brandt, now approaching his fourteenth birthday. He only had another six months training to go before he was old enough to be classed as a warrior and Æthelstan had allowed him to return home in time for the Christmas celebrations.

When he arrived at Ywer's hall in Cæstir he was disappointed to find that Irwyn wasn't there. As soon as Irwyn had left Brandt had regretted his show of petulance over his friend's elevation to warrior but the two hadn't seen each other since. Brandt was upset because they had parted on bad terms and irrationally he blamed Irwyn. Over the past couple of years it had gnawed away at him.

When he discovered that Irwyn was still away serving in Eadweard's gesith his reaction was mixed. On one hand he was relieved that now there was no risk of being rebuffed by Irwyn but, at the same time, he was infuriated that there would be no chance of reconciliation. He'd assumed that Irwyn was as preoccupied by the gulf between them as he was. The fact that the other boy wasn't even aware that there was a situation in need of resolution had never even occurred to him.

It wasn't Irwyn's fault that he wasn't there, of course, but Brandt had steeled himself to face him and he turned his frustration at the supposedly unresolved antipathy between them into resentment against Irwyn and it put him in a foul mood as he set off for the hunt.

There was little chance of finding boar so late in the year; their best chance of finding anything to smoke and store was deer. Ywer would have preferred boar as he was partial to smoked bacon and gammon but venison, provided it had been hung long enough before smoking, was a good alternative.

Once they reached the forest, they split up into three parties led by Ywer, Skarde and Wynnstan. For some reason Brandt decided to go with Ywer instead of his step-father and they set off with two of Ywer's gesith – Godric and Wilfrid - two huntsmen with hounds and a few servants who were there to gut the game and load it onto the ponies they led.

Ywer was a skilled tracker and he recoiled in surprise at the first prints that they came across. It consisted of a kidney shaped pad with five toes ending in large curved claws. Only one animal could have made that type of imprint – a bear. Whilst brown bears still existed in the more remote parts of Alba, they were thought to be extinct this far south. He dismounted and examined the spoor. From the size of the paws he estimated that it was a solitary male about seven or eight feet tall when upright and weighing anything up to fifteen hundred pounds.

What it was doing in Cæstirscīr he couldn't imagine. There had been the odd report of bears in Northumbria over the years, usually tales brought by pedlars who were known to exaggerate or even lie to attract custom.

Even if pedlars hadn't made the stories up, Ywer had put them down as the ravings of a vivid imagination. As far he knew, no one had been killed and the few reported sightings had apparently come from individuals. No one in authority had taken them seriously, whatever the gullible common folk had believed, nor had there been any verified evidence of humans or livestock being killed or even mauled by a bear.

Yet he was looking at the unmistakable marks made by a large male brown bear. He looked around and listened intently. Thankfully he heard nothing but the paw prints appeared to have been made fairly recently. He remounted his horse and silently indicated for everyone to return the way they'd come.

Brandt was full of curiosity and, despite Ywer's indication of the need for silence, he asked excitedly what the animal was.

'Bear, now shut up and keep moving.'

Ywer's whispered response was terse and heavy with reprimand. Brandt immediately took umbrage and sulked. He deliberately slowed his horse and dropped back to the rear so he could nurse his grievance privately. Instead of watching the surrounding forest and listening intently, he was so wrapped up in self-pity that he didn't notice the bear before it was too late.

By the time glanced behind him, there was a huge beast closing in at a lumbering run. He'd never seen a bear before but he knew instinctively that one blow from the beast's claws could eviscerate him. He kicked his heels into the horse's flanks and it leapt forward, not that it needed any urging. It had picked up the bear's strong scent and it bolted towards the rest of the hunting party.

Ywer's instinct was to kick his horse into a gallop and escape but his huntsmen with the dogs were on foot, as were the servants leading the ponies. Instead, he dismounted and quickly strung his hunting bow. Godric and Wilfrid followed his example and, sticking several arrows in the ground in front of them they waited.

They didn't have a clear shot at the bear because Brandt and his horse were in the way. A second later that wasn't a problem. The bear slashed his massive paw at the rear of the horse, cutting its flesh to the bone and sending it hurtling to the ground on one side of the track. Brandt was thrown clear and the bear reared up onto its hind legs before attacking him.

A moment later the boy would have been disembowelled but Ywer and his two warriors released their arrows simultaneously. The bear's fur was so thick that the arrows lost most of their momentum before the points reached the animal's skin. However, they did penetrate far enough to distract it. It stared at the three men for a second before dropping down onto all fours and lumbering towards the new threat. Ywer and his companions had saved the boy's life but only by putting their own at risk. Hunting bows were not designed to kill bears and now that it was on all fours it was far less of a target. The only parts of it the three men could see were its head and forelegs.

They sent a further three arrows towards the onrushing bear almost as one. They had little effect; one struck its massive forehead and bounced clear, merely gouging the skin covering the thick cranium, the other two lodged in its right foreleg.

They had time for one more arrow each but Ywer told them to wait. Instead of charging into them, the beast reared up so that it could use its forepaws to swipe at its tormentors.

'Now,' Ywer yelled and all three arrows hit it in the chest.

It was now mortally wounded but, before it crashed to the ground and lay still, it swung its right forepaw at Ywer, catching the ealdorman on the left shoulder and tearing five bloody grooves across his chest. He was thrown backwards by the blow and lay unmoving on the ground.

Throughout the fight Brandt had remained where he was, quivering like a leaf about to be blown off a tree. He knew at that moment that he would never make a warrior; he was too much of a coward. Perhaps another boy in his position would have admired Ywer for his courage but instead he felt aggrieved that Irwyn's father would be hailed as a hero - something he would never be.

✝✝✝

Eventually Irwyn and his five companions reached the comparative shelter of the trees. The wind had picked up as they made their way from the road to the wood, sending the snow swirling about looking like ghosts dancing. It made progress more difficult but they welcomed it as it meant that it obscured them from their pursuers and it would obliterate their tracks.

Everyone was now feeling the cold intensely, including the horses. Once in the wood Irwyn gave the order to dismount and stamped his feet to get some feeling back into them. He clapped his gauntleted hands together before putting them under his arms in an effort to generate some warmth in them. His hands were protected by an outer layer of leather with a sheepskin lining. He noticed that poor Mērerīc's were only covered by thin leather gloves. There was a very real danger of frostbite and so he pulled the boy's gloves off and rubbed his hands vigorously between his own.

When Mērerīc complained that his hands hurt like hell, Irwyn knew that circulation was returning to his fingers. Nevertheless, he told him not to be such a wimp and continued rubbing until he was certain that the danger of frostbite had passed.

If they'd been unlucky so far, that changed as, after walking further into the wood in search of shelter, they discovered a cliff with a cave at the base. It was large and deep enough for them and their horses and, as soon as they had unsaddled and rubbed the horses down with a brush, Irwyn sent the others out to find firewood whilst he and Mērerīc continued to groom the horses.

This didn't just improve the appearance of their coats, it stimulated blood circulation and natural oils which protected the skin; all of which would help them recover from their ordeal. Next, they gave them nosebags filled with oats. It was the last they had brought with them and Irwyn prayed that the storm would let up the next day so that they could reach Alseminstre where they could purchase more supplies. Furthermore, once they'd crossed the bridge they would be in Dyfneintscīr and hopefully safe from their enemies.

It took some time to get the fire going and once it was blazing away Irwyn decided that they should each take it in turns to keep watch. It was unlikely that Beornrīc's men would find them in a blizzard but he wasn't taking any chances. Besides, someone needed to keep the fire going to dry out their wet cloaks and outer clothes before the morning.

Eadsige sat and watched the sunrise. At first it was a dim orange glow seen dimly through the trees, then it grew brighter before emerging above the tree canopy and bathing the entrance to the cave in light. He looked up into the sky and was pleased to see a bright blue sky dotted by the occasional fluffy white cloud. The storm had passed leaving behind it an icy world where nothing stirred, not even the birds. It didn't last. By the time he'd roused the others and they were ready to move he could hear the tweeting of small sparrows and finches and several birds of prey wheeled and circled above the white wilderness seeking their breakfasts.

It took them three hours to battle their way through snow a foot deep to reach the road they'd left the previous day. If it hadn't been for the scrub that grew either side of it they probably wouldn't have found it. It was slightly easier going thereafter but they had to take care not to lose it when the bushes ceased and the road looked the same as the surrounding meadowland under its snowy blanket.

It was well after midday before the bridge over the River Alse and the settlement beyond came into sight. By then Irwyn was getting worried that they wouldn't reach shelter before dark. Spending a night in the open with no cloud cover would mean that the temperature would drop low enough to freeze them to death before the morning, particularly as there was no firewood around.

They arrived at the thegn's hall exhausted but glad to have survived. Irwyn decided that he would prevail on their host's hospitality until the weather improved before travelling on to their destination. He felt drained, physically and emotionally, but he was proud to have brought his little band of young warriors through the experience unscathed.

PART THREE

An Untimely Death

Heroic Elflede! great in martial fame,
A man in valour, woman though in name:
Thee warlike hosts, thee, nature too obey'd,
Conqu'ror o'er both, though born by sex a maid.
Chang'd be thy name, such honour triumphs bring.
A queen by title, but in deeds a king.
Heroes before the Mercian heroine quail'd:
Caesar himself to win such glory fail'd.

Henry of Huntingdon (1088-1157)

CHAPTER THIRTEEN

December 914 to February 915

Irwyn didn't know what to make of his cousin. On the face of it, Wælwulf was welcoming and friendly but he couldn't help feeling that behind the pleasant façade his host was cold and calculating. When he smiled it didn't reach his eyes and Irwyn had learned to distrust someone who kept his true feelings hidden.

That said, he'd made the perilous journey to tell his cousin of his suspicions about Odda's death and to warn him that Osfirth hadn't taken Wælwulf's appointment as ealdorman at all well. Whatever his reservations about his cousin, he decided to be open about his own feelings in the matter.

To his surprise, the young man neither flew into a rage nor threatened revenge. Irwyn had the nasty suspicion that Wælwulf wasn't altogether grief striken about his father's death. Perhaps they hadn't been close, he thought charitably; or more likely any sorrow he might have felt was outweighed by the fact that he was now the ealdorman.

'What will you do?' Irwyn asked when he'd finished his tale.

'Do? Well, I'll certainly be on my guard from now on – and I'm grateful to you for the warning about Osfirth's animosity. However, he's a powerful man and Beornrīc of Dornsæte is his close ally, as you know only too well. I feel somewhat isolated here as a result. Cornweal may officially be part of Wessex but its people keep themselves to themselves; trying to make them allies would be a waste of time. I therefore need to tread carefully.'

'What about Somersaete? It borders you to the north and both Dornsæte and Wiltunscīr to the east. It must be in Ealdorman

Godwin's interest to have your support against the influence of Osfirth and Beornrīc.'

'How do you know that Godwin isn't secretly allied to Osfirth as well?'

'Because his northern border abuts Mercia. I know for a fact that he's a personal friend of Lady Æthelflæd and often goes hunting with Æthelstan.'

'Perhaps,' Wælwulf said thoughtfully.

The Christmas period passed pleasantly enough but whenever he tried to raise the matter of revenge for Odda's death, Wælwulf changed the subject. As the twelve days of the Christmas festivities came to an end, Irwyn was increasingly aware that his cousin tried to avoid being alone with him. Whatever he intended to do about his father's death, he was keeping his plans very much to himself.

Irwyn enjoyed the hunt on the first day of 915 but after that he itched to get away. There was little point in staying and he had a feeling that Wælwulf was as keen to get rid of him as he was to leave. However, he didn't want to risk returning through either Dornsæte or Wiltunscīr and no ships were sailing east from Execestre at that time of year. He was beginning to feel trapped when a solution presented itself. Unfortunately, the means of travel brought with it shattering news.

✝✝✝

Cedric had felt inordinately proud at being asked by Ywer to captain the small longship that had just been completed in the shipyards at Rumcofen. Although the information he'd brought back about the attack on the north bank of Mǣresēa by the Norse king, Ragnall, had been overtaken by events, the ealdorman had been impressed by Cedric's initiative and skills. He'd expected to be allowed to serve on the snekkja he and Bēomēre had captured but instead he'd been given his own ship.

At sixteen he was young to be selected to command a warship but the small birlinn wasn't intended to fight. It was used mainly as a courier to carry messages from Cæstir to Lady Æthelflæd's palace at Glowecestre.

Her crew numbered just over twenty: Cedric, a steersman, sixteen rowers, a few archers and three ship's boys. He had no hesitation in asking Bēomēre to become one of the latter. Despite her small size and a mere eight oars a side, the newly named *Saint Werburgh* was extremely seaworthy and fast. The archers were there as a last resort; her real defence was flight.

Werburgh had been the daughter of a seventh century king of Mercia called Wulfhere. She'd been the Abbess of Ely and had been famous as a reformer of convent life. Werburgh was now the patron saint of Cæstir and Cedric felt honoured to command a ship named after her.

On this occasion he carried two letters, one for the Lady Æthelflæd in Glowecestre and the other for Ealdorman Wælwulf at Execestre. Having sailed down the coast of Wealas many times before, he was now familiar with the coast, especially the dangerous areas of rock inshore and the coves in which his ship could shelter when a storm threatened.

All had gone well until a sudden squall from the west had caught him before he could reach shelter. They'd barely had time to take down the mainsail before it hit. They'd survived well enough but if it had lasted any longer than it did, the ship would have been driven ashore. Most captains had more sense than to sail in the winter; there were too many storms and conditions in an open ship were unpleasant - to put it mildly. However, he didn't have a lot of choice in the matter.

He should have delivered the missive to the Lady of Mercia first but the squall had blown them most of the way across the Sæfern

Estuary and it seemed more sensible to visit Execestre before returning to the north and entering the Sæfern estuary.

Cedric had no intention of sailing all the way around the Cornweal peninsula with its treacherous coastline. Instead, he put into a harbour in the north of Dyfneintscīr and hired horses to travel across the shire to Execestre on the south coast. He took Bēomēre as his servant and two of the four archers as escort. The choice of companions wasn't a difficult one; they were the only members of the crew who could ride.

They reached Wælwulf's hall on the fifth of January and Cedric was shown into the ealdorman's presence as soon as he said who he was and what he was there for. He glanced around the hall as he approached the table at the far end. The building was constructed of timber and was small compared to the other halls he was familiar with at Cæstir and Glowecestre. It was no grander than that of Wynnstan at Rumcofen but the hall's lack of grandeur wasn't as much of a surprise as the identity of the person who sat next to Wælwulf. Cedric knew Irwyn by sight but he hadn't expected to see him here. He swallowed nervously. The news he brought would deeply affect Irwyn.

Cedric handed the letter from Wælwulf's mother to him, bowed briefly and stepped back. As he did so he gave Irwyn a sympathetic look which rather surprised the latter. He didn't recognise Cedric nor did he understand why he should feel sorry for him. However, when he glanced at his cousin, he gave him the same look once he'd read the letter.

Wælwulf passed it to Irwyn, who took it wondering what was going on.

To Ealdorman Wælwulf, Greetings,

My dearest son,

I hope that you are well. I find the climate up here colder than that of Dyfneintscīr but, other than that, I'm comfortable enough.

I deeply regret that my tidings will come as something of a shock. Without beating about the bush, your uncle Ywer was badly mauled by a bear a fortnight ago and the wounds became inflamed. We were fortunate that one of the Lady of Mercia's physicians – one who was originally in the service of your grandfather, Lord Jørren - had come to stay for Christmas as your father's guest. You may know him – Uhtric? When they were boys your grandfather rescued him and his brother Leofwine from Lundenburg. They were street urchins at the time but their father had been a noted apothecary and they had a gift for healing. However, I digress.

The slashes made by the claws were deep and extended from your uncle's right shoulder across his chest to just above his left hip. The blow fractured several ribs. They are healing well enough but, despite Uhtric's best efforts, the wound became infected and your uncle developed a fever. The crisis lasted for some time and he became delirious. For days we wondered if he would survive.

I'm very relieved to say that the fever has gone and he hasn't had a bout of delirium for a couple of days now. Uhtric says that his mind isn't affected and he should soon be well enough to take up a few duties, but only those he can conduct from his bed. His physical recovery is likely to take months and Uhtric doesn't hold out much hope that he will ever be able to use his right arm again.

My other brother, Abbott Æscwin, has written to both the Lady Æthelflæd and to King Eadweard to inform them of the situation and to ask the king to allow your cousin Irwyn – who I don't think you've ever met – to return home. We hope that Æthelflæd will agree to Irwyn carrying out the duties of ealdorman until your uncle recovers sufficiently and can take over the governance of his shire once more. Even then, I think that Irwyn will need to remain here as Lord Ywer will never be able to fight again and someone needs to take command of the shire's defences.

It's unfortunate in the light of what has happened that my brother never appointed another shire reeve after Skarde became Earl of Wirhealum. A thegn called Wynnstan has taken on those duties but it's only an interim measure. I fully expect that your cousin Irwyn will be made shire reeve as soon as he is able to return.

In the meantime, all we can do is to pray that my dear brother doesn't have a relapse.

Your loving mother,

Kjestin,

Irwyn read through the letter twice and handed it back to Wælwulf. Then, without saying a word, he got up and walked out of the hall.

✝✝✝

When the *Saint Werburgh* docked at Glowecestre, Irwyn sent Eadsige and Mē2 2 2 2 2 2 2 2 2 2 2 Mērerīc ashore to procure a horse. He didn't intend to arrive at the Lady of Mercia's palace on foot like a plaintiff. Cedric had no such scruples and, taking two archers as escort, he walked through the port and the settlement to the palace. He was charged to deliver Abbot Æscwin's letter about Ywer to Æthelflæd and he thought it might be better to warn her before Irwyn arrived.

Irwyn rode into the palace courtyard and dismounted, handing the reins to a stable lad who came running and bowed to him. Evidently, the boy knew who he was, despite being dressed for a sea voyage rather than a visit to the Mercian court, and he marvelled how quickly word of his arrival in Glowecestre had travelled through the palace.

As he entered her council chamber he noticed, before he bowed his head, that Æthelflæd looked older and more careworn than when he'd last seen her. He supposed that she must in her mid-forties now and the perilous times they lived in had obviously taken its toll on her. He learned later that she had been quite ill throughout November and December and was only just recovering.

She was sitting next to her daughter, Ælfwynn. Young women of her age had normally married and had several children by now. Irwyn had his own suspicions why she wasn't even betrothed yet. Her mother saw her as her successor and, if she married, her husband would want to supplant his wife as ruler of Mercia.

Æthelflæd had fought her own husband, the late Lord Æthelred, to play a part in the rule of Mercia and presumably didn't want her daughter to be condemned to the life of a brood mare.

It was one of her few blindspots; she could not see that Ælfwynn had no interest in ruling Mercia, and no aptitude for it. She was shallow, flighty and capricious. There were rumours that she had brief affairs from time to time, usually with servants younger than she was. It was even said that one of her lovers was a fourteen-year-old stable boy who accompanied her when she went riding. He shuddered to think what would happen to Mercia if Ælfwynn succeeded her mother in due course.

The only other option was Æthelstan but, despite the fact that he was Æthelflæd's nephew, the only Mercian blood in his veins came from his grandmother - and she had been married to King Ælfred. She was born in eastern Mercia, which did little to recommend her to the west Mercians, and she had supported her husband's claim to be overlord of Mercia. That was the reason that Æthelred was never allowed to call himself king and it still rankled amongst the Mercian nobility.

Whilst Æthelflæd re-read the letter that Cedric had given her, carefully considering what to do about the situation, Irwyn wondered idly where Æthelstan was. Had he been in Glowecestre, he would have expected him to be present at the meeting. However, as Irwyn later discovered, he was in winter quarters at Tomtun on the border with the Danelaw.

Irwyn stopped his daydreaming when he realised that Æthelflæd was frowning at him. He assumed that she was commiserating with him over his father's injuries and replied, hoping that he'd guessed correctly.

'Thank you, lady,' he managed to stutter. 'You are very kind.'

He breathed a sigh of relief when that appeared to be the expected response. She went on to say that, despite his youth, she was prepared to entrust Cæstirscīr to his care until his father recovered.

'Your official rank will be shire reeve as that doesn't have to be approved by the Witenaġemot. I cannot promise that you would be appointed as the next ealdorman, in the unhappy event that proves necessary, but your performance as your father's deputy will obviously be taken into consideration.'

It all sounded rather cold hearted and matter of fact to Irwyn but he supposed that a ruler couldn't afford to be sentimental when it came to the efficient administration and defence of the realm.

The next day he and his small contingent embarked on the *Saint Werburgh* once more for the voyage to Cæstir.

†††

'We're in for a bit of blow,' Cedric remarked to Irwyn.

They were sailing on a broad reach and so Irwyn turned to look aft over the port quarter from where the wind was coming. The grey clouds overhead were quickly being blown out of the way by dark black ones and he could see the rain sheeting down at forty-five degrees underneath them.

'Oarsmen get ready to hold her steady, oars out. Reef the mainsail fully,' Cedric shouted and the three ship's boys ran to lower the sail onto the deck. 'Luff up into the wind.'

The steersman brought the ship around so that it was facing into the wind, whilst the rowers pulled slowly on their oars, not to propel the ship through the water but to hold her steady. The three boys quickly tied the reefing points around the sail so that only a third of it would be exposed. They started to raise the spar from which the mainsail was suspended but they were having difficulty as the increasingly strong wind pushed it against the mast.

Without being told, Irwyn and his companions ran to help the boys sweat the spar up into position. Once it was there and the halyard secured, Cedric told the steersman to head northeast. The boys cleated the sheets home to set the sail on the new course and the ship ran before the gale-force wind. Slowly a low line of hills emerged faintly through the rain that now drenched them. As they ran closer to the coast the wind eased. Irwyn could vaguely make out hills off both the larboard and port beams and he realised that the land formed a shallow crescent. They had entered a bay of some sort.

The beach, onto which the sea crashed in foam flecked waves, lay straight ahead of them and, just for a moment, Irwyn thought that Cedric intended to run the ship up onto the sand. However, a hundred yards short of the shoreline he gave the order to drop anchor. Several of the rowers nearest the bows shipped their oars and ran to the bows from where they heaved a rock over the side. The rope attached to it ran out until it became taut and the ship swung around so that it was face on to the wind.

He saw Cedric making a sketch on a slate and, out of curiosity, he asked him what he was doing.

'You see the building near the headland at the northern end of the settlement and the watch tower beyond it?'

'Yes,' Irwyn replied, none the wiser.

'Now look at the church and the summit of the hill beyond it on the other headland. Well, as long as they both stay in line, as they do now, I know that the anchor is holding and we're not drifting into the shore.'

'Would it matter if we beached her?'

'Not if it was done gently and bows on so that we could easily push her off again but that's sometimes difficult against the wind. Furthermore, this is the coast of Wealas and the locals aren't always very friendly.'

'I see. Do you know where we are?'

'The Welsh call it Aberystwyth, meaning the mouth of the river Ystwyth.'

'Cedric, several boats are heading our way,' the man on watch shouted urgently.

'Archers, take your positions. The rest of you, arm yourselves, I don't suppose they're coming to welcome us.'

The four archers strung their bows and spaced themselves along the gunwale, an arrow nocked ready to shoot. The rest of the crew donned an assortment of padded jackets and leather jerkins and put on their helmets. They were armed with seaxes, daggers and axes, all suitable for close quarter fighting on deck, and spears were placed beside them ready to throw if they were attacked.

There were seven fishing boats, each carrying half a dozen armed men, and one small ship similar to Cedric's birlinn but shorter and wider on the beam. This was full of warriors. A large, rotund man stood at the prow. He was dressed in a highly polished byrnie, a steel helmet with a circlet of gold around it and he carried an oblong gold shield with a device painted on it that looked like a red lion.

'Anarawd ap Rhodri,' Cedric said with disbelief. 'What's the King of Ceredigion doing here?'

✝✝✝

It turned out that King Anarawd was in the far north-west of his kingdom because Aberystwyth was his only port. Another minor

Welsh king, Hwgan of Brycheniog, had abducted Abbot Egbert, who'd been Anarawd's tutor when he was a boy. He was a Mercian and therefore a subject of Lady Æthelflæd, even though he was the head of a monastery in Wealas. Anarawd was determined to get his old tutor and friend freed but he'd decided that it was the Lady of the Mercian's problem to resolve, not his.

The king was therefore on his way to Glowecestre. However, he'd only just set out when the storm blew up and he'd scuttled back into harbour. When he saw what was obviously a Mercian birlinn anchored out in the bay, he'd decided that it was a more suitable craft in which to venture out onto the high seas and he ordered Cedric to take him to Glowecestre as soon as the storm abated.

Naturally, Irwyn was totally opposed to this as it would delay his return to his father's side but, as Cedric pointed out, the tub in which the Welsh king was initially proposing to venture forth was likely to capsize the first time it met a sizeable wave.

'I have to ask myself what my sovereign lady would expect me to do. I'm sorry Irwyn,' Cedric explained.

Irwyn ground his teeth in frustration but he acknowledged that Cedric was right. It was four days before the *Saint Werburgh* saw Aberystwyth again. This time the conditions at sea were ideal. It didn't take long to put Anarawd ashore and an hour later the settlement had disappeared behind the headland as they headed back out to sea.

As soon as the birlinn had tied up alongside the wharf in Cæstir Irwyn rushed up to his father's hall. This time he was less concerned about his dignity and, far from arriving on horseback, he ran into Ywer's bedchamber smelling strongly of the sea and the accumulated odours of someone who hadn't bathed for some time.

He found his mother, his Aunt Kjerstin and his Uncle Æscwin gathered at the bedside alongside the physician, Uhtric.

Abbot Æscwin was the first to react to his nephew's sudden appearance.

'Irwyn, thank the Lord that you're here. You made good time from Ludenwic.'

'I was with Wælwulf in Execestre when I got the news. I'll tell you all about it another time,' he muttered. 'How's father?'

'Well enough to talk for himself. Come here boy; let's look at you,' Ywer called from the bed.

Irwyn went over to the bedside and was relieved to see that his father looked better than he had expected and even had some colour in his face. However, it was less encouraging to see that the bandage around his body was stained red with blood in several places, especially around his right shoulder. He bent down and gave Ywer a respectful kiss in his bearded cheek.

'By Saint Oswald's Holy bones, boy, you reek worse than a cesspit. Go and bathe and get changed.'

'Yes, father,' his son replied with a grin.

His father might still be bedbound but it was obvious that he was well on the way to recovery.

CHAPTER FOURTEEN

Summer 915

'What will you do?' Æthelstan asked his aunt after she'd recalled him from Touecestre.

The Mercian fyrd had been busy building more fortified burhs along the border with the Danelaw as there seemed little prospect of a campaign that year. That all changed when a Viking army under the leadership of two Norse jarls from the Continent – Ohtor and Hroald – landed in Gwynedd, pillaging and burning all along its south coast.

The Viking raiders had rather driven the abduction of Abbot Egbert from the minds of both Lady Æthelflæd and King Anarawd.

'We need to mobilise the fyrd in Herefordscīr and Glowecestrescīr in case the Vikings raid us as well' Æthelflæd told him. 'I want you to take command and send scouts out to track the enemy on land. When Cedric next visits here, send his ship to keep an eye on the Vikings from the sea as well. His ship is fast enough to elude their longships if they object to being watched.'

'Very well. Will you accompany me?'

'No, I have other problems to deal with. I want to visit Ywer to see how he's recuperating and then carry on to Dùn Breatann for a meeting with King Dyfnwal of Strathclyde and Constantin, King of Alba.'

She smiled at the look of incomprehension on her nephew's face.

'They've approached me for a meeting. They are concerned about the progress that Ragnall is making in subduing Northumbria. Most of western Northumbria now acknowledges him as king and he has demanded the return of Cumbria from Dynwal. You may not be aware but Cumbria was previously part of Northumbria.

'The situation over in the north-east is equally troubling. Earl Ealdred of Bernicia was driven out of his stronghold at Bebbanburg by Ragnall late last year and he fled north to Alba, where Constantin has given him sanctuary. Both the Picts of Alba and the Danes of Jorvik were content to leave Ealdred as ruler of the lands between the River Tes and the Firth of Forth as a neutral buffer zone between them. Now that Ragnall holds the area, both feel threatened.'

'I assume you'll take the Mercian fleet with you?'

'I think I'll have to; the Íralandes Sǣ is a favourite hunting ground for Norse pirates at this time of year. That's why we need Cedric's birlinn to watch what Ohtor and Hroald are up to.'

✝✝✝

'I don't want you to go!'

Astrid broke down in tears when Wynnstan told her that he'd been summoned to Cæstir. He would be accompanying Lady Æthelflæd north to Strathclyde as Lord Ywer's representative. The latter had made a remarkable recovery, although he couldn't use his right arm properly any more. He had begun to train with a sword in his left hand and a shield strapped to his right but he tired easily and Gyda forbade him to even think about accompanying Æthelflæd. Irwyn was still too young to carry much weight with the two kings in the North but Wynnstan possessed both experience and reputation as a warrior.

'Why this time? We've been separated often enough in the past?' Wynnstan asked impatiently. 'Not always by my choice.'

He regretted adding the last few words as soon as he'd uttered them. He still blamed her for the time she'd chosen to remain and serve Cuthfleda as her head of household instead of accompanying her husband. They had put that behind them and it was foolish to reopen old wounds.

The truth was he was a little fearful and he didn't like the feeling, so he'd lashed out. He'd never been so far north and didn't know what to expect. The Scots and Picts had a fearsome reputation and the Britons of Strathclyde were Celts - like the Welsh - and he didn't trust them. Had he not been apprehensive he would have shown more sympathy over his wife's reluctance to see him leave

She bit her lip. She had been on the point of telling him of her concerns about Chad and his evident lust for her but she changed her mind. Instead, she glared at him angrily and stalked out of the room.

She wouldn't have worried had Chad been going with her husband but he was staying to look after the boundary with Northumbria along the south bank of the Mǣresēa. Ever since Wynnstan had learned that he was to go to Dùn Breatann, Chad had looked like a wolf stalking its prey.

It didn't seem to matter to him that Astrid was now twenty four and the mother of two children. There were many much younger girls around who would have been glad to respond to the advances of the handsome captain of Wynnstan's warband - and no doubt several had done so. She suspected that what drove him in her case was the desire to taste forbidden fruit.

She maintained a frosty silence all evening and turned away from him when he tried to cuddle her in bed. Wynnstan felt wretched and was even more distressed when she failed to come and see him off at dawn the next day.

As soon he and his escort had riden out of Rumcofen and he felt the warm breeze on his face he brightened up. 'Let her sulk if she wants to,' he thought. 'It was her choice that we were apart for so long in the past, not mine. Now I have to leave her for a short time it seems to be my fault.'

However, his resentment faded with every mile they covered and, by the time they rode into Cæstir, he'd forgotten all about their squabble. Instead, he was totally focused on the adventure ahead of him.

Chad bided his time, his lustful eyes mentally undressing Astrid every time he saw her. On the third night after Wynnstan's departure there was a thunderstorm and he used the excuse of checking that Astrid was all right to get past the servant who slept across her threshold in the corridor.

'Who's there?' Astrid asked sleepily.

The lightning flashed and the thunder roared outside the window and it had prevented her from falling into a deep sleep. It wasn't a glazed window such as the wealthiest nobles might have but it wasn't just a simple shuttered hole in the wall. The opening was covered by a removable frame across which a thin square of leather had been stretched. It was against this faint light that she thought she saw a shadow move.

Chad sat down on her bed and pulled her to him, pushing his lips towards hers hungrily.

'Don't resist me; you know you want me as much as I want you,' he whispered in her ear.

She awoke with a start, pushing him away.

'Get off me, you moron! Wait till Wynnstan hears about this. He'll whip you within an inch of your life!'

'What makes you think he'll be coming back?' he said with a leer that looked even more chilling in the sudden light cast by another flash of forked lightning outside.

'What do you mean?' Astrid began to say but, before she could complete her query, Chad forced his mouth onto hers and pushed his tongue deep inside.

She bit down hard and he broke off the contact with a yelp of pain.

'You stupid bitch,' he shouted, slapping her hard around the head several times.

She was stunned by the incessant blows and lost consciousness. When she came to her senses, she knew from the blood and the soreness that she had been raped. Chad had evidently rolled off her afterwards and was lying beside her using a rag to try and staunch the bleeding from his mouth.

She heard a sound and looked towards the door which had been opened. Another vivid flash of lightning briefly illuminated two figures; one was the servant whose duty it was to sleep outside her door and the other was her seven-year-old son, Sicga.

He'd come to her chamber for comfort during the storm but what he saw made him forget his fright. In its place a mixture of concern and anger distorted his face. Darkness descended once more and then another bolt tore across the sky. The boy had gone, as had the servant.

A few seconds later Sicga rushed into her bedchamber clutching the small dagger that his father had given him on his seventh birthday. Chad looked up to see the boy standing over him with the dagger in his hand. Instinctively he lashed out punching the boy in the chest. Sicga was knocked flying and hit his head on a chest. He was dazed and was badly winded by the blow.

For a moment Astrid stared at the motionless figure of her son then she noticed the dagger which her son had dropped when he'd been punched. Her fingers scrabbled for it as Chad got up from the bed and went to kick and punch Sicga into a bloody pulp.

With a scream of rage Astrid stepped behind him and grabbed him by the hair, yanking his head back hard. He tried to turn and grab her but he was too slow. Astrid sawed the small blade across his throat several times. Once would have done as she'd nicked one of his carotid arteries with her first cut. When she finally let go and fell to her knees sobbing Chad had already bled to death.

She uttered a cry of relief when she saw her son stirring and she hugged him to her. He screamed in pain and she immediately let go, realising that one or more of his ribs was fractured or broken. Then the room suddenly filled with people. Astrid allowed herself to be helped to her feet and someone arranged for her to be taken to another bedchamber whilst the mess was cleaned up.

She resisted until she was sure that someone was carrying the injured Sicga to the same room. Once they'd put her down on the bed and laid her son beside her she allowed herself to lose consciousness.

It had all seemed like a nightmare and she tried to block it from her memory. Sicga wasn't badly injured and his two fractured ribs would heal in a month or two. She wasn't injured physically but her mental state was a different matter. Everyone knew what had happened and she felt ashamed, although it was in no way her fault. She was worried what Wynnstan would think most of all; if only she had told him of her fears about Chad before he left.

A few weeks later she was given cause to worry even more. She knew that she was pregnant. She was late and she was never late. It could have been Wynnstan's, of course, conceived before he went away, but she was certain deep down that it was the rapist's child.

✝✝✝

The meeting at Dùn Breatann had gone well and the three leaders were on the point of drawing up a treaty of mutual assistance when the news came that Ragnall had invaded Cumbria and was advancing towards Cær Luel. Æthelflæd had brought a total of three hundred and fifty men with her including her personal hearth warriors and the crews of her ships. They were all experienced fighters, albeit on a floating platform rather than in a shieldwall. When she was asked to join the armies of Alba and Strathclyde she felt that she could hardly refuse but she was used to commanding her own force, not being a minor player in someone else's.

Rather than be caught between the defenders of the old Roman walled city of Cær Luel and the advancing Scots, Picts and Britons,

Ragnall wisely decided to retreat. He'd intended to stand and fight on a ground of his choosing, once he was clear of the threat of fighting on two fronts, but the lack of supplies was becoming a problem.

Normally his men would have foraged for what they needed but in the land between the Firth of Forth and the River Tinan there was little in the way of crops or vegetables. It was sparsely populated and the people relied on their livestock.

The inhabitants had taken their animals and fled into the remote hills and valleys where they remained hidden from the Viking foragers. Even supply by Ragnall's fleet proved impossible because they were on the west coast and the only navigable rivers that they could have used were in the east. It would have taken too long to sail around the top of Britannia and, in any case, the Norse who inhabited the islands known as Orkneyjar, which would lie on their route, were no friends of his. He'd driven them out of the Isle of Mann and that still rankled.

Ragnall was furious when he learned that the Norse garrison he'd left in Bebbanburg had surrendered to Ealdred. Whoever held the fortress controlled Bernicia and so all the land bounded by Cumbria, Alba and the Danish Kingdom of Jorvik was effectively lost to him. Years of careful planning were about to go up in smoke. It was time to make a stand.

Æthelflæd and Wynnstan rode alongside Constantin of Alba and Dyfnwal of Strathclyde. Now that he'd recovered Bebbanburg, Ealdred had promised to join Constantin and the others just as soon as he'd mustered his nobles and the fyrd. It wasn't a promise that Æthelflæd placed much confidence in. Ealdred struck her as a man who was more interested in retaining his independence from any of his neighbours than he was in helping them.

She knew that Wynnstan disagreed with her. He maintained that it was in the young earl's interest to assist Constantin and

Dyfnwal to defeat Ragnall. If they were defeated, Ragnall would drive him out of his earldom once more.

One evening Constantin's scouts returned with the news that the Norsemen were camped alongside the River Tinan at a place called Corebricg where there were the ruins of an ancient Roman cavalry fort. Wynnstan decided that he should take a look for himself and, accompanied by three Mercian archers, he set off before dawn down the valley of the burn which joined the Tinan to the east of the ruined fort.

Mist hung in the valley so the landscape below the shallow ridge on which he lay became visible very gradually as the sun burned it off. Once he could study the camp properly, he estimated the number of Norsemen and then did the calculation again to be certain. There were no more than seven hundred warriors in the encampment. Ragnall was supposed to have near on three thousand men, so where were the rest? Even if the inevitable camp followers – whores, servants and boys – had been inadvertently included in the numbers reported by the scouts, most of Ragnall's men were evidently elsewhere.

A slight breeze lifted the banner outside the largest tent. It was black with some emblem on it. He was too far away to make out the details but Ragnall's standard was the skull of a horse mounted above a plain red cloth. This confirmed his suspicion that this wasn't the main Viking host.

As soon as he returned and reported to Æthelflæd she took him to see Constantin. He didn't believe Wynnstan – a man he didn't know – over his own scouts but Dyfnwal supported Æthelflæd's proposal that they send out scouts on a broad front to find out if Ragnall had split his army. When Constantin maintained that this was unlikely, she suggested that he might have done it in order to seek out food. He grudgingly admitted that this could explain it and half-an-hour later fifty scouts rode out of the camp in ten groups; Wynnstan and the Mercians forming one of them.

It didn't take him long to locate the first division of the Norse army and this one was led by a man whose standard was a horse's head and a red flag. This had to be Ragnall himself. He was leading a thousand warriors down a shallow valley ten miles due north of Corebricg.

When he returned, he discovered that one of the other groups had also found a large force of Norsemen some eight miles to the north-east of Corebricg. Their estimate of numbers was only five or six hundred which meant that they now knew where just over two thousand of the enemy were. This seemed to satisfy the two kings that the Norse army consisted of three columns. However, neither Æthelflæd nor Wynnstan were convinced they'd located all of them. There was probably another column of Vikings out there somewhere and they insisted it was inadvisable to commit their entire force to battle against the three columns.

After a great deal of argument, Constantin eventually agreed that the Mercian contingent should remain on the high ground to the north of Corebricg as a reserve.

Whilst Dyfnwal led his Britons and Scots against the encampment beside the Tinan, the King of Alba placed his men in two wings on the low ridge to the north of the old fort facing the direction from which Ragnall and the other column would approach. Their task was to prevent them from reinforcing the one already at the river,

At first the plan worked well. The Vikings, led by the jarl with the black banner, were trapped between the men of Strathclyde and the river. They were hemmed in and outnumbered and it quickly turned into a slaughter rather than a fight.

Constantin's own wing to the east were holding their own against the third Norse column but things were not going so well further along the ridge to the west. That was where Ragnall himself was attacking and numbers were more evenly matched.

Gradually Constantin was forced back down the slope toward the Tinan and then disaster struck. Just when the Britons of Strathclyde had won the battle in and around the old fort, their king was killed.

The Vikings didn't have many archers but one had succeeded in hitting Dyfnwal in the neck just above the top of his byrnie. The arrowhead pierced one of his carotid arteries and he fell to the ground as his lifeblood spurted all over him. A minute or so later he was dead.

It made no difference to the battle beside the river - that had already been won and decisively so – but it left the Britons leaderless. Had Dyfnwal survived he would have doubtless led his men to support Constantin. As it was, they stayed where they were and looted the dead.

The outcome lay in the balance and then it was tipped in favour of Ragnall's Vikings. The missing fourth column appeared in the east, marching along the north bank of the Tinan.

Æthelflæd faced a difficult choice: either she could commit her Mercians to support Constantin or she could attack the fourth column in the flank and hope to prevent it joining the main battle. There was a third option; she could quietly leave the battlefield and return to her ships at Dùn Breatann. It was to her credit that she never considered the latter for one second.

'I need your advice,' she told Wynnstan.

He didn't have to be told what about; he'd already worked out in his own mind what he would do. If Constantin was forced back toward the river, which seemed probable, then there was always the hope that the men of Strathclyde would rush to his support. On the other hand, if the fourth column of some eight hundred warriors attacked either the disorganised Britons and Scots by the river or the Picts on the ridge to the east, the Norsemen would triumph and their allies would be routed.

'Prevent the fourth column from joining the battle or else all is lost,' he said succinctly.

She nodded and called for the leader of her fifty archers. She quickly explained what she wanted done and they rode off to the east on the stocky garrons that Constantin had provided for them. Unlike the horses the Mercians were used to, these were hill ponies. The Mercians felt faintly ridiculous riding them as their feet nearly reached the ground when mounted but the animals were sure footed in the treacherous heather covered hills and had great stamina.

The archers dismounted a hundred yards above the advancing column and proceeded to rain arrows down on them. Most of the enemy still carried their shields on their backs and over two score were killed or wounded before they reacted and swung their shields around to protect them. The archers continued to send volley after volley down into the column and a few found spaces between the rim of the shields and exposed flesh. More importantly, some of the column had halted and about a hundred had broken away to charge the archers.

The other three hundred Mercians now arrived on the scene and formed a line to protect the archers. There hadn't been time to train the seamen to fight in a shieldwall but they were used to fighting individually and they were good at it. The first of the hundred Vikings went down to a barrage of arrows and spears. The rest hesitated but then the whole column were ordered up the slope to kill the Mercians.

Wynnstan pushed his way through to the front rank with fifty warriors of Æthelflæd's gesith led by Arne. They weren't fond of one another and Wynnstan would rather have had anyone else standing to his right but there was nothing he could do about it. They formed a shieldwall to hold the centre of the line. The tactic was for the man to your left to kill the opponent facing you as his right hand side wasn't protected by his shield. Unfortunately, Arne ignored this and Wynnstan found that he had to defend himself against the man opposite him as well as the enemy to his left.

He could only be lucky for so long and a youth with a spear managed to lunge at his chest whilst he was dealing with the axeman to his front. He felt the chain links of his byrnie part and a second or so later he was aware of a searing pain in his right side. He collapsed and the last thing he remembered was being dragged to the rear.

Arne was ecstatic. He would have happily seen his nemesis killed without the bribe that Chad had paid him to make sure Wynnstan didn't return to Rumcofen.

Æthelflæd was aware that Wynnstan had been seriously wounded but she didn't have time to worry about it. Another army had appeared on top of the ridge behind her. It had come from the north east and for a while her heart sank, believing it to be yet another Norse column. As it got closer she could see the banner being held aloft beside the man on a magnificent grey stallion. She sighed in relief when she recognised the wolf's head banner of Bebbanburg. Earl Ealdred and his Bernicians had arrived in the nick of time.

✝✝✝

'The death of Dyfnwal is a serious loss,' Constantin said as he and Æthelflæd sat together in his tent after the battle.

'As is the loss of my captain, Arne, and the wounding of Wynnstan, shire reeve of Cæstirscīr,' she retorted. 'Ragnall has retreated to lick his wounds but he still rules over western Northumbria. Although it will take him time to recover, I'm sure we haven't heard the last of him. Meanwhile I've been deprived of a suitable commander to hold my northern border. Ealdorman Ywer is still far from fit and the healers don't know whether Wynnstan will survive. Even if he does it will be a long time before he recovers.'

'Doesn't Ywer have a son?'

'Yes, Irwyn, but he's just seventeen and young for such responsibility without guidance. If it was any other shire his youth wouldn't matter so much but Cæstirscīr is the buffer between Northumbria and the rest of Mercia. It also borders the northern part of the Danelaw. I would have sent Arne to help him but somehow he was killed from behind. He's not the man to turn and run and so I'm forced to the conclusion that one of my own men slew him, although I have no idea why.'

That wasn't strictly true. She was well aware of the animosity between Arne and Wynnstan. When she learned that Arne had failed to protect Wynnstan and that was why he'd been badly wounded, she suspected that someone who saw what had happened was outraged at Arne's betrayal and had killed him in revenge.

'What will happen to Strathclyde now?' she asked, changing the subject.

'Dyfnwal has a son – Owain – but the boy is only thirteen, which is why he wasn't present at the battle. I'll arrange for a council of regency to help him rule until he's older.'

'You're not tempted to take over Strathclyde yourself?'

'No, that would only lead to conflict between us. Strathclyde consists of the Britons of Cumbria and Alt Clut and the Scots of Dalriada, whereas Alba emerged from the seven kingdoms of the Picts. We're different ethnically and culturally and, at a time when we face Norse incursions in the north and west, not to mention Ragnall in the south, a strong alliance between us is essential to our survival.'

'I agree, but I also face threats elsewhere,' Æthelflæd said grimly.

'Indeed. When will you move against the Daneland?' he asked casually.

He knew that when that started in earnest both Wessex and Mercia would be fully committed, which meant Æthelflæd wouldn't be in a position to come to his aid, even if she wanted to.

'My brother Eadweard is facing a rebellion in East Anglia and I have a few problems in the west to deal with first. Perhaps next year?'

Constantin didn't say anything but he hoped that it would be sooner rather than later, whilst Ragnall was still weakened by his failed foray against Cumbria and therefore unable to take advantage of Mercia's preoccupations elsewhere.

☩☩☩

The point of the spear had punctured Wynnstan's left lung. Quite apart from the wound itself and the detritus carried into his body, the loss of the use of one of his lungs left Wynnstan with pain in his shoulder and chest, increased heart rate and shortness of breath.

Thankfully, the monk who dealt with him was an experienced infirmarian who knew what to do. Once he'd cleaned out the wound, he inserted a stout hollow reed and pushed it into the lining of the lung. He then sucked out the excess air which had caused the lung to collapse, before sewing up the wound.

He left the tube in place for a couple of days before removing it, by which time the lung had re-inflated and the blueish tinge to his patient's skin had turned back to a more healthy colour.

'He'll need to rest and let the wound heal,' the monk told Æthelflæd when she came to see how he was.

'How long?'

The monk shrugged.

'I need to make sure there isn't a relapse. The lung could collapse again if the tear in it hasn't completely repaired itself. I would say three weeks before I can be certain that he's healed properly. Then he'll need to regain his strength before undertaking a sea voyage.'

'So you're saying a month or more? I can't wait that long; I need to get back to Mercia. Wynnstan will have to follow on when he's ready.'

✝✝✝

After Chad's assault Astrid didn't know what to do. She wished that Wynnstan would hurry up and return but then she remembered that she would have to explain the child she was carrying to him. She could lie, of course, and say it was his.

However, Chad had red hair and Wynnstan's was black. If the child was ginger he'd know it wasn't his. Besides, she didn't think she would be able to live with herself if she deceived him about the rape. Servants gossiped and he would hear about it soon after his return in any case; furthermore, it would be difficult to explain Chad's death without revealing the truth. No; she would have to tell him and tell him as soon as possible.

Another matter needed more immediate resolution. Chad had been one of her husband's companions for years. If he could betray him, who could she trust? She needed to appoint a replacement to command the garrison and Wynnstan's small warband but she didn't know who to turn to.

The solution to her dilemma came in the shape of Irwyn, now the shire reeve of Cæstirscīr. He'd heard of Chad's death and decided to attend his funeral. His aunt, Kjestin, came with him. It was an excuse for her to leave the monastery. She was relatively content living there but she was bored. She especially missed being able to go riding and hawking, two of her favourite pursuits when she lived in Dyfneintscīr. Gyda had offered her a carriage for the journey to Rumcofen but she had declined. Bouncing around in an enclosed wagon was no substitute for feeling the wind in her face and a horse under her.

As soon as polite greetings had been exchanged and Kjestin and her nephew had been shown into their chambers to change for the funeral service, Astrid asked to see Kjestin. Astrid found her being washed by a slave girl in a large wooden tub. Whilst the girl continued to wash Kjestin Astrid told her of her ordeal.

She finished just as Kjestin was being rubbed dry and the older woman embraced the younger. Astrid broke down and wept in Kjestin's arms for some time.

'I'm so sorry,' she said, pulling away. 'What must you think of me?'

'I think you have endured a terrible ordeal and have had to cope without anyone to comfort you or to confide in. Well, I'm here now and I will stay as long as you need me; until your husband returns if necessary.'

Astrid hadn't intended to attend Chad's funeral but, as Kjestin pointed out, not to do so would only increase speculation as to his cause of death. The official version was that he'd died suddenly during the night, which was true up to a point. She therefore sat and listened as Rumcofen's priest droned on about the many years of service Chad had given Mercia and how much Wynnstan would miss his friend.

She remained poker faced throughout but Sicga, sitting by her side, didn't try and keep the derision from his face. He was too young to realise that she was being raped and thought that Chad was trying to kill her for some reason. She'd warned him not to say anything or show his hatred for the man being buried but to a boy of nearly eight everything tends to be black and white. There were no shades of grey and he couldn't bear to hear the man who'd attacked his mother given a eulogy.

Eventually he'd had enough and he tore his hand out of Astrid's and ran out of the church. Astrid worried that people would speculate as to the reason but she needn't have worried. Everyone thought that the boy had looked up to Chad and was heartbroken by his sudden death.

'I've no idea when Lady Æthelflæd and your husband will return,' Irwyn said to her after Chad had been laid to rest.

There was no feast after the ceremony, which Irwyn thought a little odd, but Astrid invited Kjestin and himself to join her for something to eat.

'Who will you appoint to succeed Chad,' he asked.

It was a matter of some concern to him, as whoever was chosen would be charged with patrolling the border with the Norsemen who lived over the river, until Wynnstan returned.

'I don't know,' Astrid replied hesitantly. 'Our warband is quite small but there are several who have been with Wynnstan for some time. I'm not sure who he would want to appoint.'

Kjestin gave her a meaningful glance and when Astrid hesitated to say more, she decided to force Astrid's hand. Irwyn needed to know the facts.

'You need to tell him, my dear,' she said firmly and Astrid's face crumpled.

'I can't!' she cried. 'It's too shameful.'

'Well then, leave us alone and I'll brief my nephew; that is if you give me permission?'

Astrid nodded and ran from the hall.

'I see. Poor woman,' Irwyn said sympathetically when his aunt had finished. 'No wonder she doesn't know who to trust.'

A little later he went to see Astrid and asked who she thought Wynnstan might select, had he been there. He made no mention of her ordeal, for which she was grateful.

'Well, he's very close to Sawin, Wardric and Tidhelm. They served him as scouts when they were scarcely more than boys and they've been with him ever since.'

'If you're content to leave the matter in my hands, I'll speak to them individually and come back with a recommendation.'

'How will you decide?' she asked, looking puzzled. 'You don't know any of them.'

'Simple, I'll ask each of them who they would choose.'

CHAPTER FIFTEEN

916

Æthelflæd was furious. Negotiations for the release of Abbot Egbert had been protracted and frustrating. It seemed that King Hwgan had approached the abbot to ask for his blessing on his marriage to a pretty girl half his age. Egbert had indignantly refused, partly because the girl in question was Hwgan's niece but, more importantly, he was already married to another.

Hwgan had abducted Egbert in the hope of persuading him to change his mind and marry them. He'd repudiated his existing wife and seemed to think that by doing so he was eligible to marry again. Anarawd was determined to obtain Egbert's release. He'd been his tutor before Egbert became abbot of the only monastery in Brycheiniog. What made it even more personal was the fact that Hwgan's rejected wife was Anarawd's cousin.

The last thing Anarawd wanted was to go to war with Hwgan. He was facing internal unrest in his own kingdom and he wasn't sure to what extent he could rely on his nobles; therefore he was reliant on Æthelflæd to resolve the matter.

Presumably, King Hwgan had given up hope of getting the abbot to agree to marry him to his niece because Æthelflæd received a basket from Hwgan in early April which contained the abbot's head. She was a devout Christian and her faith mattered to her more than anything else. Murdering a senior churchman was not only an unforgiveable crime but also a profane sacrilege. Furthermore, it was a direct challenge to her and one that couldn't be ignored.

The Welsh Kingdom of Brycheniog lay across the River Sæfern from Glowecestre and it took two days to ferry the force she'd mustered over the river to Herefordscīr where they were joined by that shire's fyrd. Æthelstan was still busy supervising the construction of burhs along the line of Casingc Stræt – the boundary with the Danelaw – so she asked Deorwine, the former Hereræswa of Mercia, to take command of the army. He was now getting on in years and had retired a couple of years ago, making way for Æthelstan to take over. He was greatly respected and although now only a thegn in rank, he was probably the only person that the other ealdormen would have accepted as their commander without protest.

Deorwine brought his ten-year-old son with him. The boy, Abrecan, had been born to Deorwine and his wife, Cuthfleda, Ywer's eldest sister, late in life and it had been a traumatic birth. After Cuthfleda's death, Deorwine had decided to foster the boy with another thegn rather than raise him himself. At six, Abrecan had been far too young to send away, especially so soon after his mother's death, and consequently he'd grown to loathe his father.

Deorwine had eventually accepted that it had been an error of judgement and had tried to make amends. He'd taken the boy back a year ago and slowly trust had been restored between Abrecan and his father and bringing him along for the invasion of Brycheniog was intended to be part of that process. Æthelflæd was far from convinced that it was a good idea but she decided to allow him to stay and made the boy one of her pages for now.

The Mercian army needed to cross through Gwent to reach Hwgan's principle abode on Llyn Syfaddon. Thankfully, there was no love lost between the King of Gwynedd, of which Gwent was a part, and Hwgan of Brycheiniog and he readily gave permission for the Mercian host to cross the northern part of Gwent. However, he insisted on sending warriors to escort the Mercians to make sure there was no looting or foraging en route.

Once they entered Brycheiniog they discovered every village deserted by both people and livestock. Æthelflæd realised that Hwgan would have ample warning of their coming and would doubtless escape. She had little option but to continue her slow advance but she sent her two best scouts, Cena and Broga, to lead Banan, the captain who had replaced Arne, and fifty mounted warriors through the mountains known as the Mynyddoedd Du. Their task was to launch a surprise attack against Hwgan's crannog on the north shore of Llyn Syfaddon. This was a round hall set on a platform some distance from the shore and approached by a walkway suspended on piles sunk into the lake's floor.

Neither Cena nor Broga knew the Mynyddoedd Du at all. To make matters worse, the sun had been hidden by the clouds all day and so they had little idea whether they were headed in the right direction. They were therefore relieved when they came across a Welsh shepherd early on the second day. In return for his life, he promised to lead them through the mountains to Llyn Syfaddon. As the day wore on, the clouds cleared and the sun came out. It was only then that they realised that they were being led north instead of westwards.

The shepherd paid with his life for misleading them but that didn't change the fact that they were lost.

'I think we've probably been making no more than two miles an hour for the past five hours,' Broga said, sketching a rough map in a bare patch of ground. 'From what we've been told, these valleys and ridges run roughly north to south. I think we need to cross over the next three ranges of hills and from the top of the fourth one we should be able to see Llyn Syfaddon. If so, we can follow the valley to the east of the ridge and approach the crannog from the north.'

Banan looked at Cena for confirmation, who nodded.

'Very well, but we've only a few hours of daylight left. Our priority is to find a suitable stream beside which to camp tonight and we need to find some game.'

They carried barley and some dried root vegetables with them but it made for an insipid pottage without adding meat to it. The hillsides looked barren and there was little in the way of game. Small rodents scuttled out of their way and various birds including ravens and red kites soared above them but that was it.

They entered the next valley and to their relief a few sheep grazed here and there on the hillsides. A boy who was looking after his family's small flock fled with his two dogs, herding the rest of the sheep ahead of them, as soon as Banan's hunters appeared. Three animals were left behind and the Mercians quickly rounded them up. Cena went back to the camp with them to ensure they didn't get lost in the hills but Broga followed the boy and his sheep until he found the small settlement where he lived.

It consisted of four round huts, partially sunk into the ground, with wattle and daub walls and bundles of grass laid on a conical wicker frame for a roof. Broga didn't suppose they differed much from those lived in by their ancestors a thousand years ago.

There were two cows nearby, presumably kept to provide milk, butter and cheese, a few chickens and a fat sow with a litter of piglets. Everyone emerged from the huts when the boy drove the sheep into a crudely made enclosure. They stood around him looking alarmed as the boy pointed back the way he'd come. Obviously, he was telling them about the strange warriors.

A man cuffed the boy about the ears, yelling at him as he did so. Presumably he was bringing home to the hapless youth his stupidity in coming straight back to the settlement. Broga chuckled at the boy's humiliation and watched as everyone gathered their possessions in a flurry of activity before heading into the hills, taking their livestock with them.

The Mercians had nothing against these poor people and they represented no threat. The people who'd fled their settlement had nothing to fear but they didn't know that. The army would take what they needed but that was all. Their quarrel was with King Hwgan, not his subjects. Any wanton destruction, pillage or rape would be severely punished by Lady Æthelflæd.

It would be dark soon and so Broga quickly retraced his steps to the campsite.

At dusk the next day they climbed the final range of hills and looked down on Llyn Syfaddon. The sun reflected off its mirror-like surface, turning a broad line across the water a deep orange, as it sank in the west. The lake was a mile and a half long, half a mile wide and was shaped like a legless horse with its head lowered to drink. The crannog was just visible jutting into the lake where the horse's rump would be. Banan, Broga and Cena studied the approach to the crannog from the north and then rejoined their men by the stream in the valley below to camp for the night.

The next day they would attack the crannog and, hopefully, capture Hwgan alive.

✝✝✝

However, King Hwgan wasn't there. He and six hundred of his warriors had set out the previous day to ambush the Mercians just before the point where the River Usk turned north. The area was boggy, as was the land to the south of Llyn Syfaddon. The obvious route for the Mercians would take them north up to a saddle between two steep hills and then along the north-east shore of the lake towards the crannog.

The Welsh would be outnumbered by the Mercians but Hwgan would assume that holding the hills above the pass would give him a distinct advantage, especially as he expected that Æthelflæd's army would be spread out in a long column.

'It's an obvious place for an ambush,' Æthelflæd said as she surveyed the climb up to the saddle.

She had ridden forward with Deorwine and Abrecan. The page held their horses whilst they climbed up to the top of a hill to the south-east of the pass to get a better view.

'I agree,' Deorwine said, nodding. 'Perhaps we should ride up the other valley and take a look. Perhaps there is a more accessible route to the top of the ridge to the right of the saddle. If so, we could capture the heights on one side before venturing through the pass?'

At dawn the next day three hundred of her fittest archers and spearmen left the Mercian camp under the command of Cadda, the twenty-year-old Ealdorman of Herefordscīr. They entered the long valley to the east of the saddle and climbed the steep re-entrant that led up to the top of the ridge. The final two hundred yards were almost vertical and it took far longer than Deorwine had estimated. One man fell to his death on the rocks below and a few others broke an ankle, a leg or an arm. The rest made it safely to the top of the ridge.

What worried Cadda more than anything was that the screams of the falling man and the cries of those who had broken a bone would be heard by the enemy. Thankfully, the wind carried any noise in the opposite direction and four hours after setting out they came to the point where they could look down the southern slope of the ridge.

Cadda estimated that three hundred Welshmen were concealed in the dips and behind rocks below them. He looked over to the camp where the main body of the Mercians remained waiting for his attack to commence. No doubt the Welsh were suspicious about the length of time it had taken them to break camp but, much to his surprise, they hadn't placed a piquet on top of the ridge. There was a group of horsemen on top of the hill opposite but they seemed more interested in the Mercians below and none looked across at the ridge opposite.

He beckoned the archers forward and, as soon as they were ready, he gave the order to commence firing. Several volleys struck Hwgan's men before they reacted. With cries of rage, they began climbing up towards the archers. Cadda had kept his spearmen back out of sight of the climbing Welsh. More and more of them fell to arrows and when the last hundred and seventy breasted the crest, the archers fell back and two hundred spearmen charged into them.

The fight was brief and bloody. Those who survived fled back down the slope, several tumbling and breaking bones in their hurry to escape. Cadda estimated that no more than eighty survived to reach the bottom where they ran into the advancing Mercian main body.

Hwgan sat on his horse on top of the hill opposite the ridge which Cadda had just captured. He recognised that his gamble hadn't paid off. Instead of walking into his ambush, the Lady of the Mercians had outwitted him. He watched the battle unfolding below him with a sinking heart. It was time to leave.

The Mercians would shortly be able to cross over the saddle and make their way up the east side of Llyn Syfaddon before following the northern shore to his crannog. However, the majority were on foot. If he and his mounted bodyguard followed the valley of the Usk northwards, he could cut around the western side of the lake and reach the crannog first.

He couldn't hold it just with his bodyguard and the warriors he'd left there. He abandoned any hope of defeating the Mercians; he would have to disappear into the mountains after collecting his new wife and his children. His priority now was to get back to the crannog before the Mercians could get there. He would leave his first wife behind for Æthelflæd to do with as she saw fit. He'd repudiated her and he couldn't care less what happened to her.

Just as he was about to abandon the rest of his army to its fate, he glanced towards the lake. To his consternation, he saw a plume of black smoke drifting lazily upwards in the slight breeze. From its location it could only mean one thing: his crannog was on fire.

✝✝✝

Banan and his men had had no difficulty in capturing the collection of primitive huts that nestled along the shoreline near the crannog. They had expected opposition from warriors but the only defenders were old men and young boys. They might not have been warriors in their prime but they didn't lack courage. Seven of the greybeards and half a dozen young boys had either been killed or badly wounded before common sense prevailed and the handful that were left surrendered.

Having secured the village, Banan turned his attention to the crannog. Capturing that wouldn't be so easy. It was defended by a dozen young warriors and several of them were armed with bows. These were longer and more powerful than those that his own archers carried. He considered he was safe at a distance of a hundred and fifty yards from the Welsh archers but they soon disabused him of than. A volley of arrows struck his men, killing two and wounding three more. He and the rest quickly retreated into the huts behind them.

'Any ideas?' he asked Cena, Broga and two of his senior warriors.

'Fire arrows,' Cena suggested succinctly.

'But their bows have a greater range than ours,' one of the warriors pointed out. 'Our men would be struck down before we could get close enough.'

'Not if we shelter behind hurdles carried by other warriors,' Broga put in. 'We can cut out sections of wall from the huts. Our bowmen don't need to expose themselves; they can send fire arrows at high trajectory into the thatched roof of the large hut on the crannog.'

An hour later the defenders threw down their weapons and ran along the walkway to get away from the choking black smoke. They were followed by a handful of women and children together with a few men. The latter weren't fighters but slaves and servants.

Banan discovered that he'd captured both Hwgan's rejected wife and her replacement. Better still, five of the children turned out to be the king's offspring, including his heir. Added to the forty two women and twenty three other children that they had already taken prisoner, they would fetch a hefty sum in the slave markets. Most of what they fetched would go to pay for the cost of the campaign but he and his men would receive a share in the proceeds.

Before sorting out the captives he'd taken the precaution of deploying scouts. Now one of them came riding in at a gallop.

'Banan, riders are approaching from the south- west.'

'How many?'

'About thirty I'd say.'

'Are they ours?'

'The banner says otherwise. It's yellow with what looks like a blue bird on it.'

'A bat with outstretched wings perhaps; that's the emblem of Brycheiniog!' Banan said jubilantly. 'Perhaps we can still capture Hwgan. Get the men ready to intercept them.'

'What about the prisoners?' Cena asked.

'You stay with a dozen men to guard them. The rest of you, come with me.'

As soon as Banan's men had galloped off, one of the women attacked Cena with her bare hands and the rest followed her lead. It was futile. Cena cut her down with his sword and four others died at the hands of the other guards before the abortive escape attempt fizzled out. He cursed. Her stupid action had cost them five slaves. She'd been one of the prettier ones too.

As soon as Hwgan saw Banan and over thirty men galloping towards them he realised that his family had been captured. He could have engaged the oncoming Mercians but the chances of being either killed or captured were too high. He led his men away to the south-west, chased by the Mercians.

The Mercians began to overhaul the Welshmen initially, their horses being faster than the hill ponies ridden by the Welsh. However, once the latter had splashed across through a ford and reached the far side of the Usk, that changed. The ponies were more surefooted over the rocky ground on the far bank and their greater stamina began to show. It wasn't long before the Mercians' horses were left behind. Reluctantly Banan watched the Welsh disappear into the hills before he turned back towards the lake.

✝✝✝

'We lost just over a hundred men, including those of Banan's who were killed in capturing the crannog,' Cadda reported to Æthelflæd. 'Regretably, one of those killed was Deorwine. He died heroically whilst leading the attack uphill against the main body of Welshmen.'

Æthelflæd nodded sadly. Deorwine had been a member of her husband's gesith long before he became Ealdorman of Hwicce and then later the Hereræswa. More importantly, he'd been the husband of her greatest friend and confidante, Cuthfleda. With his loss it seemed that most of the people she had known for most of her life had now gone.

After Cadda left, she became aware of quiet sobbing that came from a corner of her tent. Abrecan was curled up in a ball and her heart went out to him. His father had been his only relative after Cuthfelda's death and now he was all alone in the world.

'Come here, Abrecan,' she said softly.

The boy rose to his feet and wiped his wet face and his snot on his sleeve before walking over to her and bowing.

'Yes, lady?'

She held out her arms and he ran into them. As she hugged him close to her he started to cry again and she comforted him until he stopped. He stepped back and she wiped his fresh tears away with a square of clean linen.

'I'm sorry, lady.'

'Don't be. I feel like crying myself. Your father was dear to me; your mother even more so. As you are now an orphan with no other adult to look after you, I've decided to make you my ward. You'll remain as a page in my household until you're old enough to train as a warrior and then if you wish, you may join my gesith.'

'Thank you, lady. I don't know what to say.'

'Then say nothing. Now go and change that filthy tunic for a clean one and bring me something to eat and drink.'

†††

Wynnstan awoke to find his body servant, Eohric, trying to dribble water between his lips.

'What are you doing?' he said, trying to sit up.

Then he fell back with a groan. His chest felt as if a horse had stamped on it.

'Lie still, lord. You're recovering from a collapsed lung, not to mention a spear wound.'

'Where am I?' he said, looking around him at the whitewashed stone walls with a crucifix as the sole decoration.

'In Hagustaldesham Monastery in Northumbria.'

'Northumbria? How did I get here?'

'You were brought here after you were wounded at the Battle of Corebricg. The infirmarian said that you're lucky to be alive.'

'I remember now, that bastard Arne deliberately left me exposed to a Danish spearman. As soon as I'm well enough I'll kill the whoreson.'

'Someone's saved you the trouble. He was stabbed in the back and killed later in the battle.'

At that moment, the door to the small cell opened and a young novice came in. Wynnstan thought that she was probably no older than thirteen. She reminded him of someone but he couldn't think who it might be.

'This is Edith,' Eohrid said, getting to his feet and bowing. 'She's been looking after you.'

As soon as he heard the name he realised who she reminded him of; she was Æthelstan's half-sister, the daughter of Æthelstan's mother and the Ætheling Æðelwold. He was an ætheling of Wessex who had died in battle after challenging his cousin, Eadweard, for the throne.

Edith smiled at Wynnstan before she changed his dressing.

'It's healing nicely,' she said as she tied the fresh bandage in place.

'How long before I can get up?'

'Not for another two weeks,' she replied. 'We can see that it's healing on the outside but we don't know what's happening inside you. You're fortunate in that Brother Alexis is far more knowlegable than most physicians in this part of the world. They wouldn't have any idea what part lungs play in keeping us alive.'

'Alexis? What sort of name is that?'

'It's Greek. He was captured during a Viking raid and brought back to Jorvik to be sold. Thankfully someone recognised that he was a gifted healer but the archbishop wouldn't let him stay, accusing him of heresy. He eventually found his way here and the abbot welcomed the knowledge he possessed with open arms.'

Well, I'm most grateful, although I'm not sure what a lung is.'

'It's like a bellows in your chest; it enables you to breathe. The air you take in contains a substance called οξυγόνο in Greek; there isn't a word for it in Ænglisc as far as I know. It passes from the lungs into your bloodstream. Without οξυγόνο you would die.'

The explanation came from an elderly monk who'd stepped into the room unnoticed. His skin looked as if he'd spent a long time in the sun and then faded, giving it a sallow look. He spoke Ænglisc well, but with a distinct accent.

'Thank you, brother. I gather I owe you my life.'

'Don't thank me, my son; thank God and His Son, Jesus Christ.'

'Nevertheless, I'm beholden to you for saving me.'

Wynnstan paused but, as the old monk turned to leave, he asked him the question which had been bothering him ever since he'd woken up.

'When will I be able to go home, Brother Alexis?'

'You can take light exercise in a fortnight and then gradually get yourself fit again. Once I'm certain that the inside of your body has healed, you can train more strenuously. As to your return to Mercia,' the monk shrugged. 'That's a question I can't answer, nor can anyone else here. We're a long way from the sea – the Íralandes Sæ and the Nord Sæ are equidistant from here, or so I'm told. The coast of one is controlled by King Ragnall of Mann and the other by the Earl of Bernicia.'

Wynnstan considered his options. Going west would be to step into the jaws of Mercia's enemy; and how would he secure passage on a Norse ship? On the other hand, whilst Earl Ealdred might help him if he went east, getting back to Mercia, or even Wessex, before the winter gales would be difficult. Going overland was even more perilous as he and Eohric would need to find their way through territory held by Ragnall.

It seemed he was marooned at Hagustaldesham until the spring.

CHAPTER SIXTEEN

Spring and Summer 917

Wynnstan stood looking out over the grey sea from the ramparts of Bebbanburg. Edith stood by his side, oddly dressed as a boy. After her mother had died she had joined her half-brother, Æthelstan, at the Mercian court but Æthelflæd had become alarmed when Eadweard had asked her to send the girl to him.

Her brother had never forgiven Edith's father, Æðelwold, for trying to usurp his throne, especially as he'd allied himself with the Danes to do so. He regarded that as the greater crime after all that his father, King Ælfred, had done to keep the Danes out of Wessex.

His loathing for Æðelwold had extended to his daughter and Æthelflæd didn't trust his motives. He was more than likely to take reprisals and sell the girl into slavery than look after her.

Æthelflæd had arranged for her to be taken to Bebbanburg and from there Eadwulf, who was the earl at the time, had sent her to the monastery at Hagustaldesham in the south-western corner of his earldom. It was the most remote place from Wessex Æthelflæd could think of.

In the past seven years, Edith hoped that memories of her father's betrayal would have faded and, given the choice between taking her vows and becoming a nun, or risking a return to her brother's side, she'd opted for the latter. She was a spirited girl, in much the same mould as Æthelflæd and Cuthfleda, and the cloistered life of a nun would have bored her to tears. She'd therefore implored him to take her with him when he left Hagustaldesham.

Wynnstan thought that a young and pretty girl travelling with only a half-recovered warrior and his body servant for protection would be tempting fate, so he'd suggested that she cut her hair and dress as a boy. Her figure hadn't yet developed as a woman and was still sufficiently boyish to allow her to get away with the deception. Even Earl Ealdred's wife hadn't discovered the truth but then the two of them hadn't come into contact much.

He'd secured passage for the three of them on a knarr carrying a cargo down to Malberthorp, a place he'd last visited when he'd been sent to recover Saint Oswald's remains from some ruins that were in the middle of Danish held territory at the time. Now the area was a part of King Eadweard's realm. From there it should be relatively easy to purchase horses, travel down into Wessex and thence back to Mercia.

He was eager to return to Astrid, who must be wondering whether he was dead or alive. There had been no means of communicating between Mercia and Bernicia and so he'd been unable to write to her. Similarly, although Æthelflæd would have told Astrid where he'd been taken after the battle, she had no means of knowing whether he was alive or dead.

Naturally, Wynnstan was also unaware of events at Rumcofen. Astrid had considered trying to abort the foetus but Kjestin had convinced her that it would be a grave sin, akin to murder, and so she'd decided to have the child and then get it adopted.

'Come, we must get ready to leave at high tide,' Wynnstan told the girl.

Over the time they'd been on the road together he'd grown fond of Edith, not in a sexual way, but like father and daughter. He worried what would happen to her once Eadweard heard that she was back in Mercia and planned to discuss making her his ward with Astrid. If she returned to Glowecestre it wouldn't be long before her whereabouts became common knowledge.

What he didn't know was that Glowecestre was no longer the capital of Mercia. During the winter, construction of the new burh at Tomtun, the ancient capital of Mercia sited just north of the border with the Danelaw, had been completed and Æthelflæd now based herself there. It would be the springboard of her invasion into Danish Mercia later that year.

Malberthorp was little different to when he'd landed there before, except there was now a jetty at which to load and unload cargoes. Five years ago ships had either to be beached or their goods had to be ferried ashore using small boats. The other change was to the occupant of the hall. The Danish jarl had been replaced by a Saxon thegn.

'The interior is still unsafe,' he warned Wynnstan. 'Although the king defeated the revolt by the Danes last year, parts of the shire are still fairly lawless. I recommend you take passage on the next ship heading south.'

He and his companions had to wait three days before a ship arrived en route to Lundenburg. It wasn't a knarr but a longship; one used as a trader, not a ship of war. The crew were Frisians, which slightly worried Wynnstan because they had a reputation as pirates as well as merchants. Nevertheless, he paid the captain and they set off the next day.

Once they were at sea his worst fears were realised. The crew didn't inspire him with confidence and one of them worried Wynnstan in particular. He was a man in his late thirties with only one eye who kept giving Edith lecherous looks. He had a nasty suspicion that he was interested because he thought that she was a boy, not that because he'd seen through her disguise.

When the opportunity presented itself he had a quiet word with the captain. They conversed in Ænglisc which most of the crew didn't understand.

'Kobe likes boys for sure,' the man said with a shrug. 'It doesn't bother me; it's his business but I'll warn him off your servant if you're worried. However, he's always generous to the boys he takes to his bed.'

Wynnstan was appalled at the captain's attitude and he began to think that it might have been better if they'd risked going overland.

He didn't know what the captain had said to Kobe but, far from putting him off Edith, he now seemed even keener on her and gave Wynnstan nasty looks whenever he saw him.

Things came to a head on the third night out but not in the way that Wynnstan had feared. The three of them had been asleep in the bows of the ship when both he and Eohric had been awoken by a commotion and a lot of swearing. He looked over towards Edith, fearing that Kobe had tried to abuse her but the girl was convulsed in laughter as Kobe stomped away still swearing vociferously.

'What happened?'

'He tried to grope my crotch,' she said with a giggle. 'When he found out that I was a girl he recoiled in disgust. I couldn't resist teasing him and so I grabbed the back of his head and kissed him on the mouth. He spat, swore a lot and wiped his mouth with his sleeve before retreating in haste.'

The story was all over the ship the next morning. The rest of the crew thought it was hilarious and made fun of Kobe. That didn't go down well with the one-eyed sailor and the looks he gave Edith and Wynnstan were venomous.

'He's likely to try and get his revenge on us for his humiliation,' Wynnstan warned the other two. 'From now on one of us will need to be awake in case he tries to kill us during the night.'

'Do you think that's likely, lord?' Eohric asked doubtfully. 'How would he explain the bodies?'

'He wouldn't need to if he tipped them over the side for the fish to feed on. Do you know how to use a knife?'

'I've gutted fish in the monastery kitchen and skinned a few animals on those rare occasions when we were allowed to eat meat,' Edith replied with a frown.

'Good. Here, take my dagger. I've got my seax as well as my sword and Eohric has a dagger. Try to wound, not kill. Although I'm certain that he'll try and murder us, killing him will not sit well with his friends.'

The first part of the night passed quietly. Eohric was on watch but, after an hour or so, he found the motion of the ship quite soporific and he began to drift off. Luckily, the sound of someone tripping over something on deck followed by a soft curse brought him back to full wakefulness. He kicked Edith and nudged Wynnstan's shoulder. Neither moved but he knew that they were now wide awake.

Suddenly Kobe's shadow loomed over him and the moonlight glinted on the blade of a knife. Eohric stabbed upwards from where he sat and had the satisfaction of feeling resistance as the dagger entered flesh somewhere towards the top of the assailant's leg.

Before Kobe could utter a sound, Wynnstan reared up behind him and clamped a hand over his mouth. The sailor struggled but the three of them pulled him to the deck and whilst Edith and Wynnstan held him down, Eohric put his hands around his throat and kept them there until he ceased to move.

'Well, so much for not killing him,' Wynnstan whispered. 'Come on let's get him over the side.'

Neither the struggle nor the splash as the body hit the water seemed to have awoken the crew sleeping further down the deck. The only man awake was the steersman and he was right down the far end of the ship.

'Now all we have to worry about is the blood he shed after you knifed him,' Wynnstan whispered.

It was difficult to see in the darkness but they were confident that it had only fallen on Eohric's cloak. It followed Kobe over the side.

✝✝✝

Æthelflæd was annoyed at having to travel all the way to Lundenburg to meet Eadweard. He wanted to co-ordinate their attack on the Daneland but he'd spent the winter there whereas she'd had to travel from Tomtun, keeping well inside the boundary marked by Casingc Stræt. Had she been able to travel down the old

Roman road the journey would have been a lot quicker and more comfortable.

When she finally arrived, she was feeling grumpy and resentful. However, her mood changed as soon as she was shown into the king's presence. She was surprised and delighted to find someone who she thought was long dead deep in conversation with her brother.

'Wynnstan, it does my heart good to see you. Not having heard anything I feared you had succumbed to your injury.'

'I would have done, lady,' he said as he got to his feet and bowed, 'had it not been for the infirmarian at Hagustaldesham Monastery, a Greek by the name of Brother Alexis.'

'Yes, yes,' Eadweard interrupted testily. 'You can tell my sister all about your adventures later. She and I need to discuss matters that are more important. You may leave us.'

'I'd like him to stay, Eadweard. I intend to appoint Wynnstan as my head of scouts for the forthcoming campaign. As such, he'll need to know our plans.'

Wynnstan's heart sank. Astrid didn't even know that he was alive and all he wanted to do was return to her side. Now it seemed that wouldn't be possible until the autumn at the earliest. Nevertheless, he forced himself to smile and thank her for the honour.

'Very well,' Eadweard agreed with a nod. 'Lord Osfirth will join us presently so I suggest we wait for him.'

'I was under the impression that you intended to replace him as your hereræswa,' Æthelflæd said with some asperity.

Her dislike for the man was well known and she had urged her brother to replace him several times. Eadweard glanced at Wynnstan and pursed his lips.

'Perhaps that's a conversation for another time,' he muttered.

At that moment Osfirth entered the room and bowed to the king. He completely ignored the other two and went to sit beside Eadweard.

'Now that we are all here, let me remind you of the latest situation,' he began before Osfirth interrupted him.

'What is this low-born thegn doing here, cyning? Should we be discussing strategy in front of him; especially as he's married to a Dane.'

Wynnstan leaped to his feet, his eyes blazing with anger.

'I've proved my loyalty to Mercia time and time again. I'll not take insults from a man who's responsible for the murder of one of his fellow ealdormen.'

He regretted the words as soon as they were out of his mouth.

'What are you referring to?' Eadweard asked coldly. 'Be very careful what you say, thegn.'

Wynnstan knew that an abject apology and a retraction was the only way he might recover from his allegation but the way that Osfirth sat back and sneered at him made him reckless.

'It's common knowledge, cyning. One of Lord Osfirth's men killed Lord Odda in battle because he was a rival for the position of Wessex's hereræswa.'

'Can you substantiate that?'

'Er, no cyning, but everyone believes it to be true.'

'Lies spread about me by Odda's son, the traitorous Wælwulf, nothing more,' Osfirth said disdainfully.

'You will leave us, Wynnstan, and confine yourself to your lodging whilst I consider what to do about you. Tell the captain of my gesith, Galan, where you are staying. You are not to leave there for any reason until I send for you. Do you understand?'

'Yes, cyning.'

He felt a fool and he sensed that Æthelflæd was furious with him. He bowed and marched stiff-backed out of the room. As he made his way back to the tavern where he and the other two had taken a room he wondered what to do. He wasn't so worried about himself but he didn't want Eadweard to know that Edith was within his grasp. He'd deliberately didn't inform Galan about the tavern; that could wait until he'd figured out what to do.

†††

'He's my subject and I'll decide what punishment is fitting. I agree that he was foolish to make an unsubstantiated accusation against Osfirth but he's correct; there is a strong rumour that he paid one of his hearth warriors to remove Odda because he feared you were about to appoint him as hereræswa. Osfirth suspected that his influence over you was waning and decided to take drastic action.'

Eadweard sighed wearily. He'd sent Osfirth away whilst he and his sister discussed the matter. He knew that Æthelflæd disliked Osfirth intensely, partially because Osfirth's sister was Eadweard's wife and mother to his heir. Æthelflæd had never ceased to maintain that the next king should be Æthelstan and he was well aware that she had proof of his marriage to Æthelstan's mother. She'd never produced it because it would severely embarrass him and weaken his position. Kings should never be caught lying.

'Perhaps, it's true; who knows? It's just a rumour and Wynnstan was an idiot to raise it, however provoked he felt. I can't be seen to let him get away with it.'

'I need him as my head of scouts. There is no one better.'

'You hardly need scouts to lay siege to in Deoraby.'

'Really? So it wouldn't be prudent to deploy patrols to ensure that Deoraby isn't about to be relieved by the Danes of Ledecestre or any of the other jarldoms in the Danelaw?'

'Well, yes, but you don't need Wynnstan for that. I'm sure you have other proficient scouts.'

'Of course, but he's the best; he's the one who's trained most of the others and he's their natural commander. Besides, I owe him a great deal for his past service – most recently at the Battle of Corebricg where he was severely wounded and nearly died.'

'I appreciate that but I can't allow the insult to Lord Osfirth to go unpunished. The only solution as far as I can see is to invite them to settle their differences by invoking trial by combat.'

She could hardly disagree with that and she realised how clever her brother had been. If Wynnstan was killed, the matter was resolved and there was nothing she could do about it; if Osfirth died then Eadweard would be rid of his troublesome brother-in-law without being blamed by the Lady Ælfflæd or their sons.

Wynnstan had almost decided to flee and hope that he would be safe from Eadweard's vengeance if he managed to reach Cæstirscīr when Eohric returned from purchasing a new cloak in the market. When he told Wynnstan that he was to fight Osfirth, Wynnstan forgot all about flight and concentrated on training for the forthcoming duel.

He remembered that he hadn't let Galan know where to find him and he sent Eohric to inform him. When the servant returned, he sent him off on a new errand: to take Edith to Æthelflæd and hand her over to her for safekeeping. He did worry about her remaining in the same place as Eadweard but Edith could more easily pass as one of Æthelflæd's pages, of whom she had several. Pages served royalty, not common thegns.

The next morning - the day of the duel - dawned fine and clear but as Wynnstan made his way to the field outside the walls where the fight would take place, clouds were rushing in from the east and the wind picked up. By the time that he arrived with Eohric the sky was overcast and rain threatened.

He breathed a sigh of relief. He was wearing boots which had been adapted just in case the grass was slippery underfoot. He'd had nails driven through the sole to make spikes. Not only would they prevent him slipping but a kick would do more damage to his opponent than a normal boot would.

His main worry was his breathing. Ever since his lung had collapsed he'd become breathless if he exerted himself too much. He would need to move as economically as possible if he was to avoid panting like an old man.

Osfirth was already waiting when he arrived. He paced up and down practicing various moves, cuts and thrusts. Wynnstan resisted the temptation to do likewise but instead he studied his opponent's technique. As he watched it began to drizzle.

A large crowd had come to watch. Lundenburg was populated by a mixture of Mercians, Saxons and Danes. The Mercians cheered for Wynnstan whilst many of the Saxons supported Osfirth but not all. The Danes hoped that they would kill each other.

Three blasts on a hunting horn announced the arrival of King Eadweard and the Lady Æthelflæd, who dismounted and took their seats on the hastily erected dais. When the king waved to indicate that he was ready, Galan gave the signal and the two men advanced towards one another just as the rain began to fall in earnest.

Both were wearing a byrnie over a leather jerkin and a helmet and each was armed with a sword and a large circular shield. In Wynnstan's case, the armour and the shield had been borrowed from one of Æthelflæd's hearth warriors.

The first attacks and counter moves weren't intended to resolve the matter quickly; they were testing each other's reflexes and learning their strengths and weaknesses. The clash of sword on sword and sword on shield rang around the arena until suddenly Wynnstan made a serious attack. He thrust his sword at Osfirth's face and, as he blocked it with his shield, Wynnstan brought the edge of his own shield down hard onto one of his adversary's shoes, breaking two of his toes.

Osfirth bit back a cry of pain as he hobbled backwards and Wynnstan was pleased to see that he'd lost his temper. However, he was out of breath himself and glad of the brief pause in the fight.

Osfirth came in and feinted at Wynnstan's face. He ducked but the ealdorman was expecting it and he brought the pommel of his sword down hard on Wynnstan's head. The helmet absorbed most of the blow but he felt dizzy and disorientated. With a cry of triumph, Osfirth thrust the point of his sword towards Wynnstan's throat.

The ground was now churned up and it was muddy underfoot; just the conditions that Wynnstan had hoped for. Osfirth slipped and his blade merely caught Wynnstan's shoulder, breaking a couple of the chainmail links but doing no damage to the man himself.

Osfirth was now off-balance and his body cannoned into his opponent's. Wynnstan was too close to him to be able to use his sword but he was able to use his shield. He was out of breath and he knew that he'd have to end this quickly before his struggle to breathe made him too vulnerable. He brought his shield up, catching Osfirth's exposed throat with the metal rim.

Now it was his opponent's turn to gasp for breath. His throat had been badly bruised by the impact and started to swell, constricting his larynx. Osfirth dropped his sword and put his hand to his damaged throat, using his shield to push Wynnstan away.

The latter saw his opportunity and stabbed down at Osfirth's right knee. He felt a jolt as the point scraped across the bottom of the patella at the base of his thigh bone and enter the soft tissue at the top of the tibia.

Osfirth collapsed with a howl of pain and Wynnstan, now wheezing badly, held a wavering sword to the other man's swollen throat. He looked up at the dais where the king and his sister sat.

'I think I've proved my accusation to be just, cyning,' he gasped. 'Do you wish me to spare him so that you can deal with him justly?'

Eadweard dithered. He would have dearly loved to be rid of Osfirth but prudence dictated that he should be merciful. Osfirth still had strong allies in the West Country. That aside, he dreaded to think what the reaction of his wife and their sons would be if he had him killed. If Wynnstan had finished him off he couldn't have been blamed for Osfirth's death. He cursed the Mercian for not doing so.

'You've made your point, Wynnstan,' he said reluctantly.

With that, the king stalked off, mounted his horse and galloped away before his escort and other nobles had a chance to follow him.

Æthelflæd beckoned Wynnstan to her side as servants and a physician rushed to the side of the wounded ealdorman. He was unable to get to his feet and had to suffer the indignity of being carried off the field of combat on the top of a trestle table.

'I think it would be prudent for you to leave Lundenburg before the supporters of Lord Osfirth arrange for you to be killed,' she said quietly. 'Cedric and the *Saint Werburgh* are moored in the port. I'll send orders for him to take you back to Cæstir. You'd better see Lord Ywer and tell him what's happened before you travel on to Rumcofen. It might also be a good idea to write to your wife before you suddenly appear; she thinks that you're dead, as we all did when we heard nothing for eight months. Oh, there's something I doubt you'd have heard yet. Astrid is pregnant and may well have had the baby by the time you get there but I'll let her tell you the tale. Now go, I can see Osfirth's hearth warriors heading this way.'

Wynnstan didn't have time to ponder what she meant by letting Astrid tell him the tale but, once he was safely at sea, having collected Edith and Eohric, he could think of nothing else. Of course, he was delighted by the news about another child but there was obviously more to it than that. He chafed with impatience as the ship made its way along the south coast, around the southern tip of Cornweal and up the coast of Wealas before finally entering the estuary of the Dēvā.

He found that Ywer had made a good recovery; he could even use a sword in his left hand but he would never be able to survive for long in a shieldwall. Irwyn had settled into his new role as the shire reeve well and had the tact to let his father carry out many of the duties of ealdorman as he was able to. However, it was obvious to Wynnstan that the son would assume those duties more and more as time went on, especially as Ywer found writing left-handed was beyond him. Clerks could write routine documents but a noble needed to be able to pen secret and personal letters himself.

A messenger had been sent to Rumcofen with the good news about Wynnstan's survival immediately after his arrival in Cæstir. He left Edith in the care of Kjestin and rode on with Eohric the following day. As soon as he arrived at his hall he rushed in to see Astrid only to find that she had just given birth to a baby boy. He'd expected a joyful welcome from his wife but, even allowing for exhaustion following the birth, he could sense that she greeted his return with some trepidation.

He was puzzled by Astrid's strange attitude to his return but he couldn't put his finger on the reason until he saw the baby. It looked nothing like him and it didn't look much like Astrid either. Then it came to him. Astrid was contrite and ashamed and there could only be one explanation. She'd betrayed him with a lover.

He stormed out of the room, ignoring his two children who'd come running to greet him as soon as they'd heard he was home, and mounted his horse. A minute or two later he galloped out of Rumcofen, his sight blurred by tears. He didn't know or care where he was going. He just had to get as far away from her and her bastard child as he could.

CHAPTER SEVENTEEN

Summer and Autumn 917

Eventually Wynnstan's horse began to tire and he slowed it down to a walk. When he came to a narrow stream that tumbled over a few rocks into a small pool before continuing the headlong journey downstream, he dismounted and tied the horse to a tree before going to sit on a rock shelf and gazing at the water below; not that he saw it. His eyes were unfocused and all he could see was Astrid wantonly welcoming another man into her arms. The man's back was to him and his body was slightly out of focus so he had no idea as to his identity.

He didn't know how long he sat there but eventually the sound of his horse snorting dragged him back to reality. His hand went to the hilt of his sword before he realised that the rider was his son, Sicga.

'What are you doing riding Eohric's horse?'

'It was the only one saddled and ready when you took off,' the boy replied apprehensively.

'I want to be alone,' Wynnstan told him, a little more irritably than he had intended. 'I'm sorry. I'm not angry at you.'

'You shouldn't be at mother either; you don't understand,' Sicga said as he jumped down from the horse that was much too large for him.

Wynnstan looked at the son he hadn't seen for the best part of a year. He was eight now but he was large for his age, looking more like a boy of ten.

'What's there to understand? She betrayed me with another as soon as I was out of sight, judging by the fact she's given birth to the brat nine months later.'

'Mother's betrayed no one,' Sicga said angrily, glaring at his father. 'You betrayed her by leaving her to be raped after she begged you not to go.'

'Raped? What are you talking about?'

'I didn't realise what was going on at the time. When I rushed to try and stop Chad hurting mother I thought he was attacking her. I'm older and wiser now. He raped her before she killed him.'

'Chad?'

Wynnstan's mind was in a whirl. For the first time he realised that Chad hadn't come to greet him as he always did.

'Chad's dead?'

'Yes, I tried to stop him but he knocked me out.'

Sicga hoped that his explanation would clear the air and that his father would ride back with him but the story of what had happened seemed to have driven his father into a stupor. He got up and wandered off in a daze. When the boy tried to follow him he barked at him to go away.

'I'm sorry, Sicga. I didn't mean to yell at you but I really do need to be alone at the moment.'

The boy, feeling depressed and angry, watched his father climb back into the saddle of the big horse – not without some difficulty – and slowly ride away.

It was two days before Wynnstan re-appeared. During that time he lived rough, surviving on berries and tickling a couple of trout to cook on an open fire. Hunger eventually brought him to his senses and he reluctantly headed back to Rumcofen.

'I understand that the baby wasn't your fault,' he said to Astrid after a tearful reunion. 'I still can't believe that Chad would betray me in this way; he must have been driven insane by lust, I suppose. However, we can't keep his bastard. We'll need to find someone to foster it.'

'At first the only thing I wanted was to get rid of it,' Astrid confessed, 'but it's not the baby's fault. I've carried it for nine months and in that time I've grown to love it. I realise that I'm asking a lot but I want to keep it.'

Wynnstan could tell by the set of her jaw that his wife was determined to bring up Chad's bastard whatever he said. However, he was equally unwavering in his resolve not to have to see the child every day. He would be a constant reminder of his wife's rape and he just couldn't cope with that.

'I'm sorry; I can't agree to that. Either we send the brat away or I'm leaving. Æthelflæd has offered me the post of captain of her scouts for the campaign in the Danelaw. I was going to decline using the excuse that I'm still not fully fit but perhaps it would be best if I accepted after all.'

'You must do as you please; you usually do,' she retorted.

She regretted the words as soon as she'd uttered them but it was too late. Wynnstan stormed out of her chamber and at dawn he left Rumcofen heading for Tomtun. He left Tidhelm, the man that Irwyn had recommended as Chad's successor, behind with most of his men. The only warriors he took with him were Sawin and Wardric, together with his body servant, Eohric.

Five days later he reached Tomtun to find that he was too late. Æthelflæd, Æthelstan and the Mercian army had already left to besiege Deoraby.

✝✝✝

'I'm sorry, Wynnstan,' Æthelflæd told him when he arrived at Deoraby, 'I've put the Ealdorman of Tamuuordescīr in charge of the scouts patrolling the approaches from Ledecestre and the North. I needed someone to warn me of any attempt by the Danes or the Norse to relieve our siege and you weren't here.

'As you probably know, Irwyn is in charge of the fyrd from Cæstirscīr. I can only suggest you attach yourself to him.'

It was a bitter blow. Far from holding the important post as Head of Scouts, Wynnstan found himself without a role. Irwyn would be keen to demonstrate his leadership abilities in his father's absence and, as shire reeve, he would doubtless resent being advised what to do by Wynnstan.

He went and found a lonely spot upstream and sat staring into the water. For the first time since he was a child he felt utterly lost. He brooded on Chad's treachery and what he saw as the irreconcilable differences between Astrid and himself over the bastard child she'd borne. He failed to understand why she hadn't got rid of it as soon as she'd found out that she was pregnant. The woman who acted as midwife had potions for unmarried girls to abort an unwanted foetus.

It didn't always work, of course, but, having given birth, Wynnstan failed to understand why she refused to send the brat away. Surely she understood that having it around whilst it grew up would only serve as a reminder to both of them of the rape and of Chad's treachery. He wondered if the intense misery he felt would fade over time but he didn't think so.

He resolved to go and see Irwyn and tell him that he wished to give up his position at Rumcofen. He would also relinquish the vills he owned along the south bank of the Mǣresēa. Whoever succeeded him would need the income they produced to maintain Rumcofen's small garrison.

Of course, that would make Astrid homeless but in his anger and self-pity he thought viciously that would serve her right. He didn't even consider what would happen to his son, Sicga, and his daughter. It wasn't like Wynnstan to be so heartless but what had happened had embittered him.

'I've been looking everywhere for you.'

The voice intruded upon his misery and his first reaction was to tell the speaker to leave him alone but then he realised who it was and jumped to his feet.

'Lord Æthelstan, this is unexpected.'

King Eadweard's eldest son came and sat on the bank and motioned for Wynnstan to join him. Reluctantly Wynnstan sat down again.

'To say how sorry I was to hear what happened to your wife seems inadequate and I suspect the last thing you want to do at the moment is to talk about it, so I'll come straight to the point. We assaulted the walls yesterday and lost a lot of men, including Bawdewyn. I find myself in need of a captain.'

'You're asking me to rejoin your gesith?'

'Yes, and to lead it once more; that is, if you're willing?'

'There is nothing I'd like more at this point in time.'

The prospect of serving his old friend once more didn't completely dispel his dark mood but it gave him something important to do instead of brooding all the time.

†††

Wynnstan ducked as someone on the walkway at the top of the palisade threw a rock down at him. It struck the man climbing up the scaling ladder just below him and he fell off, breaking a leg as he landed on the hard ground.

Æthelstan's new captain scaled the last few rungs as quickly as he could, weighed down as he was by his byrnie and the heavy shield on his back. The man who'd thrown the rock appeared with another large stone held above his head. Wynnstan had drawn his sword and looped the leather strap around his wrist so that he had two hands with which to climb. Now he desperately sought to grip it, fumbling at first, but he managed to get his hand around it before the Dane above him could bring the rock down on his head.

He stabbed upwards, not caring where the point went, just so long as his adversary dropped the rock. He felt the sword meet resistance and a split second later the Dane fell away screaming in agony. Wynnstan didn't know it but he'd stabbed him in the arm pit. The point continued until it penetrated and disabled his left shoulder. He involuntarily let go of the stone, which fell onto the man's head, crushing his skull. A second later Wynnstan reached the walkway where he was immediately attacked by three defenders - two from his left and one from his right.

He quickly swung his shield around to deflect the sword and spear of the two on his left and crossed swords with the one coming from his right. The latter was inexperienced and fell for Wynnstan's feint. A moment later he fell from the walkway, blood spurting from the gaping wound in his throat.

Another Mercian reached the walkway and, thankfully, Wynnstan was able to stand back to back with him as half a dozen more defenders came at them. It seemed a long time before they realised that they were still on their own. No more Mercians had been able to scale their part of the palisade. When the man with his back to Wynnstan was killed, he realised that it was time to go.

He launched a blistering attack on the Danes who were trying to bring him down and, as soon as he had cleared a space around him, he clambered over the top of the parapet and scrambled back down the ladder.

He stood there, gasping for breath and trying to recover from his exertions, until a rock narrowly missed him. He stumbled away from the walls of Deoraby, still struggling to breathe, in the wake of the other fleeing Mercians.

When he was a safe distance away he stopped, bent over and sucked in great lungfuls of air. His lung might have healed but his breathing wasn't nearly as good as it had been. He looked back at the Danish fortifications and was horrified at the number of dead and seriously wounded strewn on the ground below the palisade. Some might have been Danes but the majority were Mercians.

'This can't go on,' one of the ealdormen stormed. 'If we go on losing men at this rate we'll be unable to defend Mercia if the Danes launch a counter-attack against us.'

There was a murmur of agreement from the nobles and captains crammed into Æthelflæd's tent. Rain poured down outside which would turn the earth into a sea of mud by morning. That would make another attack using scaling ladders more difficult.

'Does anyone have any better ideas?' the Lady of the Mercians asked.

'The mud will make any further assaults using a battering ram even less likely to succeed than the last time,' someone said.

If Æthelflæd thought that kind of remark was unhelpful she didn't say so; she just ignored it.

'We could burn the gates down,' Wynnstan found himself saying. 'A battering ram is useless because they will have placed heavy bracing inside the gates to prevent them opening. However, if we can set fire to the gates it will burn the bracing props as well.'

'How do you expect to burn anything in this rain?' one of the other nobles scoffed.

'Obviously we need to wait until it stops,' Wynnstan said patiently. 'We need time to collect all the swine we can find in any case.'

'What do you want pigs for? Are you proposing a celebration feast to lull the Danes into a false sense of security,' another man sneered.

'No, of course not,' Wynnstan snapped, holding onto his temper with difficulty. 'We need their fat to smear on the gates to ensure they burn. If we just place bundles of faggots at the bottom, all that will do is char them.'

'We could also use pine pitch,' another suggested.

'Very well,' Æthelflæd said, forestalling any further objections. 'It's your idea Wynnstan, so I'll leave it to you to make the necessary arrangements; just keep me informed.'

✝✝✝

'Quiet,' Wynnstan whispered as he led two dozen trained scouts carrying barrels of pork fat as well as pine pitch obtained from nearby charcoal burners.

One of his men tripped whilst carrying one of the barrels with another man. The group stopped, scarcely daring to breathe, but there were no cries of alarm from above and they continued to feel their way along the base of the palisade towards the main gates.

Wynnstan had waited until there was heavy cloud cover which hid the moon. It was difficult to navigate in the darkness but they were hidden from sight. It had been ten days since the last abortive attempt to scale the palisade and he hoped that the defenders had concluded that the Mercians were content to starve them into surrender. Hopefully they had relaxed their guard against another attack, especially one at night, in consequence.

They reached the gates without further incident and they proceeded to climb on one anothers' shoulders so that they could liberally daub the gates with the inflammable fat and pine pitch. They were fortunate in that the gates were set back by a foot or so from the line of the palisade. They were therefore out of sight from a patrolling sentry with a torch.

Once the gates were coated, the first set of scouts continued along the palisade and eventually made their way back to the besiegers' encampment. They were replaced by a second group who carried bundles of kindling and firewood. As soon as this was in place Wynnstan opened a container he'd been carrying. Inside lay several hot coals. Using blacksmith's tongs he placed the glowing embers inside the kindling and, as soon as he was sure that the latter had caught light, he quietly followed the others into the darkness.

It didn't take long before the growing fire was spotted and the alarm was given. Unfortunately for the Danes, the recessed gateway couldn't be doused with water from above. The only way to reach the flames was to open the gates but this wasn't possible in a hurry because of the bracing nailed in place behind them. They watched helplessly as the gates blazed fiercely until eventually all that was left was a pile of blackened timbers.

As the sky grew lighter in the grey dawn, Æthelstan led the Mercian army in a charge towards the charred gateway. Even part of the palisade on either side had been burnt away. The Danes had made a barricade just inside the gateway using carts, furniture and even some of the charred timbers from the gates but it was soon overcome. The Mercians spread out once inside the settlement and began the usual rampage: looting, raping and killing anyone in their way. Unfortunately, quite a few of those who perished happened to be the original Mercian inhabitants.

Wynnstan was sickened by what he saw but he knew that the Mercians weren't alone in the brutal sacking of anywhere that fell after a siege; Saxons, Danes and Norsemen were just as bad. Those Vikings who were still pagans were probably the worst of the lot.

He made his way back to his tent and collapsed onto his bed.

Five days later, once an in interim administration had been put in place and jarls and the few Mercian thegns who owned vills in the surrounding shire had come in to pledge allegiance to Æthelflæd, the army moved on towards Ledecestre. Whilst on the march a messenger had reached them from King Eadweard with the glad tidings that he'd captured Steanford. He was now heading towards Snotingeham.

Wynnstan rode beside Æthelstan as they advanced south east towards the next of the five boroughs. He had been depressed after Deoraby fell and now that he had little else to occupy his mind, he dwelt on the problems he'd left behind him at home. If, as seemed likely, the conquest of the Danelaw was completed this year, he didn't know what to do next. Perhaps Æthelstan would want him to stay on as his captain but he couldn't help but feel that it was a temporary appointment. Besides, he wasn't sure he wanted to return to the peacetime existence of a bachelor member of the gesith. He was now thirty and several years older than most of the gesith. He was even three years older than Æthelstan himself.

He was still reasonably fit for someone his age but breathlessness when he had to exert himself was a problem. His old wounds troubled him and he knew his reactions weren't as quick as they used to be. The sensible thing to do was to return to Rumcofen, try and make it up with Astrid and enjoy his children and a quieter life. However, the problem of Chad's child kept rearing its head. When he was suffering moments of intense depression, he thought the best solution might be to die in battle. Perhaps the attack on Ledecestre would provide the opportunity to perish heroically. He knew it was childish but he thought that might make Astrid regret her decision to keep the brat.

In the end he was denied the opportunity to even draw his sword. The elders of Ledecestre were waiting outside the gates to surrender. They had no intention of suffering the same fate as the inhabitants of Deoraby and they'd driven out the Danish jarl – a man named Thorwald - and his hearth warriors before the arrival of the Mercian host.

However, that still meant that a powerful Danish leader was at large and he could well act as a rallying point for Danish opposition to Mercian rule.

'Wynnstan, I want you to select a hundred mounted warriors and hunt this Jarl Thorwald down and eliminate him,' Æthelflæd told him that evening. 'Lord Æthelstan has agreed to release you pro tempore and he'll help you pick the men to accompany you.'

Wynnstan wondered about the phrase 'pro tempore' – for the time being. Did Æthelstan want him to remain as his captain after the campaign was over? He'd assumed not. Then the thought occurred to him that he wouldn't have to make that decision if he managed to get himself killed during the chase after Thorwald.

Evidently Thorwald didn't think that the Mercians would bother about him after he was expelled from Ledecestre and was riding at a leisurely pace north-westwards towards the part of Northumbria held by Ragnall. Wynnstan's men caught up with them just as the Danes were making camp half an hour before dusk.

'There are only forty of them,' Sawin reported after he and Wardric had scouted the enemy encampment.

'Good. We'll move at dawn. I want them surrounded during the night so none escape. Warn the men to keep clear of the horses and to stay well back in the woods so that they don't alert any sentries. The signal will be three blasts on your hunting horn, Wardric.'

As the first rays of sunshine lit up the trees surrounding the glade where the Danes were still asleep Wynnstan told Wardric to sound his horn. Without waiting for the three notes to fade away Wynnstan charged into the encampment yelling like a Viking berserker. Both Sawin and Wardric tried to keep up with him but he'd cut down a startled Danish sentry and reached the camp before they could catch up with him.

A huge Dane emerged from his blanket clad only in tunic and trousers. He turned to face Wynnstan hefting a double bladed war axe in his hands. It had a longer reach than a sword and it was heavy enough to chop off a limb or a head with one blow of anyone foolish enough to get in its path.

The giant swung the axe at Wynnstan who, instead of jumping out of the way, threw up his shield to block the blow. At the same time, he thrust the point of his sword into the Dane's unprotected stomach. The axe splintered the lime wood of the shield and carved through the central iron boss as if it was made of paper. Wynnstan felt his forearm break and then the blade of the axe cut through his flesh to the bone.

His left arm was useless and Wynnstan let go of his shattered shield. He tried to ignore the pain and, although a stomach wound would kill in twenty minutes or so, Wynnstan gritted his teeth and pulled his sword clear, only to plunge it back into the Danes right eye socket. The man died instantly and tumbled to the earth.

'We must get you out of here, lord. You're badly wounded,' Sawin told him, trying to pull him back towards the woods.

However, Wynnstan angrily shook him off and, ignoring the searing agony in his arm and shoulder, he headed for another Dane. This one held a spear with which he was obviously adept. He had already killed one of the Mercians and wounded another.

Breathing heavily Wynnstan chopped through the head of the spear as the man jabbed it towards his face. The spearman looked surprised for an instant before he dropped the useless haft and drew a wicked looking dagger. Wynnstan batted the first thrust away easily but the pain he was in and the loss of blood was taking its toll. The Dane tried again and would have succeeded had Wardric not reached him at that point and killed him just as Wynnstan fell to the ground.

✝✝✝

Wynnstan woke up to find Eohric trying to dribble water into his mouth. His shoulder and forearm felt as if they were on fire and he felt weak and disorientated.

'Where am I? What happened?'

'You're in the house which Lady Æthelflæd has taken over for her own use in Ledecestre. You're being tended to by Uhtric, one of the Lady's own physicians. He's set and splinted your forearm and done the best he can with your shoulder, he says, but he doubts that you will even regain full use of it. You've lost a lot of blood though and you need to rest and regain your strength.'

Wynnstan grunted in frustration. 'Why did Sawin and Wardic rescue me?' he moaned. 'I wanted to die!'

Eohric looked shocked.

'Surely that would be a sin, lord. Seeking death in battle is tantamount to taking your own life and you'd be condemned to hell for all eternity. Why on earth would you want to die in any case?'

'You wouldn't understand.'

'No, I don't.'

Wynnstan neither wanted nor felt able to explain.

'I'm tired; just leave me.'

When he woke up the next time a monk he didn't know was kneeling beside his bed praying. Wynnstan had a nasty feeling that he was reciting the last rites and praying for his immortal soul. He was as devout as the next man and he didn't feel that his life was so bad that heaven would be denied him. Yes, he'd tried to die fighting in the Dane's camp but many warriors were killed in battle. What made his actions so terrible?

He drifted off to sleep again and when he next regained consciousness the small room he was lying in was deserted. He lay there for a while thinking back over his life and slowly drifted off once more. When he next awoke he discovered that Eohric was back with a bowl of broth, which he slowly fed to him. When he'd finished his servant pulled a letter from his belt.

'This came for you, lord. It's from the Lady Astrid,' he said with a smile.

'From Rumcofen? How long have I been lying here?' he asked, thinking it had been written in response to his injuries.

'Only a few days, lord. This must have been sent a couple of weeks after we set out.'

Wynnstan struggled to get into a position where he could read it. It was an effort and his struggle to sit up sent waves of pain up his arm. However, he suspected that the contents were too personal for him to ask his servant to read it to him.

'My beloved husband,'

He blinked in surprise. Astrid wasn't normally the forgiving kind – at least not quickly. He hadn't expected such a tender opening in a letter written so soon after they'd parted with such acrimony.

'I know now that you were right. I was being selfish in wanting to keep the child, however foully conceived, I had carried for nine

months. As a mother I overcame my repugnance in that time and warmed to the baby in my belly.

After talking to Lady Kjestin and to Abbot Æscwin I can see that you could hardly be expected to have the same feelings for little Tata. I'm deeply sorry that I couldn't see your viewpoint at the time. I've therefore decided to ask Lord Ywer's sister, Æbbe, if she will foster the child, with Earl Skarde's permission, of course. Kjestin is optimistic they will, especially as Brandt has turned out to be something of a disappointment to them.

Please come back to us. I miss you dreadfully. I'm afraid that you will need to mend fences with Sicga though. He doesn't understand why you ignored him when you returned and then left without saying goodbye. He flies into a temper if anyone mentions your name but he is young and he'll come round soon enough after you come back to us.

Your loving wife,
Astrid

Eohric didn't know what was in the letter and at first he thought that Wynnstan was sobbing because it was bad news. However, he knew that he was usually stoical in the face of adversity and they weren't those sort of tears.

'As soon as I'm fit enough to ride we'll be going back to Rumcofen,' Wynnstan said.

It was as much of an explanation that Eohric was going to get for his master's uncharacteristic behaviour.

CHAPTER EIGHTEEN

Early Summer 918

The last of the five Boroughs – Lincolia – had fallen and Mercia was once again united – or nearly so. Eadweard was being difficult about returning the two boroughs he'd taken, insisting that they should remain as part of his Kingdom of East Anglia. He pointed out that he was the one who had captured them and Saxon, not Mercian, lives had been lost in the process.

However, Æthelflæd had other things on her mind at the moment. She'd started to feel unwell and then an embassy arrived from Jorvik, of all places.

'Did they say what they wanted?' she asked Banan, the captain of her personal warband.

'No, lady. However, it includes Archbishop Hrotheweard, the Danish jarl who commands the garrison and several of the city's elders.'

Æthelflæd had heard of Hrotheweard, the senior prelate in Northumbria, although they had never met. He was said to be a devout man who had managed to make Christianity the primary religion of the Danish Kingdom of Jorvik, no mean feat when the previous kings of Northumbria had mostly been pagans.

The throne of the province of Jorvik, as opposed to the old Roman city itself, had been vacant ever since the last two kings, Eowils and Halfdan, had been killed at the Battle of Tatenhale eight years previously. Rather like their compatriots in the Five Boroughs of the Danelaw, the jarls of Northumbria had been content to exist without a king to rule over them. No doubt part of the reason lay in the fact that, without a ruler, they wouldn't have to pay part of the taxes they collected to him.

'Please ask Lord Æthelstan to join me and then show them into the hall.'

The delegation filed in led by Hrotheweard and a rotund man dressed in an embroidered blue tunic, baggy red trousers and black boots. The contrast between the two men couldn't have been greater. Whilst the expensively dressed Dane kept his brown hair and beard long, the archbishop was clean-shaven with barely a wisp of grey hair visible over his ears. His plain homespun black robe was unadorned except for a belt of white rope and a small silver crucifix suspended from a strip of plain leather.

His only insignia of the high office he held was the pastoral staff he carried. Even that was plain with none of the usual gold and silver adornments used by other bishops to display their wealth and importance. Æthelflæd warmed to the man instantly.

The two leaders were followed by six men, three in byrnies and carrying helmets and three wearing the long robes typically worn by merchants.

She and her nephew were sitting on two chairs on a raised dais at the end of the hall. Behind them stood Banan, Irwyn and three ealdormen. She said nothing, letting the silence do its work. The embassy shuffled their feet nervously, all except Hrotheweard who stood placidly waiting for the Lady of the Mercians to speak.

'Well, why have you come to Tomtun to see me? Are you afraid that I'll invade Northumbria now that I've succeeded in uniting all of Mercia under my rule?'

'No, lady,' the jarl in the embroidered tunic replied. 'It's not you but the pagan warlord Ragnall we fear. He has threatened to invade our lands and put all Christians to the sword, whether they be Dane, Norsemen or Angles.'

'So you want my protection, I suppose. What do you offer me in return?'

'We offer you the fealty of Northumbria, lady. Surely that's enough?' Hrotheweard responded, seemingly surprised by Æthelflæd's question.

'Correct me if I'm wrong, archbishop, but this embassy is here on behalf of the people of Jorvik, not Northumbria. If I remember my history, the region you call Jorvik was called Deira centuries ago. Northumbria includes Bernicia, ruled by Ealdred of Bebbanburg, and that part of the old kingdom to the west which is held by King Ragnall of Mann. Therefore we are talking about a third of Northumbria, at most.'

The archbishop looked uncomfortable whilst the Danish jarl beside him looked so angry she feared that he was about to burst a blood vessel.

'Bernicia is ruled by Ealdred because we allow it!' he spluttered. 'Ragnall is our common enemy. If you don't aid us, he'll take Jorvik this year and restore Northumbria to be the most powerful kingdom in the land. Surely neither you nor your brother want that.'

Æthelflæd was in a quandary. Her campaign, and that of her brother, had taken control of Western Mercia and East Anglia back from the Danes but their rule was fragile. They needed to consolidate their position and eliminate the isolated pockets of resistance that remained. If she accepted, the surrender of Jorvik, that would bring her into direct conflict with Ragnall and, if he beat her, all that she and Eadweard had gained could well be lost.

On the other hand, this was too good an opportunity to miss. Her father's grand ambition had been to unite the Anglo-Saxon peoples into one kingdom. That dream had been inherited by Eadweard, who now called himself the King of the Anglo-Saxons. However, the ancient Anglian Kingdom of Northumbria remained in Viking hands. She knew her brother would be furious if she missed this opportunity to extend their rule northwards and free the Anglian population in what had once been Deira.

'Very well. I will accept your fealty to me and I will follow you with my army as soon as possible.'

It wasn't until the delegation had sworn their oaths of allegiance to her and left the hall that she allowed herself to relax. She had a burning sensation in her chest, felt sick and had difficulty breathing; all sensations which worsened as the audience wore on. This was accompanied by an overwhelming feeling of anxiety. She staggered as she rose from the chair which had served as her throne.

Æthelstan rushed to her side but she waved him away.

'It'll pass,' she panted, her face contorted with pain. 'Probably something I ate.'

A second later the room spun around her and she collapsed in Æthelstan's arms. He told the guards to bring the top of one of the trestle tables over and they gently carried her to her bedchamber. He sent someone to fetch Leofwine the physician.

By the time he arrived she was in bed and had recovered somewhat. She was still weak and breathless but she was telling people not to make such a fuss. He quickly examined her and then took Æthelstan to one side.

'I've seen this condition before, although I don't know what causes it,' Leofwine said quietly. 'Sometimes people recover but, even if they do, there is always the danger of a second attack and that can prove fatal. I think the best thing is for Lady Æthelflæd to stay in bed and rest. All we can do is to pray that she makes a full recovery.'

'But she needs to travel to Jorvik to receive its surrender before it falls to Ragnall.'

'It's not for me to make suggestions about warfare but can't you take the army there instead? If you try and move your aunt now you'll kill her.'

'Let's see if she recovers in the next day or two,' he replied, biting his lip in anxiety. 'They've sworn their oaths to her personally, not to me or to King Eadweard.'

'Then let us hope and pray for a swift recovery,' Leofwine said. 'In the meantime I'll give her something to relieve the pain.'

†††

The nearer that Wynnstan got to Rumcofen the more nervous he became. He rode into the gates in the palisade surrounding the hall just as warm summer rain began to fall but he didn't notice it. His eyes were fixed on Astrid as she stood on top of the steps leading up to the hall's double doors. She was smiling but it seemed to him that it was rather forced, not a natural spontaneous reaction to the sight of her returning husband. However, perhaps his wife felt as apprehensive about their reunion as he did himself.

Beside her Sicga wasn't making any attempt to smile. His expression could best be described as animosity. The only person who seemed sincerely delighted to see him again was his daughter, Mildritha. She ran to embrace him as soon as he dismounted and he lifted her up and swung her around, to the child's delight. He saw out of the corner of his eye a genuine smile on Astrid's face as her daughter squealed in delight. Even Sicga's face had lightened up a little.

'I'm worried that Sicga hasn't said a word to me since I returned,' he said to Astrid when they were alone later.

'As I said in my letter to you, he took it very hard when you left without a word to him. He thinks you don't love him anymore because he wasn't able to stop Chad from raping me.'

'But he's just ten; he was eight at the time. Of course I don't blame him!'

'I've told him that – repeatedly – but it doesn't stop him from blaming himself. There's another thing; he doesn't think that Tata should've been sent away. He says it wasn't the child's fault and all of us bonded with the child before he was given to Skarde and Æbbe to bring up.'

'You know that he couldn't have stayed here,' Wynnstan said bitterly. 'He would have been a constant reminder to me of Chad's treachery.'

'I understand that. I had to make a choice between keeping Tata and losing you or giving up the baby. I chose you but I think at this moment that Sicga would opt for Tata. He doesn't understand how you feel. He sees Tata as a helpless young child who he loves and you hate. You've got a mountain to climb if you want to regain his love.'

Wynnstan sighed.

'Sometimes I think that fighting a war is simpler than keeping the peace at home.'

✝✝✝

Æthelflæd had tried to rush things. She said that she felt better on the morning of the twelfth of June and she got up and dressed against Leofwine's advice. She managed to walk to the hall, with assistance from Æthelstan, before she collapsed again. This time she screamed in agony at the pain in her chest. By the time that Leofwine reached her she was dead. She was forty-eight years of age.

Her body was taken on a cart from her new capital at Tomtun to the old one at Glowecestre where her husband, Æðelred, erstwhile Lord of the Mercians, lay buried. Because it was summer, her body had been washed and stuffed with sweet smelling herbs before being covered in mead to help preserve it and sewn into a leather sack. Despite these precautions, everyone could smell the putrefaction by the time the funeral was held.

She was placed in an ornately carved and painted wooden casket and buried at Saint Oswald's Monastery in the same grave as Æðelred. She would spend eternity on top of husband – an intimacy they'd rarely enjoyed in life.

Those attending the ceremony included King Eadweard, her daughter Ælfwynn, her nephew Æthelstan, the ealdormen of Mercia, both bishops and most of the abbots. Ywer and his brother, Abbot Æscwin, had travelled down from Cæstir but Earl Skarde of Wirhealum was notable by his absence.

When he was asked about it by Eadweard, Ywer wondered how much he should say. This was a day when they should be remembering Æthelflæd and her many achievements, not worrying about events in the north.

'He had an argument with his son, Brandt, cyning,' he replied. 'It's nothing serious but he felt he should sort it out as soon as possible.'

'What sort of argument?'

'He accused his son of being a coward. Brandt flew into a rage and struck his father. He then ran from the hall and fled with half a dozen of his cronies.'

'I see. Where is he now?'

'It's rumoured that he's joined Ragnall's army of Vikings. Skarde went after him but no one knows what's happened to either of them.'

'Where does that leave the defence of the Wirhealum peninsula?'

It was something that worried Ywer as well. Skarde had taken all of his jarls and most of his men with him, leaving Æbbe, Frida and the baby Tata practically undefended. Before Ywer had left he'd told Irwyn to send ships to patrol the coast of Wirhealum but he didn't feel he could do more without being accused of interference in a land that was outside his jurisdiction.

'You'll want to get back and sort this mess out I assume?' Eadweard asked.

'I'll depart as soon as the Witenaġemot has met to choose Lady Æthelflæd's successor.'

Privately Ywer didn't see what business it was of the King of Wessex's. It was purely a matter for Mercia to sort out. However, he didn't think it would be diplomatic to tell Eadweard not to stick his nose in where it wasn't wanted. The latter nodded and went off to talk to another ealdorman.

Ywer watched him with increasing unease. He was quietly circulating amongst the funeral guests nodding to some and having a brief word with others but he spent a long time talking to each of the members of Witenaġemot. Some seemed to agree with what he was saying; others evidently didn't and the discussion seemed to get a little heated. He wondered what was going on until Banan appeared at his elbow.

'It seems our lady's brother is trying to fix the election of her successor,' the captain of her warband murmured quietly.

'Oh? Surely Æthelstan is the obvious candidate?'

'It seems not. Oh, he has an excellent reputation but Eadweard has consistently claimed he's a bastard and that counts heavily against him. Furthermore, he's a Saxon and some Mercians won't accept a ruler whose parents both come from Wessex.'

'Lady Æthelflæd was Saxon,'

'Only half-Saxon. Æthelflæd's mother was a Mercian noblewoman; moreover she was married to a Mercian.'

'If not Æthelstan, then who? Not one of the ealdormen; they're all jealous of one another and wouldn't elect a rival.'

'No, I agree. The rumour is that he favours Æthelflæd's daughter, Ælfwynn.'

'What; but she's an empty headed harlot with no more brains in her head than a sparrow!'

'That's true. She's flighty, totally uninterested in politics and military matters and the only thoughts in her head are what dress to wear and which servant boy to seduce next. However, she'll suit Eadweard's needs admirably.'

'You mean she'll make a complete hash of it and he'll be forced to depose her.'

'Precisely. That would leave the way clear for him to absorb Mercia within his Kingdom of the Anglo-Saxons, just as he has East Anglia.'

'Thank you Banan. You've opened my eyes but I'm not sure what we can do. I think we'd better leave it there, our conversation seems to be attracting a bit of interest and I don't want Eadweard to accuse us of conspiring against him.'

✝✝✝

Banan's assessment of the situation turned out to be correct.
Many favoured Æthelstan to succeed his aunt but a slim majority
voted for Ælfwynn to become the next Lady of the Mercians. Her
opponents felt hamstrung. They could hardly list her failings and
accuse her of being totally unsuited to the role, especially on the
day after her mother's funeral, and so Ælfwynn was elected by a
majority of two.

Ywer was preparing to leave when Æthelstan sought him out.

'What a farce that was,' he complained bitterly. 'My father has
always wanted to rule Mercia directly, instead by co-operating with
my aunt. Now he's about to get his wish. I give my cousin a few
months at best before the throne is taken away from her.'

'You don't think King Eadweard intends her harm?'

'No, he needs to win over the Mercian nobility. He'll most likely
send her to a convent somewhere in Wessex before incorporating
Mercia within his kingdom. Perhaps he'll manufacture some crisis
to give him an excuse to rush to Mercia's aid?'

'What about you? Do you think your father sees you as a threat
to his plans?'

'I have no doubt of it. That's why I'd like to come with you.
Hopefully he'll forget about me in the far north.'

'I'd be delighted but I can't offer you an appointment suitable for
an ætheling.'

'Don't worry about that. My mother left me twenty vills in her
will, a dozen of which are in Cæstirscīr. I have a feeling she saw
this coming and made appropriate provision for me.'

When Ywer, Æscwin and Æthelstan arrived back at Cæstir they
found that there had been two developments; both equally
depressing. Ragnall had captured Jorvik and the archbishop had
been forced to crown him King of Northumbria. Furthermore,

Skarde was dead. The earl had apparently been killed, along with many of his jarls and hersir, through the actions of his own son. Brandt had apparently asked for a meeting with his father and had then betrayed him to Ragnall.

Ywer found himself facing a strong, united Northumbria at a time when the neighbouring province of Wirhealum had no earl. Moreover, Mercia itself was weak and divided. The Witanaġemot had hastily elected the daughter of Æðelred and Æthelflæd as the new Lady of the Mercians. She wasn't remotely like her mother and, just at a time when Mercia needed strong leadership, the nobles had elected a young woman with no idea how to rule. Ywer suspected that all of Æthelflæd's hard work over the past decade was in danger of being undone.

TO BE CONTINUED IN

THE FIRST KING OF ENGLALAND

DUE OUT IN SUMMER 2022

Historical Note

The early tenth century is a time in the history of England for which there are few written records but in the years after King Ælfred's death the two Anglo-Saxon realms which remained free of Danish or Norse control – Wessex and West Mercia – moved from the brink of survival to a position from where they could embark on the re-conquest of the Danelaw and East Anglia.

I have used the term Viking to refer to Danish and Norse warriors. Strictly speaking, it is incorrect as it refers to those undertaking an activity – i.e. sea borne raids and piracy – but saying Danes and Norsemen where both were involved would be cumbersome.

The various sources which are available often offer conflicting accounts of the same event. For example, the Battle of the Corbridge between the Norse King Ragnall and the armies of Alba and Strathclyde is recorded at taking place in 918 in several sources but in 914 in others. The Annals of Ireland refer to the alliance between Æthelflæd and the Kings of Alba and Strathclyde but it's not clear she was present at the battle. I have placed her there in the interests of the story; similarly, I have placed the battle during the summer of 915.

Whilst something is known of the events in and concerning Wessex, far less is known about this period in Mercia. The Mercian Register is a series of brief insertions included as part of the Wessex-orientated Anglo-Saxon Chronicles. Some important events are largely missing from Anglo-Saxon records. Evidently, there was much more written information about this period at one time because historians in the later medieval period refer to documentation which has since been lost. I have therefore had to rely on a somewhat patchy history on which to base the main events depicted in the book.

If the sequence of happenings – or even their existence – are debateable, even less is known about the individuals who shaped those events, their appearance or their personalities. Here I have to confess I have given my imagination free reign.

These were harsh times and they cannot be judged by modern values and ethics. Life was tough, especially so for slaves and poor farmers. A high rate of infant mortality, food shortages in winter and a primitive understanding of medicine meant the average life expectancy was around thirty years of age. Life was a little better for nobles and they might expect to live rather longer, unless they died in battle. Women tended to die earlier on average, largely because many didn't survive childbirth.

Æthelflæd died of natural causes when she was around forty eight. Together she and her brother paved the way for her nephew - and Eadweard's eldest son - Æthelstan, to complete the unification of England, but that's another story.

I am particularly indebted to the following sources:

- Ælfred's Britain – War and Peace in the Viking Age by Max Adams

- Alfred, Warrior King by John Peddie

- Pauli's The Life and Works of King Alfred translated by B Thorpe

- The Warrior Queen – The Life and Legend of Æthelflæd by Joanna Arman

- Edward the Elder and the Making of England by Harriet Harvey Wood

- Æthelstan by Sarah Foot

- Anglo-Saxon England by Sir Frank Stenton

- The Anglo Saxons edited by James Campbell

Printed in Great Britain
by Amazon